PIECE OF ᴍʏ HEART

Also by Nicole Jacquelyn

Unbreak My Heart
Change of Heart
Heart of Glass

PIECE OF MY HEART

NICOLE JACQUELYN

FOREVER

New York   Boston

Forever
Hachette Book Group
1290 Avenue of the Americas, New York, NY 10104
read-forever.com
twitter.com/readforeverpub

First published as an ebook and as a print on demand: July 2019

Forever is an imprint of Grand Central Publishing. The Forever name and logo are trademarks of Hachette Book Group, Inc.

The publisher is not responsible for websites (or their content) that are not owned by the publisher.

The Hachette Speakers Bureau provides a wide range of authors for speaking events. To find out more, go to www.hachettespeakersbureau.com or call (866) 376-6591.

ISBNs: 978-1-5387-1188-0 (ebook), 978-1-5387-1189-7 (POD)

For my mom and dad.
You're the wind beneath my wings.
I don't know what I'd do without you.

Acknowledgments

To my kids, who are ridiculously patient and ridiculously proud. You guys have no idea how much your support means to me. I wouldn't be who I am without you cheering me on. I love you.

To my parents, who supply the coffee and babysitting—I couldn't do life without you. I'm so glad I'm your favorite child.

To my sister, who is always the first one to boost me up when I'm down and kick my ass when I need it. Thanks for the shove, sis. Thanks even more for the hugs.

To Nikki who has read everything I've ever written, usually more than once, and pushes me to be better every time. Your friendship has meant more to me than you'll ever know.

To my agent and my editors, who worked tirelessly to get this book where it is today. Thank you so much for the support and patience you've shown me.

To Donna, who was the first blogger to spread the news about my work. You will always have a place in my acknowledgements. Thank you so much.

And thank you a million times to my readers. Without you, I wouldn't get to support my family while doing something I love.

PIECE OF MY HEART

CHAPTER 1

ALEX

On the day I met the love of my life, I slept through my alarm, spilled coffee down the front of my uniform, forgot to bring running shoes, and had to run five miles in my boots, all before noon. By the end of the day, I was spent. All I wanted to do was go home and watch TV in my skivvies with a six-pack of beer in arm's reach.

Just as I climbed into my truck, I remembered that I had agreed to be the wingman for my coworker Sean's double date. I didn't know the guy well, but since we'd be working together and potentially deploying together, I hadn't felt like I could blow him off when he'd asked. Most of the other guys in our platoon were in serious relationships and couldn't help him out when he'd gone around begging for the favor. I brought up Sean's contact information in my phone and called him as I pulled out of the parking lot.

"Haven't you been on a date with this chick before?" I asked as soon as Sean answered his phone.

"Hello, Alex," he laughed. "Long time no see."

"I didn't catch you before you left the building," I replied. "Haven't you guys hung out already? Why am I going to this thing?"

"Yeah, I couldn't wait, so we met up on Wednesday for drinks. I guess she'd already made plans with her friend for tonight, though, and she didn't want to cancel."

I opened my mouth to back out of the whole thing when Sean spoke again.

"You gotta come. This girl, she's so hot," he said. I could practically hear him smile through the phone.

"And you haven't sealed the deal yet."

"I never kiss and tell," he lied. "But no. I like her and she's not the type. Wants to hang out for a while first."

"Hang out or date?" I asked, switching the phone to Bluetooth so I could drive. "Because there's a difference."

"There is?" he asked.

"You're kidding, right?" I flipped on my blinker and headed toward the front gate of the fort. Living in town instead of on base had a lot of advantages, but the biggest disadvantage was that it took me twenty minutes to get home every day. I knew it could be worse, but I hated spending any time driving around. We had only a certain number of minutes on Earth, and I didn't want to waste them.

"Yeah, man, I'm kidding," Sean said. "We're dating. I'm taking her out, not inviting her over for China Buffet take-out and zombie killing on the Xbox."

"Killing zombies sounds like the perfect date to me, but it

probably wouldn't go over well with most women."

"Meet us at six, all right?" Sean said, ignoring my comment. "And shower, yeah? You smelled like ass today."

"I forgot fucking deodorant," I replied. It was one of the hazards of sleeping through my alarm.

"Right," he said. "Shower. Six o'clock at the sushi and steak place." He hung up before I could reply.

"Shit," I muttered, dropping my head back against the headrest. It looked like I was going out tonight after all.

By the time I got home it was closing in on five thirty. I stripped as I walked toward my bathroom, but carried the discarded clothes with me to the hamper and tossed them in. I'd realized not long after I'd moved out of my parents' house that if I didn't clean up my crap, I'd be living in a shithole.

After a quick shower and shave, I slapped on some deodorant and dressed in jeans and a button-down shirt. The place I was meeting Sean and the ladies wasn't fancy. A T-shirt would have worked fine, but I rarely had the chance to dress nice, and women liked when you put in some effort. I laughed as I glanced in the mirror to make sure I looked presentable. My twin brother, Abraham, would have given me so much grief if he'd known I'd put in this much effort for a blind date.

Even before he'd hooked up with our foster sister, Ani—yeah, that happened—he'd rarely made much of an effort to date, and he would never in a million years go out with a woman sight unseen. Abraham and I were opposites in almost every way, and if he knew just how many blind dates I'd gone on in the past few years, he'd shit his pants. Bram would rather have a root canal then spend the evening making small talk with a stranger.

By the time I pulled up in front of the steak house and parked my truck, exhaustion was hitting me hard. It had been a long week, and for the first time in a long time, I dreaded making nice with someone I didn't know. Usually I was up for anything, but damn, I was tired.

I forced myself toward the entrance of the restaurant and pulled open the front door, smiling politely when I caught sight of Sean and his date waiting for their table.

"Hey, Alex," Sean called in greeting, even though we'd already made eye contact and he'd wiggled his eyebrows. "This is Hailey."

"Hi, Hailey." I smiled wide, making Sean's expression flatten as he stepped a little closer to her. "Nice to meet you."

I always did that—grinned real big and stared directly into the eyes of my friend's date. You could tell a lot about a person during a first impression, and I always knew from that initial look if a woman was into my friend.

I was good-looking and I knew it. Tan skin, even white teeth, and eyelashes that annoyingly flicked against the lenses of my sunglasses. As far as I was concerned, it was a freak of genetics that didn't really matter, but I still used it to my advantage when I could. I wasn't stupid. Currently I was using those freak genetics to charm my friend's girl.

When Hailey tilted her head toward Sean just slightly, I relaxed a little. When she laughed at his reaction I relaxed more.

"Nice to meet you, Alex," she said, grinning. "Thanks for coming."

"Of course," I said, like I hadn't been thinking about a reason to bail for the last hour. I looked around the area we were standing in but didn't see her friend. "Am I making this a third-wheel situation?"

"No." Hailey shook her head and grimaced a little.

"Her friend's running late," Sean said, just as the hostess called his name. "She said she'll be here as soon as she can, though."

I nodded and shrugged. The place smelled damn good as we made our way through the tables, and my stomach growled, reminding me that I'd missed lunch. I eyeballed the sushi being prepared, and my mouth watered.

It wasn't until we'd sat down and ordered drinks that I realized we'd have to wait for Hailey's friend to get there before we could order. The good mood I'd been enjoying vanished, but I kept a polite expression on my face. I chatted with Sean about work and told Hailey some mildly embarrassing stories, but I couldn't help but keep glancing at my watch. Jesus, I was starving. Fifteen minutes passed, then thirty, and as we got close to the hour mark, even the waitress started getting a little annoyed.

Finally, about fifty minutes after we'd sat down, a petite woman with long brown hair dropped into the chair next to me.

"I'm so sorry I'm late," she said breathlessly. "There was an armadillo in the road, and I couldn't just leave it."

My interest was piqued at the sound of her husky voice, but it solidified when the woman turned toward me and I saw her face. Dark-brown eyes, a mole on her cheekbone, a sharp nose, full lips. There was a gap between her two front teeth when she gave me a small smile.

Holy fuck.

"I'm Sarai," she said, lifting her hand politely for me to shake.

I froze like a twelve-year-old who had just gotten caught staring at the pretty lifeguard at the neighborhood pool.

"This is Alex," Sean said, laughter in his voice.

"I'm Alex," I mimicked, shaking her hand and then letting go as if it were on fire. Oh, that was *real* smooth. What the hell was wrong with me?

"Nice to meet you, Alex," she said politely.

She turned back to the table, and I immediately wanted to poke her or pull her hair or make a joke. *Anything* to get her to turn those big brown eyes my way. The only problem was that my tongue seemed to be glued to the roof of my mouth.

I wasn't that guy. I didn't see a pretty face and clam up. I didn't stumble over my words or make an ass of myself. I was cool. Collected. Charming as fuck. Women loved me.

"Don't worry about it," Hailey said with a wave of her hand.

"How's the armadillo?" I asked at the same time.

"It's dead," Sarai replied.

I almost laughed. She'd said it so matter-of-factly, like I should have known the answer before I'd ever asked the question.

"And you still stopped?" I said, my lips twitching.

"Well, someone has to call it in," she said with a shrug. "You can't just leave dead animals on the road."

"Right," I replied.

"So I stopped and dragged it off the road and waited for someone to come get it."

I glanced at her hands.

"Don't worry—I washed them," she said. Smiling, she lifted her hands from the table and wiggled her fingers.

"Would you like something to drink?" the waitress asked just as Sarai's hands rested on the table again. I hadn't even noticed the woman walk up.

"Just water, please," Sarai answered. The waitress scowled.

"She's pissed because you were so late and now you're ordering a free drink," I said to Sarai as I met the waitress's eyes. I had meant it as a joke, but when I looked back at my date, her eyes were wide in disbelief and I realized how the words sounded.

Sean gave me a *what the fuck* scowl, and I grimaced, shrugging my shoulders before looking away. I was completely botching what should have been an enjoyable dinner. To be fair, I wasn't the only person at fault. *I* hadn't been the one who'd shown up late.

"I'm sorry," I muttered, running a hand down my face. "I didn't mean that toward you. I mean, you *were* late, but I wasn't trying to call you out."

"You just keep talking," Sarai said, her lips tipping up in a small smile. "But you're not making it any better."

"I'll shut up," I replied immediately. Then, like a complete jackass, I lifted my fingers and mimicked zipping my mouth closed.

Sarai laughed and looked back across the table at Hailey, dismissing me. I closed my eyes for a moment in disbelief.

I needed to turn this shit around. I waited for my moment, quietly observing the two women as they talked about their classes and professors.

"What's your major?" I asked Sarai quietly as Sean finally captured Hailey's attention again.

"I'm getting my MBA," she replied. "I graduate in the spring." She grinned and did this little celebration motion with her hands. I relaxed a little. If I could just keep her talking, maybe I could salvage her opinion of me. If nothing else, at least she'd think I was a good listener.

"Damn," I said. "That's a lot of school."

"Well, I took a couple of years off after high school," she replied. "So it hasn't seemed too bad."

"Oh yeah?"

"It turns out," she said softly, leaning toward me as if she were telling me a secret, "college is expensive."

I chuckled and she grinned.

"No kidding," I replied. "I was never very good at the whole school thing."

"Why is that?"

"Class clown," I said, pointing to myself. "I was too busy making sure everyone else wasn't paying attention to learn anything."

"Ah," she said knowingly.

"It's a curse." I shrugged.

"I'm guessing the Army beat that out of you," she said, turning toward me a little.

"The drill sergeants didn't find me amusing," I replied drily.

"I bet." She laughed.

Hailey said something, pulling Sarai's attention back across the table. Damn, just when we were getting somewhere.

We ordered our meals, and thankfully I didn't embarrass

myself again. There was something about the woman sitting next to me that made me all nervous and twitchy. I wanted so badly to make a good impression that I psyched myself out.

I watched her while we ate, trying not to seem creepy. I couldn't help myself. Everything she did, every move she made, seemed…dainty. I'd never used that word before in my life, but it fit. Her table manners were impeccable; meanwhile, my sushi rolls were falling from my chopsticks with alarming regularity.

"Do you need help with that?" she finally asked as I tried and failed to get a roll into my mouth.

"No," I mumbled, putting a hand in front of my mouth to hide the food hanging out of it. "No, thank you."

"I have just the trick," she said, lifting one finger in the air.

I sheepishly put my chopsticks in her hand when she gestured for them. I watched in fascination as she folded the wrapper from her straw and set it between the chopsticks, then wrapped a tiny rubber band from inside her purse around the whole thing.

"See?" she said, squeezing the chopsticks on one end so they opened and closed at the other end. "Magic."

"Did you just put training wheels on my chopsticks?" I asked in disbelief.

Sarai's eyes widened innocently as she pressed her lips together. "Yes?"

"I think I love you," I replied, wiggling my fingers. "Let me try them."

The woman was a genius.

"Better?" she asked, watching as I easily grabbed a roll.

"Jesus, Evans," Sean said, scoffing. "I can't take you anywhere."

"I'm taking these home with me," I replied, opening and closing them a few times.

Ground rules for wingmen in our circle meant that I was getting a free dinner. Since Sean was the one trying to impress his date, it was his responsibility to pay. I'd given up beer and video games to help him out; it was the least he could do.

Unfortunately, Sean seemed to have missed that memo and didn't reach for the check when the waitress set it on the end of our table after we'd finished eating. I gritted my teeth as I watched him smile widely at something Hailey said. I glanced down at the check and then back at him as Sarai grabbed her purse and started rifling through it. Sean still didn't pick the damn thing up. Finally, just as Sarai found her wallet and pulled it out of her purse, I reached past her and snatched the bill up.

"I've got it," I said quietly, putting my hand on top of hers for just a second. I reached for my wallet at the same time she tried to argue.

"No way," she replied. "You don't need to pay for mine."

The couple across the table completely ignored our interaction.

"I know I don't have to," I said to Sarai as I caught the waitress's eye. I pulled out some bills and handed them to the waitress when she walked over to us. "Keep the change." I'd given her a fat tip. It was the least I could do after spending so long at her table during one of their busiest nights of the week.

"Really," Sarai said, pulling some cash from her wallet. "How much do I owe you?"

Sean and Hailey were still talking to each other like they had no idea that I'd just paid for their goddamn dinner. No one was that oblivious. I was pissed, but I sure as hell wasn't going to make Sarai pay for her own meal. I'd had a good time, and I'd probably be thanking Sean later for setting this double date up, but it was the principle of the thing. The bill was his responsibility.

"Nothing," I said to Sarai, shaking my head. "Seriously, this one's on me."

"It's not like this was a real date," she said softly, her lips tipping up at the edges.

"Doesn't matter," I replied, standing up from my seat. I pulled her chair out as she finally put away her wallet and stood up, too.

"You guys leaving?" Hailey asked, suddenly out of the Sean-fog she'd seemed to be lost in.

"I still need to get the check," Sean said jovially. The prick.

"Alex already got it," Sarai said drily. "I'll see you Wednesday in class, Hailey?"

"I'll be there," Hailey said. She made no move to get up, so I guessed that was our cue to leave without them.

I followed Sarai out of the restaurant, still completely annoyed. That dipshit was going to pay me back. It wasn't as if I was hurting for money, but I definitely hadn't budgeted for paying for four expensive dinners this week.

"It was nice meeting you," Sarai said as we stepped out into the cold night. She was holding her sweater tightly around her.

"You too," I said, smiling. The night had been complete shit from beginning to end, but now that we were ready to leave, I was kind of disappointed. "Where'd you park?"

"Right over there." She nodded to her left.

"I'll walk you."

She opened her mouth to reply, then tilted her head and snapped her mouth shut again.

"Yeah, you wouldn't have been able to talk me out of it," I said jokingly. She rolled her eyes, and I knew that I'd guessed her unsaid words correctly. "My dad would kill me if he knew I let a woman walk alone in the dark to her car."

"Yeah, but how would he know?" she asked, pulling her keys out of her purse as we walked.

"I'm a terrible liar," I replied.

"Do you think he'll ask if you've let any women walk to their cars alone lately?"

"It's possible," I joked, nodding my head. "But even if he didn't"—I sighed—"the minute he answered the phone, I'd probably blurt out the truth. Guilty conscience, you know?"

"It must have sucked to be your friend when you were a kid," she said, chuckling.

"It did," I replied in mock seriousness. We'd arrived at her car, and I searched for a way to buy myself some time. I hadn't wanted to come, but now that the date was over, I didn't want to leave.

"Well, thanks for the escort," she said, smiling politely.

"You want to get dinner sometime?" I asked, grinning down at her.

"I'm really busy," she hedged.

"I could work around your schedule—"

Before I could say anything else, she shook her head.

"Thank you, but no." She unlocked her car door.

"Really?" I said, unable to hide the surprise in my voice.

She looked at me and snorted. "Yes. Really."

"Uh, okay." I stepped back, completely unsure of myself now.

Opening her car door, she turned to look back at me. "I'm focusing on school right now, but thank you for the invitation. Besides, I don't date men prettier than me," she said with a teasing smile.

After that parting shot, she climbed into her car and drove away, leaving me standing there on the pavement, a dazed look on my face. As I watched her taillights disappear, I started to laugh.

I was still laughing while I walked to my truck and climbed inside. Jesus. Getting completely shot down because I was too pretty was a fitting end to the hellish day I'd had. I mean, with the way the entire day had gone down, had I really expected that it would end any differently?

My phone rang as soon as I'd stepped through my front door, and I groaned when my brother's name flashed on the screen.

"Abraham," I answered.

"It's Ani," my foster sister, sister-in-law, and best friend whispered.

"Why are you calling from Bram's phone?" I whispered back, grinning.

"Because my phone is in the bedroom with my sweet little demon, who is currently asleep for the first time in twenty-four hours," she replied, still whispering.

"Damn, woman. Go get some sleep!"

"I am," she hissed. "I was just calling you to make sure you didn't call me."

"I wasn't planning on calling you."

"Well, how was I supposed to know that?"

"You need some sleep," I said, dropping onto my couch with a sigh. "You're acting crazy."

"Do you think Bram would find me if I slept in the bathtub?" she asked seriously. "I could put some towels in there, and—"

"Yes, he would notice. You have his phone," I replied with a laugh. "Go get in bed."

"If he asks for sex, he's coming to live with you."

"That's a little extreme," I said. "Make him live with the parents."

"He'd be too close," she said, groaning. "If I had to see his face, I'd kill him."

"He's probably already asleep," I assured her, trying and failing to take her seriously. "Just go get in bed and get some rest while you can."

"Fine." She hung up without saying good-bye, and I grinned as I dropped my phone on the couch beside me.

Ani was one of the best people I'd ever known. She'd also been right. I would have called her once I'd had a few beers. I wanted to bitch about Sean not paying for dinner, and I still couldn't get over the way Sarai had shot me down so easily, and I wanted to tell Ani about it. She'd laugh her ass off.

I knew that I wasn't God's gift to women or anything like that, but I did pretty well with the fairer sex. I'd never in my life been told no flat out when I'd asked a woman to have dinner with me. I'd heard excuses and had women give me the brush-off, sure, but never gotten a plain "No." If I was being honest, that had burned a little.

I stripped down to my boxers and grabbed a six-pack from the fridge before settling back down on the couch again. Since I didn't have anything going on the next day, I was going to drink every single one of those beers and burn off some frustration by killing some video game zombies.

Before I turned on the TV, I flipped through my text messages until I found one from Sean and replied to it, *You owe me for dinner, fuckface.*

CHAPTER 2

SARAI

School was going to kill me. I'd been working all day on a paper, and I finally had the rough draft written, but I still had to outline the next paper before I could go to sleep. Neither of them was due until Monday, but I had plans tomorrow that I really couldn't cancel. I rubbed at my forehead, where a headache was forming.

"I know, Auntie," I muttered, staring at her through the computer screen. She was complaining again about the distance between us. She didn't understand why I'd gone all the way to Missouri for school when there were plenty of good schools in New York. Why couldn't I live at home and go to school? Was I trying to get away from her? How was she supposed to check on me? I was twenty-six—wasn't it time for me to settle down and give her some babies to hold?

It drove me crazy, but I also kind of loved that she forced me to Skype her at least once a week to make sure that my cheeks hadn't thinned out. I hadn't been back home in over a year, because the tickets were so expensive and I couldn't afford to take any time off from the accounting office where I worked. I missed New York, though, and my aunt and uncle's little apartment. I missed the smells and the sounds and the food and the family that was always around when I needed them.

I'd grown up in Missouri, and it wasn't until my parents died in a car accident when I was fourteen that I moved to New York to live with my uncle and aunt. I'd expected the old familiar landmarks to feel like home when I came back to Missouri, but they hadn't.

When I decided to return to Missouri for school, I'd been so confident. I'd rolled my eyes when family and friends had told me how homesick I'd feel. After all, I'd grown up in Missouri. It was as familiar to me as New York was. Sure, I'd miss the people I'd left in New York, but it was an adventure. I'd settle easily into my old hometown.

How wrong I'd been. I hated thinking of those first two years at school. The isolation I'd felt. The homesickness. It had only been pure stubbornness that had kept me there. Sheer force of will. Everything was so spread out. I had to drive if I wanted to go anywhere, and walking to the corner store was a thing of the past. Neighbors didn't stop me to say hello and ask how my studies were going. No one cared what I was doing or where I was going. The very things I'd looked forward to when planning to move so far away were the things that depressed me.

Eventually, I'd grown comfortable again, but I still missed home, especially on days when my aunt was being nosy, and

I could hear my uncle in the background telling her how I'd never call again if she kept asking me questions.

"I'm going to a party," I told her when she grilled me about my plans for that weekend.

"What kind of party?"

"Housewarming. My friend is moving in with her boyfriend."

My aunt made a noise in her throat. "Stupid. Moving in with a guy before marriage is a bad idea. You try to do that, I'll come drag you home by your hair."

She was dramatic, but I had a feeling her words weren't far from the truth. If she found out that Hailey and Sean had been dating for less than a month, she'd have even more to say, and I wouldn't even be able to argue with her, since I thought the whole thing was insane. My aunt and uncle were young. They'd been newly married when I'd gone to live with them, and in a lot of ways we'd grown up together. They were the fun parents, the ones who'd pretended they didn't know when my friends and I sneaked cigarettes and wine or spent hours discussing boys instead of doing our homework. However, underneath the surface, they'd always taken their duties as my surrogate parents very seriously.

"I don't have a boyfriend, and I like my apartment," I said seriously.

"Good. Wait until you come home before you find a man," she replied. She'd said the same thing more than a few times before. "Easier that way." It would be easier for her, she meant. If I met my future husband in New York, she could be as nosy as she wanted and meddle until she drove me completely crazy, and she wouldn't have to worry that I'd stay in Missouri forever.

"Yeah, yeah," I muttered, searching in my closet for something to wear. "I have to go—I have a million things to do tonight."

After I promised I'd call again on Sunday, and dodged her questions about when I'd last set foot in a synagogue, we hung up. I didn't know why she still asked if I was going to temple when she knew the answer. I'd lost my faith when I was fourteen, and no nagging from her would change that.

I stuffed my phone into the pocket of my robe and stared into my closet. I should have asked my aunt's opinion on what I should wear; she'd seen nearly every item of clothing I owned. And she'd definitely have an opinion.

Jeans were always a good choice. Casual, so I didn't look like I was trying too hard, and I had a pair that made my ass look really good. I didn't know why I was so concerned with how my ass looked. Okay, no, that was a lie. I knew exactly why I had to look amazing at Hailey and Sean's party tomorrow afternoon.

Alex Evans.

I hadn't been lying when I told him that I was trying to focus on school instead of dating. But damn, it had been hard to tell him no. The man was gorgeous. Charming, too, when he tried to be.

I'd told him that he was prettier than I was, but that *had* been a lie. He wasn't pretty; he was beautiful in a way that only a man could be. Muscular, commanding, confident. If I were looking for someone to spend time with, he'd be my exact type.

Unfortunately, I wasn't looking. I was busy every day of the week and most nights. Working full-time and finishing graduate school pretty much took up every waking minute I had.

That didn't mean that I was willing to look less than spectacular when I saw him again, though. There would be a lot of people at that party, plenty of women to catch his eye, but I wanted to be the one he couldn't look away from.

I grabbed my favorite black sweater from the closet. It hung off my shoulder and gave the impression that I didn't have anything on underneath. Sexy, but not trashy. There was something incredibly provocative about a bare shoulder or a high-necked dress that showed off a woman's legs but nothing else.

As soon as I had my clothes laid out for the next day, I grabbed a cup of tea and climbed into bed with my planner. The next week was already full of reminders and timelines, but I still found a few spaces to make notes. I didn't have much to add, because I always filled the little date boxes weeks in advance, but scheduling my time and making lists calmed me. Before long, my nervousness about seeing Alex again was gone.

* * *

The next morning I allowed myself to sleep in. Since I worked full-time and took classes at night, weekends were usually filled with homework and household chores. I'd known before I'd fallen asleep that I wouldn't be able to concentrate on schoolwork before the party, though, so I hadn't set an alarm. I'd needed the sleep so badly that by the time I woke up, it was already noon.

Funny, handsome Alex Evans filled my thoughts as soon as I opened my eyes. It was ridiculous, and I knew that I had to stay on course and not get distracted by a guy, but I couldn't seem to help myself. It had been a few weeks since the awkward double date when we'd met, and I still thought about him on almost a daily basis. It was a little pathetic, really. I smiled as I remembered how he'd been so impressed by the chopsticks trick that he'd brought them home with him.

For all I knew, he had a girlfriend now. Maybe he'd show up with her this afternoon, and my outfit would go unnoticed. That would probably be for the best.

I climbed out of bed and shuffled toward the shower, stretching my arms above my head as I glanced at the sweater and jeans I'd hung over the back of my chair. Smiling to myself, I continued into the bathroom. I was definitely wearing the outfit.

It took me a little over an hour to get ready. Blow-drying my thick head of hair took almost half that time. I thought about cutting it all the time but couldn't quite make myself go through with it. My mom had loved my long hair, and she'd never let me cut more than a few inches off when I was a child. I couldn't even count the number of hours that she'd spent brushing and braiding it, telling me stories about the neighborhood in New York where she and my dad had grown up.

I checked the clock as I got dressed, but I still had plenty of time before I had to be at Hailey's new place. They were renting a house the size of a postage stamp, so it seemed a little silly to have a bunch of people over, but what did I know? I'd been in the same apartment since I'd moved to Missouri, and I rarely ever had people over.

Hailey wanted me to help her set up the food, so at three o'clock I headed over to her house. It wasn't a very long drive, but it was raining so hard that it felt like it took forever. Driving in the rain always made me nervous. I'd much rather be holed up in my apartment with a good book, wrapped in a blanket, and drinking warm soup than be out in that kind of weather.

"You're here," she yelled excitedly as I ran from my car to the front door of her house. "I've been running around like a maniac trying to get everything ready, and I'm so behind!"

"Why doesn't this surprise me?" I teased as I hurried inside. Hailey was a notorious procrastinator.

"Okay, so I mostly got stuff from the freezer section at the store," she said, taking my jacket from me and throwing it on her bed as I followed her around the house. "You know, the little pizza bites and egg rolls? But I also got chips and salsa. Oh, and some fruit and vegetables. I figured we could cut those up and put them on trays."

"How many people are coming over?" I asked as we reached the kitchen. The place was trashed. It looked like she'd been trying to prepare all the food at once, and my upbringing had me cringing at the sight. Kosher foods were carefully prepared. Meat and dairy never mixed; you couldn't even wash the dishes that held them at the same time, though most people I knew didn't follow that rule very closely.

"I'm not sure. I tried to get a head count, but nobody freaking RSVP's anymore. Especially Sean's friends. They'll probably all stop by at some point, though. I don't even know what I'm doing." She threw her hands up in the air.

"Let's start with the frozen things," I said as she glanced around the kitchen helplessly. "Where are your baking dishes?"

We baked the frozen snacks while I cut vegetables and Hailey cleaned up the mess she'd made. She explained that she hadn't gone to the store until that morning, because Sean had wanted to hang out at home the night before. She wiggled her eyebrows as she said it.

"Where is Sean?" I asked, carefully putting some sliced carrots onto a large plate.

"He's at the gym," she replied easily. "Then he was going to go grab the kegs for tonight. He said he'd be home in time to shower before everyone got here."

It seemed kind of shitty to me that the guy hadn't helped get the house ready for their big party, but I kept my mouth shut. People didn't want to hear your opinion on their significant other. If she complained to me about him, I could agree and commiserate, but otherwise it wasn't any of my business.

I didn't know much about Hailey's boyfriend beyond the one time I'd met him and the few things she'd said in passing. Sean was nice enough, I guess, but there was just something about him that didn't seem right. I couldn't pinpoint why he made me uneasy, but he did.

We worked in tandem for over an hour, getting all the food set out and the furniture reorganized to accommodate all the people who *might* attend. She'd told everyone that the party started at five o'clock, but when I glanced at my phone, I noticed it was five twenty and no one had shown up. Sean wasn't even back with the keg.

"It's five twenty," I told her, dropping onto her couch. "When's Sean supposed to be here?"

"Shit, already?" she asked, reaching up to smooth her hair.

"You look fine," I told her. "Stop messing with it."

She nodded and looked around the room. "It looks good in here," she said. "Hopefully no one goes in our bedroom, though. I haven't unpacked all of the boxes yet."

I'd seen the boxes when she'd put my coat on her bed, but I hadn't realized they were still full. The house looked finished already. It was so small, I wasn't sure where she would have room to put anything else.

"No one cares about boxes," I assured her. "You guys just moved in a week ago."

"Crazy, right?" She laughed. "It happened so fast!"

"Honey, I'm home," Sean called out as he pushed open the front door. "Hold the door for me, would you, babe?"

I stood up from the couch as Hailey hurried to hold the door, and watched as Sean carried in two kegs and set them in the middle of the floor.

"Hey, Sarai," he said with a nod. He handed Hailey a plastic grocery bag. "Here's the taps. I'm gonna hop in the shower, and then I'll get them set up."

He walked away without a word about the house or the food or any apology for being late.

Hailey set the taps on the kitchen table. "We're all ready now!"

"Hey, babe, come wash my back," Sean called, making my friend giggle.

"I'll be right back," she said, holding up one finger.

She was gone a lot longer than a minute. When someone knocked on the front door, I practically ran to it.

"I think I might have the wrong house," Alex said, grinning at me from the porch.

"Funny," I replied, waving him inside. "Please get in here."

"Where are Sean and Hailey?" he asked as he set a bottle of wine down on the coffee table. Just as he finished his sentence, a loud thump came from the direction of the bathroom, mixing in with the sound of running water.

"Taking a shower," I said, almost embarrassed that I was standing in their living room while they got busy.

"No way," he looked toward the bathroom and then back at me. "Did you just get here?"

"No, I've been here for hours, helping Hailey get ready."

"Oh, man." He laughed a little. "That's bad form."

"I mean, am I supposed to just wait until they're done?" I asked, smiling as he laughed again.

"I say we find some paper and make some scorecards," Alex replied. "Rate them as they walk out."

"Tempting," I said. "But a little creepy."

"Or we could go for a walk," he said. "The rain stopped."

"God, yes," I agreed.

I hurriedly grabbed one of Hailey's coats hanging by the door and followed Alex back outside.

"So, how's school?" Alex asked as we made our way down the sidewalk. "Are you learning all sorts of super-important smart-people things?"

I fought a grin. "Super-important smart-people things?"

"Hell, I don't even know what you're studying. Business, right? That's what an MBA is?"

"Yeah," I replied. "I'm hoping that I can get an upper-management position when I'm done. I could probably move up at the accounting firm where I work now, but I'm casting a wider net than that. I'm not sure that I want to stay in Missouri forever."

"Accounting, huh? Sounds boring," he teased. "Although, if it means you get to stay here…"

I laughed. "It is boring, but it's also kind of nice. You can work numbers to get the outcome you want, but numbers never lie. There's a beautiful symmetry to it all."

"Why didn't you become an accountant, then?" he asked.

"No way," I said, shaking my head. "That's too much pressure."

"But upper management is less pressure?" he asked, chuckling.

"Different kind of pressure, at least." I shrugged. "You want to know the truth?"

"Always," he said seriously, shooting me a sweet smile.

"I started out as an accounting major, but the professor who taught almost all the classes I needed to graduate with that degree spent every lecture discussing college sports." I rolled my eyes. "I knew I'd never be able to pass with him teaching me."

"That sucks."

"It all turned out okay," I replied. "I like what I'm studying, and I'll have far more opportunities to use it. I could work anywhere."

We'd made it almost all the way around the block, and I could see Hailey's house ahead of us as it started to sprinkle rain.

"Crap," Alex said, pulling the hood of his jacket over his head.

"I'm not running," I told him as he sped up. I pulled my own hood over my hair. "With my luck, I'd slip and fall."

"I'd catch you," he replied just as he slipped on the grass. He waved his arms around frantically, barely catching his balance before he fell.

"I'll take my chances walking," I said, laughing as he turned wide eyes in my direction. "It's safer."

"Let's forget that just happened," he whispered conspiratorially in my ear, throwing an arm over my shoulders as we reached Sean and Hailey's house.

"I don't think I can do that," I replied in mock seriousness.

The front door swung open as we started up the porch stairs, and I didn't even have time to enjoy the arm around me before it slid off my shoulders as Hailey stuck her head outside.

"There you are! Where the heck have you been?"

Alex laughed under his breath as I was pulled into the surprisingly crowded house. In the time it had taken me and Alex to circle the block, at least fifteen people had arrived, and the music had been turned up so loud I could barely hear my friend.

More people poured in the front door a few minutes later, and before long the house was packed so full that there was barely any room to stand without touching someone else. I mingled, saying hello to classmates and their dates, but I considered the less crowded kitchen the prime real estate, considering the proximity to all the snacks Hailey and I had prepared.

I noticed that the vegetable trays were looking pretty empty, so I began pulling extra carrots and celery out of the fridge. I was bent at the waist, trying to reach a container that had been shoved toward the back, when all of a sudden a hand grabbed my ass. It wasn't a brush or a pinch; it was a full-on entire-hand *grab*.

I'd spent my teenage years in New York and I'd dealt with my fair share of creeps, but I'd never been so blatantly groped in my entire life, and I was embarrassed by the way I froze in horror. My first thought wasn't that someone was assaulting me or even that I was angry someone would touch me without permission. No, my first thought was that I shouldn't have worn the tight jeans that accentuated my ass. I *knew* that was complete bullshit. It didn't matter what I was wearing. I hadn't done a damn thing wrong. Shame was almost instantly replaced with rage as I jerked away, practically diving toward the back of the fridge.

"The fuck are you doing?" Alex's angry voice thundered.

I stood up and turned just as Alex's fist met the face of a guy I'd never seen before in my life.

"You like it when people put their hands on you without asking?" Alex asked, hitting him again. "Feel good?"

"Man," the guy said, clearly drunk if his slurred speech was anything to go by. "She was shaking it right in my face—what was I supposed to do?"

Alex's expression grew even darker as he slammed the guy against the wall. "You motherfucker," he said, raising his fist again.

"Evans," a man called, pushing through the crowd. The man stopped Alex by wrapping an arm around his waist and lifting him off his feet. "Beating on civilians is a good way to get thrown in the brig."

"That fucker—" Alex replied, pointing at the bleeding idiot standing against the wall.

"I know, I know. I saw what happened," his friend said soothingly as he dragged him back a few feet. "We'll take care of him, all right?"

Alex's eyes met mine from across the room, and I felt my cheeks heat with embarrassment and something very close to gratitude. My rescuer didn't relax until a couple of guys grabbed the groper and shoved him out of the room. As the people around us went back to what they were doing before the drama, Alex mouthed, *Are you okay?* At my nod, he turned and let the big guy lead him away.

I was ready to leave at that point, but some stubborn part of me refused to show that I was shaken up. I went back to filling the vegetable trays as if nothing had happened, even though my hands were shaking. I took my time, making sure that everything was placed just so, before putting the extra food back in the fridge.

Then I walked slowly toward the living room, planning on getting my coat and making a quiet exit.

"I think everything's going good, don't you?" Hailey said, practically bouncing toward me, completely oblivious to what had happened in the kitchen.

"It looks like a success to me," I replied, my eyes straying from her to Alex. He was talking to a group of people, and they were all laughing at whatever he'd said. I was glad that he seemed to have shaken off his anger, but it also left me feeling strangely alone.

"I see you and Alex seem to be getting along," Hailey said, following my gaze. "He's so nice. He helped me and Sean move."

"Oh yeah?" I couldn't help but be distracted as Alex elbowed the big guy and then slapped him on the back. I wondered what they were saying.

"Yep, he met us at Sean's old apartment and helped carry some of the heavier stuff that I couldn't help with."

"Where'd you put your stuff?" I asked distractedly. "I haven't seen any of it here."

"I didn't bring any of my furniture with me," she said easily. "I just gave it to my roommates."

"You what?" I asked, finally paying attention to our conversation. "Why would you do that?"

She laughed. "You've seen this place! It's not like we could fit all of it in here."

"Hailey, that's—" I started to tell her what a bad idea it was for her to give away all her stuff, when Sean came up behind her and wrapped an arm around her shoulders. He was far past drunk and sliding into sloppy.

"Babe," he slurred. "Kegs'r almost gone."

"That's good, right?" she replied, looking up at him with a smile. I realized then that she must have had quite a bit of alcohol, too, because she hadn't even noticed the annoyance in his voice.

"No," he said slowly, as if she were an idiot. "People won't have anything to drink."

"We have soda," she said, laughing a little as she rolled her eyes at me. "And water."

Her face changed and her shoulders rolled in a little as Sean tightened his arm around her.

"We're not giving them soda," he said, his voice dropping. "Are you fucking kidding?"

"Hey," I said before I could think it through. "Knock it off, Sean."

"Bitch, why don't you get the fuck out—"

I took a startled step back at the vehemence in his words and ran straight into a muscular chest.

"What's going on?" Alex said from behind me. I was too rattled to move when his hand squeezed my shoulder gently and then stayed there. "Looks like the kegs are getting low, so Clover and I are going to run to the store. You have any requests?"

"Nah, man," Sean said, letting go of Hailey. "You don't have to do that. I'll—"

"No problem at all." Alex cut him off. "You can pay me back later, yeah?"

As soon as Sean nodded and moved away from us, Hailey smiled at me. "Whoops! Guess we should have planned ahead," she said happily, like the last few minutes had never happened.

"You want to ride with us?" Alex asked, leaning close to my ear.

I wasn't quite ready to leave Hailey with her asshole boyfriend, but I didn't exactly want to stay in the same vicinity as Sean, either. When he'd looked at me, I'd seen him. Not the face he showed the world, but the asshole that he tried to keep hidden. I glanced around the room, and when I saw the familiar faces of some of my classmates, I decided that Hailey would be okay if I went with Alex.

"Yeah," I replied. "I need to grab my jacket."

Alex waited while I grabbed my coat from Hailey's room, and then led me out of the house. The rain had stopped sometime when we were inside, and the air smelled fresh and clean after I'd been breathing in the scent of other people. I took a deep breath as he held my coat up so I could thread my arms into the sleeves.

I shoved my hands into the pockets of my coat, relieved that no one had stolen my wallet, phone, or keys, and followed Alex to his truck. I wasn't paying any attention to where we were going and was startled as the big guy from the party stepped out of the shadows.

"Hey, I'm Keegan," he said, reaching out to shake my hand. "I saw what happened in there. You okay?"

"Sarai," I replied. "And I'm fine." I waved my hand nonchalantly and then dropped it when I realized I was overplaying my answer.

Keegan looked back and forth between Alex and me.

"Why don't I stay here," he said, taking a step backward. "I'll help you unload when you get back."

"You sure?" Alex asked.

"Yeah, man," Keegan replied, grinning. "Your truck ain't really built for three."

He walked away with a wave as Alex opened up the passenger door. I took a deep breath as I climbed inside the truck and watched Keegan's broad shoulders disappear into the house, then Alex shut my door and went around to his side.

"All set?" he asked, starting the engine.

"Yep."

We pulled out onto the street and I tried to relax into my seat, but it wasn't really happening. I was always a little nervous riding with new people, and on top of that, I was closed in with the guy I'd been thinking about for weeks.

"Thank you for what you did earlier," I said, glancing at him.

"Of course," he replied, flexing his fingers on the steering wheel.

He didn't say anything else, and the silence stretched into awkwardness while I searched for something to say.

"I thought you told Sean that someone named Clover was going with you?" I finally asked, grasping at straws.

"That's Keegan," Alex replied. "His name's Keegan Clovis."

"But you call him Clover?"

Alex grinned and glanced at me before turning his gaze back to the road.

"You can't smile like that and not tell me why," I said, turning my body toward him a little.

"It goes back to when we first met," Alex said. "Me and Clover both got stationed here around the same time, and as the new guys, we didn't have many friends, you know? So we exchanged numbers, planning to hang out at some point, but that same night I get a call at like two in the morning." He looked at me again, and I felt my heart do this weird thump. He was really gorgeous. "Turns out, the caller is Keegan. He asks me to come pick him up at some house off base. I bitch and moan, but I do it, right? The guy doesn't know anyone but me, and I can't just leave him stranded."

"That was nice of you," I replied.

"Oh, it was worth it," Alex said. "I get to this house and all the lights are off, and I'm wondering what the hell is going on. I just happen to glance at the field across the street, and there's Keegan, doing a little shimmy in nothing but a pair of cowboy boots, using a hat to cover his junk."

"No," I said, laughing.

"Oh yeah. Turns out the lady was married, and Keegan had to bail out the window bare-assed naked." Alex laughed.

"But where did the name Clo—oh," I said as it all became clear. "He was standing in a field of clover, wasn't he?"

"Yep," Alex answered as he pulled into the parking lot. "Kind of perfect that his last name was Clovis."

I laughed. "What do you two do in the Army?" I asked as he parked and we climbed out of the truck.

"Nothing exciting," he said with a laugh. "I'm just a grunt—infantry."

"I have no idea what that means," I confessed.

"I'm just a soldier," he said with a grin as he gestured for me to walk into the store ahead of him. "That's my specialty. Nothing fancy."

Alex seemed to know where he was going, so I followed him to the coolers in the back and stood there while he loaded cases of beer into the shopping cart. He didn't let me carry anything or pay, but he refused so politely that I couldn't even argue. I'm a strong, independent woman who works out occasionally; I could've easily helped him load beer into the bed of his truck, but I kind of liked the fact that he held my door and helped me inside the cab before loading everything. It was so unassumingly sweet.

"You doing okay?" Alex asked as we headed back toward Hailey and Sean's. "You know, after all that shit earlier?"

"Yeah. I'm okay," I replied, turning my head to watch him as I remembered how he'd thrown that guy against the wall. "You didn't have to do that."

"Yes, I did," he said. He reached up and scratched where a five-o'clock shadow darkened the side of his face. "I can't stand that kind of stuff, and if no one does anything, then guys like that think they can keep doing it."

"He seemed pretty wasted," I murmured.

"Don't do that," Alex said softly. "Don't make excuses. It doesn't matter how drunk I am—I'd never touch some woman without making damn sure she wanted me to. No one else should do it, either."

"I agree," I said simply. "There's no excuse."

"Good." Alex nodded. He reached out and flipped his hand palm up.

The calluses on his fingers rasped against my skin as I put my hand in his.

"See?" he said, shrugging as he gave my hand a squeeze. "Easy as that."

I smiled as I watched his fingers thread through mine until his swollen knuckles pressed against my unblemished ones. His thumb slid gently back and forth over the back of my hand, and all my rules about distractions and my excuses for staying single flew out the window. I was pretty sure there was no way I'd ever be able to say no to Alex Evans again.

CHAPTER 3

ALEX

I liked having Sarai in my truck, especially with her fingers wrapped around mine. I'd never really been a hand-holder, but this felt good. Easy. The dark cab of the truck made it feel like we were in our own little world. I glanced over at her profile and contemplated taking the long route back to the house but decided against it. I didn't want to freak her out after the kitchen incident earlier.

When I'd seen that guy reach out and grab a handful of Sarai's ass, I'd lost it. He'd been lucky that all he'd gotten was a couple of punches. I'd wanted to knock him unconscious and then stomp as hard as I could on his hand. I was grateful that Clover had stopped me, but a part of me resented it, too.

I'd still been a little wired from the whole thing when I'd heard Sean being an asshole to Sarai, and he'd nearly felt the edges of my knuckles, too, if I was being honest. Sarai had held her own, though, even though it was clear she was rattled, and I hadn't wanted to take away from that. I belonged to a family of strong women, and I knew from experience that sometimes a good man watched them fight their own battles. Since Sean had kept his hands to himself, so had I.

"Where did everyone go?" Sarai asked in confusion as we pulled into the grass in front of Sean and Hailey's house.

The rows of cars that had been there when we left were mostly gone. I parked right out front, but when I got out, I didn't grab the beer out of the back. It was too quiet.

When we reached the front steps, I noticed Clover sitting in a lawn chair in the dark, smoking a cigar.

"Figured I'd hang out until y'all got back," he said, pushing himself to his feet. "But I'm pretty sure Ice Man in there is about to pass out."

Just as Clover finished speaking, we heard Sean start shouting inside the house. I lifted my arm and blocked Sarai from the front door.

"Stay out here," I ordered, reaching for the door handle.

"Uh, no," she argued. She scooted between me and the door and pushed her way inside.

When we walked into the living room, Sean's voice was even louder, but we couldn't see him. It wasn't until we turned the slight corner into the kitchen that he came into view.

Hailey was standing with her arms crossed over her chest, and tears were rolling down her face while Sean yelled, pointing at her.

"What the hell, Sean?" I asked, just as Sarai asked Hailey if she was okay.

"Hey, man," Sean said, dropping his hand as soon as he realized we were standing there. "Thought you left."

"Just to get more beer," Clover replied from behind me. "I fucking told you that."

It was the wrong thing to say. Hailey seemed to shrink a little as Sean scoffed.

"Soon as the beer ran out, everyone bailed," he said, pulling out a chair and dropping into it as if this were the worst thing that had ever happened.

"I didn't order enough," Hailey said quietly. She grabbed a piece of garbage off the table and held it awkwardly in her hand like she wasn't sure what to do with it.

"I thought Sean picked up the kegs," Sarai said.

"He did." Hailey shrugged. "But I had to order them first."

"Told her to get four," Sean said, rolling his eyes.

"I told you they only had two left," Hailey replied.

"Because you waited until the last goddamn minute to order them."

"Don't talk to her like that," Sarai snapped at Sean.

Sean's scowl darkened as he looked at Sarai. He tilted his head a fraction, and his fingers tapped out a rhythm on the tabletop. I knew the instant he decided to take a verbal swipe at her, and I stepped forward, ready to stop him.

"Why don't you sleep it off, Sean," Clover said, disgust clear in his voice. "You're being a douche."

"*That's* why you called him Ice Man," Sarai said to herself. "*Top Gun.*"

"What did you say to me?" Sean asked Clover, getting to his feet. "Come on over and say that to my face."

"I'm right in front of you, idiot," Clover shot back, lifting his hands in the air in a *come and get me* gesture. "You're being a douche." He enunciated the words slowly and clearly.

Sean charged forward, but I stopped him before he reached Clover. In a normal course of events, I'd let Clover beat the shit out of Sean for being a jerk to the ladies, but we were in a very confined space. There was too big of a chance that Sarai or Hailey would get hurt if the guys got into it here.

"Come on, big guy," I said, wrapping my arms around Sean in a bear hug. "Why don't you sleep it off."

"Fucking Clovis," Sean muttered, the fight going out of him.

I half carried and half dragged Sean into the bedroom. All the beer he'd consumed had finally caught up to him, and he was practically passed out in my arms. Hailey followed us in, and as soon as I'd dropped Sean on the bed, she was there, lifting his feet to pull his shoes and socks off.

I stared at Sean in disgust. I didn't consider him a friend, but I'd always gotten along okay with him. Hell, I'd even helped the dumbass move. I sure as hell wasn't doing him any favors after this debacle.

"Leave him," I told Hailey quietly as she started to take his jeans off. "He won't even notice them."

She followed me silently out of the bedroom, shutting the door behind her. As soon as we reached Clover and Sarai, Hailey started apologizing.

"I'm so sorry, you guys," she said, wrapping her arms around her waist.

"Why are you apologizing?" Sarai asked, shaking her head. "That wasn't your fault."

"It kind of was," Hailey argued.

Sarai's mouth opened like she was going to say something,

but snapped shut again. Her nostrils flared as she took a deep breath.

"You should come stay with me tonight," Sarai said after a moment. "Come back after he's sober."

Hailey shook her head. "He'll sleep until morning," she said. "Seriously, it's fine."

I could tell that Sarai wanted to argue. The look on her face was a mixture of exasperation and anger, but instead of telling her friend what she thought, she just nodded.

"Are you sure?" Sarai asked Hailey, reaching out to rub her hand up and down Hailey's arm. "I have a super-comfortable couch."

"I'm sure," Hailey replied. "I'll probably just clean up and head to bed."

We left a few minutes later. Sarai wanted to help with the cleanup, but Hailey practically ushered us out the door.

When we stepped into the cool night air, Sarai cursed quietly.

"What's up?" I asked.

"That's my car," she said with a sigh.

She gestured to a small sedan that was parked in the driveway, the bumper only a foot from the porch. The car was fine. The problem was the truck parked directly behind it. There was no way she'd be moving her car. We could call a tow truck, but that would be an epically shitty thing to do. Someone had probably drunk too much and gotten a ride home—they shouldn't have to pay for that.

"This night just keeps getting better and better," Sarai said softly.

I glanced at Clover, who was watching me with a grin on

his face. He gestured to Sarai and raised his eyebrows.

"I'll give you a ride home," I told Sarai, flipping Clover off as he gave me a thumbs-up.

"I need my car," she replied. She was still staring at it, probably trying to think of any way she could get it out of there.

"I'll bring you back in the morning to get it," I assured her.

"That's such a hassle, though," she said, grimacing. "Why would he park so fucking close behind me?"

"What makes you think it's a guy?" Clover asked, laughter in his voice.

Sarai glanced at him and back at the truck. "With tires that big, the owner of that truck must be compensating for a small penis," she said seriously.

I snickered and followed Sarai as she walked toward my truck.

"I would like that ride, if you're sure," she said, glancing up at me.

"Absolutely," I replied, trying to play it cool even though I was completely stoked that I'd get to spend more time with her.

"It was nice to meet you, Sarai," Clover called out as he took a couple of steps backward toward *his* lifted truck. "Evans, I'll see you Monday."

"It was nice to meet you, too," Sarai called back as I opened the door for her.

"Where am I going?" I asked after I'd rounded the truck and climbed into my seat.

I felt bad that she seemed so upset about leaving her car, but I couldn't help but feel a little lucky at the turn of events. I hadn't expected the chance to have her all to myself again, even for a few minutes.

"Take a left," she said, leaning her head tiredly against the headrest. "Then a right at the stop sign."

I pulled out onto the street and followed her directions.

"Have you and Hailey been friends for long?" I asked, glancing at her. It was dark in the truck, but I could see her profile clearly as she stared out the windshield.

"Two years," she answered.

I started to ask another question, trying to get her talking again, but she cut me off almost immediately.

"I can't believe you're friends with Sean," she said. "I can't believe anyone is friends with him."

"Yeah," I said carefully. I wasn't sure how to explain why I'd ever hung out with Sean. He wasn't my favorite person by any means. Most of the time, I thought he was kind of an asshole. But there was something about the relationship between fellow brothers-in-arms that civilians just didn't understand. I might not like the guy, but I knew without a doubt that when push came to shove, he'd have my back like I'd have his. It wasn't a friendship, exactly, but until tonight, he hadn't given me a reason to actively dislike him.

"I try to keep my mouth shut," she said. "I don't talk badly about him to her, even though I think moving in together was a terrible decision."

"Yeah," I said again. I'd been surprised as hell when Sean had asked me to help him move. It seemed like a bad idea, but it wasn't my business.

"But tonight"—she shook her head—"he was *such* an asshole. Why would she put up with that?"

"I don't know," I replied honestly. "In my family, that shit is never okay. You treat your partner with respect no matter how pissed you are."

"I don't like it," Sarai said. "Get on the highway here."

"I don't like it, either," I told her as I turned where she directed me. "Tonight, I thought the best course of action was to put his ass in bed. I didn't want to make anything worse, you know?"

"Yep," she said quietly. "I can imagine how Sean would act if you tried to correct him."

"Like a big toddler?" I half joked.

"Like a bully," Sarai replied seriously.

"I'll see if I can talk to him at work on Monday," I said after a few moments of quiet. "He might feel like shit about it when he wakes up tomorrow."

"Somehow, I doubt it."

I didn't reply, but I agreed with her. Sean was cocky and selfish on his best days. Alcohol only magnified his bad traits; it didn't create them.

"I have to ask," I said after the truck had been silent for a few minutes. "Where are you from?"

She looked at me and smiled. "Missouri," she said easily, watching for my response.

I laughed, because she was clearly messing with me. "That accent isn't from Missouri," I argued.

"It's true," she replied. "I was born in Missouri."

"And then?"

"And I moved to New York when I was fourteen," she said. "That's probably the accent you're hearing."

"New York, huh?"

"Yes."

"Really? That's all you're going to give me?" I was worried that we were almost to her apartment and I still barely knew anything about her. This was my chance, and once again I was kind of blowing it.

"I lived in New York with my aunt and uncle until I came back for college," she said.

"The Big Apple," I said, making her laugh.

"Both of my parents were New Yorkers," she explained.

"They were from New York and they chose to move to *Missouri*?" Wait, she said *were*?

"The heart wants what it wants," Sarai said, lifting her hands in a *who knows* gesture. "My father was an architect, and there was a firm here that offered him a good job."

"Was?" I asked carefully.

"They died when I was fourteen," she replied.

"Which is why you moved in with your aunt and uncle," I murmured in understanding. "I'm sorry to hear that."

"Thanks," she said softly. "My uncle and aunt never understood the lure of Missouri, either," she said. "They're still waiting on me to move back home."

"Is New York home, then?" I asked as she pointed to an apartment complex on the right.

"Home is…illusive. I thought Missouri was home, and so I came back."

"It wasn't what you expected?" I asked as I pulled into a parking space and put the truck in park.

"It was everything I remembered," she said, turning to look at me. "And nothing like home."

"Do you think you'll move back to New York when you're done with school?"

"I don't know. I'm keeping my options open," she said with a sigh. "I miss my family, of course, but I also like the freedom I have when we don't live in the same place."

"Freedom?"

"My aunt is a little overbearing," Sarai said, rolling her eyes. "And family is everywhere in my old neighborhood. I can't walk a block without seeing someone I know or someone who knows my aunt and uncle or remembers my parents. It's impossible to be anonymous. But if I moved back to the city and didn't live in our neighborhood, my aunt would take that as a personal attack."

"It sounds kind of great to be surrounded by people who love you," I replied. I'd been in the Army and moving around for so long I had a hard time remembering how that felt.

"It is, and it isn't." She took off her seat belt and smiled. "And I have no idea how we got on this conversation."

"It's my charm," I said with mock seriousness. "People spill all their secrets around me."

"Did I tell you any secrets?" she asked, cocking her head to the side like she was trying to remember.

"Not yet," I said.

Her hair was falling over her bare shoulder, sliding this way and that every time she shifted her head, and I was mesmerized. I wanted to touch it. Grab it. Run my fingers through it. I'd never seen anyone with hair that shiny before. Like silk.

"Not ever," she replied with a wrinkle of her nose. "But thank you very much for the ride home."

"No problem," I said, snapping back to attention. "I'll come get you in the morning to pick up your car."

"I can call an Uber," she said as she opened her door.

I quickly unbuckled my seat belt and followed her out of the truck.

"Why bother?" I asked as I met her at the front of the truck. "I don't mind coming to get you."

She paused and looked up at me. "You're walking me to the door?"

"Of course," I said. "My dad's rules, remember?"

"What would your dad say if you insisted even though the woman didn't want you to walk her?" she asked curiously.

I stopped walking. "Is that what's happening now?" I asked.

Sarai smiled. "No. You can walk me."

I let out a small sigh of relief and caught up to her.

"You know, I'm still hoping you'll go to dinner with me," I said as she started up the stairs.

She paused and stared down at me for a moment, then laughed, her eyes lighting up.

"You don't give up, do you?"

"Not usually," I confessed as she started climbing again. "Especially when I feel strongly about something."

"You don't even know me," she scoffed good-naturedly.

"I want to get to know you," I replied. "I like what I've seen, and I want to know you better."

"Well, that's honest," she said as she stopped in front of her apartment door.

"Honesty is always the best policy," I said, grinning.

"This works for you, doesn't it?" she asked, waving a hand up and down between us. "The charm and the smile and the *honesty*. It's your thing."

"Full disclosure, Sarai? I haven't asked any woman out in a long-ass time, and I haven't even been interested in anyone but you since we met."

She looked at me for a long time without replying. When she finally spoke, I wanted to punch the air in celebration.

"Breakfast," she said, tilting her chin up.

"Breakfast it is," I said, smiling happily. "What time should I pick you up?"

"Ten," she said as she unlocked her door. She opened it and stepped inside, then turned back to me.

"You're not invited in," she said, her lips tipped up in a small grin.

"I didn't think I was," I replied, my own lips curving upward.

"Good night, Alex."

"Good night, Sarai."

She closed the door, and I couldn't help myself. I spun in a circle, fist pumped a couple of times, and punched the air as if I were hitting a speed bag. A knocking sound interrupted me, and I froze, then slowly turned my head toward Sarai's apartment. She was standing in the window next to the door, laughing hysterically.

I ran a hand over my face and shrugged in embarrassment. Then, since I loved the look on her face, I punched the air a couple of times more, waved one arm like Arsenio Hall, and moonwalked out of her sight.

As soon as I reached the parking lot again, I pulled out my phone.

"I will kill you," Ani answered.

"I have a date tomorrow," I said before she went into detail about exactly how she planned on killing me. "Breakfast."

"Friend zone," she said flatly. "You called me at ten o'clock to tell me you'd been friend zoned."

"I'm not friend zoned," I argued, climbing into my truck.

"You're totally friend zoned."

"She agreed to a date," I said, pausing with my keys in the ignition.

"She agreed to breakfast."

"So?"

"Breakfast isn't an actual date unless she slept over," Ani said drily. Bram said something in the background that I couldn't hear.

"What did he say?" I asked.

"He said even he knew that breakfast isn't a date."

"It's a date," I ground out.

"It really isn't."

"Shit." I turned the truck on and dropped my phone on the passenger seat as the Bluetooth clicked on. "Are you sure?"

"Jesus, Alex," Ani said with a snicker. "Breakfast is even worse than lunch. At least with lunch, it could turn into dinner. Breakfast is like, *Let me get this out of the way before I get on with my plans for the day.*"

"She likes me," I replied stubbornly.

"She may like you, but she's not interested."

"You're wrong."

"We'll see," Ani joked.

"I have to go," I mumbled. "I'm driving."

"You're echoing, so I know I'm on Bluetooth and you can still talk to me," Ani called out as I hung up on her.

"Dammit," I said under my breath as I pulled out of the parking lot.

Ani was wrong. I was almost sure of it. Sarai wouldn't have made any plans with me at all if she was trying to blow me off. She'd had no problem turning me down before.

I really hoped Sarai wasn't putting me in the damn friend zone. I wanted to be more than friends. That sounded sappy and ridiculous, but it was true. I wanted to know her better than I knew my friends. I wanted to know what made her tick, what made her work so hard, what made her laugh and cry. I wanted to watch stupid chick flicks with her and then bitch to my brother about it. I wanted to see her naked. God, did I want to see her naked. I wanted to map every inch of her skin with my mouth, find every mole and dimple.

With another curse, I scrolled through my contacts. Whenever I was in need of advice, I went to two people— Ani, who was a complete cynic, and my sister, Kate, a self-proclaimed romantic. I usually took their advice, smashed it together, and went with something in between.

Kate answered her phone on the first ring. "Breakfast isn't a date."

"How the hell did she get to you so fast?" I asked in annoyance.

"She sent a text," Kate said, laughing.

"You both suck."

"I love you," she said as I hung up on her, too.

They were wrong. Sarai was beginning to warm to me. I could feel it.

CHAPTER 4

SARAI

I flipped onto my back and stared at the ceiling Sunday morning, my stomach in knots. Agreeing to a breakfast date with Alex had seemed like such a good idea when he was standing there with that infectious smile on his face, but now I was worrying that maybe I'd started something that I didn't exactly have the time for and wasn't really ready for. It was eight o'clock already, and I still had so much homework and laundry to do that I was going to be up super late trying to finish it all. My days were always full; that was why I'd been avoiding relationships while I was still in school. After I was done—with my degree in hand and a sweet job waiting for me—would be the perfect time to start dating again.

I'd spent the last ten years planning ahead and scheduling everything. If I said I was going to be somewhere, I went. If I didn't have time for something, I didn't overschedule and try to do it anyway. I knew from experience that things went sideways when I deviated from the plans I'd made, so I didn't do it, and when I did, my anxiety went through the roof.

But there was no way I could have planned for Alex.

I crawled out of bed and headed to the shower, my shoulders sore from how tense they'd been the night before. The party that Hailey had been so excited about had ended in disaster. I couldn't believe how Sean had behaved as if it had been Hailey's fault that all his friends had bailed. What a jerk.

I really hoped that he had a hell of a hangover when he woke up this morning, though it wouldn't be enough to pay him back for the way he'd treated Hailey. I'd hated leaving her there with him, but I hadn't been able to change her mind about coming home with me.

Men like Sean, who treated their girlfriends like crap from the very beginning, only got worse with time. They pushed and pushed, knowing that the deeper they got into the relationship, the worse they could act without repercussions. I'd seen it happen to friends in high school, and unfortunately, I'd see it again. It made me sick to watch.

I'd been lucky enough to grow up in two households where the men treated their wives like queens. My uncle worshipped the ground my aunt walked on, and was openly affectionate. My father, on the other hand, had been more reserved and quiet, but his adoration for my mother had been apparent in every look and gesture.

I knew that type of relationship was possible, so it always drove me crazy when a friend stayed with someone who didn't treat them like they mattered.

I ignored the impulse to call Hailey and make sure she was

okay as I got ready for breakfast with Alex. If she needed me, she'd call me. There was only so much you could do for someone when they didn't want your help, and alienating the best friend I had because I didn't like her boyfriend seemed counterproductive.

I took my time getting dressed and braiding my hair, but I didn't bother with much makeup. As soon as I was ready, I sat down at my laptop and worked steadily until there was a knock on my door. Alex was right on time.

I opened the door and said "Hey" as I slid on my coat.

"Hey yourself," he replied, reaching out to fix the hood that had caught on the inside of my jacket. "Ready for breakfast?"

"I'm starving," I said, grabbing my purse. "Do you care if I pick the place?"

"Not at all." He reached out, palm up, and my belly fluttered as I placed my hand in his. He must have just showered, because his hair was still damp, and as we walked toward his truck, I realized he smelled really good, too. He was wearing a nice pair of jeans and a button-down shirt under his coat, and I had to admit that I was flattered that he'd spruced up a little for our date, considering that we were just getting breakfast.

"There's a place that I used to go with my parents years ago that's really good," I told him once we were inside the warm cab of his truck. "The owners are in their eighties now, and the wife still cooks, and the husband still greets everyone at the door."

"That's awesome," Alex said, grinning.

"It is," I agreed. "Their kids are still around, and pretty

much all of them work there, but the parents are the heart of the place."

"That's how it is with my dad and uncle," he said, nodding. "I mean, they're not in their eighties yet, obviously."

"Your family owns a restaurant?" I asked in surprise. I was a little nervous now. The food where we were going was good, but it wasn't fancy. If his family was in the food business, he might not be very impressed.

"No," he said with a little laugh. "Sorry, I should have clarified. My dad and uncle own a logging business. They've handed it off to my brother and cousin, but they're still a huge part of what makes the company what it is. I'm pretty sure that they'll still be puttering around the office when they're in their eighties."

"Logging, huh?" I asked. "Take a right at the stop sign. It's in the little strip mall with the dollar store."

"Okay. I know that place." He rolled to a stop and turned to look at me. "And yeah, logging's a pretty big business back home."

"Where are you from?" I asked. I hadn't even thought about where his family was, even though I should have. I knew he was in the Army, so it made sense that he wasn't from around here; I just hadn't really connected the dots.

"I'm from Oregon," he said. "The land of Christmas trees and weed."

I let out a surprised laugh. "Well, those are interesting things to be known for."

"I know, right?" He smiled. "I think we're the Christmas tree capital of the world or something like that. It's only recently that people started owning up to the weed part."

"It's legal there now, isn't it?" I asked.

"Yeah," Alex said, turning into the parking lot. "It's legal. Most people still don't do it, though. Some employers forbid it, so you might not get arrested, but you could still lose your job."

"That makes sense, I guess."

"I don't know," Alex said, shaking his head a little. "Employers don't seem to have a problem with alcohol. Seems a bit hypocritical to me."

He put the truck in park and got out, and I laughed as he practically ran around to my side so he could open my door.

"But don't you think drugs are a little more serious than a glass of wine?" I asked, curious about his stance. I'd never really had a conversation about the ethical arguments of marijuana usage, and I couldn't help but be a little fascinated by the way he spoke about it. Marijuana was still very taboo in the circles I was a part of.

"Not really," he said with a shrug. He closed my door and set his hand on the small of my back as we walked toward the restaurant. "I know a lot of people back home who don't smoke to get wasted. A couple hits at the end of the day to relax is pretty similar to having a glass of wine. Plus, there are a lot of pain-relieving properties that people choose to ignore because of the stigma attached to marijuana."

"You seem passionate about it," I murmured as he opened the restaurant door for me.

"Eh, I wouldn't say passionate, exactly," he said quietly. "Just probably more educated on the subject than most people around here." He shrugged. "My dad has a bad back—hell, bad hips and shoulders, too. Weed's the only thing that gives him some relief. Hard not to support that."

I nodded in understanding as we stepped into the restaurant. The tone in his voice as he spoke about his dad left me feeling all warm and fuzzy. It was rare to hear men talk about their family with that type of love in their voice, especially on the first date.

"Sarai Levy!" Mr. Krakowski called as soon as he spotted me. He always said my full name like that, even though I'd been in to see him and his wife hundreds of times since I'd moved back. I suddenly realized that I probably shouldn't have brought Alex to this particular place if I wanted to keep our meal simple.

"Hi, Mr. K," I said as he kissed me on the cheek and hugged me hard. "How've you been?"

"These old bones are still holding me up," he joked, a huge smile on his face. "I can't complain." He looked at Alex beside me and stood up a little straighter. "Hello, young man."

Oh, crap. Choosing this place had been a terrible idea.

"Hello, sir," Alex said, reaching out a hand for Mr. Krakowski to shake. "I'm Alex."

"Malachi Krakowski," Mr. K replied. "Welcome to my restaurant."

I smiled lamely as Mr. K looked Alex over. Usually, he would have seated me at a table by the window by now, especially on a Sunday morning when they were busy.

"Is Mrs. K cooking today?" I asked just to break the silence.

"No, no," Mr. K said, finally turning to look at me again. "She's got the girls in there today, trying to teach them. I think it's a lost cause."

I laughed like I was supposed to and put my arm through his, leading him to the table I wanted to sit at. "Will this work for us?"

"Well, sure," he said, giving my hand a little squeeze. "Enjoy."

As soon as he'd walked away and we'd sat down, Alex started to snicker.

"He loves you," he said, unwrapping his napkin from his silverware and placing it on his lap.

"How could you tell?" I asked drily. I took my coat off and hung it on the back of my chair. "Sorry about that. I've never brought a guy in here before."

"I'm your first?" he asked, grinning.

I just rolled my eyes. "Mr. K and his wife have always been friends of my family. They kind of took my parents under their wing when they got here from New York and didn't know anyone."

"That's cool. Like surrogate grandparents."

"Sort of. I think they understood how isolating moving to a new place could be. They emigrated from Poland in the forties." I smiled as our waitress, one of Mr. K's actual granddaughters, poured us both some coffee. As soon as she moved away, I continued. "I lost touch with them when I moved, but as soon as I got back here, I stopped in. They pretty much treated me like they'd just seen me the week before."

"They must have missed you."

"Yeah." I nodded. "I missed them, too." I'd missed Mr. and Mrs. K so much that I'd come into the restaurant within the first week of being back in Missouri. I was ashamed that I'd never tried to keep in contact with them when I'd moved to

New York, but dealing with the loss of my parents had taken precedence over everything, even the old couple I thought of as family.

"Do you come here a lot?" he asked as he grabbed a menu.

"At least once a week," I confessed, grinning sheepishly. "I don't always eat, though. Sometimes I just stop for coffee on my way home from work."

I didn't tell him that the Krakowskis were one of the biggest reasons that I hadn't gone back to New York during those first two miserable years back in Missouri. Without them, I would have felt completely alone. We'd had a lot of friends when I'd lived here with my parents, but we'd known most of them from our synagogue, a place I avoided now.

"You want your usual?" Mrs. Krakowski asked as she moved slowly toward us. "Papa says you brought a man friend!"

"Hi, Mrs. K. This is Alex," I said, standing up to give her a hug. According to the photo hanging in the entryway, Mrs. K had once been a tall, curvy woman with hair that reached her waist, but now she was petite and a little hunched over, with a short haircut that she back-combed religiously.

"Hello, Alex," she said, looking him over. "This one is handsome," she said to me out of the side of her mouth.

"And he knows it," I said back the same way.

Alex laughed and said hello.

"Pancakes, yes?" Mrs. K asked as soon as I'd sat back down.

"Yes, please."

She turned to Alex and waited.

"Um." He glanced down at his menu, his eyes wide.

"I'll get you pancakes, also," Mrs. K said quickly with a nod. "Kosher?"

"Excuse me?" Alex asked.

"Kosher, yes?" She was looking at him like he had two heads.

"Yes," I replied for him.

"Good." She walked away slowly, smiling hello to the other patrons at their tables.

"Was she asking me if I eat kosher?" Alex asked in confusion.

"Yes." I met his eyes.

"Okay." He looked in the direction Mrs. K had gone and then back at me. "Because you eat kosher?"

"I try to, yes."

"You're Jewish," he said, smiling. "I'm so glad I didn't pick the place to eat."

"I can find food anywhere," I replied, shrugging my shoulders. "I'm not exactly practicing. I haven't been to temple in years."

"It sounds like there's a story there," Alex replied softly.

"Not one I'm going to tell on our first date," I said ruefully.

"Fair enough," Alex said easily. "The Krakowskis are Jewish, too?"

"Yes." I paused. "Though they aren't practicing, either."

I'd never asked why Mr. and Mrs. Krakowski chose to leave the faith. I'd always been curious about it, but it wasn't any of my business. When I'd come back to Missouri determined to never step foot in a synagogue again, I'd just been thankful for friends who wouldn't say a word about my aversion. After my parents died, my uncle and aunt had to force me to attend services. I didn't see the point of praying to someone who didn't do a damn thing to stop a fourteen-year-old from losing her parents.

"Is all of the restaurant food kosher?" Alex asked.

"Yes," I replied. "But some Jews pick and choose the rules that they'll follow. Mrs. K makes sure she follows them all. I've seen rabbis in here for lunch."

"So her question was a test, then," Alex said.

"Not a test, exactly." I smiled in apology. "More like a way to find out if you were Jewish or not."

"Is it bad if I'm not?" he whispered, leaning across the table.

"That depends," I whispered back, leaning forward, too.

"On what?"

I couldn't help myself. "You don't have to be Jewish, but circumcision is a requirement."

Alex's mouth dropped open in surprise, and I bit the inside of my cheek to keep myself from laughing.

"For you or Mrs. K?" Alex asked with a grimace.

"Me," I said through the laughter I couldn't hold back anymore.

Alex's mouth snapped shut and he leaned back in his seat. He brushed off one shoulder and looked at me smugly. "I meet the requirement."

I snorted out a laugh, making him smile.

"I knew you liked me," he said happily.

"Did you?" I asked, taking a drink of my coffee.

"I was really hoping."

"You know how attractive you are—" I began.

"Not prettier than you," he cut in, reminding me of the night we met.

I laughed and shrugged. "I was searching for excuses, and you"—I pointed at him—"were a little too sure of yourself."

"Confident," he said.

"Cocky," I replied.

"Comfortable in my own skin."

"Conceited."

"I give up," he joked, raising his hands in the air.

"You're hard to say no to," I confessed, taking another sip of my coffee. "But I'm being honest when I say I have no time. I work and go to school all week, and on my days off I clean my house and do homework."

"I'm good at cleaning," he said, his lips tipping up in a lop-sided grin.

"Are you offering to clean my house?" I asked incredulously.

"If it means I can spend some time with you, then yes."

"Done." I smacked my hand lightly on the table.

"Really?" he asked, his eyes lighting up.

"No, not really," I replied, kicking his foot under the table. "You're not cleaning my house."

"Honestly, Sarai," he said, pausing as the waitress put our plates down in front of us. "Whenever you can make time, I'll be there."

I watched him as he casually picked up his fork and butter knife.

"Look," he said, putting his fork and knife back down when he realized that I hadn't started eating yet. "You have a life and I have a life. Right now it sounds like you're busier than I am, okay? At some point, I'm going to be busier than you. That's just the way things work when you're an adult. I'm willing to work around our schedules if you are."

"I've honestly never heard anyone put it that way before,"

I told him, picking up my silverware. "Most people want to be the center of attention all the time."

"I'm in the military, and I have a huge family back home that I go to see whenever I can," he said seriously. "You're not the only one who doesn't have a whole lot of spare time."

"It's not that I don't have a lot of spare time," I said, beginning to eat. "I don't really have *any* spare time."

"You said you stop here for coffee once in a while, right?" he asked. "So I'll stop in with you. You don't want to cook? Let me know, and we can grab a quick bite somewhere and then you can go home and get things done. It doesn't have to be hard."

I thought about his words. The idea was tempting, but I still hesitated. "I only have six months of school left, Alex," I said, meeting his eyes. "And I don't know where I'll be after that." I had to put that out there. I wasn't sure what his end game was—a relationship or just a little fun. If he was looking for something long term, I didn't know if I could agree to that with everything up in the air.

"I don't want to be fuck buddies," Alex said, his voice so quiet that I could barely hear him. "If that's what you're thinking. I'm getting too old for that type of thing. I want to spend time with you, as much as I can get for however long it lasts."

"Just friends?" I asked with completely feigned nonchalance.

"Oh, hell no," Alex said quickly. "I want you. That's just not *all* I want."

I smiled. "Sweet talker."

"Give it a chance?" he asked, his eyes crinkling at the corners as he smiled at me. "If at some point you decide that it's not working, we'll walk away. No harm, no foul."

I stared at him for a long moment. It had been so long since I'd been this attracted to someone. It wasn't just Alex's looks that had me rethinking my stance on dating; it was everything else, too. His protectiveness at the party and the way his fingers felt threaded through mine, the way he opened doors and insisted on walking me in, and even the way he tilted his head when he was listening intently to what I said all seemed to pull me further and further into his orbit.

"Okay," I said nonchalantly.

"Yeah?" he asked with a huge smile.

"Yeah," I replied, smiling back. My stomach felt as if it were filled with a thousand butterflies.

* * *

I was still running on an Alex high a week later. Honestly, I hadn't come down from it since he'd dropped me off at my car after breakfast.

I'd heard from him pretty regularly since then, quick texts to tell me he was thinking about me before going to bed at night and sometimes when he woke up in the morning. Pictures of things he was doing and memes he thought were funny. Thinking about them made me smile. He knew how busy I was, so he'd kept his distance but still made time to make sure I knew I was on his mind. In return, I sent him pictures throughout the day, silly ones like a leftover tomato sitting sadly on my plate, pictures of what I was doing, well-angled selfies, and an occasional sexy bare-skinned one. They were always PG-13, but Alex didn't seem to mind. I never imagined that I'd feel giddy over a heart-eyed emoji, but I also never could have imagined Alex Evans. So far the whole thing was surprisingly simple and stress-free.

I looked at the texts again for the hundredth time, then put my phone back in the bottom of my purse, trying to control the giddiness I felt rising in my chest.

In less than six months I'd have my MBA. I'd worked so hard to get where I was, and I didn't have the luxury of losing focus. Thankfully, Mondays were always busy at our accounting firm, and I fielded phone calls all morning, a task that held my attention and made the day go by quickly.

By the time I stopped for lunch, I was itching to check my phone again.

"I'm going to lunch," I said to Elise, the other receptionist at our office.

"Sounds good," she replied, waving me off as she answered another call.

I pulled my phone out again as I walked through the front door of our building. I had another text from Alex.

I'm at Mr. and Mrs. K's restaurant for the next half an hour.

I checked the time stamp. Ten minutes ago. If I hurried, I might be able to get there before Alex left. I grinned as I speed walked to my car and climbed inside. My heart was racing. It had been too long since I'd looked into his gorgeous brown eyes.

CHAPTER 5

ALEX

I smiled at the little old lady in front of me and raised my hands in the air. "No more, please," I said with a groan. "I'm going to explode."

Mrs. K made a scoffing noise, then put more of the food that I couldn't pronounce onto my plate. It was some sort of pasta dish with bow tie noodles and little bits of onions in it. I'd had a lot of good food, but whatever she was giving me was far better than anything I'd ever had in my life.

I could see why Sarai loved this restaurant so much. When you sat down to eat, especially if you were alone, you were treated like family. They didn't serve you and ignore you; they made conversation and made sure you were enjoying your meal. Mr. K had already come by the counter twice to pat me on the back and tell me I looked sharp in my uniform. Mrs. K had stood across the counter, talking to me about the weather and what had been in the news lately, and had informed me that I needed to put a little meat on my bones in case we had a hard winter. She'd said that last part ultraseriously, and I wondered just how hard a winter they'd lived through, but I didn't ask.

I checked my watch again as I shoveled more food into my mouth. I had to leave in five minutes if I wanted to be back to work in time for a security briefing.

When I'd texted Sarai about meeting me for lunch, I'd known it was a long shot that she'd be able to come on such short notice, but I was still hoping. I'd been serious when I told her that we'd make our schedules work so that we could spend some time together. Yeah, it would be easier if we weren't so busy, but that was life. Sometimes you just had to take what it gave you and make the best of it. It had been weeks since I'd seen her beautiful face in person, but I knew that she had a lot going on. She'd sent me selfies of her doing random things—standing in front of her door with a beanie on her head and a huge grin on her face, looking bored with her head resting on her hand in what looked like a classroom, making a silly face with ice cream all over her mouth. My favorite, though, was one she'd taken of her legs in the bath, her feet propped up at the end of the tub. She may not have enough time for me at the moment, but the woman knew how to make what few seconds she had memorable. I just wished I could actually see her in person once in a while.

I hid my disappointment as I pulled some money out of my wallet and left it on the table. Sarai either hadn't gotten my text or wasn't able to meet me, and I had to get back to work. I'd kind of expected that it wouldn't work out, but I was pretty bummed anyway.

I was standing on the sidewalk stuffing my wallet back into my pants when I spotted Sarai's car pulling into the restaurant's parking lot. I lifted my hand in greeting as she drove toward me like a bat out of hell.

"Hey, Speed Racer," I called out as she parked next to my truck and climbed out of her car.

"Damn, you're leaving," she replied with a good-natured sigh. "I tried to make it in time, but all these people kept cutting in front of me!"

"They were probably trying to get out of your way. Not everyone drives twenty over the speed limit," I joked, walking toward her.

"I don't drive that fast."

"You just were," I argued.

"Well, shit." She gave me a lopsided smile. "I just didn't want you to leave before I got here."

We locked eyes, and hers were bright with excitement. As I reached her, it felt like the most natural thing in the world to lean forward and press my mouth to hers.

I'd meant the kiss to be a greeting, a small hello, but it turned into something different the moment our lips met. It probably wasn't the right moment. We'd had two actual dates, and I knew that she was trying to keep things as casual as possible. I also hadn't planned on our first kiss being on full display in front of a row of windows that looked into her surrogate family's restaurant. But damn, the moment I pressed my lips to hers, she opened right up.

My hands found her hips, and I twisted us slightly so I was shielding us from any onlookers. She tasted like mint.

"You're going to be late," she said, pulling away.

"Worth it," I replied, chasing her mouth with mine.

I'd barely made contact again when she pulled away with a small laugh.

"I'm so glad I caught you," she said. "It's been too long since I've gotten to see that pretty face of yours."

"Funny, I was just thinking the exact same thing." My hands tightened on her hips. "Fuck work. Let's run away."

She laughed, and then we stood there grinning at each other for a long moment.

"Adulting is the worst, but I can't run away today. Big test at school tonight. You'll have to go back to work," she said teasingly, making a shooing motion with her hands.

I nodded and leaned forward again, giving her a quick peck on the lips. I really was going to be late.

I took a couple of steps back, then spun on my heel and jogged around the hood of my truck.

"I'll text you later!" I called out.

"Sounds good," she replied, giving a little wave.

As I pulled away, I looked back to see her walking inside the restaurant.

I'd known that I liked her, and I'd been pretty excited to spend some time with her, but I was surprised at just how happy I'd been when she'd shown up today.

There was something about Sarai, some quality that was indefinable but present. She lit up a room. It wasn't necessarily her looks, though she was gorgeous; it was something else, like an energy. Everyone gravitated toward her whenever she was around. I'd noticed it at Sean's party, and I'd noticed it again when we'd had breakfast. People wanted to talk to her, and they went out of their way to say hello or introduce themselves. I loved it, and I wanted more of it. Before long, this whole quick-meetup thing wouldn't be enough.

As soon as I parked my truck, I texted her.

Let me take you to dinner after class tonight.

I stuffed my phone into my pocket as I hurried to my meeting.

* * *

"When you offered to take me to dinner, this wasn't what I expected," Sarai said later that night as I tucked a blanket tighter around her hips.

"I didn't expect you to agree," I confessed with a laugh. "When you said yes, I had to think of something quick."

Sarai laughed. We were sitting in the back of my truck in the middle of an open field with empty takeout containers spread out around us. It was cold as hell but the weather was clear, and I was pretty proud of our little picnic under the stars.

"You made the right decision," she said with a sigh, leaning against me. "This is perfect."

"Long day, huh?" I asked, wrapping my arm around her shoulders.

"Yeah." She nodded. "Test days suck even when I know the material."

"Do you think you did well?"

"I always do well," she said confidently. She pulled away from me so she could get to her feet. I tilted my head back to watch her as she threw her arms out and turned in a circle.

When her eyes met mine, she grinned. "And now I'm one test closer to finishing."

"It'll be over before you know it," I said, reaching out to rest my hands on her hips. "And then the world is your oyster."

"I've never understood that saying," she replied, stretching her arms above her head before gracefully dropping to her knees in front of me. "Why the hell would I want an oyster?"

"It's a Shakespeare quote," I said, grabbing the blanket she'd dropped and wrapping it around her shoulders.

"You've read Shakespeare?" she asked in surprise, laughing as I towed her toward me with the blanket.

"My sister, Kate, went through a phase when she was about fourteen," I admitted. "She went around quoting the Bard for weeks."

"Is she older or younger?" Sarai asked, resting her hands on my chest.

We were finally face-to-face, so close that I could feel her breath. Her eyes were bright with happiness and her cheeks were rosy from the cold, and I was so busy wondering if I should just lean forward and kiss her that it took me a minute to realize she'd asked me a question.

"She's younger," I replied distractedly.

"Is it hard living so far away?"

She was staring at my mouth.

Screw it.

Instead of answering her, I leaned forward and caught her bottom lip between mine, biting down just enough to make her gasp. I groaned as her hands slid up to my neck and she leaned into the kiss. My fingers were still tangled in the blanket as the kiss grew hotter and wetter, and I groaned again as I tried to use it to pull her closer.

Unfortunately, I wasn't paying attention to the way she was kneeling in front of me, because when I gave the blanket a tug, she lost her balance. Everything came to a screeching halt when one of her knees collided with my balls. The sound that came out of my mouth was something between a yelp and a squeal.

"Oh God," she said as I gasped for air and tried not to curse a blue streak. "I'm so sorry!"

"Not your fault," I wheezed as she scrambled backward.

I reached for her, pulling her back to me, slowly this time.

"Are you okay?" she whispered, her hands cradling my face.

"A little nauseous, but yeah," I replied half-jokingly, making her laugh.

"Poor baby," she said, leaning in for another kiss. The brush of her lips was so light that I barely felt it.

"My own fault," I muttered, frozen in place as she pulled my top lip, then the bottom one between hers. Holy hell, why did it feel so good? I was more of a full-contact kisser, tongue and teeth and lips working together, but hell if this wasn't more intense.

"Thank you for bringing me out here," she said, pulling slightly away so our eyes met. "I needed it."

"I'm glad you got a little time to relax."

"Me too," she said with a sigh. She turned in my lap and rested against me, her head pressed against my shoulder.

I pulled the blanket up around her shoulders and leaned my head against the cab of the truck. Even with my balls throbbing with every beat of my heart, it was still the best night I'd had in a long time.

* * *

After our picnic Sarai and I struggled to find time to see each other. I swear to God, I never had anything to do, and now suddenly it seemed like I was just as busy as she was. Sarai had classes Mondays, Wednesdays, and Thursdays right after work and didn't get home until nine o'clock. I had softball practice Tuesdays and Fridays after work for the stupid league I'd signed up for before we met. I was seriously regretting the day I'd thought it was a good idea to spend two nights a week playing softball with a bunch of guys I worked with all day, but if I was honest, my schedule probably didn't matter much. When Sarai wasn't busy at work or school, she was studying.

I had no idea how she kept up with it all. She seemed exhausted whenever we talked on the phone, but she never complained.

"You know if this woman really wanted to hang with you, she would, right?" Ani said conspiratorially through the phone. It was Tuesday night, and I was currently lying on my couch, icing my knee. I'd twisted it at practice, and it had swelled up like a balloon almost instantly. I'd been elevating and icing it for the last hour, and it didn't seem to be making much of a difference.

"I'm not taking your advice," I replied, shifting carefully. "You said breakfast wasn't a date, and you were clearly wrong."

"I wasn't wrong," she shot back.

"She's into me," I replied stubbornly.

"She's not that into you."

"She's busy."

"No one is *that* busy."

"She's got a full-time job and is working toward her MBA," I argued. "She's crazy busy."

"Fine," Ani said with a sigh, making me grin. "But, dude, seriously. Is this even a thing if you never actually see her?"

My face fell. Why did she have to ask the one question that had been rolling around in my brain the past couple of days?

"I *have* seen her—we just don't live in each other's pockets," I said finally. "Why are you so bitchy lately?"

"Jesus," she said with a groan. "I'm sorry. I'm totally bitchy."

"What's going on?"

"Nothing," she snapped, then immediately her voice softened. "Sorry, I'm just stressed."

If Ani was owning up to not having everything in her world perfectly handled, I knew that whatever she had going on had to be serious. She wasn't a complainer.

"Anything I can help with?" I asked.

"No, not really." She was quiet for a moment. "Arielle's still on a shitty sleep schedule."

"She's sleeping a little, right?" I asked. For a while, my sweet little niece had been keeping her parents up all night, every night. The doctor had told them it was purely developmental and there wasn't anything wrong, but it hadn't made their sleep deprivation any easier to deal with.

"Yeah," Ani replied. "But it's still not great, and I think it's making Bram question if we should have any more."

"What?" I sat up a little straighter on the couch. "That's nuts."

"I know that," she said. "But we were doing all this paperwork to get certified to foster—you know, so we could hopefully adopt at some point? And now Bram is dragging his feet about it."

"He's just overwhelmed and exhausted," I assured her. "You know Bram wants more kids. My idiot brother is kind of great at the whole dad thing."

"Yeah." I could hear the smile in her voice. "Who knew?"

"I did," I said smugly. "I just wasn't sure if he'd pull his head out long enough to realize it."

"You have such a way with words," Ani said drily. "Shit, Arie's awake. I'll text you later, okay?"

"Sounds good. Give my baby girl a big kiss from her favorite uncle."

"I will. She loves kisses from Uncle Shane," she said, referring to my sister Kate's husband. Ani laughed just before the phone line went dead.

"I'm her favorite," I snapped, knowing that she couldn't even hear me.

I dropped my phone and cursed as I lifted the ice pack off my knee again. The skin was tight and looked like it was beginning to bruise. I dropped my feet to the floor and let out a loud groan as I pushed myself off the couch. Dammit, I really didn't want to go to medical to get the thing looked at, but putting any weight on it was excruciating. I hobbled into the kitchen, threw the ice pack into the sink, and grabbed some ibuprofen out of a cabinet. I wished that our doctors handed out something stronger, but they rarely did, so I never had any good painkillers lying around the house.

After using my beer to wash down the pills, I made my way to the shower. I hadn't even rinsed the dirt and stink off when I'd gotten home, because I'd been in such a hurry to ice my damn knee before it got any worse.

Getting old sucked. Who knew thirty was the new seventy?

By the time I climbed out, feeling more relaxed, I was also in more pain. My knee just continued to fucking swell.

I toweled off quickly and dropped onto my bed, grabbing an extra pillow to prop up my leg. When I was situated, my mind was once again full of Sarai. The way she talked, the way she moved, the way she smiled and used her hands like they were part of the conversation.

Ani was right. If we weren't actually seeing each other, what *were* we doing? I'd thought the night of our picnic had gone really well, but I hadn't seen Sarai since, and it was messing with my head.

I lifted my phone and pulled up our text messages. I hadn't talked to her since this morning, and although that wasn't uncommon for us, it suddenly felt like a glowing red flag.

Hey, what are you up to? I texted. It was a stupid question. I knew what she was up to. It was Tuesday, and she always worked on schoolwork Tuesday nights. I could set my calendar by how regimented Sarai was.

Writing a paper, pacing, writing some more, pacing, deleting and rewriting…

Dammit. I sighed. I was doing exactly what she'd said I would do. I was fucking pouting about her busy schedule. Before I could regroup, she sent me another text.

What are you doing? Softball practice tonight, right? ?

Hurt my knee and came home early. Want some company?

There, I'd made my move. Ten minutes went by with no answer, so I sent another message.

I'll bring my cleaning supplies…

Almost as soon as I'd sent my last text, a reply popped up on my phone.

Sure. What happened to your knee? Have you had dinner?

I grinned and texted her back.

Knee's no big deal. I can grab something on my way over.

Seriously? Thank you! I'm staring at my fridge and it's pretty much empty.

On my way.

I swung my legs over the side of the bed without thinking and let out a string of curses that would have made my mother blush. Dammit. I took a few minutes to breathe through the pain, then got up and dressed. I was really grateful that I'd taken that shower earlier, because there was no way I could take one now. I was definitely going to medical tomorrow.

I thought about going to a drive-through since walking to my truck was so painful, but at the last second, I turned toward Mr. and Mrs. K's restaurant. I wasn't sure what Sarai would want for dinner, but I knew they'd never steer me wrong.

I took a deep breath as I parked in the restaurant's parking lot, then gritted my teeth as I climbed out of my truck. My knee seemed to be getting worse as I moved around, and I probably should have stayed home, but I was determined to see Sarai.

"Alex!" Mr. Krakowski called out as I pushed my way through the front door.

"Hey," I replied, smiling. I'd never get tired of the greeting I got when I walked through the front door. As I limped my way toward him, he frowned.

"What's the matter?" He hurried toward me. "Are you hurt?"

"Messed up my knee tonight," I said, grimacing as I shifted my weight to my good leg. "No big deal."

"It looks like a big deal," he replied, staring at my leg like he could see the swollen knee through my jeans. "We'll get you seated quickly."

"Actually," I said before he could walk away. "I was wondering if you do to-go orders? I'm bringing over some food to Sarai since she's studying."

"That girl studies too much," he said firmly, shaking his head.

"I agree. I was hoping you could pick something she likes?"

Mr. K grinned and wiggled his eyebrows. "Yes," he said with a happy nod. "Mama made some matzo ball soup tonight. Perfect for the rainy weather."

"Sounds great."

"You go sit. I'll get your food." He turned on his heel and made his way toward the kitchen as I sat down in a chair near the front door.

It took only a few minutes for Mrs. K to bring our dinner

out, but by the time I'd made my way to Sarai's apartment, my knee felt as if it were on fire. Sweat had made my back clammy, and I could feel my shirt sticking to it.

"Hello," Sarai sang happily, opening her door as soon as I'd knocked. She smiled until her eyes reached mine, and then her face fell. "Are you okay?"

I can't explain how badly I wanted to tell her that I was fine, not to worry, no big deal. But as I felt a bead of sweat run down my back and into my waistband, I grimaced.

"My knee's killing me," I said, gesturing to the place that was currently throbbing with every beat of my heart. "It's swollen as hell."

"Oh no." She reached for my arm. "Come in and sit down."

I followed her inside and set the soup on her countertop. Her front door opened into the kitchen, and I glanced around, taking in the little potted herbs on the windowsill and the fruit bowl in the middle of the counter with a solitary apple set in the center. We made our way into the little living room area, and I grinned at the ugly couch that looked like it was at least thirty years old and the expensive and very large TV. The woman had her priorities in order. Sarai gestured to the couch and waited for me to sit down. Then, without a word, she leaned forward and pulled off my shoes so she could gently lift my foot onto the ottoman.

"Is that okay?" she asked when she was done.

The pressure on my knee was already a little better, and I sighed in relief. "Yeah. That helps. This couch is more comfortable than it looks."

"I know, right?" she said, smiling huge. "I found it at a

garage sale. It's not pretty, but it feels like a warm hug when you sit in it."

I laughed at her description.

"I can't believe you came over when you were in so much pain," she said as she swatted my shoulder. "You should be at the hospital or at least home in bed."

"I wanted to see you," I replied, grabbing her hand. "And it's not that bad."

"You have"—she pointed to her temple and tapped it, grimacing—"sweat. Right here."

"Shit," I mumbled, reaching up to wipe off my face.

"I'll get our dinner," she said with a small smile. "What did you bring? Would you like some water?"

"You don't have to serve me," I argued, leaning forward to move my leg off the ottoman.

"Do not move," she ordered. "Stay right there."

"Sarai," I said, frustration making my voice come out lower than normal.

"Alex," she mimicked in the same tone.

I leaned my head against the couch and scowled. This wasn't exactly how I'd pictured our evening going. I hadn't gone to her house so that she could take care of me. I'd wanted to bring her dinner, do something nice because I knew how busy she was. Instead, she was waiting on me.

It took only a few minutes before she had us all set up in the living room, our bowls of soup and glasses of water on a little tray between us on the couch. Sarai sat facing me, her back against the arm of the couch and one leg folded under her.

"How did you hurt your leg?" she asked, picking up her

bowl. Both bowls had little Koozies of some sort wrapped around them, and I took a closer look at mine as I grabbed my food.

"I twisted my knee sliding into second," I said with a sigh. I sounded like an idiot.

"That sounds painful," she murmured, blowing gently on her spoon before taking a bite of her soup.

"It was stupid," I confessed ruefully. "I was joking around, and it backfired."

"What do you think is wrong with it? Are you going to see a doctor?"

"Yeah, I'll go tomorrow." I took a bite of my soup, and my eyes opened wide in horror. The liquid was so hot that it was like molten lava. I choked for a second before swallowing it down. "Holy shit," I gasped, quickly grabbing my water glass and taking a large gulp. "I didn't realize how hot it was."

"I'm so sorry," Sarai apologized, wincing. "I forgot how much the bowl sweaters fool you into thinking the food is cooler than it is."

"Bowl sweaters?" I asked, my lips twitching.

Sarai rolled her eyes good-naturedly. "Well, what would you call them?"

"Koozies?"

"Those are for beer cans," she argued. "And these are prettier."

"Why would you buy bowl sweaters anyway?" I asked, lifting a spoonful of soup so I could blow on it.

"Oh, I didn't buy them." She shook her head. "I got them from my secret Santa at work last year."

I stared at her with one brow raised.

"What?" she asked, laughing a little.

"Santa?"

"They probably don't know I'm Jewish," she said with a shrug.

"Why wouldn't you say something?" I asked with a chuckle.

"Because then I wouldn't get a secret Santa present," she said, a mischievous little smirk playing at the corners of her mouth.

"Maybe you'd get eight," I pointed out.

"I work with accountants," she replied. "They're too cheap to buy anyone eight presents."

I laughed.

"I feel their pain," I said. "Christmas gets expensive! I have a big family, so it adds up."

"I just have my aunt and uncle," she replied. "But we usually do small holiday gifts for the neighbors, too."

"Pretty tight-knit community, huh?" I asked.

"Understatement," Sarai joked. "You can't sneeze without a neighbor yelling *bless you* from three doors down."

I chuckled.

"It's nice," she admitted. "It drove me crazy when I was younger, but I miss it now."

"I know what you mean," I said with a nod. "I used to hate that my family was always sticking their noses into my business, but now I find myself calling them to tell them stuff."

"Oh yeah?" she replied nonchalantly. "Have you told them about me?"

I smiled, watching her as she looked down and then back at me, waiting for a reply. "Yeah," I said finally.

"Well," she blurted, raising her eyebrows. "What have you said?"

"That I met a woman," I replied slowly. "And she's smart and beautiful and way too good for me."

She blushed and looked back at her soup. Damn, she was cute.

"Actually," I said. "My sister and sister-in-law were convinced that our breakfast date meant you'd put me in the friend zone."

"Why?" she asked in surprise.

"Apparently, breakfast isn't a date." I shrugged.

"It felt like a date to me," she said quietly.

"Me too," I murmured, reaching out to give her thigh a squeeze.

We sat there talking long after our soup bowls were empty and she'd cleared the little table from the couch. I learned that even though she was crazy busy, she seemed to sail through academics like they were nothing. She didn't love the place she worked, but she liked the people she worked with and that was good enough for now. She had only a few good friends in Missouri, and Hailey was her best friend, but they'd barely talked lately, because Sarai couldn't stand Sean and had a hard time hiding it.

Sarai was funny and sarcastic, but I'd never heard her say anything mean. Intelligent, but she didn't act like a know-it-all, even though I knew without a doubt that she was smarter than I was.

"You're beautiful," I said, leaning my head against the back of the couch as I looked at her.

"Thank you," she replied, smiling. No argument or preening, just confidence in her own worth. "I find you very hand-some as well," she said teasingly.

"Thank you," I mimicked. But I wasn't as comfortable with compliments as she was, and I couldn't stop the small laugh that escaped my lips.

"Are you embarrassed?" she asked with a surprised chuckle. "Mr. I'm So Sure of Myself?"

"I'm not embarrassed."

"Yes, you are. You're practically blushing!" She stretched her foot across the couch and gave me a little nudge with her toes. "What happened to the guy who couldn't believe I turned him down for a date?" she teased.

"Number one," I said, grabbing her foot before she could pull away. I ran my finger along the bottom of it, making her squirm. "I'm not embarrassed. And number two…yeah, I was really fucking surprised." I laughed as she snorted.

"What?" I asked, beginning to massage her foot with both hands. "I don't get turned down much."

"Ha!" she said, getting more comfortable as she lifted the other foot so I could reach both. She stretched out on the couch and crossed her arms behind her head, leaning back against a throw pillow. "You're not *everyone's* type."

I met her eyes, my expression completely deadpan, but didn't reply.

In response, she snorted again and wiggled her toes. I liked that little snorting sound she made; it was fucking adorable.

"I don't usually ask someone out if I think they're not interested," I said, shrugging my shoulders.

"Fear of rejection, huh?" she said with a little laugh.

"What in the world gave you the impression that I was interested that night? We barely spoke."

"Actually," I replied, giving her foot a squeeze, "I try to respect people's boundaries. If I don't think someone is interested, I don't want to make them uncomfortable by making a pass. And you were interested that night—you were basically staring."

She sat up quickly. "I was not!"

"Sure you were. I could practically feel your eyes burning a hole in the side of my head while I ate." I was full of shit. She'd barely noticed me while we'd been inside the restaurant. It wasn't until we were outside that I'd thought that maybe I had a chance.

"Perhaps it was because your table manners are atrocious," she said.

"My table manners are impeccable," I shot back. "Sushi is hard to eat with chopsticks."

"Not if you have opposable thumbs," she replied just as quickly.

I laughed. I couldn't help it.

"Oh, my thumbs work just fine," I said, digging my left one into the arch of her foot. "Perfect for massages."

"And we're back to cocky," she said with a grin, flopping backward on the couch.

"I prefer to call it confident in my abilities," I said, winking at her as I rubbed her feet.

"Don't do that again," she said seriously.

I immediately let go of her feet.

"No, keep doing that," she said, nudging me with a foot. "Don't wink."

"Don't wink?"

"No. It's creepy."

I sputtered, "What?"

"Winking is creepy," she said, wrinkling her nose a little. "It's weird."

"I've never heard that before."

"Really?" she asked skeptically.

"Yes, really," I replied. "No one has ever called me creepy before."

"*You're* not creepy. Just the winking. It's like the universal disturbing gesture of everyone's weird uncle," she said, a smile tugging at the corners of her mouth.

"I really like you," I said with a sigh, smiling back at her. "But I'm not sure if this relationship is good for my ego."

"Maybe," she conceded. "But I bet your personality improves exponentially."

Dear God, I'd met my match.

CHAPTER 6

SARAI

Alex was incredible. I stared at him happily as he spoke, my feet still in his lap.

"I'm just saying," he muttered, throwing his hands in the air, "if you're putting a bunch of salt and pepper on your food, you're pretty much telling whoever cooked it that it sucks."

"That's not true," I argued, laughing as I pointed at him. "Some people like things spicier than others."

"Fine," he said. "But salt? Come on."

I opened my mouth to reply, but nothing came out.

"Exactly," he said in satisfaction.

"Okay, you might be onto something."

"I am." He shifted a little, then went back to softly rubbing my foot. "It's rude to add a bunch of seasoning."

"What about condiments?" I asked thoughtfully.

"Don't even get me started," he said with a huff.

I had no idea how our conversation had morphed into a

debate about food, but I couldn't deny how much I was enjoying it. I loved learning more about him, even little things. The smile on my face faded, though, as he shifted again, trying to get comfortable.

Alex had grown more pale as the night went on, making his tanned skin look sickly. He was trying to ignore it or maybe just hide it from me, but when he shifted for the tenth time in about fifteen minutes, I couldn't brush aside how much pain he was in any longer.

"You need to go home," I said softly, cutting off his opinion about putting ketchup on eggs.

"What?" he asked with a confused laugh.

"You need to be in bed with your leg up." I pulled my feet from his lap and sat up on the couch. "Or go to the hospital."

"I'm not going to the hospital in the middle of the night. Hospitals are for emergencies."

"Well, you need to do something," I replied, gesturing at his leg. "You're in pain."

"It's fine," he said, brushing off my concern.

"Well, it needs to be fine in bed."

"I could sleep in your bed," he said with a sly smile.

"You haven't even seen me naked," I said drily. "You're not sleeping in my bed."

"Okay." He grinned. "Strip."

"Dream on, Casanova," I said with a surprised laugh.

He smiled wide and gave an exaggerated wink, making me snicker.

"I had a really good time tonight," Alex murmured, gingerly lowering his foot to the floor. He didn't stand up, just sat there looking at me.

"So did I," I replied. "Next time we'll have to watch a movie or something."

"I'd rather watch you."

"Oh, brother," I teased. "So smooth."

"Tough crowd," he said to the nonexistent audience in my living room. He pushed himself to his feet and let out a big sigh.

"Can you make it home okay?" I asked nervously. Now that I was kicking him out, I wasn't so sure that it was a good idea to make him drive all the way home. He wasn't putting any weight on his bad knee, and judging by the strain on his face, he was having a hard time standing.

"I'll make it home fine," he said. It wasn't bravado. His tone was kind, like he didn't want me to worry.

I walked him to the door slowly, and with every step, I questioned whether I should just ask him to stay the night. How would that play out, though? My couch was way too small for either of us to sleep on comfortably—not that he'd let me sleep on it anyway. So…he'd sleep next to me when we'd only kissed a couple of times, and we'd cuddle? I wouldn't sleep. I'd be worried all night that he'd see me snoring with my mouth wide open or I'd accidentally kick his knee.

"I'll call you tomorrow," he said as we got to my front door.

"Let me know what the doctor says about your knee," I said.

"Yes, ma'am."

He rested his hand on the doorknob but didn't turn it. Instead, he used it to balance himself as he leaned down and kissed me.

It was a good kiss. One of the best I'd ever had.

Here's the thing about kissing—you could say someone does it well, but it's all subjective. A person could say that their partner kisses well because he barely uses his tongue, while another person could think that kisser is awful because he doesn't use his tongue enough. It's all about the chemistry and the dance. Kissing is a team sport, a little give and take, making sure that the other person is getting what they want while also taking a little yourself.

With all that said, I was pretty sure Alex was a good kisser no matter who you asked. He wasn't crazy or hurried; he didn't overwhelm. He just kind of waited to see what I did, and did the same thing. The kiss was leisurely and smooth, and one of his hands cupped the side of my face as he took it deeper. By the time he pulled away, my head was almost spinning, and I stutter-stepped a little as his hand left my face.

"Well, that just keeps getting better," he said huskily. He chuckled softly. "Thank you for having me over."

"Thanks for bringing me dinner," I replied quietly. "Be careful driving home."

"Of course." He leaned forward and kissed the top of my head, and then he was gone.

I stood just inside the door for a long time. Normally I would have watched him through the window, but I was afraid if I had to see him limp toward his truck, I would call him back inside. I wasn't ready for a sleepover yet. I just wasn't. I liked Alex a lot, but sleeping with someone was a little more intimate than I was ready for.

Eventually, I moved away from the door and started cleaning up our dishes. My heart was still racing, and my face felt warm from that kiss. He was right—it *was* getting better. Our first kiss had been spontaneous and sweet, full of excitement but rushed. This one had been slow and smooth. It was like the difference between a lollipop and a piece of expensive chocolate: both had their place, but the chocolate was so much better.

I'd just put our dishes away and straightened up the pillows on the couch when my phone beeped with a text message.

Home. Naked. In bed. ;)

I grinned.

Glad you're safely naked in bed. How's the knee?

Swollen.

You should have stayed off of it tonight—you probably made it worse.

Worth it.

I couldn't keep the giddy smile off my face as I turned off the lights in the apartment, working my way to the bedroom. I couldn't remember the last time I'd had so much fun just sitting at home without a good book in my hands.

I tossed my phone on the bed, stripped out of my clothes, and headed into my bathroom in my underwear. I always washed my face and brushed my teeth before bed. It was a ritual I'd started when I was a little girl. If I didn't do those two things, I found that I couldn't fall asleep. Instead, I'd just obsess about them until I crawled back out of bed and got them done.

I froze as I got a glimpse of myself in the mirror.

When Alex texted me about dinner, I'd rushed around to make sure everything was tidy before he got there, completely forgetting that I had spot treatment on a couple of breakouts. I stared in horror at the two little white spots on my jaw, one of them smeared from Alex's hands when we'd kissed.

With a groan, I got my toothbrush out and started brushing, glaring at myself in the mirror.

When I climbed into bed I sent an embarrassed text to Alex.

Why didn't you tell me I had stuff on my face?! Haha

He texted back quickly. *You did? :p*

I sent a face-palm emoji in reply.

Why would I embarrass you? No big deal, babe.

My stomach fluttered at the endearment.

Next time, let me know. LOL

I will, he replied. Then another text came through.

I'm going to try to get some rest. Sleep well, beautiful.

As I pulled the blankets up to my chin, I wondered where all of this would go. I was a romantic; I believed in happily-ever-afters and finding the person who you'd be with for the rest of your life. I'd seen it happen. Was this *it*?

I wasn't ready yet. I'd mapped out the next few years, and the plan was to graduate and be settled in my career before I found the person I wanted to spend my life with. Anxiety made my stomach churn. Maybe I could tweak the plan a little. It wasn't as if it was set in stone, and I knew I wasn't willing to say good-bye to Alex because the timing was off.

I hadn't even had sex with Alex yet, and this thing we had already felt different than anything I'd ever encountered before. There was an easiness between us, a weird feeling like I'd known him forever. I fell asleep thinking about the way his eyes crinkled at the sides when he smiled at me.

* * *

"You're seeing Alex!" Hailey sang happily as she slid into the seat next to me in our business-communications class. "Why didn't you tell me?"

"Because there isn't anything to tell yet," I replied, laughing at the wounded look on her face. "We've hung out a couple times."

"Sean said that Alex told him that you two were together," she said quietly, as if she were letting me in on a huge secret.

"Interesting," I replied, raising one eyebrow. I was surprised that they'd spoken at all. From what I'd noticed, Alex didn't like Sean.

For the next three hours, we listened to our professor make connections between the subject material and a movie he'd seen that weekend. None of his stories ever made sense, but we humored him. He was the one grading our papers, and we couldn't afford to point out that he was rambling completely off topic. Plus, I liked Professor Morrow. He reminded me of one of my neighbors from New York. The old man had spent most of his time alone, and whenever he had company, he'd talk for the entire visit, barely letting his guest get a word in edgewise.

"Well?" Hailey asked when we took a fifteen-minute break.

"Well what?" I asked, pulling an apple and some crackers out of my bag.

"Well, are you two together?"

"I guess."

"You *guess*?" she asked, looking at me like I'd grown an extra head. "Where's the excitement? Where's the joy? Where's the drama?"

"You've got enough drama for both of us," I replied, taking a bite of my apple. Hailey was all drama, all the time. That was probably why we got along so well—she was my complete opposite.

"Oh, whatever." She swept away my words with a wave of her hand. "I can't believe you guys hit it off. And all because of that double date."

"It wasn't the double date," I said around my food, shaking my head. "I turned him down that night."

"What?" Her eyes grew so wide it looked like they were going to pop out of her head. "Why the hell would you do that?"

"Because I'm busy."

"No one is that busy," she argued, stealing one of my crackers. "Alex is like a frigging unicorn. You don't tell a unicorn you're too busy—you just bask in its magnificence for as long as it allows."

"I think you're giving him too much credit," I said, laughing a little. "He's just a guy."

"Unicorn," she replied stubbornly.

"Handsome, yes."

"Hotter than the sun, you mean?"

"And charming."

"He could talk a nun into stripping out of her habit. To music. On a pole."

I burst out laughing, choking on the apple. "Stop it," I said, wheezing.

"You know it's true," she said, pointing a cracker at me.

"Well, he hasn't convinced me to strip out of anything," I said with a shrug.

"No," she whispered, her mouth hanging open. "You haven't hit that yet?"

"Ew, don't say *hit that*." I wrinkled my nose.

"He's telling people that you're together, and you haven't even had sex yet?" she asked in a whisper, completely ignoring the way I'd tried to change the direction of our conversation. "Whoa."

"We're getting to know each other," I replied with a shrug.

Alex and I hadn't had a chance to meet up over the weekend. I'd been completely bogged down with schoolwork and forced myself to stay home and get it done. It was getting harder to focus on my classes and work when my mind seemed to be stuck on Alex all the time. It turned out that he'd sprained his ACL during practice. I wasn't quite sure what that meant, but I knew it was serious enough that he had to do physical therapy to get it back to normal. I wanted to take care of him while it healed and spend more time relaxing on the couch while we learned more about each other. And frankly, I wanted sex. I could admit it. I wanted to see him naked and do all sorts of dirty things to him.

It just wasn't the right time yet. Soon, though, I hoped.

"You guys should come over for dinner this week," Hailey said, as if it were the best idea she'd ever had. "Shit, I have to pee. Be right back."

She took off in a hurry, and I knew she'd never get back before class started again. Thankfully, Professor Morrow treated Hailey like a featherbrained granddaughter and never chastised her when she was late.

I put away my snack as students started filtering back into the room. Damn, I really didn't want to have dinner with Hailey and Sean, but I had no idea how to get out of it. I knew Hailey wouldn't let it go, though. If I didn't tell her no, she'd remind me over and over until we made set plans.

The thought of eating a meal with Sean made me want to cry. Okay, maybe not cry, but it was pretty low on my list of things I'd enjoy. He was a jackass, and I wished he'd never even met my friend. Hailey had stopped talking about him as much lately, and I was pretty sure it was because there was nothing good to say. She knew that I wasn't his biggest fan, and I think she might have been afraid to say anything against him and make my opinion of him even worse.

Thankfully, Hailey didn't make it back before Professor Morrow started speaking, and by the time she slid back into her seat, the entire class was silent. She didn't have any opportunity to bring the dinner up again.

* * *

"He's such an asshole," I muttered two days later as Alex and I drove toward Sean and Hailey's little house.

I'd been correct when I'd assumed that Hailey wouldn't let the invitation to dinner go unanswered. I hadn't expected her to have Sean ask Alex about it, though.

"He'll probably be on his best behavior since he's not

drinking tonight." Alex reached over and laced his fingers through mine so he could hold my hand.

"How do you know he's not drinking?" I asked, watching Alex's thumb smooth over the back of my hand.

"We've got a fitness test tomorrow," he said. "And I'm sure he doesn't want to fail it."

"How's that going to go for you?" I asked, glancing at his knee. It was wrapped in a brace, and it still looked painful even though Alex was barely limping anymore.

"No test for me," Alex replied. "Just physical therapy for a while."

"I can't believe you hurt it during a *practice*," I teased.

"Yeah, yeah." He grinned. "At least I got out of that softball commitment, though. Now we have Tuesdays and Fridays."

"And we're spending it at Hailey and Sean's," I replied with a sigh.

"It won't be that bad," he said, laughing a little. "We'll have dinner and then leave."

"I don't understand how you're still friends with him." I leaned my head against the headrest. "He's a terrible person."

"I'm not," he said, glancing at me. "But Hailey is your friend, so I thought you'd want to go."

"Oh," I murmured in surprise.

"I had no idea what an asshole Sean was before their party," Alex said. "But I don't usually make a habit of hanging out with douchebags. It's not really my thing."

"Right," I murmured, thinking back to the way he'd handled the man who'd groped me at Hailey's party.

We pulled up to the house a few minutes later, and as soon

as Alex turned off the truck, I reached for my door handle, but I didn't get very far, because Alex was pulling my hand in the opposite direction.

"Hey," he said quietly, smiling at me. "Come here."

I leaned toward him and let out a small sigh as his free hand brushed my hair away from my face.

"I've missed you," he said against my lips.

The kiss was short, but it held the same impact as the last one we'd shared at my house. I wouldn't have been surprised if little cartoon hearts had floated out of my ears and fluttered around my head as soon as he pulled his lips from mine.

"I missed you, too," I replied, leaning forward to brush my lips against his again. "Why don't we skip this, and we can go back to my apartment—"

My words were cut off by his groan, and I laughed.

"Unfair," he said, kissing me hard and fast before pulling away completely. "But I hope you know as soon as we're done eating, I'm throwing you over my shoulder, and we're going back to your place."

I grinned as he climbed out of the truck.

"You're here," Hailey called as we walked toward her front door. She was standing there in an apron. I tried really hard not to laugh.

"We're here," I called back as we made our way toward her. "Feed me—I'm starving!"

"Oh, shit." She gave me a mock worried look. "You probably should've eaten before you got here."

"Hey, guys," Sean said, walking out of the bedroom. His hair was kind of ruffled, like he'd just woken up.

"Thanks for having us over," Alex said, reaching forward to give Sean a fist bump.

"Hey, Sarai," Sean said, giving me a nod.

"So," Hailey said, bouncing a little on the tips of her toes. "I made spaghetti. I hope that's okay with everyone?"

"Sounds good," I replied, smiling genuinely at Hailey.

We sat down at the table and let Hailey serve us, because she really wanted to do it all herself. I gave Alex a small, grateful look when he sat between me and Sean. I was actually pretty impressed when Hailey started putting out the bowls of food. Everything looked great, and she'd put it all in decorative dishes that made the table look festive. It was a far cry from the night of the party, when frozen snack food had covered every surface in her kitchen.

We'd been there for only a few minutes, but by the time Hailey sat down, I'd relaxed a little.

It all went to shit when we started eating.

"What did you put in this?" Sean asked Hailey quietly. It wasn't his tone or the inflection of his voice that immediately got my attention. It was the way Hailey stiffened, her smile turning slightly panicked.

"Ground beef," she said softly. "And the sauce you brought home."

"I brought home onions and garlic, too."

"Those are in there," Hailey said, nodding. Her shoulders seemed to relax for just a second.

"And sausage," he said.

"I didn't use the sausage," she said. She glanced at me and Alex, giving a slight shrug.

"The sausage was for the spaghetti," Sean said, as if he were speaking to a child.

"I didn't use it this time," she said simply. She reached for a piece of garlic bread and set it down deliberately on her plate.

"Jesus," Sean said, sighing and looking at us, like he couldn't believe what he was dealing with.

"It's good," Hailey said brightly. "I tried it." She looked at me, giving me a small smile. "Totally nailed it, actually."

I smiled back, but every muscle in my body was tense. I knew why she hadn't added sausage—because I didn't eat pork—but for some reason she was trying to hide that from Sean. Was she trying to shield me or something? The thought made nausea pool in my stomach.

"It would have been better with the sausage," Sean complained, making Hailey's smile disappear.

I tried really hard to keep my mouth shut. I'd been doing it for months, keeping my opinion to myself. But watching the smile fall off Hailey's face when I knew how proud she was of dinner made me snap.

"She didn't put fucking sausage in it because I'm Jewish," I ground out, staring at Sean. Alex's hand tightened on my leg in solidarity or warning—I wasn't sure which. "I don't eat pork."

The table went so silent, you could have heard a pin drop.

"Whoa," Sean finally said, raising his hands in the air in mock surrender. "Cease fire." He laughed as if it were all a big joke. "I had no idea you were Jewish."

I didn't even bother to respond. My outburst didn't have anything to do with my being Jewish. I was pissed because he was such an asshole. Because he'd embarrassed my friend. Because Hailey had been so excited about the meal she'd made, and he'd ruined it. Because he didn't seem to have any regard for her feelings at all.

"Now you know," Alex said flatly to Sean, giving my thigh one more squeeze before digging into his food.

"This bread is really good," I told Hailey, changing the subject.

"I made it with margarine," she told me quietly. "No dairy."

She knew that I didn't follow the stricter kosher rules, like never eating dairy and meat in the same meal, but she'd made sure she hadn't mixed them just in case. I sent her a thankful smile that was just between us. My best friend had put a lot of thought into our dinner, and I hated that the night wasn't going how she'd envisioned.

Alex started talking to Sean about someone they worked with, and I let myself zone out while I ate my dinner. It was really good. I was honestly impressed, considering what a disaster Hailey was in the kitchen.

After dinner, I helped Hailey with the dishes while Sean showed Alex something in the detached garage.

"Is he always like that?" I asked, handing her a plate.

"No," she said lightly, shaking her head. "I think he just really wanted things to go well tonight."

"They *did* go well," I replied. "You did a really good job."

"Yeah?"

"Yeah."

We were quiet for a few minutes as we worked in tandem.

"He shouldn't talk to you like that," I said finally, unable to ignore the elephant in the room any longer.

"I know." She sighed. "But he's not always like that. You don't see him when it's just us. He's really sweet most of the time."

"That doesn't make up for it—"

"It's only when he's around his friends," she said, cutting me off. "I think he's just a little insecure or something."

"You realize how crazy that sounds, right?" I asked incredulously. "You're saying he puts you down because he feels bad about himself? You're okay with that?" I couldn't believe what I was hearing.

"It's not as bad as you're making it out to be," she said softly as we heard the guys come back inside. "Who's the dramatic one now?"

I opened my mouth to argue but snapped it shut again when she looked nervously over her shoulder. She clearly didn't want Sean to overhear our conversation.

"Hey, beautiful," Alex murmured, coming up behind me as I set a clean pan on the countertop. "You ready to go?"

I let out a quiet sigh of relief and nodded, drying off my hands with a kitchen towel. I really hadn't wanted to be the one to cut the night short, and Alex was giving me the perfect out.

"We're going to head home," I told Hailey, giving her a tight hug. "Thank you for dinner. It was delicious."

"Thanks for coming," she replied quietly, squeezing me back. "Next time we'll come to your house, yeah?"

I nodded, even though I knew that would never happen in a hundred lifetimes. Hailey was always welcome, but I didn't want Sean in my space.

I followed Alex toward the front door, and when we

stopped to grab our coats off the couch, Sean started whining.

"Man, you guys are leaving already?" he asked. "It's early still."

"Sarai has to work in the morning," Alex said, resting his hand on my back.

"Hell, so do we," Sean replied.

"I'll see you tomorrow," Alex replied. "Bye, Hailey."

"Thanks for coming, Alex," she called back from the kitchen.

"You guys'll have to come over again soon," Sean said as he stood up. "Don't worry—we'll order takeout next time." He chuckled, and I wanted to punch him.

"Yeah, maybe," Alex said, steering me out of the house before I could say anything.

* * *

The ride back to my apartment was silent.

I was so angry and sad for my friend that I wanted to cry. Why did Hailey stay? Why did she try to justify the way he treated her? I didn't understand any of it.

I watched Alex as he drove. He was everything Sean wasn't. He complimented me constantly. He treated everyone with respect, from the waitresses at Mr. and Mrs. K's restaurant to the homeless guy who sometimes huddled at the far end of my apartment building. He didn't complain, and he'd never made me feel bad for any reason, not even when I didn't text him back or forgot to call.

"Well," Alex said as he pulled into a parking spot. "That was a shitshow."

His voice was so calm, so serious, that I burst out laughing.

"That's an understatement," I replied. "I'd rather go to the dentist than do that again."

"I'd rather slide into second again," Alex mumbled.

"I'd rather fly internationally three days in a row," I replied.

"I'd rather eat my sister-in-law's cooking every day for a month."

"She's that bad?" I asked.

"No," he confessed. "But she used to be. It was disgusting."

"But you ate it anyway?"

"Well, I didn't want to hurt her feelings," he said simply.

I think that may have been the moment I knew I was in love with Alex Evans.

CHAPTER 7

ALEX

Do you still want me to come in?" I asked as we sat in the quiet truck.

The entire night had been such a nightmare. I felt bad that I'd agreed to the whole thing and dragged Sarai along with me. The way Sean treated Hailey was disgusting, and I was embarrassed that my connection with him was how I'd met Sarai.

"Yeah," Sarai said, sending me a small smile as she unbuckled her seat belt. "I still want you to come in."

I smiled back, hiding my nervousness, and got out of the truck, hurrying around the hood to open her door. I wasn't sure why I was so nervous. The chemistry between us was electric, and I knew that the sex would be, too, but part of me worried that when we actually made it to bed, things would go south. What if it didn't go well? What if she did something that I hated? More importantly, what if

I did something that totally turned her off? I really liked Sarai, and I knew she liked me, but this was uncharted territory for us, and I so badly wanted it to be great that I was psyching myself out. Hell, maybe nothing would happen beyond some kissing on the couch and I was worrying for no reason.

I led her quietly to the front door, holding her hand until she reached for her keys. As she unlocked the door and led the way inside, my hands found her hips, and I smoothed my thumbs up under her shirt to the soft skin of her back.

"Do you want something to drink?" she asked, reaching for the light switch in the kitchen.

"No, thanks." I could barely answer her as I pulled her coat off.

The moonlight was just bright enough for me to see her head tilt back as I ran my fingers across the side of her neck. The skin was so smooth, and I could feel her pulse racing against my fingertips. When she shivered, it was all over for me. Every ounce of worry flew out the window.

"It feels like we've been waiting forever," she said quietly, unmoving, as she let me take the lead.

"I know," I groaned, brushing her hair aside so I could taste the side of her throat.

I slid my hands around her and flattened them against her belly, then smoothed them upward until I held her breasts in my palms. I smiled a little as she made a noise deep in her throat.

"Bedroom?" she said huskily.

"If we can make it there," I agreed.

She let out a small breath of laughter and laced her fingers with mine.

As she led me to her bedroom, I wished that we'd turned some lights on. There was no hesitation in her step as we walked down the short hallway and into her room, no self-consciousness as she turned on a low bedside lamp and spun to face me. Her confidence was sexy as hell.

"I have condoms," she said as she kicked off her high heels.

"So do I," I replied, mirroring her movement with my shoes. I pulled out the two condoms in my pocket and tossed them on the bed.

"Okay, good," she said, a small relieved smile on her face. "Safety first, right?"

"I don't have anything, Sarai," I told her, my mouth going dry as she slipped out of her pants. "I, uh, get tested pretty often because of work."

"You make it sound like you're in some sort of sex trade," she teased, watching as I slid my jeans down my thighs.

"Nah, but can you imagine a whole platoon coming down with gonorrhea?" I asked, immediately wincing as the word came out of my mouth. That may have been the least sexy thing I'd ever said in my life.

"We can agree not to mention any STDs by name from this point forward," she said, correctly reading my expression.

"I think that's a good idea," I joked, the last word cutting off halfway through when she pulled her shirt over her head.

Her bra and underwear matched. Holy God, they matched. They were purple, silky and lacy at the same time, and for a second I thought I could die right then and it would be the best moment of my life. Then she looked at me expectantly, and I knew there was no way I would leave the earth without seeing what was under that silk and lace. I pulled my shirt off quickly and dropped it to the floor so I could keep staring at her.

"He works out," she sang in this quiet, high-pitched tone. I recognized the song she was mimicking, and I couldn't stop the strained laugh that came out of my mouth.

"Sorry," she said, her cheeks growing rosy as she gave an awkward shrug. "I get weird when I'm nervous."

"What's there to be nervous about?" I asked innocently, flexing my pecs. Her eyes were fixed on my chest as I flexed both at the same time, then the left side, then the right. Back and forth. Left and right.

The giggle that burst out of her mouth was the best sound ever, so I kept doing it until she was full-out laughing.

"What?" I asked, watching her as she tried to keep a straight face and failed. "Is something funny?"

"Stop," she said, wheezing.

"Stop what?" I asked in mock confusion, pausing for a moment before flexing my left pec over and over so it looked as if it were jumping.

"You're crazy," she said, laughter in her voice. She fell back on the bed, giggling.

I walked over and crawled on top of her, bracing myself on my hands and knees as I looked down at her.

"Still nervous?" I asked.

"Not even a little," she replied. She leaned up as I leaned down, and when our lips met, it was all over for me.

I tried to keep my frantic hands from moving over her too

quickly, but I knew I wasn't succeeding. I wanted to touch her everywhere at once. The smooth skin of her thighs, the bend of her knee, the fragile lines of her collarbone, and the spot right under her ribs that swooped inward to her waist— I wanted it all.

Her hands weren't still, either. Her nails scraped up my back as we kissed, pressed against the muscles of my arms, gripped my ass as she pulled me down until we were as close as we could possibly get with our underwear still on.

"You are the most beautiful woman I've ever seen," I murmured, running my lips over the sweet spot between her shoulder and neck. It sounded like a line, like something that was easily said in the heat of the moment, but I meant every word.

I reached behind her and unclasped her bra, and without giving me time to pull it off, she yanked it down her arms. It got tangled between us for a second and I smiled, but then I was pretty sure that my mouth dropped open in awe when I saw her breasts for the first time. Her hands went to cover them, and my gaze shot to her face, but it wasn't nervousness or hesitation that made her press her fingers into that delicate skin. It was arousal, pure and simple. I'd been staring too long, so she'd touched them herself.

I dropped my head and used my lips to push her fingers out of the way so I could pull one of those rosy-brown nipples into my mouth.

I helped her push my boxers down my thighs and inhaled sharply against her skin when her hand wrapped around my dick. With one hand braced on the bed, I used the other to search blindly for the condoms I'd dropped. I found one and lifted my head so I could meet her eyes.

"Hurry," she murmured. Just one word and I swear the world tilted for a second.

As soon as I'd rolled the condom on, I sat back on my knees, making her whimper at the loss of contact.

I pulled her underwear off, gently pulling her legs up and out of them while she watched me silently.

Sex had never been a big deal for me. I was respectful and I treated women well, but it had never been anything more than just sex. Something that felt good and was fun.

Sex with Sarai, though? That was a game changer. It felt like a commitment. Like a promise. Like jumping over the edge of a cliff with no parachute.

I took a deep breath as I spread her legs.

Her delicate skin was slick and flushed. I wanted to taste her, but then her legs were wrapping around me, and she was whispering for me to kiss her.

I fell forward and braced myself on my elbow, kissing her hard as I lined us up perfectly. With one slow push, I was inside.

Her hands brushed my back as I pulled out and slid forward again. They gripped my sides as we found our rhythm. Her nails dug in as she got close to orgasm, and her fingers relaxed while she was in the throes of it.

I couldn't imagine sex being as good for anyone else as it was for me then. No one had felt as good as she felt; no one had experienced what I was experiencing.

I lasted just long enough for Sarai to come with a quiet moan, her head thrown back and her eyes unfocused. She was so goddamn beautiful. Seconds after I knew she'd finished, I came so hard that I made this awkward noise in the back of my throat. I'd probably be embarrassed about that noise later.

I held myself above her, gasping, my hands shaking, as she ran her fingers through my hair, soothing me as I came back down.

"We should be professionals," I joked as I rolled to the side, keeping an arm around her waist.

"I know," she said quietly, knowingly, as she pressed up against me.

She knew what I couldn't say. She knew what my joke really meant. She knew as well as I did that what we'd just done had changed everything. There was no going back now. It would be impossible to put that particular genie back into the bottle.

We lay there quietly for a long time.

"Can you turn the light off?" she finally asked.

I reached up and pulled the light cord, blanketing the room in shadows.

"I need a new bed," she said, shifting until she'd pushed me onto my back so she could rest her hands and chin on my chest. "This one is too loud."

"It is?" I hadn't noticed.

"The neighbors in the next building could probably hear it," she joked, giving me a lopsided smile.

Her hair was a gorgeous mess, tangled around her face and falling into her eyes, so I reached up and brushed it back with my hand.

"Jesus, I'm lucky," I murmured, staring at her in awe.

"What are the chances of a girl from New York and a guy from Oregon meeting in Missouri?"

She beamed. "I guess we're both lucky," she replied, her fingers tracing small patterns on my skin.

I sighed with happiness as rain started falling, the familiar sound instantly relaxing me.

"Ugh. I hate the rain," Sarai murmured, turning her head to look out the window.

"You do?" I asked in surprise, following her gaze. "I love it. It reminds me of home."

"It makes the roads slick," she muttered, turning her head back to look at me. "And it's not like when it's icy and people are extra careful."

"Is that how your parents died?" I asked quietly.

Sarai stared into my eyes for a long moment. "Yes," she said. "The driver that hit us hydroplaned and lost control."

"God, I'm sorry."

"It was an accident," she continued with a small shake of her head. "A total accident and they were both gone."

"You were in the car?" I asked.

"Yeah." Her lips trembled. "And I walked away without a scratch."

"Thank God," I whispered, the thought of never having met her like a boulder in my gut.

"I wouldn't have agreed with you back then," she said with a sad smile.

"I know that feeling," I replied, running my fingers up and down her back. "I lost my mom when I was young, too."

"You did?" she asked in confusion. "But you talk about your parents all the time."

"I was adopted when I was nine."

"What?" She looked at me like I'd grown two heads. "You've never said anything about being adopted," she said incredulously.

"It never came up…" My voice trailed off as I realized how lame that excuse was. "I don't mention it much."

"It's not like we just met," she said quietly. "I told you about my parents and that I lived with my aunt and uncle."

"I'm sorry," I replied. "It never even occurred to me. Here's the thing…" I paused, trying to figure out how to explain my reasoning. "These are my parents, okay? Kate is my sister as much as Bram is my brother. It's not 'here's my adoptive parents.' It's 'here's my parents.' I don't mention that I'm adopted, because they're just my family. It isn't any different than any other, biological family, and I don't want people to view it that way."

"But I'm not *people*," she said softly.

"You're right," I murmured. "I guess not mentioning it is just habit at this point. I *am* sorry. It didn't have anything to do with how I feel about you."

"I understand," she said, giving me a little half smile. "How did your first mom pass away?"

My *first* mom. Damn, I liked that. I didn't tell many people that I'd been adopted, but it was common knowledge in our small hometown, and I couldn't even count the times people had asked me about my "real" mom growing up. I'd hated it. Calling my biological mother my real mom was a slight to my adoptive mother. She was just as real as the woman who'd given birth to me and Bram.

Sarai watched me, waiting for my answer, and I suddenly

felt as if my heart were going to beat out of my chest.

"A broken heart," I answered, my voice grave. "At least that's what Bram and I have always thought."

Sarai made a small sound of sympathy and kissed my chest.

"This conversation has taken a surprisingly morbid turn," I joked, uncomfortable with the emotion clogging my throat.

"Thanks for telling me about your mom," she said simply, resting her chin on her hand.

"You know, Thanksgiving is next month," I said, changing the subject to the first thing I could think of. I stared at all the details that made up her gorgeous face. The strong nose and dark eyebrows, the full bottom lip and cupid's-bow top lip that were rosy from being pressed against my skin. The gap between her two front teeth that drove me crazy.

"Yep. Four days off," she murmured. "I can't wait."

"Are you going home for the holiday?" I asked, running my fingers through her hair.

"No," she replied. "My family's never really made a big deal about Thanksgiving."

"Really?"

"Really," she confirmed. "I mean, we've always had dinner, but it's not a big celebration or anything."

That was pretty much the opposite of how my family did things. Every major holiday was a celebration to the Harris and Evans clan. As I looked into her sleepy eyes, an idea formed.

"How would you feel about coming to Oregon with me?" I asked, nervousness making my words come out a bit stilted.

"What?" Her eyes widened in surprise.

"I was planning on going home for Thanksgiving, and I want you to go with me," I said. "My family will love you. Come." I watched her expression move from surprise to contemplation, and I relaxed just a little. At least she hadn't told me no right away.

"Who's going to be there?" she asked softly, laying her head down on my chest.

"My parents," I replied, wrapping my arm around her as I used my other hand to pull her comforter over us. "My brother and sister and their families." I paused, not wanting to overwhelm her, then pressed forward. "And probably my uncle and aunt and cousin Trevor and his family."

"So it's a big event, then," she said softly.

"Not a formal one," I said, smiling as she raised her knee until it was across my thighs, her foot resting between my calves. "Dinner and maybe some touch football. Some ATV riding. At least one night out so all the cousins can get hammered while our parents watch the kids."

"Sounds fun," she said, her voice even quieter.

"It is." I loved my family. I knew a lot of people who complained about their relatives back home, but I didn't. My parents were the best people I knew, and even though my brother drove me crazy, I genuinely liked my siblings and their partners. I was lucky.

"Do you want to go with me?" I asked after a while, just as I felt Sarai's body relax fully against mine.

"Sure," she said, giving my chest a kiss. "Let me know how much the tickets cost."

There was no way in hell Sarai was buying her own plane

ticket. I grinned into the darkness. She was coming home with me for Thanksgiving.

* * *

"I'm sorry," Sarai said the next morning as she followed me out the front door. We'd woken up when her regular alarm had gone off, and in a perfect world she would have had plenty of time to get ready. However, waking up naked and wrapped around another person made the mornings move a bit slower than usual. By the time we'd finished another round of sex, she'd been running late and I'd felt very guilty.

"Stop saying you're sorry," I told her as she locked her front door behind us. "I'm the one who made you late."

"I feel like a jerk kicking you out—"

"I need to go home and get ready for work anyway," I reminded her, ushering her toward her car.

As soon as we reached the driver's-side door, Sarai froze and spun toward me. "I had a really great time," she said, stretching up on her toes to give me a quick kiss. "In case you didn't know that."

"I thought you might have," I teased, nodding my head. I pulled her in for a quick hug. "I had a good time, too."

I opened her door so she could climb inside the car.

"Hey, I'm going to get our plane tickets today," I said as Sarai pushed her keys into the ignition. She paused. "Is it cool with you if we fly out on Wednesday night and home Sunday?"

I waited for her to respond for what seemed like a very long time even though it was a few seconds at most.

"Are you sure you want me to go?" she asked.

"Positive," I confirmed.

"Okay, then those dates work for me." She smiled brightly, and I wanted to do a little dance at the sight of it. "Let me know how much they cost, and I'll pay you back."

"Not a chance in hell," I said pleasantly, closing her door.

Before I could step away from the car, she'd rolled down her window.

"I'm paying for my ticket," she said, pointing at me.

"I'm paying for the tickets," I replied. "You can pay for the magazines we grab at the airport."

"I don't buy magazines at the airport. They're too expensive. I always bring a book."

"Okay, then," I said, walking backward. "You can bring a book and I'll buy a magazine at the airport."

"No you won't," she called back. "I'll buy it!"

"Good." I clapped my hands together. "Then it's all worked out."

She stared at me for a minute, then started laughing as she turned on her car. "I'm paying for my plane ticket, too," she yelled as I got farther away.

I gave her a thumbs-down from across the parking lot, then watched as she shook her head at me and pulled out of her parking spot. As soon as she'd driven away, I climbed into my truck and drove home.

Nothing was going to ruin my mood, not even the fact that I'd probably be late for work. I couldn't believe how fantastic the night had been. How well I'd slept in a bed that wasn't mine. How good the sex was this morning, even though we both went to great lengths to not let the other person smell our morning breath.

I thought about calling Ani but stopped myself. This thing with Sarai had turned into something too big to discuss with my best friend. Too private and fragile. At some point, I knew that I'd probably go to Ani and Bram for advice, maybe even ask my sister, Kate, for some, but at this point, calling them felt too much like bragging.

I didn't want to brag about my night with Sarai. I wanted to keep it to myself for just a little while. Just between us.

* * *

Work is so boring today.

I smiled as I read the text from Sarai. I understood how she felt. It was lunchtime, and most of my coworkers were at home, showering off after their testing, while I was sitting there with little to do. By the time I'd finished the paperwork I'd been in the middle of, I'd known I wouldn't have time to make it off base before everyone came back, so I'd ended up getting fast food and eating it at my desk while I searched for cheap flights home.

How do you feel about flying out at 8 on Wednesday? I asked, leaning back in my chair. Eight o'clock would be cutting it kind of close after work, but if she was all packed and ready to go, I could grab her on the way to the airport.

That works for me. We usually go home early that day so I should have plenty of time. How much are the tickets?

I grinned.

None of your business. You just worry about my magazines.

Her reply was almost instant.

I'll just start paying you back by stuffing bills in your shorts when you strip.

I sent my reply just as people started filtering in the front door.

Remind me to bring my boom box next time I come over.

"Evans," Sean called, walking toward my desk. "Must be nice to sit on your ass all morning."

It wasn't, actually. It sucked. I didn't say anything, just gave him a tight smile.

"I killed it this morning," he said, pulling up a chair and dropping into it.

"Oh yeah?"

"Yup."

I nodded but wasn't sure why he was still at my desk. We didn't really do that type of thing. He wasn't like Clover, who'd sit down and bullshit when we had time. Sean was usually trying to find a new person to impress with his epic boasting.

"So what was up with your girl last night?" Sean asked. He didn't lower his voice like he was genuinely concerned about it. Nope, he said it loud enough for half the people in the office to hear. I gritted my teeth in annoyance.

"Not sure what you mean," I replied calmly.

"She damn near bit my head off because I didn't know she was Jewish," he said, throwing his hands in the air with a laugh. "I mean, how was I supposed to know she's Jewish? Not like I can check for circumcision."

I stared at him in disgust.

"You're a fucking idiot," I replied.

"What?" he laughed like I was joking and glanced

around, like he was waiting for someone else to laugh with him.

It took every piece of willpower I had not to say anything else. If I called him out on how he treated his live-in girlfriend, I'd potentially be opening myself up to a goddamn fist fight in the middle of work. That was the type of guy Sean was—he'd never let something like that go.

"You're a fucking idiot," I repeated slowly, my voice flat.

Sean's head jerked back in surprise just as Clovis ambled over to my desk.

"What did he do this time?" he asked, jerking his chin toward Sean.

"He's all bent out of shape because his girlfriend doesn't like me," Sean said. I could see him gearing up for what would be a huge fucking blowup, when Clovis slapped him hard on the back.

"She's got good taste," he joked.

We watched Sean stomp off across the room, and I let out a sigh. I couldn't fucking stand that guy.

"Thanks, man," I said to Clovis as he leaned against my desk.

"What was that all about?" he asked, raising one eyebrow.

"Sarai handed him his ass last night, so he came over trying to save face," I said, leaning back in my chair.

Clovis laughed. "What a dick."

"No shit. He treats his girlfriend like complete garbage."

"We already knew that," Clovis murmured.

"Yeah, well, it's probably worse than what we're seeing," I said.

"That bad?"

"I don't know, man," I replied, thinking about the way Hailey had looked in the kitchen last night. "It's pretty bad."

As Clovis walked away, I stretched out my shoulders and tried to get back to work. It was hard to focus, though, when so many thoughts were racing through my head. It sucked that Sean was with Sarai's best friend, because I didn't want him anywhere near her.

* * *

"Hey, Ma," I said, smiling when she answered the phone a few days later.

"Alex! It feels like we haven't talked in weeks," she said, a smile in her voice.

"It's only been one," I replied.

"Well, I don't know why you only call on Sundays," my mom said. "I'd love to hear from you every day."

"The phone works both ways," I teased.

"Well, I know that."

"But, uh." I paused. "Don't call me *every* day, all right?"

Mom laughed but made no promises.

"How are things?" she asked. "Are you coming home for Thanksgiving?"

"That's actually what I was calling about—"

"You can't make it," she said, disappointment clear. "Damn it all."

"Mom." I cut her off with a short laugh. "Yes, I'm coming up for Thanksgiving."

"Oh, good."

"I just wanted to give you a heads-up that I'm bringing someone with me."

"You are?" she asked curiously.

"Yeah, if that's okay?"

"Of course it's okay," she scoffed. "You know you don't have to ask. Everyone's invited to Thanksgiving."

"Okay, cool." I closed my mouth and waited. It was a game I'd played with her since I was a kid. I'd give her just enough information to make her curious, and then I'd stop. The goal was to make her ask me whatever she wanted to know without my giving it up first. I rarely won, though, because she was the master.

The seconds ticked by.

I checked my watch. It had to have been at least a full minute.

"I'm bringing my, uh, girlfriend," I finally said, giving up.

"Girlfriend, huh?" she replied teasingly. "What's her name?"

"Sarai."

"Oh, that's a pretty name," she said quietly. "What's she like?"

I tipped my head back and thought of Sarai.

"She's beautiful. Funny—quick, you know."

"Oh, I know the type," she said drily. I laughed. My entire family had that sharp wit.

"And she's really smart. Way smarter than me."

"That's the best type of woman to partner up with," my mom said knowingly. "Just ask your father."

I laughed. "She's kind, too, and sticks up for her friends. Actually, she's fearless in that way."

"It sounds like you really like her," Mom said.

"Actually—" I swallowed hard. "Actually, I think I might be falling in love with her," I confessed.

"Oh, baby," she replied softly. "I can't wait to meet her."

"I think you'll love her, too."

"Oh, I have no doubt I will," she said cheerfully. Then she chuckled. "It's Ani you'll have to worry about."

CHAPTER 8

SARAI

Even though work was slow and I was bored out of my mind, I couldn't keep the grin off my face. We'd spent the night before at Alex's apartment, and even though I was tired as hell this morning, I didn't regret a single second.

I was seriously falling for Alex Evans, and despite all my early misgivings, I couldn't have been happier about it. He was everything.

"You're looking chipper this morning," Elise teased as she dropped a file on my desk.

"I am chipper," I replied, still smiling.

"That's an *I got laid this morning* smile," she said, dropping into the chair across from me. "Spill. I've been married for ten years. We never do it in the morning anymore."

I huffed out a surprised laugh as my mouth dropped open. Elise was sweet, and we'd always gotten along really well at work, but we normally stuck to safe subjects like weekend plans and family anecdotes.

"It's the new guy you're seeing, isn't it?" she said, leaning back in her seat as she crossed her legs. "Yeah, I've seen you. Checking your phone a million times a day and staring off into space. What's he like?"

"He's awesome," I gushed. I could feel my face growing warm in embarrassment at the vehemence in my words.

"That's good," she replied, waving her hand in a motion to keep going.

"He's in the Army—"

"They always are, around here." She laughed. "My man was, too."

"He's so sweet," I said. "And smart. He opens doors for me and walks me to my car and brings me dinner when I'm overloaded with schoolwork."

"He sounds great," she said, leaning forward to whisper. "What's he look like? How's he in bed?"

"He's tall, dark, and handsome," I said, pausing as she hummed in appreciation. "And he has these super-long eyelashes and this gorgeous smile that just—" I sighed.

"Makes you weak in the knees, does it?" she replied knowingly.

"It makes me weak everywhere," I joked, making her chuckle.

"And the sex?" she asked, wiggling her eyebrows.

"Insanely good," I whispered, excited to tell *someone* about it. "I've never been with someone that did everything right the first time, you know?" She nodded in understanding. "I mean, usually it takes time to figure out what the other person likes."

"Hell, there's a lot of guys that never get it right." She rolled her eyes. "If you catch my meaning."

"He definitely gets it right," I murmured in satisfaction, remembering how hard I'd come both last night and again this morning. "Usually twice."

Elise laughed. "Well, I'm glad," she said. "You've always been so serious and focused around here. It's been nice to see you happy for a change."

"I've always been happy," I replied, surprised at her comment.

"Giddy, then," she corrected. "Cheerful. Acting your age."

"Distracted, you mean," I said, grimacing.

"More like…floating around like forest animals dress you in the mornings," she replied.

"He makes me feel beautiful," I said seriously, shrugging.

"That's the kind of guy you hold on to," she replied, pointing at me as she stood up. "I better get back to work."

* * *

Time flew by in a blur of Alex, school, and work. I'd never been so busy in my entire life, and surprisingly, I didn't mind. Alex just seemed to make everything better. We'd gone from struggling to find time for each other to making time for each other, and it was easier than I could've imagined. Alex's name was written in every page of my planner.

I could feel my priorities shifting, and I started considering staying in Missouri after graduation. If I was being honest with myself, I'd never seriously planned to go home to New York, but I'd never had a reason to stay in Missouri, either. I'd just assumed that I would send my résumé out all over the country and see where I got a bite. I couldn't imagine that now, though, not if it meant leaving Alex behind. Instead, I started researching job opportunities near the university. Maybe I'd get lucky and I wouldn't have to go anywhere.

The Wednesday we'd planned to leave seemed to last a million years. Every phone call I fielded and paper I filed was just another thing holding me back from where I wanted to be. Alex had driven me to work so he could pick me up afterward. Our bags were packed and stuffed in his truck, and unbeknownst to him, I had about five magazines in my purse for the flight.

By the time I shut down my computer and gathered up my things, I was practically tapping my foot with impatience.

"I'm out of here for the weekend," I called out, though there was barely anyone left in the office to hear me. Most of the accountants had already left for the day, anxious to start their holiday weekend.

I was walking out the door to wait for Alex when my phone rang. I answered it without checking who it was.

"I'm waiting out front," I said cheerfully.

"Why are you flying to Oregon? You get a few days off and you didn't think we'd like to see you? If you have the money to fly to Oregon, why wouldn't you come home? We miss you. I tell Isaac every day how much I wish you'd come to see us. Then when you get the time, you—"

"Auntie." I cut her off midsentence. She hadn't taken even a single breath during her rant. "I see you got my email."

"Of course we got your email. You think your uncle

doesn't check his email? He uses that for work, Sarai. He opens it every day."

"I wanted him to see it," I replied, rolling my eyes. I'd wanted him to see it because I wanted them to know where I was if, God forbid, something happened and they had to reach me, but I'd kind of been hoping he'd keep the information to himself.

I'd told my aunt and uncle all about Alex. He wasn't some kind of secret. Besides, he'd been taking up what free time I had lately, and I wanted them to know what I was up to. I'd never hidden things from them—not big things. Maybe if we'd lived closer, I would have been more circumspect, but the only things they knew about my life were the things I told them, and I never wanted to get to the point where we felt like strangers because I'd stopped letting them know about my life.

"Alex is paying for our trip," I told her as I searched the street for Alex's truck.

"Well." She paused for a minute, humming. "Of course he is, since he's going to see *his* family."

I laughed a little under my breath.

"I'm still going to try to come home in the spring," I told her as I spotted Alex pulling up to the curb.

My uncle and aunt weren't exactly well off. Even though I knew they'd buy a ticket for me to come home, I refused to let them pay for my flights. I was an adult, and I had a full-time job. Plus, I was stubborn. I paid my own way. Eventually, I'd find a way to pay Alex back for the tickets he'd insisted on paying for.

"Spring is too far away," my aunt replied with a huge sigh.

"It'll go by quickly," I said. "And I'll be all done with school."

"Good," she said. "You should plan on coming home to stay. Your family is here. Your life is here."

She continued on as I climbed in the truck and smiled at Alex. He smiled back but didn't say a word, since I was on the phone. My aunt continued to talk about how I needed to go back to New York as we pulled back onto the street and headed toward the airport. Alex's hand found my thigh and gave it a gentle squeeze, and I couldn't imagine a time when I'd want to move thousands of miles away from him.

"Auntie, I'll have to call you back," I said when there was finally a break in her reasons why I should leave Missouri.

When I got off the phone, I dropped it in my purse with a dramatic sigh and turned to look at Alex.

"Sorry about that."

"No worries," he said. "How are your aunt and uncle?"

"Good." I grinned. "Mad that I'm flying off to Oregon with you when I could have flown home to New York for the weekend."

"Oh no," he murmured, glancing my way.

"It's silly. I wouldn't have flown there for the weekend, anyway," I said.

"Well, I'm glad you're coming with me," he said happily. "Do we need to stop anywhere before the airport?"

"Oh yeah," I said. "I need to stop and get my nails done. Maybe a haircut?" I lifted my hair and pretended I was searching for split ends.

"I meant for food or something, smart-ass."

"Nope." I dropped my purse on the floorboard and got more comfortable. "I'm all set."

"A few hours and I'll be back in the Northwest again," he said excitedly, letting out a deep sigh. "Just wait until you see it. Everything's green—a million different shades. And the rain makes the air smell incredible."

"I'm excited to see it," I replied, smiling at his animated description.

"You'll like my family, too."

"Yeah?"

"Oh yeah. They're impossible not to like. My dad is kind of quiet, mellow, you know?"

I nodded.

"My mom's the outgoing one. She's going to love you."

"I do have a winning personality," I said easily, making him smile.

I was a lot more nervous than I let on. Meeting new people was always a little nerve-racking, but meeting Alex's family was in a whole different universe. If they didn't like me or I didn't like them, it would be disastrous for our relationship. I'd like to say that our families didn't have any say in our lives, but I was a realist. Our families were really important to us. Their opinions mattered.

Checking in at the airport was relatively simple, and we made it to our gate with time to spare. Alex was the best person to people watch with. He pointed out things I'd never have noticed, like the woman who was looking at a crying toddler in horror but was holding a parenting magazine.

"I'd bet money that she was pregnant," he told me jokingly as we filed onto the plane and found our seats.

"No way. She probably has kids at home who are perfect

angels," I replied, sitting down while Alex put our bags in the overhead bins.

"She had that deer-in-the-headlights look," he murmured, sitting down next to me. "Like *Oh shit, what have I gotten myself into?*"

I stared at him incredulously.

"Plus, her coat opened a little and I saw the belly," he said, laughing.

I scoffed and swatted his arm. As we settled into our seats, Alex said, "I hate flying."

"Really?" I reached out and laced my fingers through his.

"Just the landing and takeoff," he muttered. "Those are the most dangerous times."

"Shh," I whispered as a woman sat down on Alex's other side. "Don't start freaking people out."

"It's a widely known fact," he said, leaning his head back against the headrest.

"That doesn't mean people want to hear about it," I said, smiling at our row mate.

Watching Alex try to stay calm while the airplane taxied made me like him more. I felt a kind of tenderness toward him in those few moments. I gripped his hand tightly, rubbing my thumb soothingly over the skin. He was unnaturally quiet until we were safely in the air, then as if a switch had flipped, he opened his eyes and grinned at me.

"I can't wait to be home," he said with a happy sigh.

"Are we renting a car when we get there?" I asked, smiling when his eyes lit up and he shook his head.

"Nope. My brother's going to pick us up."

"Abraham?" I asked. I was nervous to meet his twin, but

I was pretty curious about him, too. I couldn't imagine two Alexes running around in the world.

"Yeah, Bram. He hates driving in Portland, so I made sure to ask him specifically," Alex joked.

"You two are identical, right?"

"Yeah." He nodded. "Though it's pretty easy to tell us apart, I think. I'm the one smiling, and Abraham's the one scowling."

"Oh dear," I muttered.

"Nah, you'll like him. He's a crotchety bastard, but one minute with my niece and you'll see a totally different side of him. The guy's a softy."

"What if I can't tell you apart?" I asked, only halfway joking.

"He has a full beard," he said, giving me a smile. "You'll know who's who."

"But what if that was a thing? What if he shaved and I really couldn't tell you apart?"

"You think that's even a possibility?" he asked incredulously.

"Well, I don't know. You say identical, and I think *identical*." The real worry must have bled into my voice, because Alex shook his head a little.

"My sister-in-law, Ani, is my best friend in the world," Alex said in a low voice. "And I can tell you with absolute certainty that she's never been attracted to me—what does that tell you?"

"That you're not quite identical," I said in relief.

"You won't get us mixed up," he said firmly. "Not even possible."

"Okay."

We were quiet for a few minutes.

"You're seriously worried about it?" he asked finally.

"Not anymore," I murmured sheepishly.

Alex laughed. "Bram and I used to try to fool people," he said, still grinning. "Like *The Parent Trap*, you know?"

"I loved that movie when I was a kid," I replied, then clarified. "The original version—not the remake."

"Important distinction," Alex said in mock seriousness.

"It is."

He nodded. "When we were kids, we couldn't ever figure out why we were never able to fool anyone." He chuckled. "In hindsight it was obvious. Our personalities were so different, neither one of us could act like the other one long enough to make it believable."

Over the next couple of hours, Alex told me all about his childhood. He and Abraham had lived with their birth mother until she'd died and they'd gone into foster care. After a couple of years moving from one home to the other, they'd been placed with Liz and Dan Evans, who'd adopted them. Liz and Dan had a biological daughter named Kate, who was a year younger than the boys, and they'd continued to foster other children after Abraham and Alex had been placed in their home, but they hadn't adopted anyone else. When they were teenagers, Alex's sister-in-law, Ani, had been placed with the Evans family, and years later she and Abraham had fallen in love.

"No wonder you like me so much," I teased as the flight attendant came over the intercom system to tell us that we were beginning our descent into Portland. "Your family needed some new blood."

Alex laughed. "I'm not even done."

"There's more?" I asked.

"My aunt and uncle also fostered Shane when we were teenagers," he said, his voice a little stiff as we got ready to land.

"Shane?" I asked. Then it dawned on me. "You mean your sister's boyfriend—er, husband?" I wasn't sure if they were married or not, but I knew they had a lot of kids.

"That's the one," Alex said, dropping his head against the seat as he closed his eyes.

"Whoa," I said in wonder. "I'm a little worried I won't be able to remember how everyone is connected."

"Nah." He swallowed hard. "You'll do fine."

"Uh-huh," I murmured. I was trying to keep him talking as his muscles tensed with nerves.

"No, really," he said, opening his eyes long enough to look at me. "It'll be easy. Ani is outspoken and kind of crazy. Bram looks like a lumberjack version of me. Kate is the sweetest woman you'll ever meet, and Shane is the one following after her like a puppy. Simple."

I laughed at his descriptions and held his hand firmly as the plane landed with a bump, and then we were slowing way down as we pulled up to our gate.

"How would you describe me?" I asked teasingly as we came to a stop.

"The most beautiful woman in the room," he said easily.

"Oh, you're smooth," I joked, pinching him lightly.

"I love you," he said softly, his eyes earnest and sweet. His expression grew slightly panicked as I froze. "You don't have to say it back—" he said quickly.

"I love you, too," I said at the same time.

We stared at each other.

"Well," he said, letting out a breath of relief. "I made that awkward as hell."

I burst out laughing.

"Come here," he said, his eyes crinkling at the corners as he smiled at me. We kissed until the person next to Alex started to grumble in annoyance.

* * *

We hadn't checked any bags, so we made quick work of getting off the plane and heading toward the passenger drop-off area outside.

"It's just easier to get picked up here," Alex explained, looking around for his brother as we walked outside. "No reason to go downstairs if you don't have bags."

He inhaled deeply and dramatically dropped to his knees on the concrete.

"Oh, Oregon," he said happily. "How I've missed you."

The people around us laughed and pointed as he pretended to kiss the ground. I watched him in amusement, but when I caught him glancing at me, I realized that he was trying to embarrass me. Not on my watch, buddy.

"Yes," I yelled, raising my hands in the air. "I love the smell of rain and car fumes!" I made eye contact with a man around our age who was pulling a large suitcase behind him as he approached the doors. "Don't leave! You'll regret it!"

Alex was laughing hysterically when an SUV pulled up beside us and a petite dark-haired woman leaned out the window.

"What did I tell you two about talking to strangers?" she called out jokingly. "That man looks dangerous."

The man I'd pulled into our antics rushed away, and I smiled as Alex climbed to his feet and loped toward the car.

"You're a sight for sore eyes," he said, hugging her through the window. "Ani, this is Sarai."

"Of course when I find you, you're harassing some poor guy," she teased him, flicking him as she turned toward me.

"That was my fault," I admitted, walking toward the car. "Nice to meet you, Ani."

"You too," Ani said. She stared at me for a minute. "You're pretty." She looked at Alex. "What the hell is she doing with *you*?"

"She prefers the handsome brother," Alex replied, pulling me against his side.

"Hey now," an almost familiar voice called from the driver's seat.

I leaned down to see who was driving and met the eyes of Alex's twin brother. It was eerie, staring into those eyes. They were Alex's but not. The crinkles in the corners that Alex had from smiling were shallower on Bram, but the furrows between Bram's eyebrows were deeper.

"Hey," Bram said. His voice was deeper than Alex's, raspier.

"That's my *identical* twin brother, Abraham," Alex said, wrapping an arm around my waist.

"Huh," I murmured, tipping my head to the side. "I don't see it."

"Oh, I like her," Ani said quietly.

"Get in before people start honking," Bram ordered.

We climbed into the backseat, and just as Alex closed the door, the car was in motion.

"Where's Arie?" Alex asked as I rushed to fasten my seat belt.

"She's with Mom," Bram replied.

Ani turned around in her seat and smiled brightly.

"Baby, I get in a wreck and you're toast," Bram said, reaching out to put his hand on her leg.

"Don't wreck," Ani replied, still facing us. "How was your flight?"

"It was good," Alex said, stretching out his legs as much as he could. I didn't blame him. I was feeling a bit stiff from being in the tiny plane seats, too, and he was much bigger than I was. Hopefully his knee wasn't bothering him.

"No crying babies or smelly food," I said, making Ani laugh. "So I'd consider it a success."

"Smelly food is the worst," Ani replied, wrinkling her nose.

"I'm getting on the freeway, Anita," Bram snapped worriedly. "Sit your ass down."

"All right, all right," she grumbled.

"It's good to have you home," Bram said, glancing at us in the mirror again. "You're flying back out on Sunday?"

"That sucks," Ani announced. "You should have tried to stay longer."

"We've got jobs," Alex said in amusement. "Not all of us can paint furniture whenever we want and call it good."

"I resent that," Ani said, flipping Alex off. "I'm also raising a small human."

"And doing a fantastic job," Alex conceded.

"I can take you back to the airport on Sunday if it's in the morning, but if it's later than noon, then Trev or Dad can take you," Bram said, like the entire conversation between Alex and Ani hadn't happened.

"What do you have going on Sunday?" Alex asked, reaching out to hold my hand.

The warmth of his palm was a comfort. I didn't have anything to add to the conversation, and I didn't mind staying quiet, but I also worried that they'd think I was rude for just sitting there silently. I took a deep breath and forced my body to relax. I had all weekend to make a good impression.

"Me and Ani are going out to dinner," Bram replied.

"And?"

"And Bram promised to keep Arie so I could shower and shave things that haven't been shaved in a while. Maybe pluck my eyebrows and paint my nails if the mood hits," Ani said, leaning around her seat to glare at Alex. "It's probably going to take me *all* day."

"Ooh," Alex joked. "It's that kind of date."

"It is." Ani smirked. "We're gonna—"

"Nope!" Alex yelled, startling a small laugh out of me. "I don't want to hear anything else, thanks."

The conversation moved to the logging company, and I listened intently as Alex and Bram discussed the business. Alex had never complained to me about being in the Army; he actually seemed to enjoy it, but it was like a light flicked on when he spoke about the family business. He was animated and opinionated as he discussed potential growth opportunities and downfalls. As Alex and Bram argued good-naturedly, I smiled and looked out the window at the passing scenery. It was a gloomy day, and it looked like it was going to rain at any second, but the landscape was still surprisingly beautiful.

We'd been in the car for a little less than an hour when the SUV slowed down and pulled into a long driveway.

"Almost home," Alex said softly, glancing over to give me a sweet smile.

"This is where you grew up?" I asked in awe, leaning so that I could look out the front window.

Everything was green—from the grass and the ferns to the tall evergreen trees that seemed to go on for miles. It was beautiful and peaceful, but I couldn't imagine living so far from everything.

"Yep, the best place on Earth." Alex rolled down his window and inhaled deeply. "It's going to rain."

"How can you tell?" I whispered, rolling down my own window.

"I can smell it."

"No you can't," I argued, sniffing.

"He's right," Ani said from the front seat. "If you're around here long enough, you'll notice the smell, too."

I glanced between the two of them, trying to figure out if they were full of shit, but before I could argue anymore, we came to a stop in front of a well-kept single-story house.

"Mom must have heard us pull up," Bram said, turning off the car. A slight older woman was standing on the porch, grinning at us.

"Just leave the bags for now," Alex said excitedly as he held the door for me to climb out. As soon as my feet had hit the ground and he'd closed the door behind me, he was jogging toward the front of the house and up the two steps that led to the porch.

"Why don't you open my door?" Ani asked Bram as she climbed out of the car.

"Because you don't sit still long enough," Bram replied.

I heard them, but I didn't see them. My eyes were glued to the man and woman on the porch. Alex was hugging his mom and lifting her off her feet to swing her around in a circle.

"Sarai," Alex called, waving me over. "Come meet my mom."

Alex and his mom stepped off the porch and met me halfway.

"Sarai, this is my mom, Liz. Mom, this is Sarai."

"It's so nice to meet you," Liz said warmly, reaching out to shake my hand. "Alex has talked about you a lot."

"It's nice to meet you, too, Mrs. Evans."

"Please call me Liz," Alex's mom said with a small laugh. "Mrs. Evans makes me sound old."

"I think it sounds distinguished," Ani argued, joining our circle. "Like a proper mature lady."

"*Anita* knows a lot about mature-lady names," Alex said with a laugh.

"Like *Alexander* is much better."

They both looked to the side and laughed as Bram walked toward us. "Abraham is worse," they joked in unison.

"Ignore them," Liz told me, setting her hand gently on my upper back so she could steer me toward the house. "They're always like this at first. I swear, they won't be quiet for a full twenty-four hours, and then suddenly they'll mellow and things will get relatively normal again."

"Thank you so much for inviting me," I said, grinning as we entered the house. The walls of the entryway were covered with framed black-and-white photographs, and I made a mental note to look at them more carefully later. "I was just going to be sitting at home, watching television and eating ramen noodles all weekend."

"Of course," Liz said, smiling. "We love having a full house. Your family doesn't celebrate Thanksgiving?"

"They do," I replied as Alex, Ani, and Bram came through the front door. "We've just never made a big deal about it, so flying all the way to New York for the weekend seemed kind of silly."

Liz laughed. "Well, you're in for a treat, because we go all out. You won't be able to button your pants by the time you're done with dessert."

"Hey, where's Arie?" Ani asked, coming abruptly to a stop.

"Well, she was driving me crazy, so I sent her outside to play," Liz said jokingly about their toddler. When Ani didn't take the bait, she sighed. "She and Dad fell asleep in the recliner when they were watching a movie. You walked right past them when you came in."

"Aw," Alex said. He'd taken one step back toward the living room when Ani jumped onto his back, covering his mouth with one hand while she clung to him like a monkey.

"If you wake my child, I will make this weekend absolute hell for you," she hissed.

I watched them in fascination. As an only child, I hadn't grown up horsing around and fighting with siblings, and for the first time in my life I wondered if I'd missed out.

"I'd like to say they're usually not like this," Liz said with a sigh. "But I'd be lying. Ani, get off Alex's back before you wake the baby. Alex and Abraham, I need some wood brought in for the woodstove, and I haven't bothered your dad with it, because his back's been giving him trouble."

"On it," Alex said, helping Ani slide safely off his back. He came over to give me a quick kiss. "I'm so glad you came with me."

Bram and Alex went quietly out the back door, and Liz gestured for me to sit at the kitchen counter.

"I don't know how many jobs I have around the house to keep them occupied, but if I need to, I'll make some up," she said conspiratorially to me. "Would you like some coffee?"

"I'd love some," I replied.

"We all do that," Ani said to me, pointing at the back door.

"Do what?" Liz asked.

"Leave Bram and Alex alone to bond," Ani said, shuffling through a basket on the counter and pulling out two little individually packaged snack cakes. She set one down in front of me and opened the other.

"I was more concerned with getting the two of them out of the house before you all woke up the baby or scared Sarai off," Liz said drily. "But yes, I guess I do try to give them some time to themselves."

"I can't believe they're identical," I said, taking my coffee from Liz with a smile. "They look like brothers but not like twins."

"Right?" Ani said around her mouth full of cake. "They look totally different."

"They were a lot more similar as boys," Liz said, leaning her elbows on the counter, her hands wrapped around her mug of coffee. "But you could always tell them apart by the expressions on their faces. The scowl was Bram and the smile was Alex."

"That's sad," I blurted out. I immediately felt like I'd said something wrong, but Liz just smiled.

"I didn't mean it as an insult," she said, taking a sip of her coffee. "Bram has always seen the world a bit more cynically than his brother. It's not a bad thing, just a difference in personalities."

"I've got wood," Alex announced as he pushed the back door open with his foot. He was carrying an armful of dried firewood and had a huge smile on his face.

"Nice," Ani said, nodding.

My mouth dropped open in surprise as his mother scolded him.

"I'm pretty sure he's her favorite," Ani said to me as we watched Liz swat at Alex with a hand towel, her face completely lit up with happiness. "But none of us mind." When I glanced over at Ani, she was smiling. "Alex is everyone's favorite."

"He's my favorite, too," I murmured as Alex tripped around the kitchen laughing as he struggled to keep the firewood stacked in his arms while avoiding his mom's towel.

CHAPTER 9

ALEX

I loved being home. I liked Missouri, and I enjoyed my job most of the time, but there was something about the way the air smelled and the sound of my dad's knees cracking as he dropped into his recliner that instantly made me feel at peace. I'd joined the Army at nineteen, excited to see the world and spread my proverbial wings, but nowhere else had fit me like my parents' property in middle-of-nowhere Oregon. Bringing Sarai there to experience all of it heightened the feeling of home—like a missing puzzle piece that I hadn't realized was missing.

I looked around the kitchen happily. This, right here, was exactly what it was all about. Life, the universe, our purpose—it was all wrapped up in family. The people you chose to spend your time with, who made you comfortable and happy, they were everything.

"Dipshit," Ani said, elbowing me in the side. "I've been

talking to you for like five minutes, and you've completely ignored me."

"I was figuring out the answer to the meaning of life," I said calmly.

"Yeah, whatever."

"*The meaning of life*, Ani," I said importantly.

She looked at me as if I were an idiot. "Dude, do it on your own time."

I laughed and wrapped my arm around her head, pinning it between my biceps and chest.

"It never ends," Bram said to Sarai, nodding at us.

"Liz said they eventually calm down," she replied, her lips twitching.

"This is calm," he said with a small laugh, taking a drink of his beer.

"Why did everyone leave me sleeping in the damn chair?" my dad asked, ambling into the kitchen with a drowsy Arie against his chest. He came to a stop when he saw Sarai. "Oh, excuse me."

Sarai waved off his apology.

I let go of Ani, who hadn't even bothered to fight my hold, and stepped forward.

"Alex," he said, smiling. "Good to see you, son."

"I'll take this," Ani muttered, reaching out for her daughter. "Hey, princess. Did you have a good nap with Papa? I bet your diaper is soaked."

I wrapped my arms around my dad and slapped his back as we hugged.

"That your girl?" he asked quietly in my ear. "How'd you manage that?"

"Dumb luck and persistence," I replied, pulling away.

Dad laughed.

"Sarai, this is my dad, Dan."

"Nice to meet you, Sarai," my dad said, walking over to shake her hand.

"Damned nice to meet you, too," she said, using the curse word he'd just apologized for and giving him a lopsided smile. Dad chuckled.

"Good pick," he said to me.

"I think so," I replied, standing beside Sarai once he'd moved away.

"I like your family," she said, leaning against my side.

"They're wondering how the hell I got you to go out with me," I teased.

"Would I have to wrestle around with Ani?" Sarai asked jokingly. "Because I'm bigger, but I think she'd win."

"I'd definitely win," Ani said, joining our conversation.

"You have ears like a bat," Sarai said, her eyes wide.

"I'm a superb eavesdropper," Ani confirmed. Then she pulled Arie off her hip and held the baby in front of her. "This is Arielle. She smells much better now, and she's ready to meet you."

"Hello, Arielle," Sarai said softly, reaching out to tickle the bottom of Arie's foot. "You're adorable."

"Don't let her fool you. She's a demon who rarely sleeps and steals my food." Ani pressed loud kisses to Arie's neck, making her tense and giggle. "But she's so cute that we love her to distraction."

"Sounds about right," Sarai replied.

Arie blinked up at me curiously, and I smiled but I didn't

reach for her. It usually took a little time for my nieces and nephews to warm up to me. I'd learned my lesson the hard way the last time I'd been home, because when I'd held Arie, she'd screamed like I'd bitten her.

As Ani walked away and handed the baby off to Bram, I kissed the top of Sarai's head. I'd never imagined that Bram of all people would settle down before I did, but I had to admit that it suited him. It smoothed down his rough edges and seemed to center him.

For the first time that I could remember, I was a little jealous of my brother. I'd always wanted a family someday. Sarai laughed at something Ani said, and I tightened my arm around her. *Someday* felt a lot closer than it had before.

* * *

"You two can stay in here," my mom said later that night, pushing open the door to the bedroom my sister, Kate, used when she was home. "The other rooms have bunk beds, and I doubt that was what you were hoping for."

"I don't know," I replied. "I haven't slept in a bunk bed for years."

Mom laughed. "I'll see you in the morning. If you hear me moving around early, I'm just up putting the turkey in the oven. Don't feel like you need to get out of bed."

She left, closing the door behind her, and I dropped our bags onto the bed, grinning at Sarai.

"I know for a fact that this bed doesn't squeak," I informed her.

Her mouth dropped open in surprise. "Why would you tell me that?"

I laughed in confusion at her expression, then stopped when she began to look angry. It took me longer than I'd like to admit to realize why she was so mad.

I kicked off my shoes and jumped on the bed, raising a hand above me to make sure that I didn't smack my head against the ceiling. Been there, done that.

"There's a reason I'm the fun uncle," I told Sarai, still jumping.

Realization dawned, and she covered her face with one hand. "Duh," she mumbled.

I laughed. "You want to jump? I advise against any gymnastics, though. My nephew Keller learned that the hard way."

"Took a fall, did he?" she asked, slowly shaking her head from side to side as she grinned.

"Smacked right into the dresser," I replied, pointing to the dresser a few feet from the foot of the bed. "No blood, though, so we still considered it a successful dismount."

"Did his mother kill you?"

"Kate loves me best," I said, but I could tell she didn't believe me. "Actually, she chased me out of the house with a mop."

I stepped off the bed with a thump and wrapped my arms around her.

"I've never slept with a woman in this house," I said, tipping my head down so I could meet her eyes. "I don't bring women to meet my parents, period."

"Just me, huh?"

"Just you," I confirmed.

"Why is that?" she asked, leaning into me.

I thought about it for a second. "Growing up, my parents had to say good-bye to a lot of children that they considered theirs for a short period of time, and I love my parents enough to not bring people around that won't stay for long."

She stood quietly for a moment. "Well, they won't have to say good-bye to me."

"You're sticking around?" I asked, a smile playing at my lips.

"You're stuck with me now," she replied cheekily.

I grabbed her around the waist and threw her over my shoulder as we laughed. I couldn't remember being this happy before.

"Marry me," I whispered as I laid her on the bed.

"You're insane," she whispered back, her eyes wide with surprise.

"Maybe," I conceded. "But can you think of one reason why you shouldn't marry me?"

Her mouth opened, then closed, then opened again. "We haven't been together long enough."

"Semantics."

"You haven't met my family."

"I'll get on a plane tomorrow."

"You—I—you."

"See," I murmured, pressing my mouth to hers. "We should get married. I love you and you love me."

I was riding the high, and I couldn't think of a single reason why I'd ever feel differently about Sarai. Nothing in my life had prepared me for her. Nothing had ever felt so right or perfect.

"I do love you," she said, running her fingertips down the side of my face. She stared at me, tracing my eyebrows, nose, and lips with her index finger. "I'll marry you," she said huskily. "Yes."

"Yes?" I asked dumbly, unsure if I'd heard her correctly.

"Yes," she said again, pinching my nose as she laughed.

"Holy shit," I said gleefully.

I kissed her hard, and I loved it when she relaxed into the bed underneath me, one hand sliding around to my back while the other cupped my cheek. I held myself back a little, not comfortable with the idea of having sex in my parents' house.

However, neither of us went to bed unsatisfied that night. And later, as I drifted off to sleep with Sarai tucked close against my chest, I ignored the kernel of fear that I was rushing us into something we weren't ready for.

* * *

I woke up on Thanksgiving morning to a thunderstorm and the sound of my mom and dad talking quietly in the kitchen as they started cooking. Sarai was still completely passed out as I shifted carefully out of bed and found some clothes to wear. I was pretty sure she'd been burning the midnight oil all week in order to have her schoolwork done before we left, and now she'd finally had the chance to crash.

I tiptoed out of the room in my socks and closed the door firmly behind me, hoping she'd get the chance to sleep in. I hated that she worked so hard, but I understood the drive. Now that we were getting married, maybe I could help her relax a little. Teach her how to slow down once in a while.

I was grinning stupidly as I made my way into the kitchen.

"I told you to sleep in," my mom chastised as soon as I'd walked into the room.

"Can't," I replied, heading toward the coffeepot. "I'm getting married."

"You're what?" my dad asked, his head jerking up to look at me. He was elbows-deep in the turkey, and the whole thing jiggled at his surprised movement.

"I asked Sarai to marry me, and she said yes," I said, grinning. "Last night."

"Last night?" my mom said, her voice faint.

I looked at the absolute shock on their faces and laughed. "What? Why are you so surprised?"

"Because you never said anything," my mom said, going back to chopping vegetables. "Didn't you just start dating? I didn't realize the two of you were so serious."

"Have I *ever* brought a woman home?" I asked, a little annoyed at their reactions. I was their last holdout, the child they said they worried would never settle down. Where were the congratulations? Where was the joy and excitement?

My dad watched me for a long moment, then looked over at my mom. Their eyes met for only a brief moment, but it was as if an entire conversation passed between them. He looked back at me as he wiped his hands with a towel, then gave a slight nod. "Congratulations, son," he said, walking across the kitchen to hug me.

"Thanks, Dad." I met my mom's eyes over his shoulder.

"I think it's great," she said, her lips trembling a little as she smiled at me. "Just great."

"Thanks, Ma," I said, letting go of my dad so I could cross the room and hug her.

"Did you get her a ring?" she asked, her arms circling my waist. "What does it look like?"

"I haven't gotten one yet."

"Alex," she scolded.

"Go get one tomorrow," my dad said as he started doing ungodly things to the turkey again. "It's Black Friday."

"Jewelry stores have Black Friday sales?" I murmured, holding back a laugh. He was completely serious.

"Everyone has Black Friday sales," my mom replied. "Do you know what you want to get her?"

"A ring," I joked. Actually, I had no idea what kind of ring she'd like. We'd never even talked about her taste in jewelry. She didn't wear very much of it. She always had gold hoops in her ears and a gold necklace around her throat with a small Star of David charm that her parents had given her. Sometimes she wore gold bracelets that clinked when they knocked against each other, but that was pretty much it unless we went out somewhere.

"Well, that narrows it down," my dad muttered.

"A gold one," I said happily.

"Shit," my dad said, laughing.

The back door opened just as my expression fell and I started to panic. My cousin Trevor walked in carrying a couple of bowls covered in tinfoil.

"The jeweler will help you," my mom assured me before turning to Trev and taking the bowls from his hands. "It's their job to help clueless men."

"Jeweler?" Trev asked, raising his eyebrows.

"I'm getting married," I announced, enjoying the dumbfounded look on his face as I went in for a hug.

"To who?" he asked, slapping my back a couple of times.

"Sarai."

"Sarai?" Recognition dawned. "You mean the girl who doesn't find you funny?"

Of course *that* would be what he remembered from a conversation we'd had right after I'd met Sarai.

"She thinks I'm hilarious," I said, shoving him away good-naturedly.

"Only on your best days," Sarai piped in, coming into the kitchen behind me.

"I *am* hilarious," I replied, spinning toward her.

Her hair was up in a messy bun, and she was wearing a pair of leggings and an oversized sweater. She looked like she was about to spend a comfortable day with family.

"I'm the funny one in this couple," she said, grinning as I leaned down to kiss her good morning.

"Humble, too," Trev teased with a grin. "Hey, I'm Trevor, Alex's cousin."

"Nice to meet you," Sarai said, stepping forward to shake his hand. "Is your family with you?"

"Nah, Morgan's at home with the baby girl."

"Are you going back to get them?" my mom asked, checking under the tinfoil on the bowls to see what was inside.

"Yeah." Trev nodded. "We figured we'd let Etta sleep for as long as possible before we came over—cut down on any tantrums later, hopefully."

"Good idea," my dad said. "Why did we let Alex wake up?"

"Ha ha," I muttered. "You're all very funny."

"See? Should have let him sleep longer."

"I woke up on my own—" My mouth snapped shut as I realized that I was playing into my dad's joke.

The group laughed.

"We'll be back in about an hour, Auntie," Trev said, kissing the top of my mom's head as she went back to work on the food. "Let me know if you need me to make a last-minute run to the store for anything."

"If I need something, I'll send Alex," my mom replied, grinning. "Distraction is a good remedy for tantrums."

"You're not amusing," I said to my mom as Trev left.

"Aw," Sarai said, wrapping her arms around my waist. "Does someone need a nap?"

"Are you napping with me?" I asked, winking at her.

"Ew, quit it," she said, shoving me away.

"Why?" I asked, winking again. "What's wrong?"

"Stop doing that."

"Mom," I said, turning my head toward my parents. "Sarai thinks it's creepy when I wink."

"She what?" Mom asked in confusion.

"Not just you," Sarai clarified. "It's creepy when *anyone* winks."

"You're the only person who thinks that," I said, winking again.

"I can't take you seriously when you do that," she said with a small laugh. She moved past me, farther into the kitchen. "Do you two need any help?"

"If you could get Alex out of the way, that would be great," my dad answered. Then he winked. I wasn't sure if I'd ever laughed harder in my life.

* * *

"It's gorgeous," Sarai said later as I led her through the trees behind my parents' house. "But it's really cold and wet out here."

"Just a little further," I promised.

We were nearly at my favorite place on the property. An old fort that Kate, Bram, and I had built one summer when we'd been too old to hang out inside bothering our mom and too young to go anywhere on our own.

My brother and sister remembered the old place fondly, but they didn't seem to have the same connection to it that I did. To them, it was just a worn-down fort where we'd built fake fires and pretended that the world was at war as we hid from foreign invaders. To me, it was the place where I'd finally settled into my life with the Evans family. I'd spent hours in that tiny pocket of the property, constructing spears out of rocks and tree branches, using ferns to patch up Kate's knees when she scraped them, and building a place where my brother could feel safe. We'd never brought other kids here. It had been an unspoken rule that the three of us had followed.

Sarai and I stepped between two trees that had begun to grow together far above our heads, and through some exceptionally wet ferns that soaked us to our knees, and then we were there.

There wasn't much left of the fort. Some rotting boards were crudely nailed to a tree in a bad attempt at a ladder. There was an old metal lawn chair tipped on its side with the blue plastic seat mostly disintegrated. A few odds and ends that we'd pilfered from the house were scattered around.

"Neverland," Sarai murmured, walking into the middle of our camp. She turned in a slow circle, taking it all in.

"What?" I picked up an old spoon that was half covered in dirt and absentmindedly set it on one of the ladder boards.

"I can imagine you here," she said with a little laugh. "A little lost boy, with your fur cape and a stick taller than you in your hand."

"More like a pair of ripped jeans and an undershirt that my mom accidentally dyed pink in the wash," I replied, grinning. "My parents were real serious about wearing play clothes outside."

"I love it," she said, smiling. "This place is awesome."

"One time," I said, leaning against a tree while Sarai investigated all the little bits and pieces that we'd left behind, "Bram was in this horrible mood—he was like that, sometimes—and me and Kate dragged him out here. We made him sit in the middle of the fort in a chair, and we acted like he was a prisoner of war."

"This story is taking a dark turn," she murmured.

"So he's sitting there with a scowl on his face." I stared blankly at the branches in front of me, thinking about those days when Bram barely smiled. I shook my head to clear the memory. "Anyway, we sat him down and took turns being funny. You know, I'd make funny faces. Kate would dance really dramatically. But nothing would make him smile, not a single damn thing we did. And then Kate starts singing. I don't remember what song it was, but Bram just starts cracking up, you know? Really belly laughing. And we're both staring at him, because Kate was singing in this really sweet voice, beyond trying to make him smile at this point, just trying to make him feel better."

Sarai stopped what she was doing and looked right at me, her eyes soft.

"He wouldn't tell us what was so funny. He never said."

"You never figured it out?" she asked quietly.

"Oh, I figured it out. A couple years later, I heard the song on the radio, and it was absolutely filthy."

"No," Sarai said with a small surprised laugh.

"Oh, yeah. Kate and I had no clue she was singing a song about sex, and she'd slowed down the tempo to make it all soothing." I tried to speak through my guffaws, but tears of laughter filled my eyes. "But Bram knew immediately what she was singing about, and found it hilarious that Kate and I were so serious about it."

Sarai's laugh came from deep in her belly, and she bent over slightly, holding her stomach.

"And then," I gasped through my laughter. "He wouldn't ever tell us what was so funny, so Kate just kept singing it all soft and sweet, and Bram kept laughing, and I just stood there like an idiot, motioning for her to keep going because my brother was actually laughing and I didn't even care why."

"That's hilarious," Sarai said as our chuckles finally subsided.

"That was us." I shrugged my shoulders. "Bram was sullen, Kate was tenderhearted and sweet, and I was the clown."

Sarai moved forward and wrapped her arms around my waist. Tilting her head back, she pursed her lips for a kiss. It was an invitation I'd never refuse.

Her lips were soft and pliant, but her arms around me were firm. The feeling was *solid*. Like the kiss was sort of fleeting, just a moment in time, but the embrace was lasting. Permanent.

"I can't wait to marry you," I said quietly, there in my favorite place in the world. "I know my proposal kind of sucked, and I'll do it right when I have a ring." I brushed little pieces of hair away from her cheeks. "But I want to marry you. I want to live together and pay the same bills and wake up with you in the morning, and get you takeout when I know you barely have time to stop and eat. I want to make sure you're getting enough rest and let you patch me up when I do stupid shit like try to slide during softball practice. I want to come home to you after a shitty day and know that everything will be better as soon as I walk into our house."

Sarai was smiling gently at me, but her eyes were watery like she was fighting back tears.

"And at some point," I said, my voice starting to wobble. "I want to have babies with you. Little tan babies with dark-brown eyes and your smile. My eyelashes, because we both know mine are better."

Sarai laughed. "They are," she choked out.

"I want to get old and fat with you," I said plainly. "Because I want to be in a place with you that none of the outward stuff matters. You'll spend entire weekends with no makeup on your face, and I'll get a little bit of a gut because I know that you'll still ride me like there's no tomorrow even if you can't see my washboard abs."

"I'd do that now," Sarai said. "We don't have to be married for you to let yourself go."

I smiled at her joke. "I want to know the minute you change your shampoo just by the smell of your hair, and I want to see your feet swell up because you've been on them all day."

"That doesn't sound very fun," she whispered.

"In forty years, I want to be looking at you the way Mr. K still looks at Mrs. K."

A tear rolled down Sarai's cheek, and I brushed it away with my fingertip.

"I don't need another proposal," Sarai said, her voice hoarse. "This one was pretty good."

"I didn't even get down on one knee," I argued.

"We'll pretend you did."

I let out a mock sigh of relief. "Thank God, because my knee is throbbing from our hike out here."

My knee hadn't been bothering me much lately, but I still wore the brace. Sometimes, when I twisted just so, the thing still gave me trouble. I couldn't wait for it to start feeling normal again.

"Then you'd better sit," Sarai said seriously.

I let her pull me to the ground and sat back against the tree. She straddled my lap, making me groan as my hands went to her ass. This was exactly what I'd been hoping for when we'd left the house. Just me and Sarai in the middle of the forest.

I pressed my thumbs against the creases where her thighs and hips met, pulling her harder against me, and her mouth went to my throat, her teeth gently biting the skin there. She knew exactly what I liked, exactly what drove me crazy. It had been like that since our very first time. We moved together perfectly, seemed to instinctively know what the other person needed.

I have no idea how, because my mouth was too busy nibbling at any skin I could reach above Sarai's jacket, but we got her leggings pulled down just enough. I could feel the sweet wet skin between her thighs against the back of my hand as I unbuttoned my jeans and shoved them down.

She was tight and slick around my cock just seconds later, and I let out a sigh of relief at the contact. Our positioning was awkward with our clothes in the way, but we made it work. Her hips ground down as mine shoved up, our bodies barely moving so the contact wasn't accidentally lost.

"I love you," I said against her mouth. "Jesus."

Her lips curved as her eyes drifted shut. She murmured something I didn't understand, but it wasn't the time for explanations, so I didn't ask. In some part of my mind I knew, even though I couldn't imagine being unhappy with her, that there would be a time down the road, in some distant future, when I would think back to this moment and realize how lucky I was that she'd chosen me. That she'd agreed to spend her life with me. That my woman, who always wore makeup and looked ready to take on the world, got down in the dirt and loved me in the middle of the forest.

I came first. I held out as long as I could but eventually gave in to the inevitable. Sarai didn't complain, but I felt the way her body tensed when she realized that I'd finished.

"It's okay," I whispered into her ear, more to myself than her. "Shh."

I reached down between us and slid my fingers to her clit, willing my body not to go soft yet. She was nearly there. Her fingernails scratched at the shoulder of my jacket as I pressed, and her breath stopped as I rubbed gently, then harder.

When she came, it was with an exhalation against my throat and tremors shaking her thighs. Then the sky opened up, and the drizzle that had mostly been contained by the branches above us turned into a deluge that poured down on our heads.

"Cold!" Sarai squealed, pulling up her hood. "Oh, shit, it's running down my back."

I'd lifted her to her feet and pulled her leggings to her waist before she could say anything else. I was mostly dry because she'd shielded me from the rain, but as soon as she was up, the cold air and rain hit my lap like a cup of ice water.

"Fuck," I yelped, hurriedly pulling my jeans up. I scrambled to my feet and laughed as Sarai tried to find a place to hide from the rain. "It's no use," I told her, grabbing her hand. "Let's just go back to the house."

I took one last look around the fort, memorizing the old memories and the new ones, then led her back toward home.

CHAPTER 10

SARAI

Was I being an idiot? As we trudged back through the wet forest, our shoes sticking in the mud and our coats completely waterlogged, I wondered where the hell my new impetuousness had come from. I was a planner. I made lists. It was the only way that I could function without anxiety taking over my life.

So why had I agreed, without thought and with embarrassingly little hesitation, to marry Alex?

I knew how I'd explain it to my aunt and uncle. I loved him. He was sweet and intelligent. He made everything fun. He made me laugh. He made me feel good about myself. He made me feel like I could conquer the world. When he looked at me, I felt it all the way to my bones.

But those weren't practical reasons, and I was practical.

So why had I agreed?

My stomach twisted with worry.

Then Alex turned his head toward me and gave me a blinding smile. "Want me to give you a piggyback ride?"

"No way," I replied, my anxiety fading as I squeezed his hand. "I'm worried you won't be able to make it back to the house on that sore knee."

"Oh, is that right?" he teased. He let go of my hand and took off at a jog. "The knee's fine."

I raced to catch up, but the minute I reached his side, he sped up.

"Are we racing now?" I asked, jokingly shoving at him.

"You can't catch me," he sang, putting on a burst of speed.

We ran back to the house, laughing as we slipped and slid on the wet ground. I'd worn a pair of cute rain boots that I'd assumed would work perfectly in the Oregon weather, but on our way to Alex's childhood hangout, I'd realized they were woefully unsuited to the mud. The rubber bottoms came only about an inch above my foot; the rest of the boot was suede. Whoever marketed suede boots as rain boots surely hadn't ever actually worn them in the rain.

We reached the back porch out of breath and soaked through to the skin.

"Let's strip here," Alex said, pulling off his jacket.

"Excuse me?" I asked, not sure that I'd heard him correctly. There was no way in the world that I was going to strip outside his parents' house.

"Just the outside layers," he replied, helping me unzip my coat as my teeth started to chatter.

We quickly took off our boots and went in the back door, which led to the kitchen. We were greeted with the smell of dinner cooking in the oven and the sound of a large group having five different conversations and speaking over one another. We'd been gone so long that Alex's family had all arrived for dinner, and I was standing there with soaking-wet hair, looking like a drowned rat.

"Why in the world did you keep her out in the rain so long?" Liz scolded, her hands occupied with a pie. She pressed down the edges with her fingertips, not even bothering to watch what she was doing as she eyed our wet hair and clothes.

"I know why," Bram muttered. Ani smacked his shoulder, then paused and kissed the place she'd swatted.

"I took her out to the old fort," Alex said, sneaking a piece of sausage off one of the hors d'oeuvre platters.

"Oh, the one I was never allowed to go to?" his cousin Trevor asked. His arm was around a pretty blond woman whom I hadn't met yet, and I assumed it was his girlfriend, Morgan.

"Evans kids only," Bram and Alex said at the same time. Bram lifted his beer and saluted Alex with it.

"Then how come she gets to go?" whined Ani jokingly.

"Because they're getting married," Trevor joked back with a roll of his eyes.

There was a beat of silence.

"No fucking way," Ani yelled, her eyes wide.

"Oh, shit," Trevor mumbled. "Sorry, man."

"I was going to tell you," Alex said to Bram, grunting as Ani practically leaped across the room and slammed her body into his hard enough to make him step back. Her arms wrapped around his chest as she jumped up and down, jostling them both. "I was just waiting for you to get here so I could tell ya in person."

Bram nodded easily, but there was something in his eyes that worried me. Something that passed between them that made me uneasy.

"I didn't expect this," Ani said, letting go of Alex so she could move toward me. "But I actually like you, so I'm not going to ask all the *is this too soon?* questions." Her arms wrapped around me, and I had no choice but to hug her back.

"Alex," Dan called, turning our attention to the table where Alex's dad was sitting with his aunt and uncle. "Your girl's freezing, son. Maybe get her in a hot shower before all the introductions and announcements?"

"Shit. Sorry, sweets," Alex said, wrapping an arm around my shoulder.

As he led me out of the kitchen, everyone started laughing. I was too embarrassed to turn around, because I just knew that they were laughing at us. But then Liz's dry voice called over the chuckles, and I felt my lips twitch.

"Son, if you leave those jeans in the laundry room, I'll try and get that dirt stain off the ass of them."

"Aw, shit," Alex whispered, pushing me even faster down the hallway.

I laughed.

* * *

Later, after introductions had been made and congratulations had been handed out, we sat down to a table brimming with food. Turkey, stuffing, potatoes and gravy, multiple different types of fruit salads and cranberry sauces, some orange thing with marshmallows that looked like vomit but Alex seemed to love—there was so much food that I wasn't sure how we would even put a dent in it.

"Nothing is made with pork," Alex said quietly into my ear. "I'm not sure about all the rules, but I told my mom no pork."

I met his eyes and leaned in for a kiss. "Thank you."

"If there's anything else that you can't eat, just pass it along," he said, giving me a small smile.

"I wish Katie was here," Liz said as we passed dishes around and filled our plates.

"She said that they were going to do a big dinner with the neighbors this year," Ani replied. "So thankfully, she's not homesick."

"She's still homesick," Trevor said. "But I'm glad that she's occupied today."

"My sister hates missing family holidays," Alex explained. "But Shane's stationed in Southern California, and they have a million kids, so they can't make it to all of them."

"Too expensive," Liz said.

"Too much hassle," Bram said.

"Too many kids," Ani joked.

"No such thing," Alex's aunt Ellie scolded, smiling at her granddaughter, who'd been seated next to her in a high chair.

When I'd met Trevor's girlfriend, Morgan, before we'd sat down, I'd instantly liked her. She was quiet, and she seemed like a deer in the headlights when surrounded by this noisy family, but she was holding her own.

"Do you have a big family?" Liz asked, smiling at me.

I swallowed the food I'd been chewing and shook my head.

"Just my aunt and uncle in our immediate family," I replied. "But tons of extended family."

"Alex told me you lost your parents," she said sympathetically. "I'm so sorry."

"Thanks," I replied softly. "I'm lucky to have my aunt and uncle still."

"They're lucky to have you, too," Liz said sweetly. She must have noticed how emotional her words had made me, because she smoothly steered the conversation back around. "We don't have much extended family anymore, but our immediate family is growing practically by the hour."

"Literally, if Alex's muddy jeans are anything to go by," Bram said, quietly but not quietly enough.

I couldn't read his tone, and my throat tightened in embarrassment as I stared down at my plate. It was hard to know if Bram was teasing or not.

"Ani, you need to put out more," Alex replied conversationally as his hand found my knee beneath the table. "My brother's clearly frustrated."

"I will literally claw your face off," Ani ground out. "Don't bring me into this."

"Enough," Dan said, his voice calm. "I know good goddamn well that you didn't *mean* to embarrass anyone at this table, Abraham, but maybe you'd like to apologize anyway?" It was posed as a question, but it was absolutely an order.

"That came out wrong," Bram said instantly. "Just giving you shit, Alexander."

"Not the time or the place," Alex murmured back.

"Noted. Sorry."

The table went silent for only a second before Morgan spoke up.

"You're from New York, right?"

I raised my head and locked eyes with the only other person at the table who felt what I did. She was the only other outsider. These people were kind and welcoming, but the two of us were still finding our places in a very tight-knit family. It was like being the new kid at school, wondering where you'd fit in when everyone else already had their groups of friends.

"I was actually born in Missouri," I said, giving her a grateful look. "My parents moved there from New York before I was born."

"That must have been a culture shock," Alex's uncle Mike commented.

"Yeah, I think it was," I replied. "Moving from Missouri to New York when I was a teenager was a big adjustment."

"I bet," he said, nodding.

"It must be hard living so far from your family," Trevor said. His voice was so kind that I almost cried then and there. Alex had described Trevor as the best of their group, the kindest, the most selfless, the sounding board, and I suddenly knew exactly what he'd meant. Trevor was just…good. I couldn't explain it any better than that.

"It is hard," I said, clearing my throat. "But I like it in Missouri, and we visit each other when we can."

The subject turned to other topics, and I listened quietly, commenting here and there but never really joining any of the conversations happening around the table. Trevor was right; it was hard being away from my family. But I had to admit that it also made my life easier in some ways. I glanced over at Alex, who was laughing at something his uncle had said. I was thankful that we'd been able to get to know each other and fall in love without any family interference. While I loved his family and they'd been great, I was grateful that when we'd met and started dating, we'd sort of been in our own little bubble.

I was having fun in Oregon, and I loved meeting all the important people in Alex's life, but I wasn't ready for our bubble to include others. Even the thought of telling my aunt and uncle that we were getting married made my stomach tighten into knots. We'd be congratulated and celebrated, sure, but after that it would be a constant barrage of questions and planning for a big wedding that my aunt expected and I dreaded.

The longer dinner went on, with people laughing and joking and food being consumed in mass quantities, the more I relaxed into my chair.

This family reminded me of home. The camaraderie and inside jokes and love that were apparent in every word spoken, even when they argued. It was like sitting down at my aunt's table in New York. I let the feeling wash over me.

"You have to go with us," Ani said, pointing at me as the men got up to clear the table and bring out dessert.

"Where are we going?" I asked. I hadn't been paying attention to whatever she and Ellie were discussing.

"Black Friday," Liz said, setting down a stack of newspapers filled with advertisements. She passed them around the table. "We leave at three in the morning and hit all the best stores."

"You can look up the sales online," Ani said, digging into her paper. "But it's our tradition to look through the ads in the Thanksgiving paper."

"Be sure to set aside the comics for me," Ellie said, glancing up from her ads. "Christmas is coming up."

"She uses them as wrapping paper," Liz explained.

"I don't just shop for the holidays," Ani said, waving at us to get started looking through our own ads. "I get Arie stocked up on clothes, too, and get stuff for the house."

"We're not going to the home stores this year," Liz said. "You took hours last time."

"I needed good blinds." Ani rolled her eyes.

"And now you've got them," Ellie replied. "I'm not going in a single hardware store this year."

"You can wait in the car?" Ani said hopefully.

"Dream on," Liz murmured. "Oh, the sweaters at Macy's are fifty percent off."

I opened up my stack of newspaper ads and started browsing, but I wasn't really looking for anything. We still had to fly home on Sunday, and there was no way I was going to ship a bunch of stuff home—it would completely cancel out any deals I found while we were shopping. There were mumbled thanks handed out as the men brought coffee and pie to each of the women, but no one looked up from their papers.

"We're dragging Morgan and Sarai with us tomorrow," Ani announced. "Just so you know. Trev, you're on Etta duty."

"Sounds good," Trevor said, kissing the top of Morgan's bent head. "Get some new towels for the bathrooms, yeah? Ours are too scratchy for the baby girl."

"Our towels are fine," Morgan replied, sending him a soft smile.

"Get new ones anyway."

"Get the towels," Ani ordered. "Don't ever argue when they tell you to buy something."

"I'll remember that," Morgan said with a laugh.

"They've welcomed you into the coven," Alex teased softly in my ear as he set a piece of pie and a hot cup of coffee to the side of my newspaper. "You gonna go in the morning?"

"Do I have a choice?" I joked.

"We'll lock the bedroom door. When you don't open it, they'll leave without you so they don't waste time and miss any sales," he whispered conspiratorially.

He walked away, and I focused on my paper again. Well, maybe I'd just get a few things…

"We're going out to smoke cigars," Dan announced proudly.

"Cigars?" Liz's nose wrinkled in distaste.

"Got a few from a client," he replied, grinning. "No better way to end a meal."

"Don't come back in this house smelling like smoke, Daniel," Liz said, raising one eyebrow.

"Aw, baby," he said, still grinning. "You know I won't."

"You better not."

I glanced across the table to where Alex was standing with his brother, and our eyes met in amusement.

I felt the heat in my belly first, then in my chest, and up my neck, until I felt my face warm. This was why I'd agreed to marry him. I wanted to spend the rest of my life feeling this indescribable, inexplicable feeling when our eyes met across a crowded room. Actually, I couldn't imagine anything else.

No one ever imagines the absence of that feeling. If they did, they'd avoid it altogether.

* * *

"It can't be time to go already," I mumbled against Alex's shoulder, trying to ignore the alarm I'd set for two thirty. It was pitch black and raining outside. I groaned as I threw myself to the side and slapped at my phone. We'd been up until midnight, visiting with Alex's family and playing dice around the kitchen table. Even the two little girls had stayed up late, finally falling asleep in family members' laps. I felt like I hadn't slept at all.

"They'll be here in thirty, babe," Alex replied, his voice hoarse from sleep and full of amusement.

"I know." I slid my feet to the floor and stood up before I could convince myself to sleep for just a few more minutes.

I grabbed my toiletry bag and headed to the bathroom across the hall as quietly as I could. The house wasn't very big, and I'd noticed that sound traveled through the house like a big tunnel. That had probably helped when Liz and Dan had children living with them, but it made things a little hard when you were trying to move around without waking anyone up.

It took me only about fifteen minutes to do my makeup and hair, and by the time I'd finished, I was wide awake. I was actually kind of excited to go shopping. I liked other women. I liked spending time with them and talking about clothes and shopping for deals and making big dinners. Once, when I was young, and I came home from school angry at another girl for some reason that I couldn't even remember now, I'd said something nasty about her to my mother, and instead of giving me the affirmation I'd wanted, she'd looked at me in disappointment. *No*, she'd said softly. *Do not do that. Women are the only people on this earth who will ever fully understand your joys and pains, your disappointments and triumphs. No man can ever understand a woman's heart; only other women can do that. When you try to diminish a woman's worth to make yourself feel worthy, you're not only hurting her, you're hurting yourself. Do you understand?* I hadn't understood her words then; they'd just been another thing for me to be angry about. Later, though, as I'd grown and dealt with my own heartbreaks, her meaning had become clear.

"I made coffee," Liz said softly, smiling at me as I came out of the bathroom. "I didn't want to startle you, so I didn't knock."

"Thanks," I said in relief. "I'm exhausted."

"We all are," she snickered. "But the excitement of the deals will perk you right up, just wait."

She tiptoed quietly down the hall as I let myself back inside the bedroom.

"All ready to shop until you drop?" Alex asked from the bed as I pulled clothes out of my suitcase.

"Mostly." I glanced over my shoulder at him. He looked so comfortable in the bed, I almost crawled back in with him. "Your mom made coffee."

"She's a good egg," he replied.

"That idiom makes no sense," I muttered, looking back in my bag.

"Did you just call me an idiot?" he joked, his tone assuring me that he'd heard exactly what I'd said.

"If the shoe fits," I said, using an idiom of my own.

I looked over my shoulder again, and he was grinning.

"How long do they usually shop for?" I asked as I stood up and started getting undressed. I was glad that he didn't reach for me as I set my clean clothes at the foot of the bed. I wasn't sure I could resist letting him pull me down beside him, and I knew if I lay down, I wasn't getting back up until a reasonable hour.

"They're usually done by two or three," he said.

I looked at him in confusion for a second, then felt my mouth drop open. "Twelve hours?"

"Have you never gone shopping on Black Friday before?" he asked.

"I'm sure my mother went at some point, but I was too young to go with her," I said, pulling on my underwear and a bra. "But my aunt never went, and I haven't, either, since I've been on my own."

"Don't like shopping?" he asked.

"Don't have the money," I replied with a chuckle. "Sometimes I do the Cyber Monday sales, though. Shopping online is easier."

"But according to Ani, it's not as much fun."

"I don't know about that," I said as I pulled a pair of jeans over my hips.

"I'm pretty sure she just likes elbowing her way through crowds and stealing things out of other women's carts," he mused.

"No she doesn't," I argued, horrified.

"Not the cart part, but probably the elbowing part," he conceded.

"She's so nice," I said, pulling on my shoes.

Alex laughed, went silent, and then laughed again. "She must've been high yesterday," he joked. "Ani's not nice."

"She was nice to me."

"Probably high."

"She wasn't high."

"Fine," he said, leaning up quickly to grab my hand and pull me onto the bed with him. "She wasn't high."

I made a face, and he kissed my nose. "She's happy for me," he said. "But she's not really the hearts and rainbows type— that's Kate. Ani is more…leather jackets and sarcasm."

"That doesn't mean she's mean." I was still stuck on his description of her.

"Sarai," he said softly, rubbing his lips over mine. "She's my best friend. I'm not talking bad about her. She's full of inappropriate comments and would take someone's head off for cutting in front of her in line, but she'd also defend any of us to the death. That's just Ani." He shrugged.

A knock sounded at the bedroom door before I could reply.

"Sarai? If you're not ready, I'm telling the whole family that you forced us to go to a sex shop today and made us wait for hours while you searched for Alex's gift," Ani called, then knocked again. "Up and at 'em."

"See?" Alex whispered, his body shaking with laughter.

I gave him a quick kiss on the lips and climbed out of bed. Smoothing my hair, I grabbed my purse and opened the door. "I'll see you in twelve hours."

"Love you," he called, amused.

"Love you, too."

When I got to the kitchen, all the women were there. Liz and Ellie looked like their normal selves, neatly dressed but comfortable. Morgan was slightly rumpled and looked like I felt, and Ani appeared as if she hadn't slept, and had a slightly deranged look in her eyes.

"No coffee for you," Liz said firmly to Ani as she handed out travel cups.

"Don't need it," Ani replied, clapping her hands and shrugging her shoulders. "I've got Red Bull running through my veins."

"Did you sleep?" I asked, eyeing her wild mess of wispy short hair.

"Nope." She grinned wildly. "Arie woke up in the car and was still wide awake and playing in the living room when I left."

"Damn," Morgan murmured, looking at me in horror.

"Ani'll crash on the way home," Ellie said with a laugh as she ushered us toward the front door. "Bram will end up carrying her and her bags inside when we drop her off."

"Not this year," Ani said, pointing into the air. "This year, I'll make it home and unpack before crashing."

"No she won't," Liz said, bringing up the rear of our group as we stepped onto the front porch.

My hands were clenched as we drove into town in Ellie's large SUV. The women around me talked about the stores they wanted to hit and the early-bird deals they hoped to find, but I couldn't focus on any of that. The rain pounding on the windshield, and the bright lights that passed us on the highway held all my attention. Ellie was a good driver, but I knew that didn't mean much. My dad had been a good driver, too, and that hadn't stopped someone from hitting us. I didn't relax until we pulled into the first parking lot and slowed down to a crawl as we found a parking space.

"Get excited," Ani said as we crawled out of the SUV. She did a little dance and rubbed her palms together. "It's time to shop for things we'd never buy at full price."

"If you bring home another novelty waffle iron, Bram is going to kick you out," Liz joked.

"It's my house," Ani replied, throwing her arms out. "I'll buy as many waffle irons as I want!"

"She wasn't lying about the Red Bull in her veins," Morgan murmured, making me giggle.

I was unprepared for the madness that was Black Friday shopping. There were so many people. They pushed and shoved, practically raced down the aisles, pushed not one but *two* carts through the store. It was complete chaos.

"Okay, I'm headed to electronics and then home goods," Liz said. "Where are you all headed? Does everyone have their phones?"

"I'll go with you," Ellie said. "There were only a couple things I wanted to look at here, and they're in electronics and toys."

"Toys, clothes, home," Ani said, rubbing her hands together. "Bram can get his own electronics."

"Electronic deals are better on Cyber Monday anyway," Morgan said quietly.

"Oh, yeah?" Ani asked. "I'll check that out. Where are you guys headed?"

"Socks, shoes, and clothes," Morgan said. "Oh, and home. I need those towels."

"Nice," Ani replied. She looked at me expectantly.

"Oh, uh." I looked around helplessly. "I'll just browse."

The entire group laughed.

"Stick with me, kid," Ani said, grabbing a shopping cart.

Everyone grabbed a cart, and we headed into the throng of shoppers.

"Come on, Morgan," Ani called, waving her hand above her head. "I want to look at the socks, too, so we'll just go with you for a while."

We followed Morgan to the left as Ellie and Liz broke off and headed right.

"If you find something, you can just throw it in my cart," Ani told me as we pressed through the crowd.

"Thanks, but I'm not sure I'll find anything."

"Not your speed, huh?" Ani asked, pushing her cart around a little girl who was holding on to the back of her mom's T-shirt while the mom searched through a rack of clothes.

"Yes, this is totally my speed. Who doesn't love a good deal? But we're flying home on Sunday, and my bag was pretty full already," I said as she watched the mother struggle to calm her child. "Who would bring a kid to this craziness in the middle of the night?"

"Single moms, maybe," Ani said with a shrug. "And sometimes you just can't find a sitter, ya know? I'm just glad I've got Bram to hold down the fort."

Morgan had stopped, and she was searching through a box full of socks as we reached her.

"I took Etta shopping with me last year," she said, glancing over her shoulder to look at us. "I took her everywhere, and she was young enough that I could get her presents and she had no idea."

"I didn't mean—" I stuttered. I hoped I hadn't hurt Morgan's feelings, because that wasn't my intention at all.

"I know you didn't," she said, cutting me off with a wave of her hand. Morgan laughed. "I got some dirty looks, but most people were nice about it. It doesn't bother me—I'll take Etta into any store I want."

"And they can suck it," Ani piped in.

"Exactly," Morgan said with a smile. "But it *is* nice to leave her home this year. Especially since we came in the middle of the fucking night."

"Early bird gets the worm," Ani said. She was kind of fidgeting as she looked around where we were standing, her head nodding to the music coming over the store's sound system.

"I need whatever you had," I said, laughing as her hips did a little twist. "It'll help me stay up late to study."

"Just energy drinks," Ani said, smiling. "I'm excited. I love this. I'm not crazy about the amount of people in here, but if you look hard enough, you can find some killer deals, and I'm all about saving money."

"Amen," Morgan replied, still searching through the socks.

"So, how did you and Alex meet?" Ani asked me as she scooted in next to Morgan and started rifling through another box of socks.

Why was she asking something that she already knew the answer to? I watched her for a few seconds, then my lips tilted a little. "I ran into him with my car," I said easily.

Morgan jolted, but Ani didn't show any response at all.

"Once I got him to the hospital and knew he wasn't in any serious danger, that was it," I said happily. "We were in love."

"You're so full of shit," Ani said, looking at me over her shoulder.

"You're Alex's best friend. You already knew how we met," I replied.

"I was working up to the hard questions," she said, shaking some socks at me. "You're welcome."

I got tired of standing behind them, so I found a spot on the other side of the boxes and dug in. "What are we looking for?" I asked.

"These," Morgan said, holding up a package of little girls' socks. "But I need the next two sizes. Etta's feet are growing really fast."

"I'll take the ones in your hand," Ani said, grabbing the socks from Morgan and throwing the package into her cart. "Arie's in that size."

"So, ask me the hard questions," I said, searching for the socks.

"Okay. What do you love about Alex? Have you ever been married before? Engaged? What do your finances look like? Health insurance? Is your family wealthy or poor? Has Alex met your family? How did that go? He's not Jewish and you are—is that going to be a problem for you? How will you raise your children? We're not really churchgoers, but we believe in sweet little baby Jesus. Do you even want kids? How many? Have you talked to Alex about it? Because it's kind of important to get that stuff figured out. You know that Alex isn't going to be in the Army forever, right? I mean, it's great for now, but eventually, he'll want to move home and help his brother and Trev with the family business. Are you cool with that? How do you feel about living closer to family? We're kind of all up in each other's shit, but we also are a huge help when you need it, flip sides to the same coin."

I stared at her in shock, my mouth hanging open.

"You wanted the hard questions," Morgan said with a chuckle.

I took a deep breath. "I've never been married or engaged. I have health insurance through the company I work for; it sucks, but I have it. My finances are shit, but I'm not in a crazy amount of debt. My family isn't wealthy or poor— they're somewhere in between. I'm not sure why that matters—I pay my own bills and have since I moved out. I was raised Jewish, but I'm no longer practicing, so it doesn't matter what Alex believes in." I paused for a moment, then clarified. "Actually, even if I was practicing, I don't think I'd care."

I stopped there, mostly because I couldn't remember exactly everything she'd asked, but also because she was asking a lot of questions about things I hadn't even discussed with Alex yet.

Ani gave me a small smile. "You'll do," she said.

"Found them!" Morgan announced triumphantly, holding up a couple of packages of socks.

"Sweet," Ani replied, turning toward her cart. "Because the woman on the other side of me has been up my ass for the last five minutes instead of waiting her damn turn."

My cheeks heated in embarrassment as the woman gasped,

and I moved away quickly, following Ani and Morgan as they walked toward the shoe department. When I caught up to them, Morgan was laughing, but Ani was scowling.

"Did you see that?" she asked. "I could literally feel her breath on my neck as she tried to look over my shoulder."

"Why didn't you just move?" I asked, eyeing the rain boots on sale. Those wouldn't stain; you could just spray them off with a hose.

"Because," Ani said, bumping me with her hip. "I had to see if you were going to answer any of my questions or chicken out and change the subject."

"I never chicken out," I replied, reaching for a pair of purple boots in my size.

"You'll fit in just fine," Ani said, chuckling. "Now hand me that blue pair."

CHAPTER 11

ALEX

Honey, I'm home," I called as I pushed through my brother's front door. He'd moved in with Ani when they got together, and since Ani loved sprucing up the old house, it was always a work in progress. As I looked around the space, I noticed that the baseboards along the wall were missing. She must've decided to replace them with something she liked more, but she hadn't finished the job yet.

"Hey," Bram said, coming around the corner, carrying Arie. "Watch where you step. We've been tearing out the baseboards, and Ani isn't real good at keeping track of the nails."

"That seems safe when you've got a baby crawling around," I replied drily.

"We've got a gate set up," he said, walking toward the living room. "She can't get out of here."

I followed him around the short wall and stepped over the

gate, blinking as what little sunlight we had poured through the large windows at the front of their house.

"How's it going?" I asked, dropping onto the couch as Bram sat Arie on the floor with some toys.

"I should be asking you that," he said as he lay down on his side and propped himself on one elbow by his daughter. "So you're getting married, huh?"

"That's right." I grinned. Someday, we'd have a house like this, and I'd be the one lying on the floor while my kid ignored me in favor of a multicolored lion with no legs.

"You sure about it?" he asked.

I jolted. "Of course I'm sure," I replied, scoffing. "I wouldn't have asked if I wasn't sure."

"Don't be that guy," Bram said, his voice low.

"Don't be *what* guy?" Okay, I was surprised by his last question, but now I was getting kind of pissed at his insinuation.

"The guy who gets married on a whim and gets divorced just as fast," Bram said.

"What makes you think I would be?" I sat forward on the couch. "Just because I didn't have kids with her first—"

"Watch yourself," he warned, glancing at Arie. He and Ani had been together before Arie had come along, but when Ani had decided to adopt her without Bram's agreement, it had caused some major problems. Of course, once Bram met his daughter, all his doubts flew out the window. Since then, you had to pry him away from the two of them.

"I want to marry Sarai," I said, staring at my brother. "I love her, and I want to marry her."

"Where are you gonna live?" Bram asked, unswayed by

my declaration. "You two planning on kids? How many?"

"We'll figure it out," I replied. We hadn't discussed any of that yet. My apartment was nicer, but Sarai's was bigger. I wasn't sure which she would choose, but it was a nonissue for me. I didn't care where we lived. I'd already mentioned kids and she hadn't argued, so that discussion could come later, way later.

"Man, you have to know that shit," Bram scolded.

"Like you and Ani knew any of that when you got together?" I said snidely.

"Ani and I weren't engaged," he said, looking at me as if I were an idiot. "And do you really want to go through what I went through?"

"Out of everyone in our family, I figured you'd be the hardest sell, but I didn't think you'd bust my balls," I said in disgust.

"I'm not busting your balls, jackass," Bram shot back. "I'm asking you if you've thought this through."

"I've thought it through, all right?" I said. "I know what I'm doing."

Bram stared at me for a long moment, then nodded. Jesus, he looked like our dad when he did shit like that.

"All right," he said. "I'll drop it."

"Thank you."

We were quiet while we watched Arie play with her toys, babbling at them and then throwing them to the side to grab a new one. Damn, she was cute. Every time I saw her, she was so much bigger than the last time. It was hard living so far away, especially now that everyone had kids running around and growing up without me.

"Ani didn't sleep last night," Bram said finally, laughing a little. "I bet she's hell on wheels today."

"Why didn't she sleep?" I asked, leaning back into the couch again.

"Arie woke up as soon as we got home, and didn't fall back asleep," Bram replied. "Ani's gonna be pissed when she finds out that the little monster fell asleep right after she left."

"And that you got some rest and she didn't," I said.

"Yeah." He nodded. "But she'll nap when they get home, and I'll have to wake her up for dinner."

"Better you than me," I said.

"I don't know," Bram said. "She's getting used to surviving on little sleep. Once Arie starts sleeping through the night, Ani's not going to know what to do with herself."

"Maybe you'll finally get laid again," I said slyly.

"I pray for it daily," Bram replied, deadpan.

"And then you'll adopt another one, and the whole process will start all over again," I joked, making Bram jerk his head up to look at me.

"Ani's been talking to you?" he asked. "About the adoption shit?"

"Not in a while," I replied, watching his expression. "You guys get that figured out yet?"

"Yeah, maybe," he said, looking back at Arie. "It's just a lot, you know? I love Arie, but it's a lot of work."

"It won't always be so hard," I murmured, thinking of my older nieces and nephews. "If scatterbrained Kate can do it, you've got it handled."

Bram laughed. "You make a good point."

"Don't take it for granted, man," I said, meeting his eyes. "You're a lucky motherfucker."

"I don't," he replied seriously. He picked up a cardboard book and threw it at my head. "And watch your mouth around my kid."

"Hey," I said, dodging the book. "You're just as bad!"

"I'm the parent—I get a pass," he said flatly.

I scoffed. "Hey, you, uh, feel like going into town with me today?"

"Oh hell no," Bram said immediately.

"Come on," I wheedled. "I need to get Sarai a ring, and I don't want to go to the jewelry store by myself. I'll end up buying something I can't afford and Sarai will never wear, and you know they don't take returns on that shit."

"Ask Trev to go with you. He'll do it."

"I don't want Trev," I replied. "I want my brother there."

Bram laughed. "You already asked him, didn't you?"

"He turned me down flat," I confessed. "He said that Etta slipped in dog poop outside and got it everywhere and he couldn't leave the house until all the evidence was cleaned up."

Bram laughed.

"And not to tell Morgan," I said, laughing with him. "Because she asked him to clean the shit up the day before yesterday, and he didn't do it."

"Animals are a pain in the ass," Bram said.

"I'd still like a dog, if I wasn't gone all day every day," I replied.

"Yeah, me too." He stood up. "Maybe once this one's a little older and wiping her own ass. I can only clean up so much shit in a day."

"You *just* threw a book at my head for cursing," I accused, putting my feet up on the coffee table. "My niece is going to have a filthy vocabulary if you and Ani don't start filtering yourselves."

"Fuck off," he replied, knocking my feet off the table. "I'm gonna get dressed so we can go."

"Missed you," I said, smiling up at his scowl.

"Missed you, too, asshole."

* * *

A few hours later, I sat on my parents' couch, staring at the ring I'd found for Sarai. It hadn't taken me long to find it once Bram, Arie, and I walked into the jewelry store, but it had taken me a long time to buy it. The place was like a damn car dealership. The salesperson had shown me practically every other ring they had before finally selling me the first ring I'd liked.

It was simple. A round diamond, a little over a carat, so it wouldn't look ridiculous on her hand. I also stashed away another simple gold band that matched it for when we got married. The engagement ring felt heavy when I held it, and it cost more than I wanted to think about, but I was sure Sarai would love it. It looked like something she'd wear. God, I really hoped she liked it. She'd have to wear it for the next forty years or so.

I sighed and leaned my head back, tapping the ring box on my knee. I hadn't heard from Sarai in a couple of hours, and I couldn't wait for her to get back. My dad was hanging out with my uncle, and I had the house to myself. I hated having the house to myself. Being alone was normal in my apartment, but my parents' house was supposed to be noisy and filled with people. It felt lonely when I was the only one in it.

I scrolled through TV channels for over an hour before I heard my aunt's SUV pull into the gravel driveway. Slipping the ring box into my pocket, I headed toward the front door, then pulled a pair of my dad's slippers on and walked outside.

"Oh, good, Alex! I need your help," my mom called, waving at me from the back of the vehicle.

I jogged toward her. "What's up?"

"I bought a fridge," she said, staring at the box in the back of my aunt's SUV. "The nice men at the store loaded it up, but it's too heavy for me to lift it out."

"You bought a *fridge*?"

"It's just a mini-fridge," she said.

"Why would you buy a mini-fridge?" I asked, sliding it toward me. Whoever had shoved the box in the car must've really wanted it gone. The thing was wedged in there.

"I was thinking I could put it in our room," she said, watching me. "Don't drop it."

"I'm not gonna drop it." My aunt Ellie, Morgan, and Sarai were now standing behind us while I tried to pry the box out of the trunk. "Why exactly would you need a fridge in your room?"

"In case I get thirsty," my mom replied.

"You can't," I grunted as I lifted the fridge, "walk fifty feet to the fridge in the kitchen?"

"Maybe I don't want to walk fifty feet," she said, leading me toward the house so she could open the front door for me. "Maybe I want to grab myself a drink without having to put any clothes on. It gets drafty at night."

"Aw, Mom," I groaned in disgust.

"Well, you asked," she said, pointing where she wanted me to set it down. "Don't ask if you don't want to know the answer."

"Lesson learned," I replied, following her back out of the house.

"Every year, this happens," my aunt Ellie complained, searching through the bags. "Why do we always get the same crap?"

"Because we've got good taste," my mom replied, walking over to help her.

"I'm so exhausted," Sarai murmured, slumping against me as I wrapped an arm around her shoulders. "We went to about fifteen stores."

"I see you got a few things," I said, pulling the bags from her fingertips.

"Just a couple." Her eyes were closed as she leaned against me. "Really good deals."

"Oh yeah?"

"Yeah. I decided that I'm getting you Hanukkah gifts this year and you can get me Christmas. We'll cover both holidays."

"There's no way you're getting me a bunch of gifts and I'm getting you only one," I replied, leading her into the house. As soon as I'd gotten her onto the couch, I jogged back out to help my mom carry in her loot.

"Thanks, baby," Mom said as we hauled in at least ten full bags. "Just don't look in them, okay? I got a bunch of Christmas presents."

We waved to my aunt and Morgan as they pulled out of the driveway, then made our way inside. Sarai was still on the couch, but she'd slipped off her shoes and was curled up on her side.

"Your fiancée did well," Mom said, laughing. "She didn't fall asleep until after we were home."

"Ani crashed again?" I asked.

"Out like a light the minute we left the parking lot," Mom confirmed. "I don't know why she drinks those energy drinks. As soon as they stop working, she shuts down like a dead battery."

"Did Bram have to carry her inside?" I asked.

"Well, you know she wouldn't wake up," Mom joked. "Just leave those there, son. I'll come grab them in a minute. Put Sarai in bed so she can get some rest."

I rounded the couch as my mom walked away, and lifted Sarai into my arms, startling her.

"I can walk," she protested, dropping her head to my shoulder.

"I can carry you," I replied.

I walked back to our room and set her on her feet so she could strip out of her pants and coat and slide on a pair of pajama pants before crawling into bed.

"I really don't want to be a rude guest," she said as she got comfortable, her eyes already closed. "But I have to nap, or I'm going to feel like shit later."

"You're not being rude," I replied as I pulled the ring box out of my pocket and slid in next to her. "My mom will nap, too, once she goes through her haul and writes down all the presents she's gotten."

"She writes them down?" Sarai asked sleepily, curling up against my side.

"She's got a lot of kids and grandkids to buy for. She writes everything down so she can keep track and she doesn't miss anyone."

"That's sweet," Sarai mumbled.

I lifted her hand and traced it with my index finger, debating with myself whether this was the moment I wanted to show her what I'd been doing all day.

"I got you some presents today," she said sleepily, patting my chest. "So don't look in my bags, okay?"

"I won't," I said.

I quietly snapped the lid of the ring box open and pulled the ring out, holding it between my fingertips for a moment before I spoke.

"I went shopping today, too," I told her softly.

"Really?" she mumbled. "Where'd you go?"

I slipped the ring onto her finger without a word, the rest of my body frozen and tense as I waited for her to open her eyes. I didn't have to wait long.

"Oh, Alex," she whispered, pushing the ring farther down her finger until it rested at the base of her knuckle. "It's gorgeous."

"Yeah?" I rasped out. I'd been less nervous when I'd asked her to marry me. That...well, that had been a spur-of-the-moment thing, though I'd never admit it. I hadn't had time to worry that she'd say no. This ring had been in my pocket for hours while I worried.

"It's simple," she said, still staring at her hand. "Classic."

My stomach rolled. "That's good?" I asked tentatively.

"Yes." She laughed a little, her eyes locked on mine. "Every day women get the popular engagement rings, the ones that are in style that season. My ring—" She looked back at her hand, tilting it this way and that. "My ring will always be in style. It'll still be as beautiful when I'm as old as Mrs. K."

"I'm really glad you say that," I replied, relaxing with a huff. "Because I can't return it."

Sarai jokingly smacked at my chest before lying down again, her head resting on my shoulder and her soft breaths tickling my neck.

"I love it," she said, her eyes already closing again.

I fell asleep with her curled up against me, my fingers entwined with hers on my chest, and happiness pulsing through my body.

* * *

I woke up later to the light fading outside and Sarai saying my name. Her body was still pressed against mine, but when I opened my eyes, I realized that she'd been awake for a while.

"Did you sleep?" I asked, my voice hoarse.

"Yes." She stared at me, her serious eyes trailing over my face.

"What's wrong?" I asked, all sleepiness disappearing in an instant.

"Let's get married," she said.

"That's the idea," I replied, looking at her in confusion.

"This weekend," she clarified.

"Uh." I coughed, choking on my own saliva. "What?"

"Let's get married this weekend. Let's just do it."

"Just do it," I murmured.

"That didn't come out right," Sarai mumbled with a little laugh.

"You want to get married this weekend?" I repeated back to her. "*This* weekend. In the next two days?"

"Yes," she confirmed with a nod.

My mind raced. I wanted to marry her—of course I did, or I wouldn't have asked her. But this was crazy...wasn't it? We'd just gotten engaged. She'd just met my family. I hadn't even met hers yet.

Our eyes met, and a million things passed between us, from the first night we'd met to the moment I'd slid her engagement ring on. The times we'd texted late into the night, the times I'd stopped by her place just to bring her dinner while she'd studied, and I'd had to force myself to leave again. The nights I hadn't left, and we'd stayed tangled up in the sheets until the sun rose the next morning. The moment she'd met my parents. The way she'd kissed me that morning. The way she'd ridden me the day before in the forest. All of it.

"Okay," I said, reaching up to brush her hair away from her face.

"Most of your family is already here," she said, her lips tipping up at the corners.

"Your family isn't."

"That's okay," she said quickly with a shrug. "You can meet them afterward."

Her nonchalance rang false, but I didn't argue. The feeling of her hand on my chest and her legs tangled with mine made me look past how odd I found it. I shouldn't have ignored that feeling, but I did.

"Shit," I said after a few seconds of smiling at each other. "You can't just get married in Oregon," I explained, dropping my head back against the pillow. "You have to file for a license first."

"And everything is closed for the holiday," she said with a deflated sigh. She lay down next to me.

As we stared at the ceiling, an idea formed. I studied it from all angles, thought about the balance in my bank account, thought about my family, counted the number of hours I had until I had to report in again on Monday morning.

* * *

My dad always made turkey-noodle soup with our Thanksgiving leftovers, so later that night my brother and Ani brought the baby over for dinner. My sister-in-law was dragging ass, and I couldn't help but laugh when she walked into the house.

"Lookin' good," I called out from my place next to Sarai on the couch.

"I look fantastic," Ani grumbled, pulling her beanie farther down her forehead. "You try staying up all night and shopping all day."

Sarai turned toward Ani's voice so we were both looking over the back of the couch, and before I could block it, Ani's hat came sailing through the air and hit Sarai in the face.

"You suck," Ani said, pointing at Sarai.

"What did I do?" Sarai asked, laughing as she threw the hat back. Ani's hair was sticking up at all angles. She looked like she'd stuck her fingers in a light socket.

"You put makeup on," Ani accused, like she'd been betrayed. "This is the day after Thanksgiving. How could you?"

"I—" Sarai looked at me for help. "I wasn't supposed to?"

"How the fuck should I know?" I asked. "I don't wear makeup."

My mom came down the hallway, her hair wet from the shower but neatly pulled back.

"You too?" Ani gasped.

"I didn't want Sarai to feel out of place," my mom replied, smiling our way. She was wearing lipstick.

"It's like I don't even know you people," Ani bitched, stomping toward the kitchen.

"What was that?" Sarai asked, watching Ani leave with wide eyes.

"We usually just do dinner in our pajamas," my mom said, grinning. "But I realized I hadn't told you before you two fell asleep, so I decided to mess with Ani a little."

"I ruined tradition," Sarai said with a grimace.

Mom laughed. "You didn't ruin anything. Ani's a beast when she hasn't had enough sleep. She'll be even funnier by the end of dinner, scowling at everyone and practically falling asleep at the table."

She turned to walk away, and I reached out to grab her hand. "Hey, Ma," I said, stopping her. "I just realized that I'm supposed to report back in Sunday night, not Monday morning." My mom's smile fell. "We have to leave tomorrow night instead of Sunday."

"Oh," she said, looking a little deflated.

"Sorry, Ma," I said, guilt causing a sharp pain in my gut.

"You gotta do what you gotta do," she replied, giving me a small smile. She leaned down and kissed the top of my head, then followed Ani into the kitchen.

"Um," Sarai murmured, drawing my eyes to her. "Were you going to tell me that we had to be home earlier?"

I grinned. "We don't," I whispered.

I watched her expression become even more confused as she tried to figure out what the hell I was doing.

"I found us a different flight," I said easily, leaning forward to kiss her.

"Okay," she said, kissing me back. "Why?"

I pulled away slightly and stared into her eyes. "This one stops in Vegas," I replied.

"Las Vegas?" She still didn't understand.

"Las Vegas," I confirmed, smiling. "Where you can walk into any chapel and get married on the spot."

"Oh," she breathed, her eyes widening.

"We'll get there tomorrow night, and our flight leaves at noon the next day."

"That must've cost a fortune," she said.

"It wasn't too bad," I lied. "I got us a room, and we're all set."

"When did you do all this?" she asked with a chuckle.

"When you were breaking tradition," I joked.

"I've never been to Vegas," she said, her lips tipping up at the edges.

"Sorry," I replied, my smile growing. "But we won't have time to sightsee this trip We'll be finding the first chapel and then spending the rest of the night in bed."

"Can't wait," she murmured, leaning forward to kiss me.

* * *

The next twenty-four hours flew by. Time at home with my family always went by quickly, and leaving a day earlier made that feeling even worse. It was tempered by excitement, though.

We kept our plans to ourselves as we said our good-byes, but I felt Ani's suspicious eyes on me more than once. She knew something was up, and she didn't buy the story that I'd mistaken the day I was supposed to be back in Missouri. She kept her mouth shut, though.

"Are you coming home for Christmas?" she asked, hugging me good-bye.

"Not sure yet," I replied, surprising her. I never missed Christmas.

"Oh," she said finally in understanding. "I didn't even think that you'd have to coordinate plans with your new lady."

"I'm not sure if she wants to go home for the holidays," I said with a small shrug, even though the idea of missing Christmas bummed me out.

"Ooh," Ani said. "Maybe she'll take you home to meet the family."

"Maybe." I glanced over at Sarai, who was saying good-bye to my parents. They both hugged her, and my dad said something in her ear that made her laugh.

"You did good," Ani said, following my gaze. "I like her."

"I knew you would."

"No you didn't," she scoffed. "It could've gone either way."

"Not true."

"You have shit taste in women," Ani said.

"I do not." I looked at her in disbelief. "And I've never even brought any women to meet you."

"Exactly," she said, nodding. "Because you knew they were shitty."

"That's not—"

"Jesus," Bram cut in, shaking his head as he stepped beside us. "You two are like twelve-year-olds."

"No we're not," Ani and I both replied at the same time.

"Jinx, you owe me a Coke," we both said at the same time again.

"I rest my case," Bram muttered. He wrapped his arms around me and slapped me on the back a couple of times as we hugged. "Make sure you get some pictures," he said quietly in my ear. "You know mom will want some."

My mouth dropped open in surprise as I pulled away. "How did you know?"

"You'd never forget when you had to be back," he said, his voice low as Ani made her way over to our parents. "Figured you were probably taking a detour."

"Were you looking in my phone?" I asked suspiciously. There was no way that he'd put it all together himself.

Bram laughed and shook his head. "Nope. I just knew what you were up to as soon as you said you were leaving tonight instead of tomorrow."

"Woo-woo twin shit?" I asked. It happened very rarely, but sometimes we just knew things about each other that made no sense. It wasn't telepathy or anything like that; it was more of a feeling.

"Must be," Bram said with a shrug.

"Not even sure if we'll go through with it," I said, guilt rising up in my chest. I had no idea how to explain to my brother that the thought of marrying Sarai in a quiet ceremony without the entire family watching and weighing in felt…right. I wanted it to be about me and her, not putting on a show for everyone else.

"Alex," Bram said, stopping my apology. "Do what's best for you guys, all right?"

"You're the best brother a boy could have," I replied, grinning.

"You're a shithead, and if you try to hug me again, I'll punch you."

"Abraham," I sang as I wrapped him up in a bear hug. "I love you, brother!"

"Knock it off," he groused, laughing as he tried to push me away.

"I can't," I yelled. "I can't contain it!"

"You damn well can," he huffed, shoving at me while I clung to him. He was laughing so hard that barely any noise came out.

"Boys," my mom called as we tussled, my hands grabbing hold of anything I could grip as Bram did his best to shove me away. "You're going to fall and get all muddy."

"I'm okay with that," Bram called back, out of breath. "My house is five minutes away. Princess here can fly"—he paused for a split second—"*home* covered in mud."

"You're such an ass," I said, laughing as I finally let him go.

Bram shot me a lopsided grin as he settled his coat back on his shoulders.

"We better go," my dad said, giving my mom a kiss on the lips. "Or they're gonna miss their flight."

I jogged over to my mom and pulled her into a hug, spinning her gently in a circle before putting her on her feet again.

"Thanks for coming home, baby," she said, smiling even though her eyes were watery. "Love getting to see you, even for a couple of days."

"We'll be back soon," I promised, smiling back.

"Make sure of it," she replied. She turned to Sarai. "It was so good to meet you, sweetheart."

"You too," Sarai said, smiling as my mom pulled her into a hug.

As soon as they'd separated, I laced my fingers with Sarai's and tugged her toward the truck.

"Love you," I called over my shoulder to my mom.

"Love you, too. Call me this week."

"I will."

We climbed into my dad's truck, and I turned to smile at Sarai. "You ready?" I asked as my dad backed out of the driveway.

"Yes," she murmured, grinning excitedly.

CHAPTER 12

SARAI

I swallowed painfully, smoothing down the front of my white sundress as I waited for the receptionist to start the music. After Alex and I had split up and found clothes to wear for the ceremony, it had been pretty easy to find a chapel. It was nothing fancy, and the small building had only a few people working, but they'd fallen all over themselves trying to make sure everything was perfect for us.

They'd stuffed a bouquet of fake flowers in my hand in the reception area and ushered Alex to the front of the chapel to wait for me, and the moment he was out of eyesight, my stomach twisted painfully with nerves. Was I doing the right thing? We hadn't told anyone what we were doing. In theory it had seemed really romantic, but now that it was actually happening, it felt…sneaky. Like we were doing something wrong.

My aunt and uncle were going to lose it. I couldn't imagine getting married any other way, but convincing them of that would be impossible.

"Are you ready?" the grinning receptionist asked me. At my nod, she started the music and gestured for me to move through the door to the chapel.

My heart was thumping heavy in my chest, and my feet felt like lead as I moved forward, but the second I saw Alex's wide smile and the way he fidgeted, clearly nervous himself, I calmed down.

This was what I wanted.

When I reached Alex, he leaned down so our foreheads touched, and let out a shaky breath, his excitement palpable.

"Ready?" he whispered.

"Ready," I whispered back.

As we turned to face the officiant, Alex's hand found mine. We held hands through the entire ceremony.

* * *

I was married.

Married.

I stared down at my ring while Alex took his shower, and finally let the gravity of the situation sink in. I had a husband. I was a wife.

Any important decisions I made would forever have to be discussed with another person. I twisted the rings around my finger. I was going to have to share my space, change my schedules, and worry about someone else whenever I made plans.

Panic seeped in until I heard Alex singing happily in the shower.

I would always have someone to come home to, someone to share expenses with, someone who would kill spiders and change light bulbs. I'd never have to worry about putting an extra blanket on the bed, because sleeping with Alex was like sleeping with a space heater. I smiled to myself.

He also hogged the blankets.

"Well, wife," Alex called out as he stepped from the shower and began to dry off. "Are you ready to head back to reality?"

I really wasn't. Missouri was school and work and schedules and deadlines. It was calling my aunt and uncle and breaking the news that I'd gotten married when they hadn't even known that I was engaged.

Growing up, I'd had my wedding planned out. I'd get married in a synagogue to a boy that my parents loved. My mom and aunt would help me get dressed, and my dad would walk me down the aisle. We'd have a big party afterward, and then my husband and I would go on some extravagant honeymoon that my parents had gifted us for our wedding. The details had always been vague, but the idea had been solid. It was how things were done in our community. Long engagements, fancy weddings, fabulous honeymoons.

Imagining any of that now made me want to scream. So I'd pretty much done the exact opposite. My aunt was going to lose her mind when she found out. I swallowed hard as I felt myself break out in a cold sweat. To say that I was dreading that conversation would be an understatement. Was there something worse than dread? Because the feeling in the pit of my stomach was definitely worse than that.

Aunt Adinah would be heartbroken if I told her how

painful it was to even think about planning a wedding without my mother. That the thought of walking down the aisle by myself or with Uncle Isaac made me want to cry. She'd be understanding, and she'd never make me feel bad about it, but I knew it would hurt her. I was the only child she had, and I'd never want her to feel like she wasn't enough. No, it was better this way. I would rather have her angry with me than sad.

"I am," I said, standing up to slide my shoes on as he got dressed. "Are you ready to get back on a plane?" Our landing in Las Vegas had been bumpy, to say the least. The woman sitting next to us had said that it was pretty common when flying in and out of that airport. I'd thought Alex was going to vomit.

"Not looking forward to it," he said with a humorless laugh. "But I'm ready to be home."

"Missing work?" I asked, checking the room for anything we'd missed when we'd packed our things. We'd been there for less than twelve hours, but somehow the contents of our bags had exploded around the room.

"I'm just ready to be married, I guess," he replied sheepishly. "You know, all the normal stuff. Getting you all moved in, coming home from work to see you on the couch with a frown on your face, going to see the Krakowskis, all of it."

"Wait," I said. "Why would I have a frown on my face?"

"Because you're doing homework," he replied easily.

"Oh." That made sense. I was getting close to the end of school, and I definitely had what Hailey called "senioritis." I was tired of the homework, tired of all the time I spent at the university, and tired of stressing about my grades. I was more than ready to graduate.

"It's cute," he said, coming up behind me as I bent to look under the bed.

I shot up like I'd been electrocuted when he lightly pinched my butt.

"I wish we had more time," he murmured, fitting himself against my back.

"Me too," I replied, letting my head drift back to rest against his shoulder as he rolled his hips.

"We should come back for our anniversary," Alex said, kissing my neck before pulling away. "Go to some shows, gamble a little—you know, do Vegas right."

"Sounds fun," I replied, but my mind was already wandering back to the fact that I was married and no one knew it yet.

We left the hotel and got into a cab that took us to the airport. It was late November, but the sky was clear and bright as we wove in and out of traffic. Ironically, Alex didn't seem at all nervous that our cab driver was a maniac, but he nearly lost the contents of his stomach when we hit a little turbulence on an airplane. I was the exact opposite. I hated riding with bad drivers, and the only saving grace of the whole ride was that it wasn't raining.

By the time we got on our flight and settled into our seats, I'd calmed down and Alex was all wound up again.

"Almost home," I said with a sigh, giving his knee a squeeze.

"So I was thinking," he said, lacing his fingers with mine as we taxied down the runway. "We should mail some of our wedding photos to my parents."

"No," I replied, elbowing him.

"It would be hilarious," he argued, his lips tipping up in a small smile as he grew more and more tense. "That's how we could announce it."

"Not even you could think that was funny," I replied, staring at him in disbelief.

"Can you imagine the looks on their faces?"

"You mean your mom crying?" I asked dubiously. "I'd rather not."

"She won't cry."

"She's definitely going to cry," I muttered. Everything had happened so quickly, and I'd been so caught up in the excitement that I hadn't worried about how Alex's mom was going to react. I'd known that my family would be angry about our marriage and how we'd gone about it, but I hadn't given much thought to how Alex's family would feel, because he'd been so supportive of the whole idea. Now I was really regretting not warning them.

"They'll get over it," Alex said, opening his eyes even though his skin was pale and we weren't at cruising altitude yet. "Don't worry—my sister will think it's romantic, and she'll convince everyone else."

"Somehow, I can't imagine your brother thinking that anything is romantic," I replied.

"Bram already knew," Alex said with a shrug.

"What?" I asked, my eyes widening. I'd thought that we'd agreed not to tell anyone yet.

"Wife," Alex said softly, leaning down to catch my eye, "I didn't tell him—he just knew."

"How would he just know?" I asked suspiciously.

"Twin shit," Alex replied. "Sometimes we just know things. He didn't believe our story, and he put the pieces together."

"Twin shit," I muttered, leaning back in my seat.

"It doesn't happen all the time, mostly just with big stuff," Alex explained.

"And what did he say?" I asked, turning my head to look at him. "You know, about the elopement."

"He said to do whatever is right for us," Alex said, giving a little shrug. "My brother's kind of an ass, but he's a good guy under all of the bluster."

"I liked him," I confessed, laughing a little at Alex's surprised look. "What? He's interesting. He might be grumpy, but you can tell he loves you guys."

"Yeah," Alex said, grinning. "Me best."

I laughed.

"No, but you could tell, right? That he loves me best?"

I shook my head in exasperation as Alex's smile grew.

"He does," Alex continued. "Everyone knows it." His voice dropped to a whisper. "He just doesn't let it show so he doesn't make anyone else jealous."

"Yeah," I murmured back drily. "Ani was obviously in a distant second place."

"This is why I love you," Alex replied, putting an arm around my shoulder so he could tuck me against his side. "Because you see through all the bullshit into the heart of things."

"You're so full of crap," I muttered, unable to keep the smile off my face.

"And that's why you love me," Alex replied.

* * *

The next week was a blur of school, work, and packing. Alex mentioned not telling our families about our marriage until we were all settled in, and I gladly took the reprieve. I struggled with how I was going to break the news to my aunt. My uncle was the calmer of the two, and I knew that even though he was going to be disappointed in how I'd gone about things, it was my aunt who was going to be the angriest. I wasn't looking forward to that conversation at all, and the longer I waited, the more anxious about it I became.

By the next weekend, Alex and I were tripping and stubbing our toes against boxes, but all my things had been moved into his apartment across town. We were officially living together, and though I'd been nervous about it at first, I was thoroughly enjoying it when I woke up pressed against his bare back.

"Hey, roomie," Alex mumbled, lifting my hand to kiss my fingertips. "Sleep good?"

"Yes," I murmured against his back. The skin was smooth under my lips, and I kissed him there once, then twice. Yeah, I was enjoying married life very much.

"We need to call our families today," Alex said, stretching his arms above his head. "Waiting a few days so we could get settled in is one thing, but waiting any longer makes it look like we were hiding it, don't you think?"

"Yeah," I replied, my voice coming out like a croak. "Yeah, you're right."

"Let's do breakfast first, though," he said, kissing me quickly before he hopped out of bed. "I'm starving."

I watched his bare ass leave the room, then fell back against the pillows and stared at the ceiling. It was judgment day, the day I'd spent all week trying to ignore.

I forced myself out of bed and took a shower, barely noticing my surroundings as I rehearsed exactly how I was going to break the news to my family. No matter how I looked at it, I couldn't imagine our conversation ending in anything but tears. I hoped, though, that Aunt Adinah would at least let me try to explain before she completely lost her composure.

"You hungry?" Alex asked, standing in front of the stove in nothing but a pair of sweatpants. "I'll make you an omelet."

The idea of food made my stomach roll, and I shook my head. "No thanks." I'd been dealing with a nervous stomach all week, and this morning was no different.

"I wonder if you caught a bug on the plane or something," Alex said, leaving the stove to come over and rest his palm against my forehead. "You don't have a fever."

"I'm okay," I said, leaning against his chest.

For all my anxiety and worry, I didn't regret getting married the way we had. I'd never imagined how comforting it would be to have a husband. It was as if the moment we'd signed our names on the paperwork, I'd suddenly had a person who would always be in my corner. It was a heady feeling, knowing that he wasn't going anywhere, that this relationship was permanent no matter what. I was glad that we'd gotten to that point without all the unnecessary stress of a big wedding.

"Let's call my parents first," Alex said, still holding me in the middle of the kitchen. "Then we can call your aunt and uncle."

I nodded and went to sit on the couch while he grabbed his phone. As soon as he'd dropped down beside me and pulled my legs over his lap, his fingers were moving across the screen.

"Hey, Ma," he said, wiggling his eyebrows at me. "Yeah, I'm good. Is Dad with you?" He paused. "Yeah, I wanted to talk to you both at the same time." He waited again, and then his face broke out in a smile as he put her on speaker.

"You got married, didn't you!" Liz was saying, her voice loud and excited. "Dan! Get in here. Alex got married!"

"What?" we heard in the background.

"Mom," Alex called, laughing. "What if that wasn't what I was going to tell you?"

"Yes it is," she said, like she had him all figured out. "Isn't it?"

"Yeah," he replied, locking eyes with me.

"I knew it! He got married," she said to Dan, whom we could hear asking "What the hell is going on?" in the background.

"Congratulations," Dan said, his voice suddenly clear. "And you're in deep shit."

Alex laughed again. "We decided to elope," he explained, relaxing into the couch. "We didn't want to make it a big thing, especially since our family is all over the place."

Well, that was as good of an excuse as any. At least he hadn't told them that I was the one who'd wanted to do it right away.

"Still," Dan said, his voice happy but serious. "You know your mom lives for that stuff."

"We can have a big party next time we're home," Alex promised.

"I'll rent the grange," Liz said. "And we'll invite everyone to a reception. If that's something Sarai would like?"

"That sounds good," I replied, relief making me almost giddy.

"I can't believe you two," Liz said, exasperation in her voice. "You know your dad and I would have come."

"I know," Alex said. "But then we would've had to invite everyone—"

"And it would've turned your little wedding into a huge production." Liz finished his sentence with a sigh.

The next half an hour was filled with more phone calls and more congratulations from the rest of Alex's family. Ani complained that Bram had known and she hadn't, Trevor had laughed and given his congratulations without reservation, and Alex's sister, Kate, had cried because she hadn't even met me yet. They were all happy for us, though. Not a single person held back as they told us how happy they were, how I fit right in with the family, and how they didn't know how Alex had managed to get me to marry him.

I was jealous of how easily Alex's family had accepted our decision to leave them out, even when I could tell that some of them were really disappointed that we hadn't included them in our big day. His family was so genuinely nice that I dreaded calling my own.

By the time we sat down at the kitchen table and turned on my laptop, I was a nervous wreck and trying not to let Alex see how anxious I was. I would have preferred to call my aunt and uncle privately because I knew exactly how the conversation would go, but after being included in Alex's announcements, I couldn't think of a good excuse to leave him out.

"I haven't spoken to you in weeks," my aunt said, her home office coming into focus as she answered the video call. "Where have you been?"

"Hi, Auntie," I replied, turning my laptop until both me and Alex were in the camera's frame. I was really glad he'd decided to put a shirt on for our video chat, since my aunt was surprised enough to see him sitting next to me. "Alex," I said, "this is my auntie Adinah."

"Alex," Aunt Adinah murmured. "It's nice to finally meet you."

"You too, ma'am," Alex replied, clearing his throat and showing just how nervous he was under his cool exterior.

"How is everyone?" I asked, trying to pull her attention away from my husband. I knew my question hadn't worked, because her eyes were still moving over the screen as she took in the details of Alex and our surroundings.

"They're well," she replied. "Where are you, Sarai?"

"We're at Alex's apartment," I said, my palms beginning to sweat. Then, because I was a fool, I just blurted it out. "*Our* apartment, actually."

"Excuse me?" she asked sharply as my uncle came into view room behind her.

"It's our apartment," I replied as Alex's strong fingers laced with mine under the table.

"You moved?" my uncle asked, his voice calm but suspicious as he sat down next to my aunt.

"Yes." I swallowed hard. I needed to tell them that we were

married; it was the entire purpose of our call, but with them staring at me in disbelief, I couldn't find the words.

"We actually called to tell you the good news," Alex said, his voice calm as my heart raced. He squeezed my hand in solidarity, and I opened my mouth to speak, but no words came out. I was frozen with fear.

"Sarai?" my aunt asked, her brows drawn together.

"We got married," I finally said, lifting my hand to show off my ring. I tried and failed to smile as my aunt snapped backward as if I'd slapped her.

"You what?" my uncle asked, his voice lower but no less calm.

"Tell me you're joking," Aunt Adinah said, pursing her lips. "Tell me this is a joke."

"I'm not joking," I said, my throat burning as she paled.

"Sarai Levy," she said, tears in her voice as she stared at me. "You didn't even tell us you were engaged."

Alex's hand tightened around mine, but I couldn't look away from my aunt and uncle, who were visibly disappointed.

"Why would you call to give me this news?" my aunt asked. "You clearly don't care what I think if you ran off and got married to a stranger without a word to anyone."

"He's not a stranger," I whispered.

"He's a stranger to me," she shot back, her voice trembling.

"I know that you'll love him," I replied. "He's a good man."

My aunt huffed and waved her hand as if she were brushing me away. When she stood up and walked out of the camera's view, I had a hard time holding back the sob that rose up in my throat.

"Give her time," my uncle said with a sigh. "She's heart-broken." He reached forward and closed the laptop without saying good-bye, and I knew that my aunt's heart wasn't the only one I'd broken.

I stared blankly at the black screen. I'd known they'd be angry. I'd prepared myself for that. But I hadn't anticipated how hurt they'd be. I'd screwed up.

"Well, that went well," Alex said jokingly, his hand coming up to rest on my back.

My laugh turned into a painful sob, and once the tears began, I couldn't control them.

"Shit," Alex murmured, pulling me onto his lap. "I'm so sorry, baby," he whispered against my hair, his hand rubbing my back in long sweeping strokes. "It'll be okay. They'll come around."

I didn't have the heart to tell him that he might be wrong. That my aunt still carried grudges from high school, and that even though my uncle had seemed calmer than her, he was feeling this betrayal just as deeply.

We stayed there in the kitchen, with me curled up like a child in Alex's lap long after my sobs had turned to silent tears. I thought about my parents, and I couldn't stop myself from imagining that they'd be happy for me. That they'd give Alex a chance. Maybe it was wishful thinking, but I day-dreamed about how the news would make my mama's eyes light up, and how my dad's would grow teary, but he'd pull me into one of his warm hugs and whisper in Hebrew how happy he was for me.

It was useless, but I let myself drift in that place, the dream of them alive and well and celebrating with us. I didn't let myself dwell on the fact that if they'd lived, I'd be a completely different person. Maybe I wouldn't have ever even met Alex. Maybe I wouldn't have distanced myself from the faith I'd grown up in, and I'd already be married to a boy that my parents had introduced me to. I surely would've never imagined eloping if my parents had still been with me. If my dad had been alive to walk me down the aisle.

"I know that this hurts," Alex said, resting his cheek against the top of my head. "But once they get to know me, they'll love me," he joked gently. "Everyone does."

I laughed because I was supposed to, but I didn't feel it. I was raw, stripped bare, and it felt like I would break at any second. Shatter into a million pieces and float away with the dust motes in the kitchen.

"Have you ever dusted in here?" I asked, sitting up and sliding off his lap as I wiped the makeup from under my eyes.

Alex looked around the room, then shrugged. "Nope."

The word came so easily that a real laugh popped out of my mouth before I could stop it.

Alex smiled wide and stretched out his legs. "Why don't you call Hailey and tell her the big news?" he asked.

"Good idea," I said, reaching for my phone. I found her name and pressed SEND as I walked out of the room.

"Hey, stranger," Hailey answered happily, her cheerful voice an instant balm on my emotions. "It feels like we've barely talked since Thanksgiving."

"I know," I replied. We'd been preparing for finals and barely had time to visit. "Did you have a good holiday?"

"Puhlease," she said, dragging out the word. "It was boring. I was here. I want to hear about your big trip! How did it go? Did you have fun?"

"It was good," I replied, dropping down on the edge of the bed. "Alex's family is awesome."

"Well, that's no surprise. Look at Alex," she said easily. "He's one of the nicest guys ever."

"Yeah, he is," I said softly, thinking about the way he'd held my hand during the conversation with my aunt and uncle.

"Is everything still good with you guys?"

"Um, that's what I was calling you about," I replied. "I have some news."

"You better not have broken up with the unicorn, Sarai," she said seriously.

"The opposite, actually."

"What?" she asked in confusion.

"We got married."

"What?" she shrieked happily, making me laugh. "No you didn't!"

"Yeah, we did." I couldn't stop the grin that had taken over my face. "We went to Vegas."

"No you didn't!" she yelled again.

"Yep. We stopped there on our way home from Oregon, and we've spent the week moving me into Alex's apartment."

"Holy crap," she exclaimed. "Where the hell did my best friend go? You know, the fuddy-duddy that never does anything spontaneous?"

"She's still here," I replied ruefully. "I'm still as boring as ever."

"Yeah, but now you have a husband to be boring with," she squealed. "Congratulations."

"Thanks," I said, tears coming to my eyes as she whooped and made celebratory noises. This was exactly the type of reaction that I wished I could've gotten from my aunt and uncle. I hadn't expected them to be happy, but damn, it would've been so nice.

"I'm so freaking happy for you," she said, her voice calmer than before. "This is awesome news." Before I could reply, she spoke again. "Crap, I gotta go. I just spilled shampoo all over the floor—don't ask. Call me later and give me all the juicy details?"

"Sure."

After she'd hung up, I stared at the phone in my hands, wishing I could call my aunt and have a do-over. I wanted her to be excited for me, to squeal and yell and tell me how happy she was that I'd found someone as great as Alex. I wanted to go back in time and introduce them before I dropped the marriage bomb so she could've been more accepting.

I rubbed at my sore eyes, trying not to cry.

"What did she say?" Alex asked, poking his head around the doorway.

"When she got done screaming in excitement?" I asked, making him chuckle. "She said congratulations."

"I'm sorry you didn't get that from your uncle and aunt," he said softly.

"I didn't expect them to break out the champagne," I replied with a shrug. I would *not* cry again. I'd known that they were going to be upset with me; now I had to live with it.

"Hey, all this excitement made me hungry," Alex said.

"How about we run down to the restaurant and grab some lunch?"

I nodded because I knew exactly what he was doing. After the disastrous conversation with my aunt and uncle, Alex was doing the only thing he could to cheer me up. He was taking me to see the other half of my family, the ones who loved me by choice and never had a bad word to say about anyone. He was bringing me to Mr. and Mrs. K, who would be happy and full of congratulations when they heard about our marriage.

* * *

"Do you think you got food poisoning?" Alex asked later that night, running a washcloth under cold water in our bathroom sink so he could press it against the back of my neck.

"I don't know," I mumbled, too tired to care if he saw me vomiting.

I'd been in the bathroom for hours, with no end in sight, and I finally came to the conclusion that I'd just have to be mortified later. I was too busy feeling awful now.

"There's no way Mrs. K gave me food poisoning," I said, swallowing back the bile that rose in my throat. "She's so careful."

"That's all you've eaten today," he replied with a sigh. "Maybe it's a virus?"

"I don't know," I ground out, laying my head on my arms. "Does it matter?"

"Yeah." He sat down behind me and began rubbing my

back. "I think food poisoning goes away once whatever's making you sick is gone. A virus could last a lot longer."

"Great," I whined, tears threatening as I swallowed again.

"You're going to get dehydrated," he said, reaching for the bottle of water he'd put on the floor next to me. "Have a drink."

"I'll just throw it up," I said, not even bothering to take it from his hand.

"Come on, baby," he tried again, wiggling the bottle from side to side. "Just one small sip."

I knew before I took it from his hand that the water was going to come right back up, but I couldn't stand the worry in his voice, so I let him uncap the bottle. I rolled a tiny amount of water around in my mouth for a minute, hoping that somehow it would keep me from gagging as I swallowed it. That didn't work. Less than a minute after I'd let the cool water run down my throat, I was heaving, bringing it all back up again.

"I'm sorry," he whispered, holding my hair back. "We'll try again later, okay?"

Later came and went, and I was still vomiting. By midnight, I was completely drained and lying on the bathroom floor.

"Okay, we're going to the hospital," Alex announced, stuffing his phone into his pocket as he entered the bathroom.

"Were you looking things up on the internet?" I asked groggily. "You know those doctor websites always make it seem worse than it is."

"Nope," he replied, leaning down to lift me off the floor. "I called my mom."

"Alex," I whined. Ugh, I wasn't a whiner, but the situation definitely called for it. "Why would you do that? Now she's going to be worried."

"Because I knew she'd know what to do."

"We don't need to go to the hospital," I argued as he sat me on the edge of the bed.

"You're dehydrated, and you can't keep any water down," he said, pulling one of his sweatshirts over my head. "Maybe they can give you an IV."

"I don't want an IV," I replied, pushing my arms through the sleeves.

"Too bad," he muttered, sliding socks and my new rain boots onto my feet. "Let's go."

All the movement had made my stomach start churning again, so I froze and started shaking my head slowly from side to side.

"I got you covered," he said, pulling me gently to my feet. He handed me a plastic container to vomit in, and I felt my face heat in embarrassment. This was an all-time low.

I didn't start heaving until we were in the truck on our way to the hospital. Thankfully, there was nothing left in my stomach to throw up, so the plastic container was still empty by the time we pulled into the parking lot. I'd take the pain of dry heaving over the smell of vomit filling the cab of his truck any day.

It took a while to get me checked in and even longer for us to be escorted into a little room, but it didn't take long for a doctor to come in and check me out.

"How are we doing?" he asked, looking down at a clipboard as he stopped at the foot of my bed. "I'm Dr. Landry."

"Hi," I mumbled, curled up on my side in the sterile bed.

"She's been puking since this afternoon," Alex said, his knee bouncing up and down nervously. "She can't even keep any water down."

"Small sips?" the doctor asked.

"Tiny ones," I clarified.

"Okay." The doctor came over and pressed gently on my stomach, looking for tenderness, but beyond the soreness of my abs from throwing up, nothing hurt.

"Might just be a virus," the doctor said, making me look pointedly at Alex. "But I'm going to run a couple of tests just to make sure. When was your last menstrual cycle? Is there any chance you could be pregnant?"

"No," I replied quickly. "I have an IUD. I haven't had a period in a long time."

"We'll check just to make sure," he said, smiling. "Okay?"

I shrugged. I didn't care what they did, as long as they could stop the rolling and cramping of my stomach. He hadn't mentioned an IV yet, but I was starting to hope for one. Maybe they could give me anti-nausea medicine.

I peed in the little cup they gave me and let them take a blood sample, then Alex and I settled in to wait. The TV in my little room was broken, so I closed my eyes and drifted off while Alex played on his phone and absentmindedly ran his fingers through my hair.

About an hour later, I opened my eyes as Dr. Landry came back into the room.

"Blood tests were all normal," he said, smiling at me. "And it looks like you did test positive for pregnancy."

"No." I chuckled a little, my voice hoarse. "No, I have an

IUD. You must have mixed it up or something."

"I can assure you, we didn't," Dr. Landry said kindly.

"I have an IUD," I said again, my words slower and overenunciated.

Dr. Landry's eyes met mine, and he gave me an understanding smile that I wanted to knock off his face. "I assure you, the test was positive. I'd like to do an ultrasound to see how far along you are and check on that IUD."

"Why would we need to check on it?" I asked. "It's clearly not doing its job."

"Sarai," Alex said, his hand covering mine. "It's okay."

"Are you kidding?" I spun my head to look at him and immediately regretted the movement. Alex had the little kidney-shaped tray under my chin as soon as I started dry heaving again.

"I'll be back in a few minutes with that ultrasound machine," Dr. Landry said, stepping back out of the room.

"This isn't possible," I mumbled, breathing heavy as I tried to calm my nausea with shallow breaths through my nose. "I have an IUD."

"Let's just get the ultrasound," Alex said, his voice subdued. "Then we'll see where we're at."

"It's not going to show a baby," I said, scoffing. "They screwed up somehow. I have an IUD."

I felt like if I said the words enough, told enough people that I had an IUD protecting me from this exact scenario, then I would be in the clear. I wanted children, but I didn't want them yet. I barely had time to eat dinner; I really didn't have time for a child. I didn't graduate until June, and after all the hard work I'd put in, I *had* to graduate in June.

The doctor came in, rolling the ultrasound machine, and squirted some goo on my belly. Then he was shifting the little wand against my skin, pressing and twisting it until a very faint heartbeat came through the system. I stared uncomprehendingly at the screen.

"You *are* pregnant," the doctor said, typing a few things into the machine. "Let me get some measurements, and then we'll check on that IUD."

Fuck the IUD. Who the hell cared where that useless thing was?

"Look at that," Alex said, whispering in my ear. "That's our baby."

I didn't respond. I couldn't.

"I'm going to put you at about seven weeks, four days," Dr. Landry said. "That would put your due date in mid-July. The eighteenth."

"After you graduate," Alex said, squeezing my hand.

"I don't understand how this happened," I said dully, staring at that little flicker, flicker, flicker on the screen. "We were careful."

"If your IUD isn't where it's supposed to be, it wouldn't work correctly," the doctor said, moving the ultrasound wand around as he stared at the screen. He was patient with my arguments and denial, but there was a thread of exasperation in his voice.

"Sarai," Alex said, his voice low. There were a million questions in the way he'd said my name, but I wasn't ready for any of them. I wasn't ready for *this*. The pillow made a swishing sound as I dropped my head against it and stared at the ceiling.

"Ah," the doctor said. "I see the problem. The IUD was displaced. It happens, but not often. We can take it out in a few minutes." He stood up. "And I'd like to give you some fluids before we send you home."

"Thanks, Doc," Alex said.

It was silent in the room as soon as the doctor left. I was numb, barely able to feel the blanket that covered my legs or Alex's fingers brush over my knuckles. Even my stomach seemed to have stopped churning.

I let the nurse hook me up to an IV without even looking at her, choosing to continue staring at the ceiling instead even though the fluorescent lights made my eyes burn.

"You're scaring me," Alex said after the nurse had gone. His voice was soothing, comforting even, but it still grated. "Sarai, this is good news, right? I mean, this was the plan. A little early, but we talked about having kids."

Plans. I wanted to laugh. *I* was the planner. Alex seemed to just take each day as it came, but I didn't do anything on impulse. I scheduled every piece of my days, spent hours making sure that everything I needed to do was written in my calendar, knew exactly how much money I needed each month to cover bills, food, fuel for my car, and possible unexpected expenses.

And then, in a fit of insanity, I'd started dating a man who'd made me lose all of that. I'd traveled instead of getting ahead on my schoolwork. I'd gotten engaged and married in the same week. I'd lost myself, and now I was pregnant. What the hell had I done?

"Say something," Alex said sharply, his voice still soft.

"I had an IUD," I murmured. I couldn't think of anything

else to say. It was the root cause of all of this. I'd had an IUD, and it hadn't worked. Clearly my hormones had caused me to do all these things that I normally wouldn't have done. That tiny piece of plastic had failed me spectacularly.

"Jesus," Alex said with a sigh. He set my hand gently on the bed and stood from his chair. "I need some air."

When I didn't reply, he left the room.

CHAPTER 13

ALEX

I pushed open the emergency room doors and inhaled deeply, letting the cold night air calm my temper. I was trying not to be angry—I really was—but I was so close to losing my cool that I had to leave Sarai's room. It didn't help that I felt shitty for leaving her in there alone even though I wanted a little distance between us.

I knew that she didn't feel good. I knew that we hadn't expected a baby. I knew that she'd probably felt even more overwhelmed than I had when the doctor told us she was pregnant. I knew she was stunned—hell, *I* was stunned. But I was having a really hard time accepting her complete lack of response when we'd seen that heartbeat on the monitor.

That was our child in there. *Our baby*. Sure, it wasn't much to look at, but that was our kid. A little human made from equal parts Sarai and Alex. Even if we weren't prepared or ready for this, it *was* happening. How was she so indifferent?

I pulled my phone out of my pocket.

"Hey, brother," Kate answered. "Everything okay?"

"Sorry I'm calling so late," I said, pacing back and forth across the sidewalk.

"No worries, Shane and I are just watching a movie."

"If you're busy, I can just call you back tomorrow," I mumbled. I shouldn't have called her. I knew that Sarai wasn't anywhere near ready to let people know, since she wasn't even accepting the truth herself, but God, I needed to talk to someone.

"No way," Kate shot back. "What's up?"

"I had to bring Sarai to the hospital tonight because we thought she had food poisoning or something," I said with a sigh.

"Oh no," Kate replied. "That sucks. Is she okay?"

"She's pregnant," I blurted out, getting right to the heart of why I'd called her.

"Oh," Kate said. "Uh, congratulations? Is this a good thing or a bad thing? Because you sound like it's a bad thing."

"Christ, I don't know." I rubbed my forehead, where a headache was forming.

"Wait," Kate said suspiciously. "Is this why you ran off and got married?"

"No," I replied quickly. "Hell no. We got married because we wanted to get married. No other reason."

"Okay," she said, drawing out the word. "Well, you're married, so you're both clearly committed, and you both have good jobs. What's the issue?"

"Sarai," I said, hating myself for throwing her under the bus like that, but dying for some support.

"What is she worried about?" Kate said, her voice low and calming.

"I don't know," I replied, thinking of the look on Sarai's face when she'd found out she was pregnant. "She just keeps saying that she had an IUD."

"Ah," Kate murmured.

"What?"

"I can understand that." Kate had accidentally gotten pregnant when she and Shane had a one-night stand. Everything worked out in the end, but it hadn't started out well. "Try to imagine it from her point of view. She thought she was protected from pregnancy, and now she's growing a human she hadn't planned for. Pretty scary."

"Did you—" I wasn't even sure what I was asking. "How did you react?"

"I yelled," Kate said. "I think I called Shane a bunch of dirty words. Threw up a couple of times."

"Sarai just went silent," I replied. "After arguing with the doctor."

"She's just in shock," Kate said soothingly. "Give her a little time, and then see where her head's at."

"Yeah," I said. "Yeah, that's a good idea."

"Where are you?" Kate asked. "Still at the hospital?"

"Yeah, I walked outside for a few minutes," I replied. "Sarai's dehydrated, so they're giving her some fluids."

"Well, get back in there, Dad," Kate scolded. "She's probably scared out of her mind, and you're outside calling me."

"Shit," I muttered.

"It'll all work out," she promised. "Give Sarai a hug for me, and tell her to call if she wants to talk or anything. I'm kind of an expert on babies."

"Will do." I turned back toward the doors. "Hey, Kate—"

"I won't tell anyone," she said, cutting me off. "It's your news to share."

"Thanks, sis."

"Anytime."

I hung up the phone and dropped my head back, staring at the dark sky. Sarai's behavior made me antsy and anxious. There was something about the way that she refused to believe in our new reality that scared me, but I couldn't figure out why. She'd calm down and everything would work out—I knew that—but it didn't stop the knot of fear in my stomach from growing.

I took a deep breath and shook out the tension in my arms as I walked back inside.

"How you feeling?" I asked as I stepped through the door of Sarai's room. I'd been gone only a few minutes, but she looked worse than when I'd left her. Pale, with dark circles under her eyes, and curled up in the fetal position, she looked like a scared teenager.

"The heaving has stopped," she said, pulling the blanket farther up her shoulder. "For now at least."

"That's good," I said as I sat down next to her on the bed and smoothed her hair away from her face. "The news sinking in?"

"I can't believe I'm pregnant," she whispered. "How the hell did this happen?"

"My sperm is clearly too powerful to contain," I replied. The joke fell flat.

"I have months left of school," she said, staring at the wall. "I had plans."

"You heard the doctor—she'll be born after you graduate," I pointed out. "Nothing is changing yet."

"*Everything* is changing," she snapped. "I knew before that first date that this was a bad idea. I knew, and I went anyway, and now look."

I jerked back at the verbal blow.

"You realize we're married now," I said, letting my shaking hand fall away from her hair. "This wasn't some *whoops, now we're stuck together* thing. You *married* me."

"I know that," she replied dully, pulling the blanket tighter around her shoulders. "Believe me, I know."

"Then what?" I asked, trying to keep my voice even. Yelling would solve nothing, and I'd be an asshole if I raised my voice, but Jesus, I wanted to. "You think I ruined your life? That our wedding was a mistake?"

"I didn't say that," she replied defensively.

"I can read between the lines," I shot back.

"You're not even trying to see this from my point of view."

"I am," I said, shaking my head. "But I'm not under-standing it. We got married. Moved in together. Yeah, this baby is way earlier than we were hoping, but it's *here*. So we change our plans. It's not the end of the world."

Sarai scoffed. "You haven't given up anything," she said. "Of course you're happy. This doesn't change your life at all."

"You're kidding, right?" I asked dubiously.

"Your family will be so excited," she said, her voice wob-bling. "Your mom will probably start sewing baby clothes or something equally grandmotherish."

"That's a bad thing?"

Sarai just shook her head.

"You're pissed because my family is supportive?" I asked in confusion.

"It's all just so easy for you," she whispered angrily.

Comprehension dawned, and my chest ached sharply as I watched her hold back tears.

"Aw, baby," I said softly, lying down on the bed behind her, my feet hanging off the side. I curled my body around hers. "Your aunt will come around. She loves you."

"You heard Uncle Isaac," she said. "I broke their hearts."

My jaw clenched in fury as I held her tighter. Her aunt and uncle had every right to be disappointed, but I hated how shitty they'd been to Sarai. "This is going to change things," I murmured against her hair. "You'll see. Just wait until they find out that you're going to give them a grand-baby to love. Babies are like magnets—they won't be able to stay away."

"How am I supposed to tell them?" she asked. "I came back to Missouri to go to school. They've been waiting for me to come home for years, and now I'm building this whole other life here."

"Do you want to go back?" I asked, keeping my voice even. I dreaded her answer, but I needed to know. My re-enlistment was coming up, and we were going to have to make some important decisions soon. In the back of my mind, I'd assumed that if I got out of the Army, we'd move to Oregon. Most of my family was there, and I was ready to be close to them again.

"No," she said softly. "No, I don't."

"We'll figure it out," I said, kissing her head. "We have time to figure it all out."

"I'm really scared," she admitted, her fingers lacing with mine.

"I know," I replied, giving her fingers a squeeze. "But I'm not scared of anything," I boasted. "So we'll be fine."

"I hope so," she said.

I pressed my lips against her hair and held them there, letting the tiny strands brush against my face. I'd do whatever it took to make sure that we were okay.

"Let's remove that IUD," the doctor said as he and the nurse came back into the room.

Sarai reached for my hand, and I cringed as they helped her feet into the stirrups.

"Try to relax," the doctor said as Sarai's fingers tightened around mine.

There was a sheet covering what the doctor was doing, but I still broke out in a cold sweat as he worked.

"You okay?" I asked, leaning down to kiss Sarai's forehead.

"It hurts," she breathed, squeezing her eyes shut.

My stomach churned.

"All done," the doctor said a few minutes later, reaching up to pat Sarai's knee as he stood up. "How're you doing?"

"Okay," Sarai said, letting out a deep breath.

"The worry we have when someone becomes pregnant while using an IUD is ectopic pregnancy," he said, taking off his gloves. He walked to the sink and washed his hands, then turned to face us. "But the ultrasound showed everything progressing appropriately in your uterus."

"What's an ectopic pregnancy?" I asked, glancing between the two of them.

"It's when a baby starts growing in a fallopian tube," Sarai replied.

"And that's bad, right?"

"Yes," the doctor said. "Ectopic pregnancies aren't viable. They can be very dangerous if they progress too far. There's a danger of the fallopian tube rupturing and causing internal bleeding."

"Rupturing?" I asked, feeling the blood drain from my face.

"Alex," Sarai said, tugging on my hand. "You heard him say everything is fine."

"It could've—" I shook my head a little and looked back at the doctor. "That would've been really bad, right?"

"But it wasn't," the doctor said calmly. He clapped me on the shoulder as he moved toward the door. When he got there, her stopped and turned to face us. "Everything looks good. Once you've had some fluids, you can head home."

"Thank you," Sarai said.

I couldn't say anything. My tongue felt as if it were glued to the top of my mouth as I stared at Sarai's hand in mine. She could've been really hurt. The difference between what would have been *not viable* and our currently growing baby was what—only a few inches? And what had he meant by "rupturing"? Like, exploding? Sarai's fallopian tube could have exploded? I wasn't a doctor, but that sounded *really* bad.

"Alex," Sarai said, trying to meet my eyes. "Everything is *fine*."

"But it almost wasn't," I blurted. "You could have exploded."

"What?" she asked in confusion.

"Your fallopian tube could have exploded," I said dumbly, staring at her in horror. "Why weren't we more careful?"

"How could we have been more careful?" she asked, cocking her head to the side.

"I could've worn a condom," I said in frustration, running my hand over my face. My hand was shaking. "Jesus, I should've—"

"Alex," she said softly, pulling me toward her. "Come here." She pulled me down until our cheeks were pressed together, her lips brushing my ear. "It's okay," she said gently. "Everything is fine."

Jesus, she'd been right to be afraid. What if something went wrong? What if something bad happened?

I closed my eyes and pressed my forehead against hers, turning so that I could kiss her.

"This wasn't a bad idea," I murmured. "I promise. I know that shit is moving faster than you wanted, but we're not a bad idea. I love you so much."

Sarai sucked in a sharp breath. "I didn't mean it," she said, her voice wobbling as her hands came up to cradle my face. "I'm so sorry."

"You're the best decision I ever made," I rasped. "I don't know what I'd do if something happened to you."

"I love you," she whispered, pressing her lips to mine. "Everything's going to be fine."

* * *

After Sarai was discharged from the hospital early that morning, she went to bed and slept for almost twenty-four hours. We didn't talk about the baby; actually, we didn't really talk about anything. We went back to our jobs, and Sarai studied and went to school. We ignored the elephant in the room, and I swallowed back the questions I had. Did she really think we were a mistake? She'd apologized for saying it, but that didn't mean there hadn't been a kernel of truth in her words. Maybe it made me a coward, but I was afraid to ask her about it.

I was waiting for her to bring the baby up, but she didn't. She just continued on with her normal day-to-day life as if nothing were happening. As if she weren't growing a human. Thankfully, after the night we'd spent at the hospital, she didn't seem to be feeling bad or having any morning sickness. I wasn't sure if that was normal or not, but I wasn't about to rock the boat by bringing it up.

We got used to married life slowly, and as weeks went by, our lives melded together and I slowly stopped thinking about the things she'd said to me at the hospital. I picked up dinner on the nights that she was studying, and ate fast food on the nights she was at school, and we took turns cooking on the nights she was free. Those nights were few and far between. It seemed like Sarai had buckled down even harder on her schoolwork.

Sarai still hadn't heard from her aunt or uncle. They were freezing her out, and as much as I tried to be understanding and give them the benefit of the doubt, the longer it went on, the more pissed I got.

"I'm so glad we can sleep in tomorrow," I said, dropping

next to Sarai on the couch. It was Friday night, and I was beat.

"I know," Sarai said, leaning against me as I set my feet on the coffee table. "This week was awful."

"How much homework do you have this weekend?" I asked.

"Not much," she said with a sigh of relief. "Just planning out the next couple of weeks and finishing up a paper."

"We should do something fun," I said.

"Like what?" she asked, tipping her head back to look at me.

"My normal ideas would include booze, tattoos, or skydiving," I replied, grinning. "But I guess those things are out."

The smile on her face froze, but she rolled with the conversation starter. "I don't even like to drink, and I'd kill for a beer," she joked, rolling her eyes.

"Oh yeah?" Relief filled me as she shrugged good-naturedly.

"And at work, someone was eating a bacon, lettuce, and tomato sandwich, and I almost tackled her for it."

"Now that, I can help with," I laughed. "I'll pick some turkey bacon up at the store."

"It smells different," she muttered.

"Are you really going to give up a lifetime of kosher eating for a BLT?" I asked. "I'm not judging." I lifted my hands in the air. "I mean, if you're going to do it, go hog wild."

"Nice pun," she replied, her lips twitching.

"I'm very punny," I said, nodding.

"And no, I'm not going to start eating pork products. I can still enjoy the smell, though."

"I'll cook bacon every day, just for you."

"If you eat bacon in front of me, I'll cut you," she replied, settling back against me.

"Fine," I replied, sighing in fake disappointment.

"I've noticed you've been trying to keep our meals kosher," she said nonchalantly.

"What gives you that impression?" I asked. She was right; I had been trying to follow the rules I'd found on the internet. I was doing my best, but I knew I was forgetting things. I'd even printed a list of foods she wasn't supposed to eat and kept it folded up in my wallet.

"The disaster you make in the kitchen," Sarai said. "So many different bowls and spatulas."

"Yeah, thank God we have double what normal people have," I said sheepishly.

"You don't have to go to all the trouble," she replied. "I mean, there's certain things I won't eat, but I'm not going to freak out if you use the same sink to wash dishes that aren't supposed to be mixed."

My eyes widened in horror. "That's a thing?"

"That's a thing," she confirmed, chuckling at the look on my face.

"You're supposed to use a different sink?" Had my voice just risen an octave? I cleared my throat. "We only have one sink."

"Alex," she said, patting my leg. "It's a nonissue."

But it wasn't. Not to me. I was trying to make things easier for her, trying to train myself to follow the guidelines she'd lived by all her life. I still felt completely clueless about Judaism beyond what I'd learned in my extensive internet searches, but I was trying damn hard.

"It'll get easier," she said, somehow reading my mind. "You'll see how I work in the kitchen, and it'll make more sense."

"So you *do* follow the rules," I said, pointing at her.

"I do it without thinking," she said, swatting at my finger with a laugh. "It's just second nature for me."

"Then it'll be second nature for me," I replied stubbornly.

"We'll see," she said.

I hummed to myself and decided that I was going to look online at food-preparation etiquette the first chance I had.

"I haven't really had any cravings beyond that BLT," she mused. "I wonder if that comes later or something."

"I'm not sure." God, I loved that she was finally talking to me about her pregnancy. I wanted to know everything. I was so curious about it all, but I hadn't wanted to ask her questions when she wasn't ready to discuss it. "You could ask my sister—she knows all about being pregnant."

"Kate?" she asked.

"Yeah." I nodded. "She's only been pregnant once, but the older kids' mom was her best friend, so she was the support crew on those pregnancies."

"I guess we should probably tell people soon," she muttered, picking a piece of lint off her pants.

I didn't tell her that Kate already knew. Now that we were finally communicating, I really didn't want to bring up my freak-out at the hospital. It wasn't the time. I'd tell her in a few years, when all of this was just a fond memory.

"I'd really like to tell my parents," I admitted. "But we can wait a little longer, if you want."

"I—" She paused for a long moment. "Can we just keep it to ourselves a little longer?"

"Sure," I replied, trying to hide my disappointment.

"I'm sorry," she said quietly, leaning against me. "I just don't want to tell your family and not tell mine."

"They're still not taking your calls?" I asked, familiar anger burning in my gut.

"Not yet," she murmured. "I can't believe they've held out this long."

"Me either," I said.

"I'm sure that they'll call this week," she replied. "My aunt won't be able to keep avoiding me."

"I hope so, baby," I said, planting a loud kiss on her forehead.

"Hailey invited us to a party they're having next week," Sarai said, groaning.

"She's planning that far in advance?" I asked in surprise. Honestly, I was more surprised that they'd invited us at all. Sean had been keeping his distance at work, and I couldn't imagine him willingly inviting Sarai to come over, since he knew she disliked him.

"I know, right?" Sarai said, biting her lip. "I'm kind of worried about her."

"Because she's planning in advance?" I joked, not understanding why she would be worried about a party. Sarai didn't smile.

"Actually, yes." She nodded. "She's been showing up to school on time, too."

"Shit, better call the Army." I was still making jokes, but Sarai didn't find our conversation even remotely funny.

"She's a notorious procrastinator," Sarai explained. "She doesn't plan ahead, because she always thinks she has more time. I've known her for years and that's never changed, so why now?"

"Maybe she decided she doesn't want to be late anymore," I replied. I wasn't really seeing the problem.

"You're not taking this seriously," Sarai complained, standing up.

"Hey, come back," I said, reaching for her. She dodged my hand.

"I'm really worried about her, Alex," she said, crossing her arms over her chest. "She's not acting like herself. It's weird."

"It's probably nothing," I replied as she walked toward the kitchen. "What is she, twenty-three or something?" Damn, that made me feel old. "She's probably just finally getting her shit together."

"Is that why she cut her hair?" Sarai asked. "Is that why she barely texts me anymore? Is that why all of her assignments are suddenly done on time? Is that why she barely goes out and hasn't even asked to see my new apartment?"

"All of that would be easily explained by a little maturity, yes," I called, getting to my feet. "Why, what do you think is wrong?"

"I think it's Sean," Sarai said, glaring at me as I strode into the kitchen. She took a bite of ice cream straight out of the carton.

"He's helping her get her life on track?" I asked, my tone a clear indication that I thought she was crazy. "The guy is a douche." I didn't understand why Hailey stayed with an asshole like Sean, but I wasn't seeing the connection between Hailey getting her shit done on time and her relationship.

"I don't know," she replied, sounding annoyed. "I just know something is wrong. I can feel it."

"Then why don't you ask her about it?" I asked, opening my mouth so she'd give me a bite of her ice cream.

"Because," she replied, pushing a spoonful into my mouth. "If she wanted to tell me something, she would. Whenever I comment on the changes, she just brushes me off."

"Okay then," I said, shrugging.

Sarai made a disgusted noise and spun toward the fridge to put the ice cream back.

"Baby, I'm sure she's fine."

"We both know that Sean is a jerk," she pointed out as she cleaned her spoon.

"Well, yeah. But what does that have to do with your friend finally taking care of her shit?"

"Don't call her *my friend* like that," she replied.

"Like what?"

"Like she's not your friend," she mumbled.

I laughed. "Really, that's where this discussion is going?"

"Well, she's your friend, too," she replied loftily.

"Okay, fine, she's also my friend," I said. "Because she's your friend."

"I just think we should be aware of it," Sarai said, walking away again.

I followed her into the bedroom and watched her as she stripped out of her work clothes and threw on a tank top and a pair of shorts so short they made my mouth water.

"What am I supposed to be aware of, exactly?" I asked, staring at her bare thighs.

"That Hailey is acting weird," Sarai replied, snapping her

fingers to get my attention. "That something's wrong."

"I'll keep my eyes open," I promised. I wasn't really sure how I'd do that, since Sean usually avoided me, but if Sarai was worried, I'd try.

As she pulled her hair into a ponytail, my attention shifted and I licked my lips. Goddamn, my wife was hot.

"You've already moved on to other things, haven't you?" she asked, rolling her eyes.

"You just got undressed in front of me," I replied honestly. "If you were trying to keep my attention, you should've kept your clothes on."

"I'll remember that for next time," she said, trying to edge around me.

"Hey now," I joked, wrapping an arm around her waist as soon as she was within reach. "Where are you going?"

"Back to the living room to zone out with some television," she replied, giggling when my lips tickled the edge of her ear.

"I think we should zone out in the bedroom," I murmured, moving my lips down her neck.

"I mean, we could," she said slowly. "But your lack of imagination is a little disappointing."

"Hey," I replied, jerking my head up to meet her eyes. "You've never complained about my imagination before."

"It's been a problem for a while," she said mockingly, her lips twitching as she pulled out of my arms. "I just haven't wanted to hurt your feelings."

She shrieked as I lunged for her, chasing her out of the bedroom and down the short hallway to the living room. When we got there, she spun around to face me, and we both froze.

"You can run," I said, smiling. "But you can't hide."

"I got you into the living room," she boasted, her hands on her hips. "Why would I hide?"

I took the last step that separated us and reached around her, grabbing her ass as I lifted her against me. Her legs wrapped around my waist as she laughed, and she braced her arms on my shoulders, our noses just millimeters apart.

"I love you," I breathed. "I haven't said that enough."

"You say it every day," she whispered back.

"Still not enough."

After the teasing and the race into the living room, when our lips finally met, the kiss was surprisingly soft.

I let go of her with one hand to brace myself on the arm of the couch, then lowered us down until she was straddling my lap, her legs still around my waist. It wasn't as smooth as I'd imagined it in my head, but she didn't complain. She held still until I was seated, and then her hands were all over me. She pulled my T-shirt over my head and scratched down my chest, running her hands lightly over my belly and more firmly up my arms to my shoulders.

"You're wearing too many clothes," I murmured, pulling her tank top off. "All of this needs to go." I unhooked her bra and sighed when her breasts were finally bare.

"They're not any bigger," she mused, leaning forward to kiss the notch in my collarbone. "I was actually looking forward to that part."

"They're just the right size," I said, pushing her away so I could take a nipple into my mouth.

I breathed in the scent of her skin and traced the delicate bumps of her spine with my fingertips, my heartbeat racing.

I tried to take hold of her hips as she shifted, but let her go as she climbed off me and pushed her shorts and underwear to the floor. She stood there, staring, while I followed her lead, stripping my bottom half.

Then she went to her knees, and the room spun for a second.

Her mouth was warm and wet and pretty much the best thing in the history of the universe. I closed my eyes as I threaded the fingers of one hand through her hair, the other hand gently wrapping around the side of her neck. It felt good. So good, in fact, that I was getting close just a couple of minutes later. I gave the signal, tried to warn her, but she didn't listen. Then I called her name through my gritted teeth, but she still gave no response beyond a hand that patted my knee softly, as if she was telling me to go ahead. I came in a rush of euphoria and nerves.

"I tried to warn you," I blurted as she got up and climbed onto my lap.

"I got the warnings," she muttered, laughter threading through her words. "I was ignoring them."

"Oh." I wrapped my arms around her as she laid her head against my shoulder. "It's your turn," I murmured, my fingers trailing lightly down her back.

"I'm too tired," she replied with a sigh. "Can we just cuddle for a while?"

"Of course." I pulled her tighter against me and stared at the black TV screen in front of me. I didn't really understand the concept of being too tired for sex, but I knew it wasn't just an excuse when her breathing evened out and her body relaxed against mine.

I carried her into the bedroom and put her in bed. She barely stirred as I pulled the covers up around her neck and crawled in beside her.

"Sorry," she mumbled sleepily. "You can do dirty things to me tomorrow."

"Looking forward to it," I replied. I rolled onto my belly and propped my head on my folded arms so I could watch her as she drifted off to sleep.

Sarai was right—her breasts hadn't grown much, but they had become a little firmer, the tiny blue veins more pronounced. Her cheeks were just a fraction rounder, and her back arched just a little more as she walked. Her belly was slightly curved in a way that no one else would notice unless they were obsessed with her naked body the way I was.

I'd noticed other things, too. Changes in mannerisms and food preferences. Frequent midnight trips to the bathroom. The way she fell asleep the minute her head hit the pillow, when before it had always taken her a little while to wind down from the day.

It was kind of amazing, the things I noticed now that I was looking for changes. Now that I knew our baby was growing inside her, I paid more attention than I ever had. I mentally catalogued everything she did, every move she made. I tried to hide the way I watched her, but I had a feeling that she was beginning to notice. She didn't call me a creeper outright, but more than once she'd closed the bathroom door while she did her makeup, or turned away while she ate her breakfast, to give herself a little privacy.

As Sarai let out a little snore, I smiled and carefully climbed back out of bed to make sure the doors and windows were locked. A lot of things had changed since Sarai and I had gotten married, and even more changes had happened once I knew that we had a baby on the way. It was as if I was seeing everything differently now. For the first time in my life, I paid attention to expiration dates on the food in our fridge. I bought organic. I followed speed limit signs. All of a sudden I remembered to turn the fan on when I was taking a shower, every single time because I was afraid of mold. There were a million different dangers in the world, and it felt as though I had just discovered every single one.

It wasn't only the little things that I noticed; I was also struggling with the big things. My re-enlistment was looming, and I still didn't know what decision I was going to make. I hadn't brought it up with Sarai yet, because I knew that she was already dealing with more stress than she should have to. We would have to have that discussion soon, though. The thought of being away from her for a long period of time put my stomach in knots, but the idea of getting out of the Army and losing my health insurance and income was just as scary. I'd deployed twice already, and I wasn't exactly looking forward to doing it a third time, but if my life hadn't changed, I wouldn't have even considered staying home.

But my life *had* changed. It was terrifying and exciting in equal measure.

"I woke up and you weren't there. What are you doing?" Sarai asked in confusion. I'd been standing at the same window for a few minutes, my hand on the sill.

"Just making sure the windows are all locked," I said softly. She swayed sleepily on her feet but smiled.

"Well, come back to bed. I'm cold."

She probably *was* cold, considering that we were both standing there fully naked, and it was the beginning of winter.

"I'll be right there," I replied. I still had two windows to check.

She walked away, and I hurried through the apartment, checking the last couple of windows and turning off all the lights on my way to the bedroom. I hit the bathroom, too, so I could take care of business and brush my teeth. By the time I crawled back into bed, Sarai was starfished in the middle, just dozing off.

"Bed hog," I teased, pulling the blankets back.

"I wanted to make sure I knew when you came in," she said, grinning as she scooted to the side.

"I'm here," I said, getting comfortable. I rolled onto my side, stuffed one arm under my pillow, and rested the other across her waist.

"Good. I can't sleep without you." She threaded her fingers through mine, and we held hands, our arms wrapped around her belly.

I closed my eyes and smiled. *Do you feel us, baby?* I thought. *You're not even born yet, but Mommy and Daddy are already hugging you.*

CHAPTER 14

SARAI

I love him," I reminded myself as I drove to work. I was almost late, again, because Alex had started checking my car out before I left every morning. Today, he'd even lain down on the pavement to look underneath it before he'd let me leave. His worry was driving me crazy.

Oh, he was still the easygoing, joke-telling goofball I'd fallen in love with, the life of any party, but lately he'd been so nervous about everything that it was beginning to make me nervous. He watched me. It wasn't like glancing over at someone once in a while; it was actual staring. It drove me crazy because I was used to having my own space. Privacy was hard to come by in a one-bedroom apartment even when your spouse wasn't acting like a lunatic.

I didn't remember feeling so closed in when I'd lived with my aunt and uncle, and our apartment hadn't been much bigger even with an extra room. We'd given each other plenty of space to do our own thing, and we'd spent a lot of time outside, which had helped.

I let my irritation with Alex simmer while I drove to work, but in the back of my mind I knew why I really felt so anxious. I'd finally agreed to tell our families about the baby. Hanukkah and Christmas were coming up soon, and he wanted to spread the news before everyone started gathering for the holidays.

Alex had asked if I wanted to go to New York for Hanukkah and try to make peace with my family, but I'd decided against it. I just couldn't make myself go begging on their doorstep for forgiveness when they'd been so awful. When I'd asked Alex if he wanted to go to Oregon, he'd shaken his head and said that we'd just seen his family. As if he didn't want to see them every chance he got. I wasn't sure if he was trying to make me feel better or if his finances looked as bleak as mine after our spur-of-the-moment wedding and move, but we'd come to the conclusion that we'd stay home in Missouri this winter and spend the holidays as newlyweds.

I got to work on time, barely, and sat down at my desk. I sighed as I booted up my computer and put my purse away. It was going to be a long day of work and homework, and I'd been exhausted lately.

I knew the exhaustion was because of the baby, and I should probably be trying to get more rest, but I didn't have the time. I was still planning on graduating on schedule and at the head of my class. If I could just keep up the pace until graduation, I could rest for the last month of my pregnancy. That was the plan, anyway.

Now that I'd had more time to get used to the idea, I was feeling more optimistic about our new addition. I'd always planned on having a family, and complaining about the timing began to feel petty after those first few days. Women would kill to have the life I led: a handsome and kind husband, a good job, and a safe place to live. When it came right down to it, I'd just been overwhelmed by all the changes that had happened so quickly.

I hadn't been good with change in a very long time, not since my parents had died and my entire world had been upended.

I jumped when my phone rang from inside my desk, and I scrambled to grab it when I realized I hadn't silenced it for the day. I was too preoccupied lately.

"Hello," I said quietly, leaning over a little so no one could hear me.

"You never answered if you were coming to the party," Hailey said, her voice coming through the speaker like a megaphone. "I'm trying to get a head count."

A head count? Who was this, and what had she done with my best friend?

"What day is it?" I stalled for time, wondering how I could get out of going without hurting her feelings.

I loved Hailey, and if she'd asked me to do anything else, I'd have said yes in a heartbeat. However, spending time with Sean sounded like torture, especially now, when all I wanted to do was lie around on the couch when I had any time to spare. I sighed. Even though I dreaded it, I'd still go. I wasn't about to miss my best friend's party, no matter how much I hated her boyfriend.

"It's on the twenty-third," Hailey said. "And you have to come. It's a white-elephant party, so you and Alex each need to bring a present."

"I'll be there," I said, my voice low as I glanced around the open office again.

"Yay," Hailey said. "I swear, I never see you now that you're a married lady."

"I see you in class twice a week," I replied.

"Oh, you know what I mean," she said. "You'll be there?"

"We'll be there," I confirmed.

"Excellent!" She said with a whoop. "I'll let you get back to work now."

"Thanks," I replied drily, hanging up. I silenced my phone quickly and tucked it away just in time as one of the partners walked up to my desk, asking for a client file.

The waistband of my skirt dug into my belly while I searched through a filing cabinet. I just needed to get through the day, and then I could change into some leggings. And then, of course, I had to call my aunt and uncle to give them the good news. My stomach rolled.

* * *

"We can do my family first, if you want," Alex said that evening while unpacking a bag of takeout. "And then yours."

"That works," I replied, swallowing hard.

"Okay, good," Alex said happily. He was practically bouncing with excitement and trying to hide it. I guess I wasn't doing a very good job hiding my nervousness, either.

"Did you get to work on time today?" he asked as we ate, grimacing as I looked up at him.

"Yes," I said, drawing out the word. "Barely. You know you don't have to check my car every day, right? It's a little excessive."

"It's not a big deal," he replied, smiling. "Happy to do it."

I looked at him in disbelief. I don't think he understood what I was trying to say, so I tried again.

"It just takes up so much time, you know?" I said. "Waiting for you to be ready so we can walk out together. Especially on days when you'd normally leave later than me."

"I don't mind leaving early," he said with a shrug. "And we get to leave together, which is kind of nice."

"It's driving me nuts," I finally blurted, making his eyes widen in surprise. "It takes ten extra minutes that I don't have unless I wake up earlier."

"Oh." He paused with his fork halfway to his mouth. "Okay. Well, don't wait on me tomorrow—just leave whenever."

I watched him as he dug into his food. His agreement had come too easily.

"You're just going to do it before I'm ready to leave, aren't you?" I asked.

"Yes," he replied with a nod, not looking up from his food.

I watched him eat, love and tenderness for him washing over me in a wave. He was the sweetest person I'd ever met. Knowing that I'd almost turned away a man that cared so much about me that he checked my car every morning made my chest ache. What a horrible mistake that would've been.

"It's my brother," he said when his phone rang. He looked at me with big questioning eyes.

"Go ahead," I said, laughing. God, he was too cute for his own good.

"Abraham!" he answered happily, his eyes meeting mine as he smiled. "What's up?"

He waited for a second, then chuckled. "Yeah, man, I'm fine."

Silence again.

"I was actually going to call you tonight."

I dropped my hands to my lap and clenched them together. We'd taken for granted that his family would be happy about our news and mine wouldn't, but what if we'd been wrong? What if Alex's family wasn't as excited as we'd assumed they would be? What if they thought we were idiots? What if they said something that took away the shine of excitement in Alex's eyes, made his smile disappear?

"We're having a baby," Alex announced.

I watched him carefully, looking for any change in expression, but none came.

"Yeah, the doctor said July." He paused. "Ha ha. We took all the precautions, but clearly my sperm are superior."

Alex reached over and put his hand over mine, rubbing along the white knuckles.

"Thanks," he said into the phone. "We're pretty stoked." He scoffed. "I can say *stoked*. You can't, because you're a grouchy old man in a young man's body."

Alex dropped the phone to his shoulder. "He's going to get Ani," he whispered, practically giddy. "I'll put her on speaker so you can hear her reaction."

"He's happy for us?" I asked, just to be sure.

"Yeah." Alex leaned forward and kissed me. "He knew something was up," he said, wiggling his eyebrows. "More of that woo-woo twin stuff, but he was waiting for me to fill him in. He finally lost patience."

"That's so weird," I murmured.

"Makes it hard to keep a secret," he replied. Then his eyes widened, and he put his phone on speaker.

"Hey, asshole." Ani's voice rang out. "What do you want?"

"You're on speaker," Alex replied. "Can you at least act like you like me?"

"You're pregnant!" Ani yelled. "I mean, Sarai's—hell, you *know* what I mean."

"How the hell did you figure that out?" Alex complained, laughing.

"Because you put me on speakerphone, idiot," Ani replied. "And you already eloped. What the hell else would you have to tell me?"

I couldn't fault her logic. Alex smiled at me and I tried to smile back, but my face felt frozen. Why was I so nervous?

"That's awesome! When are you due?" Ani asked. I felt the muscles in my shoulders relax a little in relief.

"July," I answered, my voice coming out a little rough.

"Wow, you guys didn't waste any time," she replied laughing. "Congratulations."

A couple of minutes later, Alex hung up and then called his parents. My worry disappeared as his mom squealed and cried, and his dad told us that he was "real excited" for us in his calm, quiet way. They were surprised, but there was nothing but excitement and happiness in their responses.

Alex was enjoying this, telling everyone that we were having a baby. He loved sharing the news, and I felt tears hit my eyes more than once as he proudly talked about how we'd already heard the baby's heartbeat and how he thought we were having a girl because I wasn't sick and any boy of his would already be wreaking havoc from the womb.

Alex's sister, Kate, didn't answer her phone, so he left her a message telling her to call him because he had news. I had a feeling that she was going to know exactly what he wanted to tell her, the way Ani had. I laughed as he tried to make his information seem really mysterious.

"Okay, just Trev left," Alex said, taking a deep breath. "I'd call my aunt and uncle, but I have a feeling my mom has already called Aunt Ellie."

"She seemed pretty excited," I replied while Alex scrolled through the contacts on his phone.

"Oh yeah," he said. "She loves kids, and grandbabies are even better."

I smiled, but my stomach still churned with nervousness. This wasn't as hard as I'd thought it would be, but the phone call I was dreading loomed. If Alex wanted to make only one more call, then it was almost my turn. I looked at the clock and realized that Alex had been talking to his family for almost two hours already.

"Trev?" Alex said, putting the phone to his ear. "Hey."

He waited, leaning back in his chair until the front legs came off the floor.

"Yeah, I was just calling to tell you the news."

He smiled.

"Really? Okay, sure," Alex said. He held the phone out to me. "Morgan wants to talk to you."

"What?" I whispered, not reaching for the phone. "Why?"

"I don't know," he whispered back jokingly. "Maybe she wants to congratulate you?"

I took the phone and put it to my ear. "Hello?"

"Hey, Sarai," Morgan said. "Congratulations."

"Thanks." I couldn't think of anything more to say than that.

"You freaking out?" Morgan asked, her voice low.

I glanced at Alex and gave him a small smile.

"A little," I said. What an understatement.

Morgan laughed quietly. "Yeah, I've been there."

"Yeah." I glanced at Alex again. "It took a minute for it to sink in."

"Been there, too," Morgan replied. "Look, everything probably seems scary right now, but thankfully it takes forty weeks to grow a human, so you have time to figure it out."

"Okay."

"And you've got a good guy, which makes things easier. At the very least you'll have someone to run to the store for late-night cravings. I don't know how many times the corner-store guy saw me in my pajamas."

I chuckled. She was so frank that I was instantly at ease. I also felt grateful. Unlike Alex's sister, Kate, who I'd never met in person but who had already texted me a few times just to chat, Morgan was reserved. The fact that she'd asked to speak to me felt special, I guess.

"Just a few words of advice," Morgan said. "Don't join any mommy groups—those women are barracudas. Find a doctor that you like, because all sorts of weird shit is going to happen, and you want to be able to tell them anything without feeling self-conscious. And just so you know—because I didn't—you're going to come home from the hospital still looking about six months pregnant."

"Good to know," I replied.

"Oh, and if you're interested in cloth diapering—"

"People still do that?" I asked in confusion.

"Yep. They still do it. I've cloth diapered Etta for years. Super easy, cheaper than disposables, and saves the environment."

"It's not gross?" I asked, intrigued.

"Your definition of *gross* is going to change dramatically," she said, chuckling. "It's really not a big deal. We used pockets on Etta for a long time, but I've just discovered flats and wool, and I'm in love. I've got an awesome hookup in Germany that makes the cutest baby pants and diaper covers that I can send you to, if you decide to go that route."

"I only understood about half of what you just said," I confessed. What the hell were pockets and flats? And why would I need wool?

"One thing at a time," Morgan replied. "But I'm going to be honest: knowing another mom who cloth diapers would be awesome. I tried to get Ani to convert, and she acted like I was crazy."

"Uh," I said. It *did* sound kind of crazy. "I'll let you know if we decide to do that."

"Do what?" Alex asked, trying to eavesdrop.

"Use cloth diapers," I replied. He wrinkled his nose in disgust, and I nodded.

"Just worry about getting rest and eating healthy," Morgan said. "The rest will come in time. Everything happens in stages, you know? You don't have to figure it all out at once."

"Thanks," I said, making a mental note to call Morgan the next time I was freaking out. She seemed to know exactly what questions I had without me asking.

"I'm really happy for you guys," Morgan said. "Crap, Etta let the puppy out of his crate. We'll talk soon, okay?"

"Okay."

She hung up, and I set the phone down on the table in front of me.

Now that we were done calling Alex's family, it was time for me to break the news to my family, and I had a feeling that the congratulations were over.

"You want me to grab the laptop?" Alex asked. "Is it in your bag?"

"No." I shook my head. "I'll just call this time, okay?"

"Whatever you want to do, baby," he replied, dropping forward so the legs of the chair thumped back onto the floor.

I pulled my phone out of my pocket and stared at it for a moment before calling. The minute it began to ring, I felt my heart start to race.

"Hello?" my aunt answered, her voice subdued.

"Hey, Auntie," I replied. I bit the inside of my cheek to keep from crying. "How have you been?"

"Good," she said. She didn't elaborate or offer any more information.

"Is Uncle Isaac home?" I asked. "I wanted to talk to you both."

She didn't reply, but I heard her calling my uncle. A few seconds later, his voice came through the line.

"Sarai," he said. "Hello."

"I was calling"—I forged on before I lost my nerve—"because I have some news." I paused, but they didn't respond. "I'm going to have a baby. Me and Alex, we're going to have a baby."

The silence was deafening.

"I'm due in July," I rambled on, afraid of the silence. "So I won't have the baby until after I graduate. The doctor said that everything looks good, but I have to go back next week."

"Mazel tov," my aunt replied stiltedly.

"We were just headed out, actually," my uncle murmured uncomfortably. "Thank you for calling, Sarai."

I tried to swallow the lump in my throat. "Of course," I whispered. I wanted to say something else, anything that would keep them on the line. I wanted to fix what was broken, but I had no idea how. Hanging up, I set my phone down carefully next to Alex's on the table.

I stared at the two, side by side, marveling at how the phones looked so similar but had caused such opposite feelings when we'd used them tonight.

"That wasn't so bad," Alex said tentatively.

My eyes watered when they met his, and I felt so much love for him at that moment that it was almost as if my skin heated from the inside out.

I wiped at my eyes and waved a hand in the air. "It could have been worse," I said lightly.

"What did they say?" he asked.

"Congratulations," I replied. "But my uncle said they

had plans, so they had to cut the conversation short."

Alex's gaze moved over my face, searching. "Still not quite what you were hoping for," he said in understanding.

I stood up from my spot at the table and moved to him, stepping between his knees so I could wrap my arms around his neck. Without hesitation, his arms circled my hips.

"I'm happy," I said, the realization coming later than it should have. "So if they aren't happy for me—" I shook my head and cleared my throat. "I'm married, and I'm having a baby. They can be a part of that if they want, but I won't force them."

"You shouldn't have to force them," Alex replied. It was the first thing he'd said that was even remotely disparaging of my aunt and uncle. He treated them with respect when they came up in conversation, even when I knew that he didn't like how they were treating me. I was thankful for that.

"No, I shouldn't," I said. "They're angry now, but they'll come around eventually."

"Yeah, they will," Alex confirmed. "And then you won't be able to keep them away."

* * *

"We're really good at that," Alex murmured as he rolled to the side, his sweaty skin sliding against mine. "And practice seems to be making us Olympians."

I laughed as I tried to catch my breath. Somehow, in our rush to touch and taste everything we could, we'd knocked the pillows off the bed, and we were currently lying naked in the cool room, too lazy to pull the blankets up around us.

He ran his hand down my side, and I shivered. It seemed like my skin was extra-sensitive lately, which delighted Alex to no end.

"Sexual Olympics," I replied. "I like it."

"Olympic coitus," he said.

"Olympic intercourse."

"Erotic Olympics."

"Olympics of intimacy."

Alex opened his mouth, paused, and then laughed. "I've got nothing else. You've turned me into an idiot with your feminine wiles."

"Someone's been reading," I teased.

"I can use *wiles* in a sentence. I say it all the time," he argued, leaning up on one elbow.

"Try it again," I replied.

I laughed when he couldn't come up with another sentence. After dinner I'd gone into the bedroom to study so that Alex could use the television without worrying that he was going to bother me. I'd felt relieved that the announcements were over and I could finally relax, assuming that my focus would improve and I'd start sailing through my assignments the way I used to.

I hadn't actually been able to concentrate until Alex had come quietly into the room and sat down beside me on the bed. I didn't think either of us had realized how raw we were still feeling until we'd settled into separate rooms to do our own thing.

"Hey, Hailey called me," I said, turning my head to face him. "She was checking to see if we're going to their Christmas party on the twenty-third."

"You don't celebrate Christmas, so we obviously won't go," he replied quickly.

"Nice try," I said. "They're doing a white-elephant gift exchange, too."

"Oh, fun," Alex mumbled. "We'll come home with a popcorn popper we'll never use and a personal massager that someone thought was hilarious."

"I notice that you didn't say we'd never use the massager," I replied.

"Well, that's useful," he said innocently. "Your shoulders get sore after hunching over a computer all day."

"I don't hunch."

"I love you sweetheart, but you hunch."

I grinned. "You've never called me sweetheart before."

"You like that?" he said, smiling back. "Thought I'd test it out, see how it felt."

"It would have felt better without the hunching part," I shot back.

"Your shoulders would feel better without the hunching, too," he said with a shrug.

I laughed and poked him in the side, making him jerk.

"Are you ticklish?" I asked, my eyes wide with newfound power.

"Absolutely not," he replied, stiffening.

"Yes." I poked him again and got the same jerk in response. "You are."

"This is a fight you'll lose," he warned, tilting his head to the side as he watched me. "Are you prepared for that?"

"I was born prepared," I replied.

Alex's laugh came out in a huff. "It's *ready*, I was born *read*—"

I took advantage of his distraction by digging my fingers into his sides, making him practically leap off the bed. As he scrambled to get away from me, he fell off the side, ass first. I laughed so hard that my eyes began to water as his feet got tangled in the blankets and sheets so he was hanging awkwardly from the bed.

Knowing retaliation was coming as soon as he worked his way free, I slid off the other side of the mattress, still laughing.

"Funny, huh?" he asked, hopping to his feet. He was breathing heavily, and the hair on his head was sticking out at a million different angles.

I began to nod, and he chose that moment to leap over the bed.

I screamed in surprise and ran. I wasn't even sure why I was running, but I was down the hallway, through the living room, and on the far side of the kitchen island in seconds. When I spun to face him, he wasn't even chasing me.

"You're pretty fast," he said easily, walking down the hall. He'd somehow found the time to put his boxers back on. "But should you really be running like that while you're with child?"

My mouth dropped open in surprise. "With child?" I asked.

"You're also naked," he said, raising one eyebrow and pointing at me, his hand making a little circle.

I huffed and crossed my arms over my breasts.

"Come on," he said, reaching out his hand. "I won't get you."

"I don't believe you," I replied, staying on my own side of the island.

"Promise," he said, his eyes crinkled with laughter. "I stopped thinking about payback when I was watching your ass bounce as you ran away."

"You're awful," I said, moving toward him to lace my fingers with his.

"I have a healthy attraction to my wife," he replied, wrapping his arms around my waist as he danced me around the kitchen. "Nothing awful about that."

"I guess not," I agreed.

Our dance slowed until we were swaying, our feet barely moving.

"Hey, Alex," I said quietly.

"What's up, sweetheart?"

"I don't regret marrying you," I murmured, kissing his bare chest. "I'm sorry for what I said at the hospital."

He pulled me closer and kissed the top of my head. "It's already forgotten."

*   *   *

After moving past the stress of telling our families about the baby, I felt my excitement grow a little more each day. I couldn't help it. My clothes were getting a little snug, and I hadn't dealt with any nausea since my visit to the hospital. Even my exhaustion seemed to be getting better as long as I went to bed before eleven.

Alex and I grew closer every day. I was always learning new things about him, some that I liked (he always threw his laundry straight into the hamper) and some that I didn't (his socks were almost always inside out, and I had to fix them before I threw them in the wash). He was unflaggingly easygoing. Nothing seemed to bother him. Even when I did something like accidentally wash a pen with his uniforms, leaving blue splotches on everything, he didn't get mad about it. He'd just make a joke and move on even though I knew it must have frustrated him.

We'd begun to make plans for the future. He was trying to decide whether he should re-enlist in the Army, and though I tried not to sway him in either direction, I was terrified for him to leave on a deployment. I needed him here with me, not in danger halfway around the world. I couldn't imagine having our baby without him there. If I was being completely honest, I couldn't even imagine going a day without seeing him. He'd become as necessary to me as breathing.

We agreed that no matter what he chose to do, we'd keep our apartment at least until I graduated in June. After I had my degree, I'd have a lot of options career-wise, and I could find a management job anywhere once the baby was old enough to go to day care. Alex was a little more limited in his job choices, which was why we'd started discussing what he'd do when his career in the Army came to an end.

He hadn't made a final decision, but I had a feeling that Alex was leaning toward getting out of the military and moving back to Oregon to be near his family and join the family business. I tried to stay neutral when we discussed the pros and cons of moving to Oregon, but I was pretty sure he saw right through me. I loved the idea of raising our child surrounded by aunts, uncles, and cousins.

It was kind of crazy, especially for someone who'd started making five-year plans when she was sixteen, but I hadn't really thought very far into the future when we'd gotten married. I'd been concerned only with the immediate changes in our lives. Now I couldn't stop planning for our future, even when I was supposed to be focusing on other things.

"Do you think if we lived near your parents, your mom could keep the baby while I worked?" I asked, looking up from the paper I was writing. I'd thought that Alex would be a distraction, but I'd had no idea how a baby would completely shift my focus. I was learning to deal with the constant bombardment of thoughts that didn't have anything to do with what I was working on, but it still drove me a little crazy.

"You're supposed to be writing," Alex replied, pulling his headset off and pausing the video game he was playing.

"I know, but I was just thinking that we'll have to find childcare," I said, leaning back and stretching my arms above my head. Alex had been right—I did hunch over my keyboard. "But we don't know anyone here."

"That's a long way off," he said.

"I'm a planner," I replied. "It's what I do."

"Yes," he said. "If we lived near them, my mom would love to keep the baby while you work. She kept Arie for Ani and Bram while Ani was still working."

"So that's a mark in the pro column," I murmured to myself.

"You want me to get out of the Army?" he asked, setting his controller down. "I need to make the decision soon."

"I'm not making that decision for you," I replied.

"But you're making pro/con lists?"

"Just a running tally in my head," I confessed.

"Well, let's hear it."

I looked at him closely, making sure he really wanted to hear it before I spoke.

"Cons," I said, saving my work and then closing my laptop. "You have really good health insurance. You've been in the Army for a long time already, and it would be a shame to stop now when the retirement benefits are so good."

"I'm only about halfway to retirement," he said. "That's a long time to be a military wife."

I nodded in agreement. "Also, if you get out now, you'll still be living in Missouri until I graduate, and we can't survive on one income." I'd barely been surviving on my single income; there was no way I could pay his bills, too. "Plus, your health insurance is so much better than mine."

"I'm not staying home while you work," he said, shaking his head. "I'll find something. What are your pros?"

"Pros are that you wouldn't deploy." I sighed. "We could move near your family. You could work in your family business with your brother, which I know you'll love."

"I don't know about that," Alex joked. "Bram's a pain in the ass."

"Your mom could keep the baby while I work," I continued. "We could buy a house. We wouldn't have to move from place to place."

"Are you worried about that?" he asked softly.

"Not yet," I replied. "But eventually the baby will be in school and making friends."

"Lots of military kids do just fine," he said.

"And we'll make it work, of course," I replied quickly. "These are just on the pro/con list."

"Fair enough."

"There are arguments for both decisions," I said, setting my laptop down on the coffee table so I could scoot into the spot next to him. He wrapped an arm around my shoulder and pulled me against his side. "It needs to be your decision. What do *you* want to do?"

He took a deep breath and exhaled loudly. "I want to get out."

"Really?" I glanced up at his face to see if there was any indecision in his expression, but found a smile.

"Yeah." He shrugged. "I've done my part. I'm at the point now where I want to be home with you. I want to have a nine-to-five job that I can leave at the end of the day. You know, be able to coach baseball and all that shit."

"Baseball?" I wrinkled my nose. What a boring sport.

"Yeah." He gave me a squeeze.

"Okay," I replied with a sigh, like the thought was depressing.

"And I can come home to you every night," he murmured, pushing me gently until I was lying on the couch. He hovered over me, his lips almost touching mine. "And we can leave the kids with my parents and go have sex in the woods."

"Kids, plural?" I asked with a little laugh.

"Hell, if we're going to have one, we might as well give her a couple of siblings," he said, grinning huge.

"Let's see how we feel after this one," I replied.

"Anything you want," he said, brushing his lips against mine. "I'll give you everything."

"In that case, I'd like a pony," I said in mock seriousness. His chest rumbled with a barely repressed laugh.

"I can make that happen." He leaned down and kissed my chin, then smoothed his lips down my throat. "Any other requests?"

"I want a house," I said, since we were dreaming now, wrapped around each other in our warm home while the wind blew outside. Nothing could touch us here in our little piece of the world. "Only one floor, but with plenty of bedrooms."

"A ranch," he said.

"No, I was joking about the pony," I whispered.

"No, that's the style of house you're talking about. It's called a ranch style."

"Oh." I closed my eyes as his lips tugged on my earlobe, then kissed the sensitive spot just behind it. "And I want a garden with lots of flowers and food that we can go out and pick in the summer."

"That sounds perfect," he whispered in my ear.

As he tugged my shirt over my head and ran his fingers gently over my belly, I thought that life couldn't get much better than it was right then. It was beginning to look like the best things in my life had been the things I hadn't planned for.

CHAPTER 15

ALEX

You never see the big stuff coming, not really. You may think you've prepared, you may think you know what's next, but life has a way of slapping the smug look off your face at regular intervals. Sometimes it's a love tap, like when you've filled your gas tank the night before, but your car gets a flat on the way to work. Other times, the slap damn near knocks you out.

"You should have told them to come tomorrow," Sarai scolded, leaning toward the mirror as she put lipstick on. "We'll have to leave the party early."

"That's what I was hoping for," I replied, stepping out of the shower. "This way we have an excuse for leaving."

My family hadn't taken the news that we were staying in Missouri for Christmas very well. They'd been understanding because that's the way they were, but my mom hadn't been able to hide her disappointment. The next day,

Ani had called to let us know that she, Bram, and Arie were flying to Missouri to spend the holiday with us. I think her exact words had been "Buy an air mattress, asshat—we're coming to you." Since none of the kids would be in Oregon, my parents had decided to fly down and spend the holiday with my sister's family in San Diego.

"You picked up the white-elephant gifts?" Sarai asked for the fifth time that morning.

"They're in the truck," I replied as she walked out of the room. "I even put them in gift bags."

I was trying to snap myself out of the pissy mood I'd been in, but it wasn't working. When I'd let my commanding officer know that I wasn't going to be re-enlisting, I'd gotten a lecture about priorities with a heavy dose of guilt trip thrown in. I understood the sentiment, and I knew he'd been counting on me, but I wasn't going to change my mind. My priorities had shifted. Unfortunately, the whole thing had left a bad taste in my mouth, and I couldn't seem to shake it.

Sarai was blending a smoothie when I walked out of our bedroom, fully dressed and ready to go.

"I'm going to eat and brush my teeth, and then we can leave," she said, ignoring my comment. "Do you want some?"

I looked at the green slime she was pouring into her glass. "No thanks."

"It's just green because of the kale," she said. "You can't even taste it."

Before I could reply, her phone rang, interrupting us. She reached for it and accidentally knocked over the blender, sending pureed fruit flying across the countertop.

"Shit," she hissed, bringing the phone to her ear. "Hello?"

I wasn't really paying attention to her conversation as we both tried to mop up the mess, but when she went still beside me, the hair on the back of my neck stood up.

"Of course," she murmured, her eyes meeting mine. "We'll be right there."

"What is it?" I asked as she hung up the phone.

"We need to go get Hailey," she said, tossing the towel she'd been using to clean up onto the counter. "Right now."

"What happened?" I asked, following her to the bedroom.

She grabbed her coat and purse from the bed and shook her head. "She said Sean freaked out. He was angry about something—I didn't understand that part, but she said he went nuts. She needs to get out of there."

"You're not going over there if he's acting like a douche," I said, planting myself in our bedroom doorway. "I'll go get her."

"She said he took off," Sarai replied. "He's not there anymore."

"Then why does she need us to come get her?" My mind was racing. I wasn't real excited about walking into a situation that I wasn't sure about, and I damn sure wasn't going to let Sarai anywhere near it.

"She said she's had too much to drink—"

"It's eleven in the morning," I said flatly.

"And?" Sarai asked, pulling on her coat. "I told her I'd come get her."

"Okay," I said, grabbing a coat out of our closet. I knew

I wasn't going to be able to stop her without a fight. "Then let's go."

We were quiet as we drove over to Hailey and Sean's house.

I should have been preparing myself. I should have been paying closer attention to my surroundings as we'd pulled up to their house. I should have planned ahead and thought about worst-case scenarios, but I didn't.

I wasn't prepared when Hailey met us at her front door, her face covered in bruises.

Fury hit me so hard and fast that I took a step backward so I wouldn't scare her. I was going to fucking kill Sean.

"I packed a bag," Hailey said, swallowing hard. She was mumbling like it hurt to speak. "I got most of the important stuff."

She stepped onto the porch without inviting us in.

"Oh, God, Hailey," Sarai murmured, her breath catching on a sob as she reached for her friend. "Are you okay? Your poor face."

"I just want to go, all right?" Hailey replied, shying away from her touch. "Can you drive my car? I'm afraid if I leave it here…" Her voice trailed off.

"Of course," Sarai said, glancing at me. "We can do that. Whatever you need."

"Is there anything else you want me to grab?" I asked Hailey, trying to keep my voice level and calm. She was glancing around like she thought Sean was going to jump out of the bushes, and she didn't need me to lose my shit and scare her even worse.

"No," she said. "Thank you, but no."

"Okay," Sarai said, putting her hand gently on Hailey's arm. "Let's just go."

I took Hailey's bags from her and carried them to her car, stuffing them in the backseat while she and Sarai climbed into the front.

"I'll follow you home," I told Sarai, closing the back door so I could lean in the driver's side.

"Sounds good," she said. She was preoccupied with sliding the seat up so she could reach the pedals, so I closed the door without kissing her. It was raining and I didn't want her to get wet, but I should have kissed her.

I climbed in my truck and started it up as Sarai backed out of the driveway. Putting the truck in reverse, I turned to look out the back window with one arm over the passenger seat.

The tail end of Hailey's car pulled out into the quiet street, and I watched in horror as a truck going twice as fast as it should have been plowed into the driver's side. My heart stopped as the car spun in a wild circle and the sound of crunching metal and breaking glass filled the air. It happened so fucking fast.

Later, I wouldn't remember putting the truck in park or running toward the accident, but I must have done both. I also wouldn't remember reaching through the driver's-side window to unlock the door so I could get to Sarai, but the long cuts on my forearms from broken glass would prove I did that, too.

Someone called 9-1-1, but it wasn't me. Someone pulled Hailey out of the car, but it wasn't me. Someone also tackled Sean to the ground as he tried to run away from the scene, but that wasn't me, either.

I was too busy trying to wake Sarai up and yelling at any-one who tried to touch or move her.

"You're okay," I said, using my pocket knife to rip a hole in the airbag so it would deflate faster. "Sarai, sweetheart, you're okay."

Her wrist was bent at a weird angle, but I tried not to fo-cus on it as I checked the other parts of her body. She had a goose egg on the side of her forehead where it must have hit the window, and it looked like her nose was broken, but I couldn't find any other injuries, at least none that were bleeding or noticeable.

"Hey," I said, gently moving her hair away from her face. "Baby, wake up."

She didn't stir.

"Sarai," I said, louder. The rain began to fall harder, and I tried to shield her from it with my body. "Sarai, wake up."

"Dad?" she groaned, breaking my heart in two. She went to lift her hand to her face, then cried out in agony.

"Don't move, sweetheart," I ordered, my voice cracking. "Don't move. The ambulance is coming." Someone had to have called, right? Why couldn't I hear sirens yet?

"Alex," she said, her dazed eyes meeting mine. "My face."

"Just a bump," I assured her. Was I crying? I couldn't tell with the rain running down my face.

"Hurts," she mumbled, her eyes filling with tears.

"I know," I choked out. "It's okay. We'll get you all fixed up, okay? You're good, baby. You're fine."

"Get me out," she said, panicking as she finally realized where she was. "Get me out of here."

"We just have to wait a couple more minutes," I said, holding her still as she tried to shift out of her seat. "Stay right there, okay? Don't move yet."

"Why?" she asked, her breathing turning frantic. "Why?" Her eyes scanned the crowd around us as she began to sob.

"You were in an accident," I said, putting my face near hers. "You're okay."

"Get me out," she said again. "Get me out. Get me out."

"You have to stay still until the paramedics get here."

"Alex," she said, the fear in her voice almost bringing me to my knees. "Get me out of here."

"Sir," a voice said behind me. "Please step back."

"Fuck off," I replied, shrugging off the hand on my shoulder.

"Sir, you have to let us help." There was something about his tone, or maybe the firm way his hand met my shoulder again, that got my attention.

I turned my head to find a fireman and a paramedic standing side by side, waiting for me to move. I took a step back, making Sarai call out my name in a panic.

"It's okay," I told her, moving back just enough to let them reach her but staying close enough that she could still see me. "They're going to help you."

It seemed like it took hours for them to get her out of the car, but it must have been only minutes. I hated the way they moved with calm efficiency. Didn't they realize that she was my life? Why were they moving so slowly?

I let them speak to Sarai, calming her down in a way that I hadn't been able to. I took a step back as they helped her out of the car, but when she sat down on the stretcher so they could buckle her in, I lost all feeling in my legs.

I'd been to war. I'd seen things that would never leave me, things that had given me nightmares, things that I wouldn't wish on my worst enemy. I'd lived through them and done my best to move past them. But nothing in my life had prepared me for the sight of the blood covering the back of Sarai's light-gray pants.

"She's pregnant," I choked out as my knees hit the pavement. "My wife's pregnant."

* * *

"You did a number on these," the doctor said as he added another stitch to my arm. "When I'm finished with this one, I'm also going to put a couple in the cut near your elbow."

"Do what you need to do, Doc," I murmured, staring into the hallway. After we arrived in the ambulance, they'd tried to put Sarai and me in separate rooms. When I finally convinced them that I wasn't leaving her side, they'd agreed to let me get fixed up in her room while they took her away for some tests.

She'd been gone for thirty minutes already.

"You're going to need to keep these clean," he droned on. "So they don't get infected."

I didn't bother to reply. My mind had wandered back to the scene of the accident.

As I'd gotten to my feet again, I'd heard Sean screaming at Hailey.

"You thought you were gonna leave me? You stupid bitch."

A three-hundred-pound police officer had pulled me off of him, but not until after I'd broken his jaw. I was damn lucky that they hadn't arrested me but instead had shoved me toward the ambulance so I could ride to the hospital with Sarai.

"Your wife should be back soon," the doctor said as he started cleaning up his tools. I guessed he was finished patching me up. I hadn't even realized when he'd started on the cut by my elbow. "They'll bring her right back here when she's done."

I nodded. I wasn't even sure what tests they were running. I knew they wanted to check her head and x-ray her arm, but no one had said anything about the baby yet. I knew deep in my gut what they'd say, though. The amount of blood I'd seen…I shook my head to clear it. I'd wait until the doctors gave me some answers.

My phone rang as I pushed myself up off the chair.

"Hey, dipshit," Bram said. "Where are you?"

I cursed and looked at the clock. We were supposed to pick Bram, Ani, and Arie up fifteen minutes ago. Goddamn it, we'd already been at the hospital for hours. Where the hell was my wife?

"I'm at the hospital with Sarai," I said, rubbing my forehead. "I'm sorry."

"What?" Bram asked worriedly. "What happened? Is she okay?"

I could hear Ani in the background asking the same questions.

"There was an accident."

"What kind of accident?"

"Car accident," I said, my voice wobbling. "She was backing out, and a truck hit her doing forty on a residential street."

"The fuck?" Bram snapped angrily.

"It was bad," I said. I cleared my throat. "She's going to be okay, but we'll be here for a while."

"No problem," he said. "We'll rent a car."

"I'm sorry, man," I said with a sigh. "I didn't even think to call you."

"Shut the fuck up," Bram replied. "You've got bigger things to worry about."

"There was a lot of blood, Bram," I said, my voice breaking. "I don't think the baby—"

"I'm on my way," he replied. "Which hospital?"

I gave him the name of the hospital and hung up just as I saw Sarai being wheeled down the hallway.

"Hey," I said, stepping aside so they could push her bed into the room. "How're you feeling?"

"My head hurts," she said softly, reaching out to grab my hand.

"I bet," I said, leaning down to brush my lips against hers. Her hair was still damp from the rain, and I pushed it away from her face. "You've got quite the goose egg."

"They fixed my nose," she said. "Can you tell?"

I leaned back and tilted my head to the side. "Is it supposed to still be crooked?" I joked. I chuckled hollowly as she rolled her eyes.

"It hurt when they did it," she said as the nurse fixed her IV and plugged in her monitors. "But afterward, it felt a lot better."

"They should've waited until I was with you," I said.

"You would have been a nervous wreck," she replied. "It was better that you weren't there."

"That's not true."

"You almost punched the paramedic when he started my IV."

"Remember that, do you?" I asked, giving her a small smile as I sat in the chair next to her.

"It left an impression," she replied.

We stopped talking when the doctor came into the room. He was very matter-of-fact while he explained all her injuries. Her wrist was splinted for now, but they'd have to do surgery to set it. She had a mild concussion. Then I watched as his entire demeanor changed.

"I'm so sorry," he murmured. "But the trauma of the accident has caused you to miscarry."

Sarai froze.

"We're going to keep an eye on things here," the doctor said. He continued speaking, but I blocked him out.

I stared at the gray-flecked linoleum under my feet, trying to control my breathing as he went on and on. Didn't he realize that we didn't care what he was saying? Neither of us was paying any attention while he spouted medical terms and tried to explain something that didn't make any goddamn sense.

I lifted my head when I heard his footsteps leave the room.

"Sarai," I said quietly, trying to get her attention. "Sweetheart?"

She ignored me. Her face was pale as she stared at the empty doorway, the bruises under her eyes and along the side of her forehead becoming more apparent by the minute. She began to tremble as her fingers tightened painfully around mine, and then quietly she began to moan.

The sound was like nothing I'd ever heard before.

She gasped, and then the sound came again, deeper than before, almost animalistic.

"Shh," I murmured, coming to my feet. "It's okay," I lied. I wasn't sure what else to say.

Her breathing sped up, and the long moans turned to rapid-fire gasping and moaning. It terrified me. She shut her eyes tight, and suddenly a loud sob burst out of her mouth.

"Shh," I whispered, leaning over her and pressing my cheek to hers. Our fingers were still entwined against the scratchy sheets. "It's okay. It's okay."

My words had no impact, but I hadn't expected that they would. They didn't mean anything. Nothing I could say in that moment would mean a goddamn thing. There was nothing I could do for her, nothing I could fix.

"I didn't want it," she said through gritted teeth, her voice so low I barely heard her. "I didn't want it."

I jerked in surprise but didn't move my cheek from hers.

"I was worried about school, and I didn't want it."

"Yes you did," I said finally. "You were just surprised."

"And now it's gone," she said, ignoring my words. "What did I do?"

"You didn't do anything," I argued, my chest so tight that I was having a hard time drawing a breath. "This isn't your fault."

"I didn't want it, and now it's gone," she wailed.

"No," I said into her ear. "No."

"It's gone, Alex," she said with a sob. "Our baby is gone."

"I know, sweetheart," I whispered back, my voice catching on a sob.

I'd never understood pain before. I realized that as Sarai continued to tell me over and over again that our baby was gone.

The nurses gave us privacy for a while, but before long they came quietly back into the room. I dropped into the chair, and Sarai stared blankly at the ceiling, tears rolling down the sides of her face as they lifted the blankets and checked the pad they'd placed under her. I nearly vomited when they slid the pad out from under her and I saw the blood before they quickly wadded it up and threw it in the trash.

Somewhere in that bloody pad or the clothes they'd stripped off her in the ambulance was our child, too small to see even though I'd heard her heartbeat.

The nurses were efficient and kind, and they had Sarai quickly tucked into bed again, but I couldn't forget that bloody pad. I stared at the trash bin marked BIOHAZARD as they left the room again.

"Knock, knock," a quiet voice called from the hallway. I looked up to find Ani's concerned face peeking around the doorjamb. "Can I come in?"

I looked over at Sarai, and she nodded.

"Hey," Ani said, hugging me as I got to my feet. "How are you guys doing?"

"Shitty," I murmured with a sigh.

"The baby?" she asked quietly.

I shook my head as I let her go.

"Goddamn it," she whispered. Turning to Sarai, she gave her a gentle smile. "Hey, Rocky, nice shiner."

"Hi, Ani," Sarai replied. Her lips trembled. "Sorry we didn't pick you up."

"Shut it," Ani said with a wave of her hand. She leaned against the bed and awkwardly grabbed Sarai's good hand, giving it a squeeze. "How're you holding up?"

"Okay," Sarai said. The word came out warbly and soft.

"Bullshit," Ani said, leaning forward. "I'm going to hug you, but I'll be really careful."

As Ani wrapped an arm around Sarai, my wife started to cry in big body-shaking sobs. I took a step forward to intervene but stopped when I saw the way Sarai's hand had fisted in the back of Ani's shirt. Ani murmured to Sarai as I stepped quietly out of the room.

I found Bram and Arie in the emergency room waiting area. The baby was asleep for once, bundled up in her car seat, and as I walked toward my brother, he got to his feet. He met me halfway in a hug so tight I felt my spine pop.

"How's Sarai?" he asked, still holding on to me.

"Not good," I replied hoarsely.

"Awake, though, yeah?" he said, his hand patting my back in the way my dad had always hugged us as kids. "She's gonna be okay."

"Yeah." I nodded, my chin knocking into his shoulder. "She's awake."

"The baby?" Bram asked.

I shook my head.

"Aw, man," he said with a sigh. "I'm sorry, brother."

"Me too," I ground out. I let go of him and stepped back. "It could've been way worse," I said, rubbing a hand over my face. "We got lucky."

"Don't do that," Bram said. "You don't have to do that."

"Do what?"

"Pretend like you're feeling lucky," Bram said flatly.

I scoffed.

"There's nothing wrong with being upset," Bram said, his eyes boring into mine.

"I know that."

"Okay." He let it go, but I could tell that he was itching to say something else by the way his jaw flexed. "So what happened?"

I followed him to the chairs lining the wall and sat next to him, with Arie at our feet. I stared at my niece for a moment, thinking about all the things I was never going to do with my daughter or son, then shook my head and looked back at Bram.

"We went to pick up Sarai's friend Hailey because her boyfriend beat the shit out of her—"

"Motherfucker," Bram muttered. I nodded.

"Sarai was going to drive Hailey to our place, and I was following in my truck." I paused and took a deep breath, remembering those horrible few seconds when I'd seen Sean's truck barreling toward Hailey's car. "They were backing out of the driveway, and I was in my truck, ready to follow them, when Hailey's boyfriend rammed his truck into the driver's side."

"Deliberate?" Bram asked in surprise.

"Didn't even slow down," I confirmed. "Sped up, even. He

hit the back fender and back door, thank God, but he hit it hard."

"Son of a bitch."

"Yeah." I stared at the floor. "Thankfully, the entire neighborhood came out to help, and someone called 9-1-1 because I was too busy trying to get to Sarai."

"That how you fucked up your arms?" he asked, gesturing to my bandages.

"Cut them on the window," I replied. "Trying to get the door unlocked."

"They arrest the boyfriend?" Bram asked, leaning forward to rest his elbows on his knees.

"Yeah, but not before I broke his jaw."

"Good man," he murmured.

"He works with me," I said, making Bram whistle through his teeth. "He'll be court-martialed."

"Military prison, hoorah," Bram said, his lips twitching.

"Less than what he deserves," I muttered.

"No kidding."

Ani walked through the door and looked around the room, then headed toward us. "Hey, the doctors are wanting to do surgery," she said. "You might want to get back there."

"Her wrist?" I asked, getting to my feet.

"I think so," she replied.

"I—" I glanced around helplessly.

"Just go. We'll wait out here."

"I don't know how long I'll be—"

"Go," Bram said. "We'll wait."

I nodded and jogged back toward Sarai's room.

* * *

"Alex," Hailey called, hurrying toward me as I waited for Sarai to get out of surgery that night. "Is she okay?"

I winced as I met her eyes. The bruises on her face had gotten worse, and her jaw looked painfully swollen.

"She's okay," I rasped, getting to my feet.

"Oh, thank God," she whispered, coming to a stop. "I was so worried. They took me to a different hospital. Where is she?"

"Her wrist is broken, so they're doing surgery to set it."

Hailey's lips trembled as she nodded. "What about her face?" she asked. "I saw her in the car. I saw—there was something wrong."

"She broke her nose, and she's also got a concussion." I took a shuddering breath. "And she lost the baby."

"No." Her hands flew up to cover her mouth, and her eyes filled with tears. "Oh, God. I'm so sorry."

"It's not your fault."

"I shouldn't have called you," she said, shaking her head. "I shouldn't have pulled you into my mess."

"No," I said, cutting her off. "You needed help and you asked for it. That's exactly what you should've done."

I could tell she didn't believe me, but she didn't argue. For a while she sat beside me while I waited, but I could tell she was in pain. Between the beating she'd taken and the car accident afterward, she should've been in bed. After a while, she reluctantly left with a promise to call Sarai.

* * *

They discharged Sarai the next morning. Bram and Ani had driven over to Sean's place to pick up my truck and left it at the hospital for me so we'd have a way home, and they were waiting for us as Sarai shuffled through the doorway to our apartment.

"Let's get you into bed," Ani said, immediately taking over. She must have seen how completely overwhelmed I felt. I'd been trained in rudimentary field medicine, but I wasn't a doctor. How the hell did they expect me to watch over Sarai when I wasn't even sure what I was supposed to be watching for?

"How's she doing?" Bram asked as he followed me into the kitchen.

"She's tired," I said. I looked around the room. Ani must have cleaned up the spilled smoothie that we'd left in our rush to get to Hailey.

"Her wrist bothering her?" he asked, sitting down at the counter.

"No," I replied. "They gave her some good pain meds."

I wasn't sure if it was a curse or a blessing that we hadn't started buying anything for the baby yet. I knew it would have hurt to have the reminders around the apartment, but I thought that not having anything felt worse. It was as if he or she had never existed.

"Where you at?" Bram asked, waving a hand in front of my face.

"I'm fine," I muttered, running a hand down the back of my neck. "Tired."

"Why don't you go take a nap?" he suggested. "Ani and I will take care of dinner tonight."

"You sure?"

"Yep. Give me the name of that restaurant you guys like, and I'll pick something up."

I told him how to get to Mr. and Mrs. K's restaurant, then made my way into the bedroom. By the time I got there, Ani had already helped Sarai get into a pair of pajamas and was sitting next to her on the bed.

"Room for me?" I asked, kicking off my shoes.

"Change your clothes first," Ani ordered.

I looked down at myself and realized that there was blood all over me. Suddenly I felt grimy as hell, but I was too exhausted to take a shower.

"I'll strip," I said tiredly, pulling my shirt over my head. "Once you get out."

"They're always kicking me out," Ani told Sarai, giving her a small smile. "Like they've got anything I'd want to see."

"You've seen it all," I said. "Bram and I are identical. Now scoot."

"You sound like your mother," Ani bickered, rounding the bed. "And you and your brother definitely aren't identical."

"Close enough," I muttered as she left the room, closing the door behind her.

Sarai closed her eyes as I pulled my pants and socks off, and she didn't move as I climbed into bed beside her.

"Do you need anything?" I asked, pulling the blankets up to her shoulder.

"Just sleep," she said dully.

I watched her as her breathing slowed and finally evened out, but I couldn't fall asleep. Since the moment she'd gotten back from surgery the night before, something had been off. It was like she'd shut down. There weren't any more tears, but there wasn't any conversation, either. She barely said a word even when I asked her direct questions.

She'd completely closed herself off from me.

CHAPTER 16

SARAI

I woke up from my nap to the sound of voices in the living room. Alex wasn't in bed beside me anymore, and I let out a little sigh of relief. I didn't know what to say to him. I didn't know what to say to anyone, really, but it was worse with him.

The last twenty-four hours felt so unreal. I didn't understand any of it. I'd known that Sean was an asshole, but I never could've predicted how crazy he'd turned out to be.

I slid my hand over my stomach and stared at the ceiling.

"You're awake," Ani said, peeking around the door.

"Yes," I said, using my good arm to push myself up.

"You've got someone out here who wants to see you," she said. "Do you want to stay in here or come out?"

"I'll come out," I replied, wondering who it could be.

The sky had darkened while I'd slept, and rain dripped down the window, making me shudder. I lifted a hand to my hair, expecting it to feel wet, then remembered that it had dried overnight at the hospital.

"You have a robe?" Ani asked, coming into the room. She opened my closet and found what she was looking for, then helped me put it on.

Ani was pushy. She didn't wait for my permission, just waded in and did what she thought was best. For some reason, though, I liked it. I didn't have to worry about her feelings or try to make her comfortable; I just had to let her have her way, which was fine with me. There was no pressure to do or say the right thing.

I followed her out of the room, trying to ignore the pad that bunched and moved with each step. Every time it rubbed against my skin, it was a reminder of what I'd lost, like someone tapping on my shoulder to point it out.

"Mom wants to know if you want her to come," I heard Bram say as we neared the kitchen.

"Tell her thanks, but no," Alex replied. "I think Sarai has enough company for now."

"She wants to check on you, too," Bram said.

"I'm fine," Alex said firmly.

Well, I was glad that one of us was.

"Sarai," a familiar voice said as I rounded the corner.

Mrs. K moved across the room and met me in the middle, her arms coming around my body in a surprisingly tight hug. Her head barely reached my shoulder—she was so tiny—but the familiar smell of her perfume was instantly comforting, and I sagged against her.

"Well now," she murmured, reaching up to smooth my hair. "Well now, it's all right."

I shuddered, but no tears came. My eyes had been dry since I'd woken up from surgery, no matter what thoughts bombarded me. I didn't know what was wrong with me.

"I brought you some dinner," she said, pulling back from our hug. "Sit, sit."

She ushered me to the table and sat me down. For the next hour, I ate what Mrs. K put in front of me and stared into space, letting the conversation flow around me.

"Mrs. K," I said, putting my hand on hers as she tried to take my plate. "You don't have to take care of me."

"Papa is enjoying the time to himself," she said, nudging me with her arm. "So he can sneak a TV dinner he thinks I don't know about."

I smiled for her benefit, but exhaustion was starting to weigh me down. I didn't want to talk to anyone or see anyone, and the sound of little Arie babbling was starting to really bother me. My baby would never do that. She'd never keep me up at night or cry for me or lay her head on my shoulder the way Arie was lying on Ani. She'd never do anything.

I stood from the table as Mrs. K walked toward the sink, and the conversation around me stopped.

"What do you need?" Alex asked, coming to my side, his hands out in front of him as if I were going to fall over or something.

"Just tired," I replied, never meeting his eyes. "I'm going to go back to sleep."

I shuffled back into our room and crawled into bed, leaving my robe on as I pulled the blankets up around my shoulders. I stared at my cast as I lay there, running my fingers over the ridges and the smooth cotton that peeked out near my thumb. I'd never broken a bone before, not even a finger. My dad had called me Gumby because he'd said that my bones must have been able to bend, considering the number of times I'd fallen out of trees and crashed my bike as a child.

I missed them so much. My mom would know what to say right now. She'd know exactly what to do. *Please take care of her, Mama*, I thought, sending it out into the universe. *Love her until I get there.*

It hadn't been a good idea to come back to Missouri. In hindsight, I realized that it wasn't where I wanted to be. I'd wanted to somehow bring back the feeling I'd had when my parents were alive, but I'd never found it. Twice now, this place had completely shattered my life, and I was left trying to find all the pieces.

If I closed my eyes tight enough, I could almost imagine that I was somewhere else, somewhere that didn't constantly bombard me with bad memories.

* * *

The next few days went by in a fog of prescription pain medication and lack of interest on my part. Alex and his brother put up a Christmas tree, and I sat in the living room to open presents before going back to bed. Even Arie's excitement wasn't enough to hold my attention.

Hailey showed up to visit, unharmed from the accident, and I could barely look at her. I knew that none of this was her fault. I *knew* that. But it was still so goddamn unfair that she'd somehow come out of it all unscathed, but my world had been shattered.

I existed. Nine days after the accident, after Bram's family had flown back to Oregon and I'd gotten the okay from my doctor, I went back to work and school. Just like that, as if nothing had changed.

I studied and I did my job, but nothing and no one could pull me out of the fog. I just didn't care. My drive was gone, and I couldn't seem to get it back.

I barely spoke to Alex, and after I'd flinched away from him enough, I was glad when he'd finally stopped trying to touch me. I didn't want to talk to him. I didn't want him to keep bothering me. Couldn't he see that I was holding everything together by a thread? Why did he always have to *push*? Why couldn't I just be left alone to heal?

"I don't know how to help you," he finally said, standing in the doorway of our bathroom as I pulled the plastic bag off my cast. I knew I'd locked the door before I'd gotten into the shower, and I glared when I realized he must have broken in somehow.

"I don't need your help," I replied, stepping into my underwear. I'd finally stopped bleeding.

"You need something," he said, frustration making his words heavy and painful. "You barely talk. You barely leave the house."

"I go to work every day," I said calmly, brushing off his concern. He didn't know how hard it was for me to even sit in the driver's seat of my car.

"You don't talk to *me*," he said. "Maybe you should see someone. If you can't talk to me, maybe you could talk to a doctor."

"I'm fine," I replied. "I don't need to talk to a shrink."

Ignoring the sadness in his eyes, I edged around him and walked back to our room. I couldn't take on his sadness. Didn't he see that? I was barely functioning with my own. I went to bed and didn't wake up until the next afternoon.

My husband continued to talk to me, telling me random things about his day, what his mom had told him on the phone, and whatever food he'd brought for dinner, but he didn't expect responses, and I didn't give him any. His last day in the Army was the following week, and even though I knew that the change was going to be difficult for him, I didn't bring it up. I didn't initiate any conversations anymore. I didn't go to his going-away party, either.

I'd curled into myself like a potato bug, hiding all my soft parts behind a hard outer shell. It was the only way I could make it through each day. I knew how bad I was hurting Alex; I could feel it chipping at me a little more each time we spoke, but I couldn't seem to stop. He was so good, so steady and strong, that I was afraid that the minute I let him back in, I'd completely fall apart because I knew he'd be there to catch me. I couldn't let that happen. I was terrified to let go of my tightly held emotions.

It was two and a half weeks postaccident when the quiet little world I'd built was flipped on its axis. I woke up midafternoon to voices I knew very well.

"Sarai Levy," my aunt scolded as she strode into my room. "Get out of bed." She went to the window and opened the curtains wide.

"No," I murmured, pulling a pillow over my head.

I hadn't seen my aunt and uncle in person for over a year, and I hadn't seen them on a computer screen in months, but

I felt nothing. Blankness. I wasn't sad or happy, excited or disappointed. I was just existing.

"Sarai," my aunt said softly, realizing that her scolding had no effect. She crawled onto my bed and lay down so that our faces were level. "I've missed you so much."

I let that sink in for a moment, trying to find some relief that my aunt was just inches away and that she had finally forgiven me, but there was nothing. She'd abandoned me for months because she'd been angry; the fact that she'd shown up because of the accident seemed hypocritical. She hadn't been happy about Alex or the baby anyway, so why was she trying to comfort me when she'd gotten what she wanted?

"Missed you, too," I replied honestly. "Poor timing for a visit, though." I wasn't ready to give her more than that. My trust was gone.

"I'm sorry for how I reacted when you told me you'd gotten married," she said softly, brushing her fingers through my hair. "And when you told us about the baby. But I'm here now." She paused, waiting for a response that I refused to give her. "God has a plan, Sarai," she said. "You'll have more children. Later, when you're ready."

My whole body went hot as I opened my eyes. No. She didn't get to act as if this were all part of a big plan, like my child had been a mistake. "God didn't kill my child," I replied flatly. "A man did. He's currently rotting in a military jail for it."

"I didn't mean—"

"I know what you meant," I said, cutting her off.

"I'm so sorry," she said, sighing as she ran her fingers along the cast covering my wrist, like she could heal the bone beneath it with just her touch. "I'm not sure what to say."

"Don't say anything," I muttered, closing my eyes again. "There's nothing to say."

She was quiet for a while, and I felt sleep pulling me under again.

"Your uncle is here, too. He's in the kitchen with your husband." My heart gave a weak thump at her use of the word. At least she'd acknowledged our marriage.

"Good," I replied. For the first time in a while, I felt something resembling hope. Maybe if they spent some time with him, they'd grow to love him like I did.

"Aren't you going to go out and save him?" she teased.

"No," I said easily. "Alex can take care of himself."

* * *

I sat at the table later that night, picking at my food while my aunt and uncle tried to pull me into their conversation. I responded when I was supposed to and asked for clarification when I knew I should, but they must have known that I had no interest in hearing stories about the people I used to know. New York felt so far away now, like an alien planet.

"Maybe you should come home with us," my aunt said. "Stay for a while."

"Adinah," my uncle said firmly, cutting her off.

"New York isn't home anymore," I replied, not looking up from my meal.

"Of course," my aunt said. "I just thought maybe some time away would help."

"Well, it wouldn't," I snapped. I glanced at Alex. Did he

realize what she was doing? Did he understand the implication of her words? She hadn't invited us both.

"Sarai only has a few months of school left," Alex said easily. My uncle and aunt didn't notice the way his jaw flexed as he gritted his teeth, but I did. "Maybe we could come for a visit after she graduates."

My aunt bristled. "Do you speak for my niece now?"

"Adinah," Uncle Isaac bit out. "That's enough."

"No," Alex said, his hand finding my thigh beneath the table. "Sarai is more than capable of speaking for herself. It was just a suggestion."

"I'm sorry," Aunt Adinah murmured. She straightened her shoulders. "That was rude of me."

"Well, if you can't be rude to family," Alex said, extending an olive branch, "who can you be rude to?"

Aunt Adinah smiled slightly. "Is your family rude, then?" she asked almost teasingly. I felt my shoulders slowly relax.

"No," Alex said, shaking his head as he went back to his food. "Well, my sister-in-law is borderline rude."

"That's not true," I interrupted. I looked over to my aunt. "Ani's just very outspoken."

"She says whatever pops into her head, and damn the consequences," Alex continued. "Once, she yelled at a guy wearing expensive shoes because he ignored a homeless man panhandling on the street." He shook his head. "The guy turned out to be the person she was supposed to be meeting for an interview." He paused. "She didn't get the job."

I could imagine Ani doing that. My lips twitched, and Alex caught it, smiling back at me.

"She also used to tell people that I didn't understand English," Alex said, still looking at me. "So I'd have random people speaking to me in Spanish—which I don't understand."

A laugh escaped my lips before I could stop it.

"I bet that was uncomfortable," Uncle Isaac said wryly, looking back and forth between us.

"Yeah," Alex said, looking back down at his food. "Ani enjoys that type of thing. She thinks it's funny."

"Sarai had a friend like that," my aunt said, joining the conversation. "What was her name?"

"Mary," I replied.

"Right. Mary. She married the Rebenowitz boy last year. Did I tell you that, Sarai?"

Of course she had. She'd given me details of the wedding, the reception, and Mary's new apartment when she'd been trying to convince me to come back to New York after graduation. Our family had gotten an invitation, but, I hadn't been able to go.

"She's pregnant now," my aunt said, making a knot form deep in my belly. "A little boy."

"That's nice," I choked out.

"Adinah, enough," my uncle practically hissed.

Aunt Adinah's head shot up, and she met my eyes from across the table. "I'm sorry," she said, shaking her head. "I didn't mean to—"

"It's okay," I murmured.

"How was your Hanukkah?" Alex asked, interrupting us.

"It was good," Uncle Isaac said. "Maybe next year you guys can come to New York and spend it with us."

"We could do that," Alex said, raising his eyebrows questioningly at me. "Maybe?"

"Maybe," I confirmed.

"Passover?" my aunt asked, smiling gently at me. "Then we wouldn't have to wait so long to see you."

"Sure—" Alex began to say before I cut him off.

"Not this year," I corrected with a small shake of my head. "I'll still be in school."

By the time we were done with dinner, I just wanted to crawl back into bed. It had been a long day even with my afternoon nap, and seeing my aunt and uncle was draining. I wished that I felt excited or even happy that they were there, but I didn't. I was searching every word they said for hidden meanings.

Alex was fully capable of handling them himself, and I wasn't really worried that they would hurt his feelings. No, it was embarrassment that had me listening to every inflection and watching every facial expression. The Evans family had welcomed me with open arms, no reservations, and I was afraid that my own family wouldn't extend the same welcome to Alex.

"I'm very tired," I said as Alex began to clean up the dishes. It was rude, and I'd been taught better, but I still left that sentence hanging in the air until my aunt and uncle understood my meaning.

"We should be getting back to the hotel," my uncle said to my aunt finally, while she looked at me in surprise.

"Sleep well," my uncle said, kissing my head. "We'll see you tomorrow."

My aunt was next, and she held me for a long time before speaking. "Sometimes I'm not very good at saying the right thing," she whispered. "But I love you so much."

"I love you, too," I replied as I pulled away.

I turned to walk toward the bedroom, then paused.

"Good night, Alex," I said softly.

"I'll be right behind you," he said, looking over his shoulder as I walked past him. "Just going to finish up here."

I nodded and let my hand touch his back in solidarity, just for a second.

I stripped to my underwear and got into bed, forgoing my nighttime routine. Who cared if my teeth were unbrushed or my face unwashed? I was too tired for it to bother me.

As I settled into bed, I heard Alex and my aunt and uncle talking. I froze when I heard my name, barely breathing as they discussed me as if I were a child.

CHAPTER 17

ALEX

Have you seen her?" Sarai's aunt asked, glaring at me. "She's skin and bones, and she has dark circles"—she gestured to her face—"under her eyes."

"Why do you think I called you?" I asked, leaning against the kitchen counter. "She's a mess."

"Is she still going to school?" her uncle asked, calmer than her aunt but still clearly worried.

"She's still going," I confirmed. "I don't know how well she's doing, though. She used to do a lot more homework than she's doing now."

My stomach sank as I realized how true that statement was. I hadn't seen Sarai do any homework in a long time. As far as I knew, she was still going to class, but when she was home, she almost always went straight to bed.

"We should take her home," her aunt said. "She should heal with her family."

"I *am* her family," I ground out.

I'd done everything I could to help my wife, but nothing seemed to be helping. Calling Sarai's aunt and uncle had been my last resort, and I was pretty sure it had been a mistake.

Sarai's aunt scoffed. "You barely know her," she said condescendingly.

"I'm her husband," I argued.

"A mistake," she replied. "One that is easily fixed."

It took every piece of self-control my parents had instilled in me not to throw them out of my house then and there.

"We're worried," Isaac said, shooting his wife a look. "She doesn't look good. Sleeping all day isn't normal for her."

"I know," I replied, scratching at the hair on my face. I'd let it grow since my last day in the Army, and I already couldn't understand how Bram let his get so long. It itched like crazy.

"Adinah and I are just worried because we can't stay here to watch over her," Isaac said kindly. "I know you're trying your best."

I nodded.

Shortly after, they left for their hotel, and I breathed a sigh of relief. I knew that her aunt and uncle were worried, but I hated that they believed that they knew what was best for Sarai. They acted as if there were a problem between us, like she would get better if they separated us, but I knew that wasn't true. Sarai treated everyone with the same detachment.

I didn't know what to do.

My stomach twisted with anxiety as I opened our bedroom door. Sarai was asleep. I didn't turn on the light as I walked into the dark room, and I ended up tripping over her laptop bag as I moved across the room.

I glanced at Sarai as I lifted the bag and pulled out her laptop. I'd seen her sign into her accounts a thousand times, and it was easy to find her school emails, even though it made me feel like an asshole. Ignoring the guilt that settled in my stomach, I started snooping. I had to know how bad it was.

Scrolling through random updates and announcements, I started to feel a little relieved until I realized she hadn't opened any of them. Near the bottom of the first page was an email from one of her professors. When I opened it, I let out a disappointed breath.

Sarai was falling way behind. She'd been going to classes, but she wasn't turning in her work and her grades were dropping. I ran my hand over my face and read the email again.

"Shit," I breathed as I closed the laptop and stuffed it back in her bag.

I walked back out of the room and closed the door behind me. I was scared. When Sarai snapped out of this depression, she was going to be absolutely devastated. She'd worked so goddamn hard.

I pulled my phone out as I dropped to the couch.

"Hey, Mom," I said when she answered.

"Hi, son," she replied. "Is everything okay?"

"I can't call you on a Wednesday night?"

"You can call me anytime," she said. "You just usually don't. What's wrong? How's Sarai?"

"She's good," I replied automatically. Then I laughed, because trying to hide how depressed my wife had become was completely idiotic. "Actually, she won't get out of bed."

"Oh, Alex," my mom murmured. "I'm sorry. Has she been to the doctor?"

"Yeah, but they don't notice anything wrong, and she won't let me go with her."

"I—" She paused. "Honey, I don't know what advice to give you. I know that counseling helps, seeing a psychologist."

"She won't go. When I brought it up, she brushed me off," I said. "I'm just not sure what to do. I've been applying for jobs, but I haven't found anything yet, so I'm just kind of sitting around the apartment while she goes to work and school. When she's home, she barely talks to me."

"At least she's still going to work and school," my mom said. "That's something."

"I looked through her email account tonight because I realized I hadn't seen her doing homework in a while."

"Alex," Mom scolded. "That's not okay."

"She's falling behind, Mom," I replied, not getting into the ethics discussion. Honestly, I'd snoop and look through everything she owned if I thought it would help. "She might be going to class, but she's not doing any of the work."

"Shit," my mom murmured.

"I think I should just bring her home," I said, the words coming out of nowhere. As soon as I finished speaking, though, I realized how *right* the idea seemed. Sarai's aunt and uncle were leaving in two days, and then it would just be us again, living like a couple of roommates with nothing to say to each other.

I needed to find a way to change things, a way to shock her into living again. And if I was being honest, I needed my family.

"You want to bring her here?" my mom asked.

"Yeah," I replied. "Can we stay with you?"

"Of course," she said. "But before you make any plans, I think you should discuss it with Sarai, son. She might be having a hard time, but that doesn't give you the right to make decisions for her *or* look through her computer."

"I hear you," I mumbled.

"How are you doing, baby?" she asked. "Feeling free as a bird?"

"Kind of bored, actually," I replied, making her laugh. "I'll be happy to find another job."

"And how are you doing with everything else?"

"I'm…" I paused, trying to find the right words. "I'm okay."

"You're *always* okay," she replied. "But how are you really?"

"Mom, really." I scratched at my jaw. "I'm doing okay. Worried about Sarai, but fine otherwise."

"You can talk to me, you know," she said gently.

"I know that."

"Or your brother. You know you can talk to him."

"I know."

"Or your dad," she said hopefully.

"Mom," I replied. "Stop—I get it."

"Well, I'm just saying," she muttered in exasperation.

"I know what you're saying. Thank you, but I'm fine."

We talked for a few more minutes, and I promised her that I'd let her know what we decided to do after I'd talked to Sarai. She was worried, for Sarai and for me. I knew she hated being so far away and was really excited for us to move closer, but she was doubtful that Sarai would agree to the move when she still had months of school left. She hadn't seen my wife lately, though. She had no idea how little Sarai cared about anything.

I dropped my head against the back of the couch and sighed. I'd lied to my mom. Of course I wasn't fine. How could anyone be fine after what we'd gone through? I was fucking devastated. I replayed the scene of the crash over and over, trying to figure out if I could've done something differently. If I'd volunteered to drive Hailey's car, then Sarai would've been safe in my truck. If I'd backed into the road first, maybe I could've blocked Sean from hitting them.

There were a thousand scenarios that didn't end with Sarai losing our baby, and that *killed* me because I couldn't change a goddamn thing. And now I was terrified that I would lose Sarai, too.

* * *

"Are you hungry?" I asked the next morning as Sarai came out of our room ready for work. "I can make you something real quick."

"No thank you," she said, setting her laptop bag on the table. The sight of it reminded me of what I'd found last night, and I glanced at the clock to see how much time I had.

"I want to run something past you," I said. I waited for her to look at me before continuing. It was frustrating as hell when I couldn't tell if she was paying attention or not. "I think we should move."

"To where?" she asked.

"I think we should move to Oregon."

Sarai scoffed.

"Sarai," I said, taking a deep breath. "You're falling behind at school."

"What?"

"I read your emails."

"You got on my laptop?" she asked. She was irritated, but the normal anger I would have encountered for the breach of privacy just wasn't there. Her lack of real emotion grated.

"Yes," I snapped. I knew she was struggling and depressed, but the apathy was hard to endure day after day. "I looked in your emails, and you're going to fucking fail if you don't ask for a leave of absence or something."

Sarai rolled her eyes, and for a split second she looked like the woman I'd married.

"Do you want to completely fail out of that program?" I asked in disbelief.

"You worry about you," she replied dully. "I'll worry about me."

"Goddamn it, Sarai," I sighed.

"Don't swear at me," she replied forcefully. My eyes widened in surprise.

"Then get your head out of your ass," I said, trying my best to provoke her.

"My head is in my ass?" she shot back. My heart raced as she took a step forward. "I'm sorry that you don't seem to feel anything, but I'm having a harder time with all this."

"Me?" I replied dubiously. "You're the one who walks around here like you don't care about a goddamn thing."

"I care," she argued.

"Really? Because from what I can see, you've completely given up since the accident."

"Don't you talk to me about the accident," she spat.

"Why, because I didn't get hurt?" I asked. "Do you have any idea what it was like, trying to get to you? Having to watch it all?"

"I'm sure it was much harder than living it," she replied sarcastically.

"If we hadn't gone to rescue your fucking friend, none of this would have happened," I blurted.

"If your friend wasn't psychotic, I wouldn't have had to rescue her!" she yelled back.

"He's not my friend. He's a guy I worked with."

"I told you that there was something wrong with him," she said. She was shaking, her hands balled into fists at her sides. "I told you that something was going on, and you acted like I was crazy."

She was right. I'd brushed off her worry when she'd tried to tell me that something was wrong with her friend. I hadn't taken it seriously. We'd known that Sean was an asshole, but that hadn't necessarily meant that the guy was abusive. I couldn't have predicted how crazy he would turn out to be.

"I went with you." I threw up my hands. "I went to help her just like you asked. I didn't want to, and I didn't want *you* to, but we went anyway."

"And I did want to go," she said, deflated. "And our baby died because of it."

"No," I said, shaking my head. "No, that's not what I meant. You said—"

"But it's what you think. It's what everyone thinks." She

glanced at me and then looked away. "I put us in danger."

"Sarai," I said, taking a step toward her. She didn't want me to touch her—I knew she didn't—but it took everything I had not to wrap my arms around her. "I don't think that."

"I wanted to run to the rescue," she said dully. "Because Hailey finally decided to leave him."

"You didn't do anything wrong," I replied. "You had no idea what Sean would do. None of us had any idea."

"I don't want to talk about this anymore," she said, taking a step backward. "I have to go to work."

I watched her as she retreated, pulling on her coat and picking up her laptop bag before she headed toward our front door. As she reached it, she paused.

"I'll talk to my adviser," she said, her back to me. "Call a moving company. There's nothing left for me here."

* * *

The next two days with Adinah and Isaac were a marathon of keeping my mouth shut and holding myself back whenever they said something to upset her. Sarai seemed to do just fine dealing with them, but I still couldn't stand the way they tried to bulldoze her. There was no doubt in my mind that her aunt and uncle loved her and were worried about her, but they were so controlling that it overshadowed everything they did.

After speaking with her adviser, Sarai was able to get a leave of absence like we had discussed. It had taken only a doctor's note and some paperwork, and she was officially no longer required to attend classes. I thought that it would be hard for her, that she would be upset about the change in plans, but I should have realized it would be like anything else—she just didn't care.

We didn't tell Adinah and Isaac that she'd decided to take some time off from school, and I made plans for the move when they weren't with us. It might come back to bite us on the ass later, but we didn't want to add any more tension to the already strained visit. Plus, I wanted to get Sarai to Oregon before she changed her mind. Instinctively, I knew that staying in Missouri wasn't an option. Sarai wouldn't get any better here.

* * *

Three days after her uncle and aunt left, we packed all our personal items in the truck and left our apartment behind. I'd bought a canopy for my truck, and it had been a tight fit, but I'd made it work. Later, if we decided to stay, we'd hire movers to bring Sarai's car and the rest of our stuff. I wasn't about to deal with that shit now.

"What did your boss say when you quit?" I asked, glancing at Sarai as I got on the freeway. We'd barely spoken in the last few days, but I was hoping that the close proximity in the truck would force her to acknowledge me.

"She said that she was sorry to see me go and asked me to call a temp agency and find a replacement," Sarai replied, looking out her window.

"So she was real broken up about it," I joked.

"We weren't close," she said.

"She was a bitch, huh?" I teased. Sarai hadn't talked about

her coworkers much, but I knew she'd liked them.

"No." She looked at me in disbelief. "She was twenty years older than me. We didn't have much in common."

"I bet she was the one who bought you the bowl sweaters, wasn't she?" I said, still teasing her. "Old ladies are weird."

"She wasn't weird," Sarai said, looking back out the window. "She was nice."

Neither of us spoke for a minute.

"And I think she made the bowl sweaters—she didn't buy them," Sarai said finally.

I laughed. "No way."

Sarai just shrugged.

The first day of driving was long and exhausting. Sarai didn't talk much, but I didn't let it bother me. We still had a couple of days to reconnect.

I'd planned out our trip, so we knew exactly how far we had to go each day. I'd even made reservations so we wouldn't get stuck trying to find a place to sleep each night. But when we got to our first motel, I grimaced at the outside. It wasn't exactly the Hilton. There was a taped-off area where the sidewalk had cracked in half. The building needed a fresh coat of paint about ten years ago, and the parking lot had only one light working.

"Come inside with me," I said to Sarai as I put the truck in park. "This place is sketchy."

I grabbed our overnight bags out of the backseat and opened Sarai's door, helping her out. I held her hand as we crossed the parking lot. She didn't pull away, which I considered a win, but I didn't expect that anything had changed.

"Hey, I have a reservation for Evans," I told the night clerk.

She looked bored and irritated that I'd shown up, but she nodded and immediately searched my name in the computer behind the desk.

"It looks like someone overbooked," she said, grimacing.

I stood up straighter. No way in hell were they going to turn us away after we'd just spent all day driving. I had no idea where the nearest hotel was, and I wasn't going to search for a new place to stay this late at night.

"I have a room," she said in relief. She looked between us, then met my eyes. "It's only got one full bed in it because we're waiting for the other one to be shipped," she said quickly. "But it's newly remodeled. You'd be the first people in there."

"Fine," I said, setting my credit card on the counter. "I'm guessing the change in rooms will change the price?"

"Of course, of course," she said, typing.

A couple of minutes later Sarai and I had our key, and we were walking toward our room. All the doors were outside the building, and I glanced at the windows as we passed. Most of the curtains were closed, but a few were open, and I could see families in the rooms, probably travelers like us, and it made me feel a little better.

When I opened the door to our room, I laughed in disbelief. The place was tiny, smaller than any other hotel room I'd ever seen. There was space for the other full bed the clerk had told us they were waiting on, but I wasn't even sure how they'd fit a nightstand.

I also didn't think either of us had realized just how small a full-sized bed was.

"You're going to hang off the end," Sarai said, setting her

purse down on the dresser as I closed the curtains.

"I'll make it work," I said with a sigh, dropping my duffel on the floor. "Sat on my ass all day and I'm still beat."

"You can have the bathroom first," she said with a small smile of thanks when I set her bag down in front of her.

"I'll be quick," I replied. Normally, I'd insist that Sarai go first, but I wanted to check it out before Sarai got in there. I'd seen some nasty hotel bathrooms.

Thankfully they really had just remodeled our room, and that included the bathroom—everything was clean and bright. As I looked around, I grimaced at myself in the mirror. I was still growing my beard because I finally could, but I looked like a damn hobo.

After taking care of business and a quick shower, I wrapped a towel around my waist and went back into the room to find Sarai sitting on the bed. She wasn't watching TV or playing on her phone. She was just staring at nothing as she ran one finger back and forth over the edge of her cast.

"You okay?" I asked, trying not to let her hear the worry in my voice. I knew that just because we'd left our apartment behind, she wasn't going to suddenly turn into the woman I'd married, but I'd hoped for some change, no matter how little it was.

"I'm fine," she said, turning to look at me. "Are you all done in there?"

I nodded.

As she walked into the bathroom, I realized something. Sarai was wearing makeup for the first time in weeks. I smiled a little to myself as I pulled the sheets to the foot of the bed, checking for critters. Maybe leaving the apartment *had* helped.

I was rethinking that an hour later as Sarai and I tried to get comfortable on the bed. I hadn't touched my wife, really touched her, in more weeks than I cared to think about, and trying to keep my body away from hers on that bed was nearly impossible. When I tried to roll onto my side, my ass pressed against her hip. If I rolled onto my back, our elbows bumped into each other and my shoulder pressed against hers. When she rolled onto her side, it was even worse. There was no way in hell that I'd be able to sleep with *her* ass pressed against *me*.

There was nowhere to go. The clerk had said they were buying a second new mattress for the room, but they clearly hadn't replaced the one we were sleeping on. It sank down so far in the center that unless we held on to the edges, we naturally slid toward each other. Sarai was doing her damnedest to keep some space between us, but it wasn't working, and her anxiety was feeding my own.

I was seriously debating sleeping on the floor when she huffed out a breath.

"This is ridiculous," she murmured, flopping onto her back and accidentally elbowing me in the side. "Sorry."

"Why do they even make beds this size?" I grumbled, wiggling my feet. I was so far up on the bed that my hair brushed the headboard, but my heels still hung off the end. "Who could be comfortable like this?"

"I don't think it's meant for two people," she said seriously.

"I don't think it's meant for adults," I replied.

"Short ones, maybe," she muttered.

We were quiet for a while, neither of us comfortable enough to actually fall asleep.

"Still happy that we're moving to Oregon?" I asked, then cursed silently. "I mean, okay with it?"

"I'm happy," she said unconvincingly. "I like your family."

I lay there for a moment, then asked the question that had been rolling around in my head for days. "Do you wish that you'd gone back to New York with your aunt and uncle?"

Her answer didn't come right away, and my heart raced while silence filled the dark room.

"No," she said finally. "I'm not a child, and if I went back with them, they would have treated me like one."

"I wasn't sure," I murmured. "If you wanted to go, I wouldn't have argued."

"Did you want me to go?" she asked quietly.

"No," I replied quickly. "No, I want you with me."

She didn't reply, and even though it was the truth, I wasn't sure if I'd said the right thing. Everything was so messed up with us. I didn't know what I was supposed to say or do anymore. I'd always been the easygoing one, the person who put everyone at ease and made them laugh. But I wasn't that person for Sarai. My jokes had no effect on her anymore, and my words always seemed to come out wrong.

We lay there in the silence for a long time. Then, without a word, Sarai reached out and grabbed my hand. She rolled onto her side and pulled me with her until I was pressed against her back, my knees notched behind hers. I was so overwhelmed that I had a hard time controlling my breathing. Finally, she was in my arms.

I wrapped my arm around her waist and inhaled the scent of her hair. I'd missed her so goddamn much.

* * *

We slept together like a couple of spoons, but when we got up the next morning, nothing had really changed.

I'd married her planning on forever, and that hadn't changed for me. I didn't for a second wonder if we would get divorced, because I didn't consider it an option. We'd promised to stick it out through the good and the bad, and right now was really bad. We just had to get through it.

I wondered if Sarai felt the same way, though. She didn't even seem to like me anymore, much less love me the way I loved her. The thought made nausea pool in my gut.

"We're making good time," I said as the light started to fade. We were almost to the hotel I'd planned on staying at. "Do you want to stop for the night, or should we keep driving?"

"Didn't you make a hotel reservation?" she asked, turning her head to look at me. It was the first time she'd even acknowledged me in hours.

"That doesn't mean we have to stay there," I said, wiggling my eyebrows. "We can go where the wind takes us."

"We should probably follow the schedule," she said, looking out the windshield again.

"Schedule smedule," I replied. "This is a road trip. We make the rules."

"I say we stop where you made the reservation," she said flatly.

"Oh, come on," I teased. "It's barely dark yet."

"If you plan for something," she snapped, losing her temper, "then you should follow the plan! That's what plans are for. You follow them so you know what you're doing. Why even make a plan if you aren't going to follow it? That's just stupid!"

My eyes widened in surprise.

"Sarai," I said, completely confused. "It's a crappy motel reservation. They don't care if we stop or not."

"I care," she yelled, making me jerk. "I care that we follow the fucking plan."

"What the hell?" I replied, glancing over at her in disbelief. "What's your deal?"

"Some of us make plans for a reason, Alex," she hissed. "Some of us make plans because we like knowing what's next. We like knowing where we're going to sleep that night. We like knowing when we'll be to our destination."

"We'll stop," I conceded, raising one hand in surrender, trying to calm her down. "I didn't realize it was such a big deal."

"Of course you didn't," she ground out. "Because you just do whatever you want and everyone just has to go along with you. You don't care about how anyone else feels."

"You're kidding, right?" I asked, flipping on my blinker so I could take the next exit.

"No, I'm serious," she said derisively. "You're the one who likes to make jokes."

I pulled off the freeway and stopped in a gravel parking lot set up for big rigs. I threw the truck in park and spun to face her.

"I've been really fucking understanding," I said, my hands clenched on my lap. "But don't treat me like shit."

"I'm not treating you like shit," she shot back.

"The first time you've opened your mouth all day and you start in on me about how I don't care about your feelings," I said. "How I don't care about your plans. What the fuck do you think I'm doing here, Sarai?"

"We're driving to Oregon to see *your* family," she said flatly.

"That's such bullshit," I growled. "I've done everything I can for you. I asked if you wanted to go back to New York, and you said no. I try to make you happy, and you fucking scowl at me. I can't touch you, because you flinch away. I can't talk to you, because you don't respond. How in the fuck am *I* treating *you* bad?"

"I told you that I didn't have time for a relationship," she said, crossing her arms over her chest. "I told you that I had goals and plans that I wanted to follow through on."

"We're back to that?" I said tiredly. "Really?"

"Everything comes back to that," she replied, her eyes not meeting mine.

"I didn't force you to spend time with me," I said, my breathing choppy as I stared at her. "I didn't force you to do anything. You're the one who wanted to get married, so we eloped. I tried to make everything easy on you. I—"

"If you would have just left me alone, then none of this would have happened," she said accusingly, her eyes filling with tears. "I had plans. I knew what I was doing."

"So you just wish that we'd never met?" I asked, my throat tightening as I struggled to speak.

"No," she said, shaking her head. She lifted her hands to her face and let out a small sob.

"Then what do you mean?" I asked. We'd had this discussion at the hospital, but I'd let it go. I'd known that she was in shock, and I'd thought she hadn't meant it. But now she was saying the same things all over again, and I felt as if my chest were cracking open. "You act like I ruined your life or something. *If I'd just left you alone?* What the fuck?"

"This wasn't supposed to happen," she cried. "None of this was supposed to happen." She clenched her jaw and spoke through her teeth. "This is what happens when you don't follow a plan—everything gets messed up."

"What are you even talking about?" I asked. Was she talking about the baby? Our marriage? School? She wasn't making any sense.

"I was supposed to stay the weekend," she said suddenly. I stared at her in confusion. "But I was homesick, so I called my mom and asked her to pick me up."

"Sarai," I said quietly, trying to get her attention, but she was a million miles away.

"So my parents came to pick me up. Of course they did," she said with a sigh. "They had to get me early so we could go to temple. If I just would have stayed like I was supposed to…" She turned to me and shrugged her shoulders. "They shouldn't have even been on the road yet. That wasn't the plan."

It all became clear as she stared at me dully.

"And you think if you wouldn't have asked to be picked up…," I said, my words trailing off.

"It wouldn't have happened," she said faintly. "We were on

our way home so my mom could finish getting ready. She had hot rollers in her hair, with a scarf over them because she wasn't planning on getting out of the car." She looked down at her hands. "She would have hated that people saw her like that."

"I bet she would've just been relieved that you were okay," I murmured, covering her hands with mine. "That's what parents are like."

"If I would have just kept to the plan...," she mumbled.

"That's bullshit. You have no idea if they would have gotten into an accident even if they hadn't picked you up," I replied, making her jerk in surprise. "Sweetheart, don't you think they'd be grateful that they got to see you one last time before they died?"

"They wouldn't have even been on that road," she rasped.

"Sarai." I gave her hands a squeeze. "You can't plan for everything."

"I can try."

"Yeah, you can," I conceded with a sigh. "But some of the best things happen when you don't plan for them."

She didn't reply.

"Did you know that I didn't want to go to that stupid double date?" I said, taking a risk by bringing up Hailey and Sean. "I was *planning* on playing video games in my underwear."

Sarai rolled her eyes.

"But I went and met you."

"And I blew you off," she said.

"And made me even more interested," I confessed.

She shook her head. "You're twisting it."

"No, baby," I said softly. "I think you're the one who's twisted it. You can't plan for everything. Life doesn't work that way."

I sighed and dropped my head against the back of the seat, suddenly completely worn out. Nothing I was saying would make her change her mind.

"Are you sorry you married me?" I asked finally. "Because I can't live like this. I need to know if you're staying or going."

"Of course I'm not sorry I married you," she replied, her voice wobbling.

"You keep bringing it up," I replied. "If only I hadn't ruined your plans."

"No," she said, shaking her head. "That's not what I meant."

"Then what did you mean?"

"I meant—" She paused. "I meant that—"

She couldn't find the words, and I couldn't let her off the hook. I needed to know.

"I'm not sorry I married you," she said again. "But everything that happened, it's because I deviated from my plans." She didn't sound as sure of it anymore.

"You lost the baby because Sean is a fucking douche," I replied. "It didn't have anything to do with your plans."

"Yes, it did."

"Jesus," I murmured. "That's not how it works, Sarai."

I put the truck in drive and whipped around, pulling back onto the road so I could get back on the freeway.

"Your plans were still set," I said, changing lanes. I didn't even bother looking at her. "You were still planning on graduating in June. That hadn't changed. Our marriage had changed where you lived, but you were still on track. The baby wasn't even going to be born until after you were done with school. Nothing fucking changed until we lost her."

"You don't understand," she said again.

I tried to take a deep breath but couldn't. Her inability to see reason made my chest tight, and I lifted my hand to rub at it.

"Alex?" Sarai said cautiously. "What's wrong?"

"I—" I snapped my mouth shut and swallowed. Shit, what the hell was happening? I inhaled again, this time inflating my lungs.

"Are you okay?" she asked, leaning toward me.

Her words triggered a memory, and my hands began to shake.

"Are you okay?" Bram asked, pushing past me into the room where my first mom lay on the floor, her round belly pointing toward the ceiling.

I couldn't stop the sound that came out of my throat.

"Alex, you're scaring me," Sarai said. "Pull over."

I nodded and took the next exit. By the time we were parked, I'd started sweating.

"I need a minute," I blurted, climbing out of the truck.

I lifted my hands and laced my fingers behind my head as I took deep breaths of cool air. *Jesus.* Was I having some sort of panic attack? I'd never had a panic attack in my life.

"What's going on?" Sarai asked, rounding the truck.

I huffed, willing the tears at the back of my eyes to disappear. "Remember when I told you that my mom died from a broken heart?" I asked. When she nodded I continued. "What I didn't tell you is that she lost a baby."

"What?" Sarai gasped, wrapping her arms around herself.

"She gave up, Sarai," I said, my eyes on hers. "She just *gave up*, and we lost both of them."

"You won't lose me," she said softly.

A choked sob came out of my mouth, and I brushed at my face in embarrassment.

"I'm right here," she said, taking a step forward.

All the panic, the incessant need to check the windows and doors to make sure they were locked, to inspect Sarai's car every time she drove it, all of it made sense now. My skin felt tight as I flexed my shoulders and stretched my neck from side to side. I barely remembered the night my sister arrived stillborn, but it must have stuck with me, because I'd been obsessive about keeping Sarai and the baby safe.

And it hadn't done a damn bit of good.

I looked at my wife, terrified that history was repeating itself.

"It's cold out here," she said softly, reaching her hand out to me. "Let's get back in the truck."

I nodded silently and took her hand, leading her back to her side.

"Everything's going to be okay," she said as I helped her into her seat. She reached out and put her hand on my cheek.

I nodded and pulled away. A few minutes later, as we pulled back onto the freeway, her hand slid across the seat and came to rest on my thigh. I took that as a step in the right direction, but I was too raw to do anything about it.

CHAPTER 18

SARAI

I didn't know how to explain to Alex how things had become so jumbled in my mind when I couldn't even make sense of it myself.

Whenever I'd thought about the past month, one thing had popped into my head. I hadn't planned for any of this. I hadn't been prepared to be pregnant. I hadn't been prepared to get into a car accident. I hadn't been prepared to lose the baby whom I'd just begun to accept and want. If I'd only known it was coming, then maybe it wouldn't have hurt so badly.

I knew it didn't make sense, but during those first few days after the accident, it was all I could think about. It was how I'd rationalized it in my head—that something horrible had happened because I'd deviated from my planned route. If only I hadn't done that, the rest of it wouldn't have happened.

It didn't help that it seemed to be affecting me far worse than it did Alex. I couldn't understand why I was so upset when he wasn't. He'd been the one who was excited for the baby, and I'd been the one left brokenhearted when that baby didn't exist anymore. It didn't seem fair.

But I'd had no idea about his mother. My heart ached when I remembered the bleak look in his eyes when he'd told me about her.

I rubbed my thumb against Alex's jeans as we flew down the freeway, unable to open my mouth and apologize to him.

I turned a little and leaned against the seat sideways, closing my eyes as Alex drove. It had taken me a long time to become comfortable in a car again. It was only when it rained that I felt the old panic rise up inside me.

As we pulled into the motel, remorse made my throat tight. I shouldn't have yelled at Alex about where we were staying, especially since I didn't actually care where we slept.

"I'll grab a key," Alex said, pulling under the little archway near the office. "I'll be right back."

I took a deep breath once he was gone. I hurt. Every place inside of me hurt. My weariness was bone deep and exhausting.

Our room turned out to be a lot nicer than the one we'd stayed in the night before, and I glanced around in relief as Alex carried our bags over to the dresser and set them on top. There were a king-sized bed, a table with a couple of chairs, and a flat-screen TV that was bolted to the wall.

"You can take the bathroom first," Alex said quietly, gesturing toward it.

We were both so raw from our conversation earlier that I

didn't have the courage to bring it up again. Instead, I hurried to get my toiletries and closed myself in the small room. The tears didn't hit until I was hidden away in the shower.

* * *

"I don't know what to do," Alex said quietly after we'd turned off the lights and crawled into the huge bed. The space between us was massive, but I didn't know how to bridge the gap. "I want to help you, but I have no idea what to do."

"You are helping," I said, my words slightly muffled by my pillow.

He had no idea how much he was helping by just being there. Solid and strong. He also had no idea how much his presence hurt. I didn't know why both things were true, but they were.

I wanted to be close to him constantly, but I could barely stand to touch him most of the time. I didn't want him to leave, but I didn't want to talk. I knew it was unfair to him, but I couldn't seem to claw my way out of this whirlpool of conflicting emotions. I needed him with me to feel safe, but I was afraid if I let him get too close, I'd lose what little composure I'd managed to hold on to.

"I couldn't understand why you weren't sad," I finally said, halfway hoping that he was asleep and wouldn't answer me. "Why was I so upset when you weren't?"

"What?" he asked in confusion. He leaned up on one elbow, the light from the bathroom illuminating his face. "What are you talking about?"

"I just can't get out of this pit," I said, the words a relief as

I said them. "I try and move past it, but I just can't. The baby was barely anything, barely even there, but I can't stop thinking about it. Missing it. How did you do it?"

"You thought I didn't care?" he said, his voice choked. "Why?"

"You said you were fine," I replied. "You *keep* saying you're fine."

"I'm not fine," he said instantly.

His words were firm and direct, and something in my chest tightened and loosened at the same time. How had I missed it? He seemed okay. He always seemed okay. I was falling apart, and he just went on with his life like nothing had happened.

"I'm devastated," he said, his words quiet. "I'm…I'm shitty. Horrible."

"But you said—" I began to argue.

"Sarai, you were barely talking, baby," he said gently, his words choked. "You were barely living. Who would take care of you if I lost it?"

"What?" I said in disbelief, my nose stinging as my eyes started to water.

"One of us had to be okay," he said. "It's my job to make sure *you're* okay."

"No, it's not," I said.

"I'm your husband," he said, his voice wobbly. "That's my most important job."

Tears ran down my cheeks as I stared at him. I'd been so sad, so wrapped up in my own feelings, that I hadn't realized what it was doing to him. How had I been so blind to it? I'd watched him smile at my aunt and uncle, knowing how uncomfortable he was, but I'd been completely oblivious when he'd acted okay in front of me. I hadn't even bothered to search below the surface.

"I thought you didn't care," I whispered hoarsely. "I thought you were fine."

"You're my life," he said simply. "I'm sad about our baby, and I loved it, but you're still here, and I needed to take care of you. I couldn't lose you, too."

"I'm so sorry," I choked out.

"Sarai," he breathed, reaching across the bed to cup my cheek in his hand. "I love you. There's nothing to be sorry for."

The sobs burst out of my throat no matter how hard I tried to contain them.

"Shit," Alex said, crossing the wide expanse of the bed to take me in his arms. "Don't cry, baby."

"You just kept saying you were fine," I said in confusion, my lips brushing against his chest. "You just kept saying it, and I was drowning. I didn't understand what was wrong with me, why I couldn't move past it."

"No," he said, his hand rubbing firmly up and down my back. "God, no. I was so disappointed. I was so upset that we lost our baby. I just…" He shook his head, his beard rubbing against the top of my head. "You needed me, so I just…" He couldn't seem to find the words.

"You pretended like you were fine," I whispered, my stomach clenching at how horrible that must have been for him.

"I didn't pretend," he said. "Not exactly. I just—I don't know—ignored it, I guess. Pushed it down, put it in a box, and kept going."

"I needed you." I hated to put that on him. It wasn't fair and I knew it, but I had to get it out. "I needed you to be with me. I needed you to be in bed with me in the dark. I needed you to feel it, too."

"I was there," he whispered. "You didn't see me, but I was right there."

"I thought I was all alone," I whimpered.

"You weren't," he murmured, pressing his forehead to mine. "I was with you the whole time."

* * *

We were physically and emotionally exhausted by the time we arrived at Alex's parents' house the next night. By un-spoken agreement, when we'd woken up that morning, we'd stopped talking about all the wounds that were still open and raw. Instead, we just drove in companionable silence for most of the day, listening to music and holding hands across the seat.

I think we both needed time to adjust and reflect on the revelations we'd dealt with the night before. We were careful of each other, more considerate than we'd ever been, and fi-nally fully conscious of each other's pain.

As we drove up Liz and Dan's winding driveway, Alex rolled down his window and hung his arm outside, letting the rain soak him.

"The rain," I said quietly, staring out the windshield as the house came into view. "It'll take some getting used to."

"It's okay," he said. "We'll figure it out together." He rolled up his window and sent me a small smile. "We're home."

I remembered thinking the last time I was there that I'd never want to live somewhere so secluded. As I stared out at the warmly lit house and surrounding trees, a sense of peace filled me. The same seclusion that had seemed so unappealing before comforted me now.

I pulled the hood of my sweatshirt up as Alex opened my door, and I followed him as he jogged to the porch.

I couldn't help but grin at Liz through the open door, her smile was so bright.

"Get inside—it's freezing out there," she ordered with a wave of her hand.

The house was just as warm and inviting as I remembered.

"I'm so glad you're here, sweetheart," she murmured as she gave me a long hug. "How was the drive? Long and boring?"

"It was okay," I said, letting Alex help me take my sweatshirt off. "I've never seen so much of the US."

"It was long and boring," Alex joked. "She's putting a nice spin on it, though."

"You were bored?" I asked.

"I'm never bored with you," he said, putting on the charm. Then he mouthed *Bored* to his mom, making no sound.

"Well," she said with a laugh. "I'm glad you two are finally here and the trip was uneventful."

I met Alex's eyes. It had been far from uneventful.

"You're here," Dan said, coming out of the bedroom with a newspaper in his hand.

"Thank God you used the master bath," Liz said with a laugh. "Because I guarantee they both need to use the other one."

"Oh, yeah," Dan said, his cheeks turning a little pink. "Stay out of there for a few minutes."

Alex laughed as I realized that suddenly I wasn't a guest anymore. I was part of the inner circle. Just one of the kids.

"I'm going first," I said. I threw my arm out in front of Alex so he couldn't race in front of me as I kicked off my shoes.

"We'll eat in a few minutes," Liz called as I hurried down the hallway. "I ordered Chinese food!"

I took my time in the bathroom, carefully washing my hand around my cast and smoothing down my hair before I joined the group in the kitchen. When I walked into the room, Dan was standing across the island from where Alex and Liz were sitting. She was rubbing Alex's back as he spoke quietly.

"It was the worst moment of my life," he said quietly. "I saw him coming a split second before he hit, but I couldn't do anything about it."

"That must have been terrifying," Liz murmured.

"It was," Alex said. "The car spun and I just went running. The airbags had deployed, and Sarai was knocked out." He put his arms out in front of him, showing off his newly healing scars. "She'd locked the doors, but thankfully the window was broken, so I was able to unlock it."

"Abraham didn't tell us you'd been hurt," Dan said, his voice gruff.

"It was nothing," Alex said, brushing him off. "It was minimal to what Sarai went through."

"Don't do that," I said, walking farther into the kitchen. "Don't minimize it."

"We've been talking about that," he told his parents with a self-deprecating chuckle. "Saying that I'm fine when I'm not isn't going to fly anymore."

"Nice work," his mom said to me, turning to wrap an arm around my waist as I stood next to her. She gave me a squeeze. "That always drove me crazy. He never admits when he's upset."

I smiled wanly. I hadn't heard Alex's memory of the accident yet, and I was disappointed that I'd interrupted him telling his parents.

"I didn't even realize what had happened," I finally said, continuing when he stayed silent. "I just remember getting to Hailey's house and then riding to the hospital in the ambulance. Alex nearly broke the paramedic's arm when he gave me an IV."

"Did they get there pretty quick?" Dan asked, leaning his elbows on the counter.

"I don't know," Alex said, shaking his head. "Felt like it took hours, but it must've been only a few minutes."

"Can't imagine," Dan murmured.

"They got her out of the car," Alex said, his voice cracking. "And there was so much blood." He stopped speaking and shook his head. Clearing his throat, he looked at me. "I knew before we ever got to the hospital."

I swallowed hard. I hadn't known that. I hadn't been aware of anything beyond my splitting headache and throbbing wrist. It was only later that I'd known that something bigger was wrong.

"Oh, son," Liz said as her arm tightened around my waist. "I'm so sorry that this happened to you two."

When Dan started unpacking the food boxes, I stepped out of Liz's hold and went to help him.

"How're you doing, sweetheart?" he asked quietly as Alex left the room.

"Not great," I said truthfully, glancing over at him.

"Admitting it is half the battle," he said kindly, reaching out to gently squeeze the fingers poking out the end of my cast. "Then you can start healing."

I nodded, blinking away the tears that threatened.

"I'm real sorry," he murmured. "Real sorry."

"Thank you," I whispered.

He nodded as Alex came back into the room.

"Hey, baby," he said, a shy smile on his face. "I thought since your hand is in that cast…" He lifted his arm, and I started crying when I saw the chopsticks I'd rigged for him the first time we met.

"You kept them?" I asked incredulously.

"Of course," he whispered, pulling me into his arms.

I let the tears fall as he held me tightly against his chest, swaying slightly from side to side. When they finally started to wane, I felt Liz's hand on my back.

"Food's getting cold," she said gently, kissing the back of my head with motherly affection that almost had me in tears again. "Let's eat, huh?"

As I pulled away, Alex snapped the chopsticks together a few times. "These are dirty," he said, like he'd just realized it. "You probably shouldn't use them."

I giggled at the look on his face, my heart lightening. "I can make another pair," I replied.

"Cool." He handed them to me. "Make me one, too, okay?"

* * *

We stayed up talking late into the night with Alex's parents. Eventually, we moved into the living room, where Alex and I curled up together on the couch. The closeness was like a balm, soothing all the surface hurts while we focused on the deeper ones.

Sometimes we talked about the accident, and sometimes we talked about what we planned to do for the next couple of days, but no one brought up the future. I don't think Alex or I were ready to make any big decisions yet. We were still licking our wounds, still raw from the past couple of days and all the days that had come before.

We slept in the same bedroom we'd shared at Thanksgiving, and I woke up the next morning feeling refreshed in a way that hours spent in bed had never given me. I think what I was feeling was hope, but at the time I was too nervous to give that feeling a name.

Over the next few days, Alex and I went on long walks through the forest. We spent time quietly and gratefully falling further in love with each other. I told him stories about my parents, and he told me about his birth mother and what it had been like when she'd fallen into a depression so deep that even her twin sons hadn't been able to pull her out of it.

I wasn't blind to the parallels in our stories, and I held Alex's hand a little tighter as we walked slowly through the trees. He'd lost his first mother because she hadn't been able to climb out of the dark pit she'd fallen into, and after that, my husband had felt responsible his entire life for being the person who made others happy. He'd taken on that role with Abraham, and though I knew he wasn't ready to hear it, I came to realize that he'd done the same for me.

His family gave us the space we needed to get back on our feet, but by the end of the week, our alone time was up.

"I missed you," Ani said, rushing through the front door of Liz and Dan's house, Abraham carrying Arie in behind her. She hugged me hard, then pulled back to get a good look at me. "You're doing better," she said. "Good. You looked like shit before."

"Thanks," I replied with a small laugh. I was beginning to learn how to read between the lines with Ani. Sometimes she said exactly what she meant, and other times you had to search for the hidden meaning in her words. She'd been worried about me.

"You," she said, pointing at Alex across the room. "I called you like four days ago, and you never called me back."

"I was busy," he replied, backing away.

"Don't make excuses," she bitched, walking toward him.

Bram stopped in front of me, and as he gave me a tender smile, I finally saw the strong resemblance between him and Alex. "Hey, little sister," he said, wrapping one arm around my shoulders. "Okay?"

"Almost," I replied honestly.

"You'll get there," he said, giving me a squeeze.

We congregated in the kitchen, since that seemed to be where the Evans family always ended up, and for the first time in so long, I was able to relax. I laughed at the way Ani teased Bram and Alex, complained good-naturedly when Dan told Bram and Ani about how much I hated winking and they all started doing it, and leaned against my husband, enjoying his strong arm around my shoulders.

"You should see a counselor," Liz told me later that night as we scooped ice cream for everyone. She laughed a little at the surprised look I gave her. "Maybe not the best way to bring up the subject, but is there a good way?" She shrugged. "I just know from experience that sometimes you need to think about this stuff when you're feeling good, because when you're feeling bad again, it'll be hard to imagine anything helping."

"You're right," I murmured, scooping out another spoonful of ice cream. "And kind of sneaky."

She laughed.

"You just countered any argument I could have made by acknowledging that I'm doing better before I could use that excuse."

"Honey, I've raised a lot of kids," she replied, bumping me with her hip. "There isn't any excuse you could make that I haven't heard before."

"I think you're right," I said quietly, thinking back to Dan telling me that admitting I wasn't okay was the first step to being okay. I really wanted to be okay again. I looked at Liz. "I think Alex should go, too."

"I think you're right," she replied.

* * *

"Come on," Alex said, tugging me along behind him. He thought he was going to surprise me, but he was seriously underestimating my memory, because I knew exactly where we were headed.

We'd been at his parents' house for nearly a month, and things were going well. We had good days and bad days. Sometimes I still had a hard time getting out of bed in the morning, but we were actively working on getting better. It helped that Alex had started working at the logging company and his health insurance allowed us to see a really nice counselor once a week. My cast was gone, which was a relief.

I'd also been talking to my aunt and uncle again. Things weren't the same as they had been before, but knowing that they loved me made a huge difference. Even though I'd been pretty lost in my own world when they'd come to see me, I'd still recognized how much they cared. Once I'd been able to see it from the other side, I'd made an effort to repair my relationship with them.

"Alex," I said, huffing as he pulled me along. "These boots are going to give me blisters if you keep making me walk so fast."

"Sorry," he said, grinning back at me. "I'm in a hurry."

"I can tell," I said, slowing down so he was forced to also.

A few minutes later, I could see something flickering in the trees, and I watched in confusion as the light got brighter.

"What did you do?" I asked, laughing as I realized there were candles hanging from at least twenty branches.

"They're LED candles," he said proudly. "Don't worry— I'm not starting any fires."

"I wasn't worried," I mumbled as I stepped between the trees and into his old hideout.

There was a picnic laid out in the middle of the clearing, on what looked like an old green sleeping bag. A thermos held whatever we were drinking, and a box of doughnuts sat off to the side.

"I remembered the lights and the sleeping bag," he said, laughter in his voice. "But I forgot the food, so Mom helped me out."

"I think it's perfect," I said, smiling at him as I moved to the sleeping bag. "Is this yours?"

"It was either mine or Bram's," he said with a chuckle. "They were both exactly the same."

"I love this," I said, sitting down.

"Wait!" he said. "Stand up."

I wobbled as I pushed myself up again, and searched the ground, thinking that I was about to sit in something or there was a rodent or spider.

I was still searching for whatever had made him panic when he dropped down on his knees in front of me.

"What are you doing?" I asked, my lips twitching.

"Sarai Levy," he said, holding up his hand to stop me from correcting him. "I promise to always tell you when I've had a bad day."

I bit my lip, trying to hold back my smile.

"I promise to bring you dinner when you go back to school, because we both know you're not good at making time for necessities like food." We'd discussed my finding a program in Oregon where I could transfer my credits, but I wasn't ready for the stress of that yet. Maybe someday.

"I promise to turn my socks right side out before I throw them in the hamper, because even though you've suffered in silence, I know it drives you crazy." I couldn't hold back my laugh, and he grinned proudly.

"I promise to always try to make you laugh, even when you're mad. I promise to share my family with you. I promise to support you in everything you do. I promise to never let you feel alone. I promise to give you children when the time is right."

My eyes watered. He wasn't done.

"I promise to always open your doors when we go on a date. I promise to learn how to cook that matzo ball soup that you love. I promise to get along with your family even when they piss me off. I promise—"

"That's a lot of promises," I said, cutting him off with a watery laugh.

"Remember what I told you?" he asked, wrapping his arms around my hips and resting his chin on my stomach.

"What?" I whispered, smiling down at him.

"I'll give you everything," he whispered back.

And he did.

EPILOGUE

ALEX

I was really hoping you'd do a Jewish wedding," Ani said as she leaned against the wall beside me. "I wanted the whole step-on-a-glass, mazel-tov thing."

"Sorry to disappoint you," I replied drily, taking a drink of my champagne. "Sarai wasn't comfortable with that. She did invite her rabbi to the party, though. So that's something."

I smiled as I watched my wife dance across the room with Shane and Kate's son Keller. She was laughing at something he'd said, and Keller's face was so full of mischief that I chuckled. He was probably hitting on her, the little punk.

"Has she been to church yet?" Ani asked.

"Nope." I shook my head slightly. "Just long conversations with Rabbi Stevens at a coffee shop for now."

"Well, good for her. Baby steps, right?" Ani said seriously. Then she grumbled, "I can't believe she made me wear a bridesmaid dress when you didn't even have an actual wedding."

"Why are you over here harassing Alex?" Bram asked as he brought Ani a drink. "It's his wedding reception—give the guy a break."

I tuned them out as they argued, and watched as Sarai spun in a circle, her wedding dress floating out around her. The dance floor was full of friends and family, but I knew that somewhere in the crowd Clover was doing his damnedest to woo Hailey. After we'd left Missouri, they'd formed a friendship that was as close as that of any couple I'd ever seen, but my old buddy was holding a torch. It would be interesting to see how that all played out.

"What are you guys doing over here?" my little sister, Kate, asked as she came to stand beside me. "You're like a bunch of wallflowers."

"Just enjoying the show," I said, pointing with my champagne flute at her son, who was currently wiggling his eyebrows at Sarai.

"Oh, good grief," she said with a laugh. "He can barely speak to girls his own age, but when he gets around older women, he thinks he's Mr. Smooth."

"The boy's got game," Kate's husband, Shane, said, joining us. "Gets that from his dad."

"Oh, you're so full of shit," Ani barked, laughing.

"You wish you had game," Bram said to Shane, grinning.

"He does," Kate argued. She turned to Shane. "You totally do."

I chuckled. "Do you guys mind?" I asked. "I'm trying to ogle my wife."

"You can ogle your wife at home," Ani replied with a wave of her hand.

"And so can everyone else," Morgan said as she and Trevor walked up. "You need to get some blinds on your windows. Me and Trev stopped by the other night, and we could see right into the house."

"That's because we live in the middle of nowhere," I said in exasperation. "We shouldn't have to put blinds on the windows."

"You built your house on the family property," Bram replied, reaching past Ani to shove good-naturedly at my shoulder. "That's just asking for family members to show up whenever they want."

"Sarai wanted to be close," I murmured as I watched her raise her hands above her head and clap. The smile on her face was so bright, I swore it lit the entire room.

We'd come a long way from the two broken people who'd shown up on my parents' doorstep looking for a place to heal. Our counselor said that people were a constant work in progress, and I guessed that was true, but I didn't think I'd ever feel happier than I did in that moment.

She turned toward me, grinning, then raised her eyebrows as her gaze moved over our group. When she strode toward me, I pushed myself away from the wall.

"Is this a private party," she joked, "or is anyone invited?"

"I guess you can hang with us," Morgan joked as I pulled Sarai toward me for a kiss.

"Kind of you," Sarai murmured, glancing at Morgan right before our lips met.

"Picture!" my mom called out, interrupting us. "You're all in one place! Don't move!"

We all laughed as we turned toward her.

"I want one, too," Sarai's aunt yelled, lifting her camera in the air. She hurried toward us.

Sarai giggled as she turned toward them and leaned back against my chest. After months of conversations and a couple of trips out to see us, I finally got to witness the loving relationship Sarai had with her aunt—free of hurt feelings and arguments. It was awesome.

"Okay, Shane and Trevor, scoot in," my mom ordered, making the guys grumble.

"No, scoot," she ordered again. "Closer." She looked through her camera lens. "Ani, I can't see you. Why are you behind Morgan?"

"I can crouch down," Morgan said questioningly, turning her head to look at Ani.

"Bram, you're stepping on my dress," Ani grumbled. "Move."

"Crap, sorry, baby," he replied.

"Mom, my face is starting to hurt," Kate said through clenched teeth.

"Then stop smiling," I said, shaking my head. "Wait until she's ready."

"I can't," she muttered, still smiling.

"She's afraid she'll be making a weird face," Shane said. "It always happens."

"You're fine, Kate," I said as the couples on my other side shifted around some more. "Stop smiling."

"No," she ground out.

"Okay, we're ready," Ani said. "Wait! Bram, you're on my dress again!"

"Shit," Trevor said. "Sorry, Ani, that was me."

"Move, Trev," she barked. "You're pulling it down!"

I laughed at the chaos surrounding me and leaned down to kiss Sarai's bare shoulder. Leaving my lips there for a minute, I slid my hand over her belly.

Later, when all the reception photos were developed, that photo would be the one we chose for our wall. From left to right, Shane smiled happily; Kate frowned as she lost the struggle to keep the smile on her face; Bram grinned proudly, his eyes on me; Trevor grimaced, looking at his feet; Morgan stared at Ani in horror; and Ani glared at the camera as she clutched at the top of her strapless dress. And right in the center, Sarai beamed while I kissed her shoulder and pressed my hand against the spot where our son was growing.

Did you miss Kate and Shane's love story?

Please turn the page for an excerpt from
Unbreak My Heart.

Prologue

SHANE

"Why are we going to this shit again?" I asked my wife as she messed with her makeup in the passenger-side mirror.

"Because it's important to your cousin."

"She's not my cousin," I reminded her, switching lanes.

"Fine. It's important to *Kate*," she answered, losing patience. "I don't understand why you're being a dick about it."

"How often do we get out of the house with no kids, Rach? Rarely. I'd rather not spend our one night alone at some fucking coffeehouse filled with eighteen-year-olds."

"Damn, you're on a roll tonight," she murmured in annoyance. "Kate asked me to this thing weeks ago. I didn't know you'd be home."

"Right, plans change."

"I promised I'd go! I drop everything for you every time you come back from deployment. You know I do. I can't believe you're acting like a jackass because of *one night* that I had plans I couldn't change."

"I highly doubt Kate wants me here," I mumbled back,

pulling into the little parking lot that was already filled with cars. "She's going to hate it when I see her crash and burn."

I hopped out of the car and walked around the hood to help Rachel out of the car. I never understood why she insisted on wearing high-as-fuck heels while she was pregnant—it made me nervous. She looked hot as hell, but one day she was going to fall and I was terrified I wouldn't be there to catch her.

"You really have no idea, do you?" she said, laughing, as I took her hand and pulled her gently out of her seat. "How in God's name did you grow up together and you still know so little about Kate?"

"You know I didn't grow up with her." I slammed the door shut and walked her slowly toward the small building. "I moved in when I was seventeen and left town when I was nineteen. She's not family, for Christ's sake. She's the spoiled, *weird* niece of the people who took me in for a very short period of time."

Rachel stopped short at the annoyance in my voice. "She's my *best friend*. My only friend. And she freaking introduced us, in case you've forgotten."

"Not on purpose."

"What's that supposed to mean? What wasn't on purpose?"

"She was pissed as hell when we got together."

"No, she wasn't," Rachel argued. "What are you talking about?"

"Never mind. It's not important."

"Can you please, *please*, just be nice and not act like you're being tortured when we get in there? I don't know what your deal is with her—"

"I don't have a deal with her, I just wanted to take my gorgeous wife out to dinner tonight, and instead we're going to watch her friend sing for a bunch of teenagers. Not exactly what I was hoping for."

I reached out to cup her cheek in my palm and rubbed the skin below her lips with my finger. I wanted to kiss her, but after all the lipstick she'd applied in the car, I knew she wouldn't thank me for it.

"We'll go somewhere else afterward, okay? I think she's on first, so we won't be here long," she assured me with a small smile, her eyes going soft. She knew I wanted to kiss her; my hand on her face was a familiar gesture.

"Okay, baby." I leaned in and kissed the tip of her nose gently. "You look beautiful. Did I tell you that yet?"

"Nope."

"Well, you do."

She smiled and started walking toward the building again, and I brushed my fingers through the short hair on the back of my head.

It wasn't that I disliked Kate. Quite the opposite, actually. When we were kids, we'd been friends, and I'd thought she was funny as hell. She had a quirky, sometimes weird sense of humor, and she'd been the most genuinely kind person I'd ever met. But for some reason, all those years ago, she'd suddenly focused in on me, and the attention had made me uncomfortable.

I wasn't into her, and her crush had made me feel weird, uncomfortable in my own skin. I didn't want to hurt her feelings, but shit, she just didn't do it for me. She was too clean-cut, too naive and trusting. Even then, I'd been more attracted to women who were a little harder, a little darker, than the girl who still had posters of fairies on her walls at seventeen.

So I began avoiding her as much as I could until she'd brought home a girl wearing red lipstick and covered in tattoos after her first semester in college. I'd ignored the way Kate had watched me with sad eyes as I'd monopolized her friend's time and completely disregarded her hurt feelings. I'd never liked Kate that way, and I hadn't seen anything wrong with going after her new friend.

I'd ended up married to her roommate, and from then on I'd acted like Kate and I had never been friends. It was easier that way.

"Come on, baby," Rachel called, pulling me into the darkened coffeehouse. "I see a table, and my feet are killing me."

Why the fuck did she insist on wearing those damn shoes?

"Can I get you anything to drink?" a small waitress asked us. Like, really small. She was barely taller than the bistro table we were sitting at.

"Can I get a green tea, please?" Rachel asked.

"Sure! The green we've got is incredible. When are you due?"

"Not for a while."

"Well, congratulations!"

"Black coffee," I ordered when the friendly waitress finally looked my way. Her smile fell, and I realized my words had come out shorter than I'd intended.

"Sure thing!" she chirped with a tight smile before walking away.

"Seriously, Shane?" Rachel growled in annoyance.

"What?" I knew exactly what. I'd been a jackass, but I wasn't about to explain that the crowded coffeehouse was making me sweat. People were laughing loudly, jostling and bumping into each other around the room, and I couldn't see the exits from where we sat.

"Hey, San Diego," a familiar voice called out over the speakers. "How you guys doing tonight?"

The room filled with cheers, and Rachel's face lit up as she looked past me toward the stage.

"Aren't you sweet?" Kate rasped with a short chuckle. "I dig you guys, too."

The crowd grew even louder, and my shoulders tightened in response.

"There's a coffee can being passed around, who's got it?" She paused. "Okay, Lola's got it now—back there in the purple shirt with the Mohawk. When you get it, add a couple dollars, if you can, and pass it on."

The crowd clapped, and Kate chuckled again over the sound system. "I better get started before you guys riot."

I still hadn't turned to look at her. Frankly, I didn't want to embarrass her if she sucked. I didn't—

The clear notes of a single guitar came through the speakers, and I froze as the entire room went silent. Completely silent. Even the baristas behind the counter stopped what they were doing to watch the stage as Kate began to sing.

Holy shit. My head whipped around, and I felt like I'd taken a cheap shot to the chest.

Her voice was raspy and full-bodied, and she was cradling her guitar like a baby that she'd held every day of her entire life. She was completely comfortable up there, tapping her foot and smiling at different people in the crowd as they began to sing along with her.

It was incredible. *She* was incredible. I couldn't look away. This wasn't some silly idea she'd had on the spur of the moment. She knew exactly what she was doing, and these kids knew her. They freaking loved her.

And she looked gorgeous.

Shit.

Her hair was rolled up on the sides in something Rachel had attempted a few times. I think they were called victory rolls? I'm pretty sure that's what Rach had called them when she couldn't figure them out. Her skin was smooth, and she wore deep-pink lipstick that made her teeth bright white under the spotlight. She was wearing a T-shirt that hung off her shoulder and ripped jeans that were so tight, I wasn't even sure how she'd managed to sit down.

I blinked slowly, and she was still there.

"I tried to tell you she was good," Rachel said smugly from my side.

"Did she write that song?" I asked, turning to look at my wife.

"Babe, seriously? It's a Taylor Swift song."

"Oh."

"This one's a Kenny Chesney song."

"I know this one," I murmured, looking back toward the stage. "Does she only sing country?"

"Hell no. It's mostly other stuff, but it's usually got a theme. Tonight is obviously about kids…teenagers, since the donations are going to some stop-bullying charity."

I nodded, but my eyes were on the stage again as Kate

danced a little in her seat, tapping out the beat of the new song on the front of her guitar. Had Kate been bullied? I didn't remember anything like that, but like I'd told Rachel, I'd only stayed with Kate's aunt and uncle for a little over a year before I left for boot camp. Maybe I'd missed it. The thought made me grind my teeth in anger.

Kate pursed her bright lips then, blowing a kiss with a wink for the crowd.

My breath caught.

Jesus Christ.

I pushed my seat back from the table and grabbed Rachel's hand, pulling her over to sit on my lap.

"What are you doing?" she whispered with a laugh.

"If I've gotta stay here, I'm getting some perks."

"Oh yeah?"

"Yeah." I leaned in and kissed her hard, ignoring the lipstick I could feel smearing over my lips. I slid my tongue into her mouth and felt her nails dig into my shoulder as she tilted her head for a better angle. God, kissing her still felt as good as it had the first time I'd done it. I hadn't known that loving someone so much was even possible before I'd met her.

"Rain check?" she asked against my lips as she reached out blindly and grabbed a couple of napkins to clean off our faces. Her face was flushed, and I wanted nothing more than to leave that fucking coffeehouse and get her alone.

My wife was the most beautiful woman I'd ever known, and it wasn't just her looks. She'd grown up like I had, scrounged and fought for every single thing she'd needed— and I was proud of the family and the life we'd built together.

We'd come a long way from our nasty upbringings.

"Can we go home yet?" I replied with a smirk as I wiped my face.

"Hey, you two in the corner!" Kate called into the mike, interrupting the incredibly sexy look Rachel was giving me. "None of that, I've got kids here."

The crowd laughed, and I glanced sharply at the stage.

Kate was smiling so brightly that she looked giddy. "That's my best friend, right there. Isn't she gorgeous?"

The crowd cheered as Rachel laughed softly in my ear and blew a kiss at Kate.

"I wanna know who the guy is!" a girl called out from across the room, making everyone laugh.

"Eh, that's just her husband," Kate answered flatly, making the crowd snicker. She met my eyes and winked, then grinned before looking away and starting in on the next song as if she hadn't just made my stomach drop.

We watched her for almost an hour as she fucking killed it on stage. Then I ushered Rachel out of the building without saying good-bye, making excuses about wanting to beat the rush of kids.

I had the distinct impression that I knew very little about the woman I'd been avoiding for the past ten years, and I wondered how I'd missed it. She wasn't the awkward girl I remembered, or the sloppy woman in sweats and tank tops that Rachel occasionally invited over to the house when I was home.

The Kate I'd seen on stage was a fucking knockout—confident and sassy. I knew then that I'd continue to avoid her, but for an entirely different reason than I had before.

About the Author

When Nicole Jacquelyn was eight and people asked what she wanted to be when she grew up, she told them she wanted to be a mom. When she was twelve, her answer changed to author. Her dreams stayed constant. First she became a mom, and then, during her senior year of college—with one daughter in first grade and the other in preschool—she sat down and wrote a story.

You can learn more on Twitter (@AuthorNicoleJ) or at Facebook.com/AuthorNicoleJacquelyn.

Printed in Great Britain
by Amazon